SARTOR RESARTUS

Thomas Carlyle was born at Ecclefechan in Dumfriesshire on 4 December 1795. The son of a stonemason, he was educated in the village school and at Annan Academy. In 1809 he entered the Arts Faculty at Edinburgh University, graduating in 1813 with a distinction in mathematics. His parents had hoped that he would be a minister, and indeed he spent the next year studying to join the strictly Calvinist Secessionist Church. But his own religious doubts would not let him continue and he left to work as a teacher in his old school at Annan and then at Kirkcaldy. 1819 saw Carlyle back in Edinburgh as a law student, but this did not last and he turned to private tutoring and his own studies in German language, literature and philosophy. Prone to insomnia and depression he underwent something of a spiritual crisis during these years, a crisis later recounted in *Sartor Resartus* as an encounter with the 'Everlasting No', followed by a determination to embrace instead the affirmation of life and continual striving. Living near his parents in Ecclefechan (where they had turned to farming) he made friends with Edward Irving, a charismatic religious figure of the day through whom he met Jane Welsh, a local doctor's daughter, who became his wife in 1826. Jane's support was to prove invaluable to this difficult and sometimes tormented man, and the letters of this intelligent and independent-minded woman are rightly famous.

Carlyle was becoming known for his interest in German culture. He translated Goethe's *Wilhelm Meister's Lehrjahr* (1824), his *Life of Schiller* (1825) and in 1827 four volumes on *German Romance* and a translation of *Wilhelm Meister's Wanderjahr*. The couple moved to Edinburgh, but could not afford to live in the city, and so retired to Craigenputtoch, a Dumfriesshire farmhouse belonging to Jane's family, where they spent the next six years. Carlyle continued to write and to wrestle with what he saw as the mechanistic and utilitarian materialism of the day. A key essay 'Signs of the Times' was published in Francis Jeffries' *Edinburgh Review* in 1829; he planned a massive and dynamically written history of the French Revolution; and the serial version of *Sartor Resartus* appeared in 1833–4. In fact it was an American publisher who first produced this briliant and idiosyncratic work in book form in 1836. The Carlyles moved to London in 1834 where they were to live in a little house in Cheyne Walk for the rest of their lives. At the age of forty Carlyle's growing reputation as a critic of his age brought him the friendship of Emerson, Browning, Tennyson, Dickens and Arnold.

His output was prolific and dense. *The French Revolution* appeared in 1837 and a four volume collection of his essays the following year. He gave lectures on the history of literature which appeared in print in 1838; *Chartism* was published in 1839 followed by another book based on a series of public lectures, *On Heroes and Hero Worship* (1841); his critique of politics and social issues was devoloped again in *Past and Present* (1843). His interest in the role of key individuals in history produced the letters and speeches of Cromwell (1845) and a massively researched six volume work on *The History of Friedrich II of Prussia, Called Frederick the Great* (1858–65). During the 1840s Carlyle's acerbic intellectual position had been strongly tinged with the democratic sternness of his early religious upbringing, but by the 1860s this was turning to an increasingly authoritarian position, secure in his reputation as 'the sage of Chelsea'. His beloved wife died in April 1866, only weeks after he had been honoured as Rector of Edinburgh University. In the aftermath of that crucial and painful loss he remembered his early years and their life and times together in a series of vividly realised sketches. Edited by his biographer J. A. Froude, these were later published as Carlyle's *Reminiscences* in 1881, shortly after his death in February of that year.

THOMAS CARLYLE

Sartor Resartus

The Life and Times of Herr Teufelsdröckh

Introduction by Alasdair Gray

ILLUSTRATED BY
Edmund J. Sullivan

CANONGATE
CLASSICS
107

First published as a Canongate Classic in 2002 by
Canongate Books Ltd, 14 High Street, Edinburgh EH1 1TE.
First published in 1898.

Explanatory Notes © Peter Sabor and Kerry McSweeney
1987. Reprinted from Thomas Carlyle: *Sartor Resartus*
edited with an introduction and notes by Kerry McSweeney
and Peter Sabor (Oxford World Classics, 1999) by permission of Oxford University Press.

10 9 8 7 6 5 4 3 2 1

The publishers gratefully acknowledge general subsidy from
the Scottish Arts Council towards the Canongate Classics
series and a specific grant towards the publication of this
volume.

Typeset in Monotype Plantin by Hewer Text Ltd, Edinburgh. Printed and bound by Cox and Wyman, Reading.

British Library Cataloguing-in-Publication Data
A catalogue record for this book is available
on request from the British Library

ISBN 1 84195 278 8

www.canongate.net

Summary of Contents

BOOK ONE

Chapter 1: Preliminary   5

No Philosophy of Clothes yet, notwithstanding all our Science. Strangely forgotten that Man is by nature a *naked* animal. The English mind all-too practically absorbed for any such inquiry. Not so, deep-thinking Germany. Advantage of Speculation having free course. Editor receives from Professor Teufelsdröckh his new Work on Clothes.

Chapter 2: Editorial Difficulties   11

How to make known Teufelsdröckh and his Book to English readers; especially *such* a book? Editor receives from the Hofrath Heuschrecke a letter promising Bio-

the fifteenth century. By what strange chances do we live in History! The costume of Bolivar's Cavalry.

Teufelsdröckh's Theorem, 'Society founded upon Cloth;' his Method, Intuition quickened by Experience. – The mysterious question, Who am I? Philosophic systems all at fault: A deeper meditation has always taught, here and there an individual, that all visible things are appearances only; but also emblems and revelations of God. Teufelsdröckh first comes upon the question of Clothes: Baseness to which Clothing may bring us.

The universal utility of Clothes, and their higher mystic virtue, illustrated. Conception of Mankind stripped naked; and immediate consequent dissolution of civilised Society.

A Naked World possible, nay actually exists, under the clothed one. Man, in the eye of Pure Reason, a visible God's Presence. The beginning of all wisdom, to look fixedly on Clothes till they become transparent. Wonder, the basis of Worship: Perennial in man. Modern Sciolists who cannot wonder: Teufelsdröckh's contempt for, and advice to them.

Nature not an Aggregate, but a Whole. All visible things are emblems, Clothes; and exist for a time only. The grand scope of the Philosophy of Clothes. – Biographic Documents arrive. Letter from Heuschrecke on the importance of Biography. Heterogeneous character of the documents: Editor sorely perplexed; but desperately grapples with his work.

BOOK TWO

men. Irony and its consequences. Teufelsdröckh's Epitaph on Count Zähdarm.

Teufelsdröckh gives up his Profession. The heavenly mystery of Love. Teufelsdröckh's feeling of worship towards women. First and only love. Blumine. Happy hearts and free tongues. The infinite nature of Fantasy. Love's joyful progress; sudden dissolution; and final catastrophe.

Teufelsdröckh's demeanour thereupon. Turns pilgrim. A last wistful look on native Entepfuhl: Sunset amongst primitive Mountains. Basilisk-glance of the Barouche-and-four. Thoughts on View-hunting. Wanderings and Sorrowings.

Loss of Hope, and of Belief. Profit-and-Loss Philosophy. Teufelsdröckh in his darkness and despair still clings to Truth and follows Duty. Inexpressible pains and fears of Unbelief. Fever-crisis: Protest against the Everlasting No: Baphometic Fire-baptism.

Teufelsdröckh turns now outwardly to the *Not-me*; and finds wholesomer food. Ancient Cities: Mystery of their origin and growth: Invisible inheritances and possessions. Power and virtue of a true Book. Wagram Battlefield: War. Great Scenes beheld by the Pilgrim: Great Events, and Great Men. Napoleon, a divine missionary, preaching *La carrière ouverte aux talens*. Teufelsdröckh at the North Cape: Modern means of self-defence. Gunpowder and Duelling. The Pilgrim, despising his miseries, reaches the Centre of Indifference.

encompassed by them; lives and works by them. Theory of Motive-millwrights, a false account of human nature. Symbols of an extrinsic value; as Banners, Standards: Of intrinsic value; as Works of Art, Lives and Deaths of Heroic men. Religious Symbols; Christianity. Symbols hallowed by Time; but finally defaced and desecrated. Many super-annuated Symbols in our time, needing removal.

Heuschrecke's Malthusian Tract, and Teufelsdröckh's marginal notes thereon. The true workman, for daily bread, or spiritual bread, to be honoured; and no other. The real privation of the Poor not poverty or toil, but ignorance. Over-population: With a world like ours and wide as ours, can there be too many men? Emigration.

Teufelsdröckh considers Society as *dead*; its soul (Religion) gone, its body (existing Institutions) going. Utilitarianism, needing little farther preaching, is now in full activity of destruction. – Teufelsdröckh would yield to the Inevitable, accounting that the best: Assurance of a fairer Living Society, arising, Phœnix-like, out of the ruins of the old dead one. Before that Phœnix death-birth is accomplished, long time, struggle, and suffering must intervene.

Courtesy due from all men to all men: The Body of Man a Revelation in the Flesh. Teufelsdröckh's respect for Old Clothes, as the 'Ghosts of Life.' Walk in Monmouth Street, and meditations there.

Destruction and Creation ever proceed together; and organic filaments of the Future are even now spinning. Wonderful connection of each man with all men; and of each generation with all generations, before and after: Mankind is One. Sequence and progress of all human work, whether of creation or destruction, from age to age. – Titles, hitherto derived from Fighting, must give way to others. Kings will remain and their title. Political Freedom, not to be attained by any mechanical contrivance. Hero-worship, perennial amongst men; the cornerstone of polities in the Future. Organic filaments of the New Religion: Newspapers and Literature. Let the faithful soul take courage!

Deep significance of Miracles. Littleness of human Science: Divine incomprehensibility of Nature. Custom blinds us to the miraculousness of daily-recurring miracles; so do Names. Space and Time, appearances only; forms of human Thought: A glimpse of Immortality. How Space hides from us the wondrousness of our commonest powers; and Time, the divinely miraculous course of human history.

Recapitulation. Editor congratulates the few British readers who have accompanied Teufelsdröckh through all his speculations. The true use of the *Sartor Resartus*, to exhibit the Wonder of daily life and common things; and to show that all Forms are but Clothes, and temporary. Practical inferences enough will follow.

The Dandy defined. The Dandiacal Sect a new modification of the primeval superstition Self-Worship: How to be distinguished. Their Sacred Books (Fashionable Novels) unreadable. Dandyism's Articles of Faith. – Brotherhood of Poor-Slaves; vowed to perpetual Poverty; worshippers of Earth; distinguished by peculiar costume and diet. Picture of a Poor-Slave Household; and of a Dandiacal. Teufels-dröckh fears these two Sects may spread, till they part all England between them, and then frightfully collide.

THOMAS CARLYLE

Introduction

The Carlyles were a fiercely independent family of farmers and tradesmen in Ecclefechan, a small Scots market town near the Solway Firth. Here Thomas Carlyle was born in 1795, eldest of eight children. His father and uncles were stone-masons, his mother had been a house servant, both parents believed in the literal truths of the bible and read it daily. Carlyle's dad belonged to a Calvinist sect because it allowed landowners to appoint local clergy. He inclined to the stern hellfire aspect of religion; Carlyle's gentle mother favoured Christ's loving mercy. Their son seems to have doubted their faith from an early age, once shocking his mother by asking if God Almighty had really come down and made wheelbarrows in a shop? But when he was nearly fourteen they sent him to Edinburgh University hoping he would become a minister of religion: not an unusual thing for a son of a Scots farmer or tradesman in those days. Carlyle never became a minister but never openly rejected the faith he knew had helped his parents, and many other working-class Scots, endure hard lives with courage and dignity. This partly explains his quarrel with the eighteenth century, which in later years he could hardly mention without explosions of contempt.

In that century most leaders of British politics and fashion
had profited by science, trade and warfare in a way they
thought would last forever if religious enthusiasm did not
upset it. Dean, Swift, Pope, Sterne and Dr Johnson were
practising Chritians, yet only mention religion in their writings when mocking its departures from common sense.
There were reasons for this fear of strongly worded faith.
In the previous century a bible-conscious parliamentary
army had beheaded a king, disbanded the House of Lords
and briefly made Britain a republic. The restored lords (if we
omit bishops who sat among them) mostly thought the bible
a poor guide for their own pleasant lives and a dangerous
guide for their underlings, yet they supported state churches
to keep the faith of the labouring classes within governable
limits. They even tried to penalise those who would not
attend such churches. Their efforts failed. By the 1730s so
many working people avoided church that John Wesley, an
Anglican clergyman, began preaching to them in the open
air. The Church of England expelled him as a rabble-rouser.
Carlyle never became a clergyman but believed everyone
should have a strong faith and declare it, so eighteenth-
century civilisation struck him, not as a great achievement,
but as a great sham, and the nineteenth century in some ways
worse.

He might have thought differently had his family prospered by enclosures of land, or by new steam-powered
machinery, or by wars with France and the resulting colonial
expansion. On the other hand poverty did not drive them to
early deaths in mines and factories, or starve them when the
Irish potato crop failed. While aware of Britain's huge
increase of wealth and poverty, Carlyle avoided both by
teaching, by writing for an Edinburgh encyclopaedia that
became *The Britannica*, and by mastering the main European
languages until he was Britain's principal translator of foreign literature. Through many works of philosophy, history
and poetry he searched for a faith that went beyond his

parents' bible, for though incapable of religion he had the instincts of a passionate preacher. An incident from his youth as a schoolmaster in Kirkcaldy shows this.

When addressing a class he used the word *virtue*. A senior master present asked him to define it. 'Sir,' said Carlyle, 'if you have no notion of virtue within your own breast I despair of ever communicating to you any adequate conception of it.' A Christian could have defined virtue as *loving the Lord your God with all your heart and mind and soul and your neighbour as yourself*, but many Christians had used these words to justify hurting or killing neighbours with whom they disagreed. A British philosopher had joined political economy to virtue by saying it was *what had led to the greatest happiness of the greatest number*, but by 1820 British economists believed that what led to the happiness of the greatest number in one generation (well-paid work, good food and housing) must cause famine in the next by letting far too many working-class children survive. They got the idea from Malthus, an Anglican vicar, who wrote that *only vice and misery* kept the poor in check: so magistrates were wise to have thieves hanged and poachers sent to Australia, fools if they worked to reduced widespread hunger and unemployment. This pleased a government chosen by big landlords who saw Britain as a statistical machine profiting those who owned it by grinding down those who served it. Comfortable churchmen called the machine a God-given construct. Comfortable atheists thought it a natural one. Carlyle thought it disgustingly unfair and wasteful.

He also rejected atheists and sceptics like Rousseau and Voltaire whose ideas were held responsible for the French Revolution. They had done good, he thought, in helping to undermine a corrupt society, but could not help to build a better. So he looked to Germany, then a cluster of many rural kingdoms and tiny city-states. They possessed forty universities, no modern factories or far-flung colonies, but were united by a language and growing literature. Germany existed as an idea that hoped to become a nation so her poets and philosophers thought societies were shaped and driven by ideas – Christian, feudal, imperial and democratic ideas. This meant that the mercantile processes described in Adam Smith's *Wealth of Nations* were made by human thoughts and actions, not by God-given or natural laws, though mercantile governments enforced them as laws. Moreover our ideas, feelings and appetites (in combinations variously labelled *intelligence, self-consciousness, mind, soul,* or *spirit*) are part of the energy driving our body through its growth, activity and decay. And are not all the things we see, from the smallest flowers to the vastest stars, the outward form of an energy driving these, too, through growth, activity and decay? Is not this energy the shaping spirit or nature or mind of the whole universe? If so, another name for it is God.

Coleridge, Byron and other British poets called Romantic were also anti-materialists who identified the human spirit with unenclosed landscapes, skies and mountains. *I am the eye by which the universe beholds itself and knows it is divine,* wrote Shelley. But these poets had messy love lives and when most inspired had supported the French Revolution. The same Revolution had led to Napoleon's dictatorship and defeat and the restoration of decrepit monarchies. German Romantic writers blended hope for the future with what was then harmless nationalism and praise of domestic virtue. By the age of thirty-five Carlyle, after years of patient wooing, had firmly, finally married intelligent and attractive Jane Welsh. He was now ready to start *Sartor Resartus.*

The Latin title means *The Tailor Retailored* and began as an essay on metaphors – words displaced from their original uses to represent or signify something else, as when we talk of *loud* colours, *black* depressions, *sour* faces, *golden* opportunities. But all words, spoken or written, are signs representing thoughts which cannot be shared unless *clothed* in words. Ideas need noises or printer's ink, as rich establishments depend on what is common and cheap. Gold in the vaults of banks and The World Trade Centre represent the wealth of nations, but can only do so when themselves represented by paper money and plastic credit cards; nor could a nation exist without flags and the clothes and uniforms of many trades and professions. In Goethe's drama *Faust* the world is called a garment woven by nature for God, so that we can see him. Carlyle realised an essay on the science of signs (nowadays called semiology) could expand into a book about everything – an impossible book! But by pretending that a foreigner had already written it, and by writing about it, Carlyle could say what he wished about anything. He had already introduced works by Goethe, Schiller, Hoffman and Jean Paul Richter to the British. He now introduced the life and opinions of Herr Teufelsdröckh, Professor of Things in General at Weissnichtwo University and author of a great work on the philosophy of clothes. Two of Carlyle's favourite books were Sterne's *Tristram Shandy* and Swift's *Tale of a Tub*. Both grotesquely parodied academic learning. The second described Christianity as an overcoat God had given to his Catholic, Calvinist and Anglican sons who each retailored it to suit himself. In fantastic academic German diguise Carlyle wrote his own life and opinions.

Readers tackling *Sartor* for the first time will not be surprised to hear that seven years passed before Carlyle got it published in Britain. It lost *Fraser Magazine* subscribers when serialised in London. The vocabulary is a queer blend of erudition, slang and words Carlyle invented. The grammar in Scottish-Germanic, the prose clotted with metaphors and allusions to other obscure literatures, and why so many cryptic references to shit? Teufelsdröckh is German for devil dung. See on pages 142 and 143 the Latin epitaph he wrote for a great nobleman. The book is in three sections, the first and last pretend to describe Devil Dung's character- and clothes- philosophy; the middle one his biography; but the whole is a patchwork of digressions linked by an idea that most laws, educations, churches and governments are as temporary as old clothes, and no longer fit the nations and public bodies using them. The supposed editor's apologies for the book's revolutionary tone is an evasion because the editor is author in diguise. See pages 182–4 for how he views modern armies. The name he gives to the British solidiers' home village (Dumdrudge) is an incitement to mutiny.

So the book was first published in the USA which, sixty years before, had made itself a republic without an official religion, and where many liked iconoclastic ideas dressed as hoaxes. The first complete British edition appeared two years later in 1838. By then Carlyle's *French Revolution* had appeared, so *Sartor* was published in greater and greater numbers till the early twentieth century, being famous as the first great outcry of a voice all intelligent folk should read and understand, if only a little. George Eliot said it was impossible to imagine nineteenth-century literature without Carlyle, so hugely had he influenced his contemporaries: Dickens, Browning, Tennyson, Ruskin, Eliot herself, Disraeli (who Carlyle detested) and in the US (where the Transcendentalists revered him) Herman Melville, Emily Dickinson and Whitman.

He made an impact because he addressed his readers like Micah or Isaiah addressing the Jews, declaring that states where great wealth flourishes alongside great poverty *should* be reformed peaceably and fairly by rulers or *will* be changed violently and horribly by the ruled. This was because the French Revolution had not (as many prosperous folk believed) been finally defeated, but was being continued by a commercial and industrial revolution. His message was effective because told in a tone of passionate sincerity varied by grotesque irony and grim humour. He also suggested democracy and social justice could coincide, while doubting the value of ballot boxes. *The French Revolution* was banned by European Monarchies. British Tories thought his works harmless because no British worker could read prose that resembled Milton's *Areopagitica* more than Tom Paine's

Rights of Man. They were not wholly right. Patrick McGill's autobiography *Children of the Dead End* tells how, when a young navvy, he read the Natural Supernaturalism chapter of *Sartor Resartus* while sitting on the footplate of a flying ballast train.

Politics are only part of this book. Says George Eliot: 'The character of his influence is best seen in the fact that many of the men who have least agreement with his opinions are those to whom the reading of *Sartor Resartus* was an epoch in the history of their minds.' Most nineteenth-century thinkers whose parents were not aristocratic came, like Carlyle, from Christian families but had lost faith in a good spirit mastering the universe. Unbelief is so common now that perhaps a majority of comfortable people find the world good enough for them without it, but religion is still widespread among a majority whose lives are not comfortable at all, and perhaps nobody can feel life deeply satisfying without some vision of goodness greater than themselves. In three chapters, *The Everlasting No, Centre of Indifference, The Everlasting Yea,* Carlyle-as-Teufelsdröckh tells how, by doubting the value of all things, he finds one that, while he exists, can be depended upon: his soul or self which is free to serve only what he respects. The discovery gives him only bleak satisfaction until one day, seeing smoke rise from cottage chimneys where poor women are making meals for their families, he sees he is not unluckier than many others, and with love and pity, should work to serve them. I think these were the chapters which meant most to the biologist Huxley, Darwin's chief supporter who also invented the word *agnostic*. He suffered greatly from depressions until (he said) 'Sartor Resartus led me to know that a deep sense of religion was compatible with an entire absence of theology.'

Carlyle's dad once likened a young minister having trouble with his sermon to a *fly wading through tar*. His son knew many readers would have that sensation with *Sartor*, so forestalled the worst possible criticism by putting four other writers' reactions at the start of the 1838 British edition, heading them *Testimonies of Authors*. Ascribed to *Highest Class Bookseller's Taster* and dated 1831, number I is an extract from the report of a reader working for Murray, the London publisher who rejected the manuscript that year, or it may be a Carlyle forgery pretending to be one. He was capable of such jokes. II is an extract from a British review of the magazine serial version, singling out the obscurest sentence in the book (see footnote on page 177). III is an extract from a facetious American review giving translations of the book's farcical German names. Number IV is the Preface to the United States edition by Carlyle's friend Ralph Waldo Emerson. His emphasis on *purity of moral sentiment* contradicts Carlyle, who called it a cynical extravaganza.

This Canongate Classics edition is based on the most visually pleasant version we could find, the 1898 version illustrated by Edmund Sullivan. We have kept his own introduction as a pleasant thing which shows the influence of Carlyle's prose style upon an intelligent fan.

POSTSCRIPT

After 1840 something went wrong with Carlyle's notion of virtue. He defended negro slavery, Prussian militarism and an unscrupulous dictator of Paraguay, Dr Francia. George Orwell was probably right to call him sadistic. He remained sure that government by commercial interests had nothing to do with duty and was preparing terrible catastrophes, but died in 1881, long before the First World War and all that sprang from it.

Alasdair Gray

A Letter of Introduction from the Illustrator

WITH THE
DRAWINGS TO `SARTOR RESARTUS´

HAMPSTEAD,
*October 27*th, 1898.

MY DEAR DOCTOR,
Now that my holiday task is over, I wish to do myself
the honour of dedicating it to you in memory of
certain nights that we spent together with our feet
in your fender, and our heads somewhere among the
stars. The faces in your fire were always of the
friendliest.

It is appropriate that a labour of love, as this is,
should be dedicated to you; the good wish is the
greater part of a gift: and I beg your acceptance of my
little drawings as the token of much goodwill.

It has always been a wonder to me that 'Sartor Resartus' should never have been illustrated: and I addressed myself to the undertaking because I saw in it an opportunity to make drawings almost entirely for their own sake, as a holiday from the conditions that so often bind the modern artist to the prettinesses and trivialities of the moment; and, quite apart from my love of the book itself, I was attracted to the illustration of it because the subject left so much elbow-room. Was I a realist? I could be as realistic as I chose. Was I an idealist? I could idealize to the top of my bent. A caricaturist? Who could complain? In fact, the subject was the history of mankind, and his relation to infinity: his greatness and his nothingness.

In the conception of an idea no bounds are set: yet in its execution the limits are most grievous. The large conception dwindles to nothing in its execution.

An illustrator who cared to devote himself entirely to the realistic or quasi-realistic passages in 'Sartor' would find abundance of subjects ready to his hand. The village of Entepfuhl, the mysterious stranger, the Blumine episodes, and the rest all make subjects which contain delightful possibilities. But then, the chief characteristics of the book are hardly to be found in these passages; they are the clothes-pegs only: and the more important part of the book would have been untouched.

Again, I set a limit on my work by rejecting the illustration of many of the most vivid passages: for instance, lovers of 'Sartor,' on opening this book, will probably turn first of all to see what has been made of the famous passages, opening with 'Often in my atrabiliar moods,' concerning Royal Ceremonies and the House of Lords: and be astonished to find absolutely nothing by way of illustration.

So far from accepting the blame for what will

probably be called a sin of omission, I may claim a little credit for my restraint: since everyone sees the subject so luminously for himself that in my view an illustration is unnecessary, and would probably clash with the reader's own conception. And again, while the subject to be presented is 'Indecorum,' the limits imposed upon the illustrator would of necessity reduce the drawing to a representation of the very opposite – for all the world as decorous as a County Council swimming bath.

I confess that, in my sketch book, a skit may be found of my Lord Duke of Windlestraw, clothed as described in the book, with the small additions of an eye-glass and the order of the garter: upon which the 'Honi soit qui mal y pense' seemed to me appropriate enough.

As to the treatment, the German accent of the book is mimicked more or less in the drawings: I have pretended here and there that clothes were the serious business of the book: a thin pretence of Carlyle's own: sometimes I have adhered to the text, sometimes only to the general spirit of the book, and the fancies stirred by it; in some cases, perhaps, the drawings may be considered obscure or far-fetched: the drawings themselves must apologize as best they can.

> With all best wishes,
> Believe me, my dear Doctor,
> Yours always sincerely,
> EDMUND J. SULLIVAN.

DR. JOHN COLBORNE,
HASTINGS.

List of Illustrations

Testimonies of Authors

This questionable little Book was undoubtedly written among the mountain solitudes, in 1831; but, owing to impediments natural and accidental, could not, for seven years more, appear as a Volume in England; – and had at last to clip itself in pieces, and be content to struggle out, bit by bit, in some courageous *Magazine* that offered. Whereby now, to certain idly curious readers, and even to myself till I make study, the insignificant but at last irritating question, What its real history and chronology are, is, if not insoluble, considerably involved in haze.

To the first English Edition, 1838, which an American, or two Americans had now opened the way for, there was slightingly prefixed, under the title '*Testimonies of Authors*,' some straggle of real documents, which, now that I find it again, sets the matter into clear light and sequence; – and shall here, for removal of idle stumbling-blocks and nugatory guessings from the path of every reader, be reprinted as it stood. (*Author's Note, of* 1868.)

1. HIGHEST CLASS, BOOKSELLER'S TASTER

Taster to Bookseller. – 'The Author of *Teufelsdröckh* is a person of talent; his work displays here and there some felicity of thought and expression, considerable fancy and knowledge: but whether or not it would take with the public seems doubtful. For a *jeu d'esprit* of that kind it is too long; it would have suited better as an essay or article than as a volume. The Author has no great tact; his wit is frequently heavy; and reminds one of the German Baron who took to leaping on tables, and answered that he was learning to be lively. *Is* the work a translation?'

Bookseller to Editor. – 'Allow me to say that such a writer requires only a little more tact to produce a popular as well as an able work. Directly on receiving your permission, I sent your *Ms.* to a gentleman in the highest class of men of letters, and an accomplished German scholar: I now enclose you his opinion, which, you may rely upon it, is a just one; and I have too high an opinion of your good sense to' &c. &c. – *Ms. (penes nos),*[1] *London,* 17*th September* 1831.

2. CRITIC OF THE SUN

'*Fraser's Magazine* exhibits the usual brilliancy, and also

1 *penes nos*: in our possession

the' &c. '*Sartor Resartus* is what old Dennis used to call "a heap of clotted nonsense," mixed however, here and there, with passages marked by thought and striking poetic vigour. But what does the writer mean by "Baphometic Fire-baptism"? Why cannot he lay aside his pedantry, and write so as to make himself generally intelligible? We quote by way of curiosity a sentence from the *Sartor Resartus*; which may be read either backwards or forwards, for it is equally intelligible either way: indeed, by beginning at the tail, and so working up to the head, we think the reader will stand the fairest chance of getting at its meaning: "The fire-baptised soul, long so scathed and thunder-riven, here feels its own freedom; which feeling is its Baphometic baptism: the citadel of its whole kingdom it has thus gained by assault, and will keep inexpugnable; outwards from which the remaining dominions, not indeed without hard battering, will doubtless by degrees be conquered and pacificated." Here is a' – . . . – *Sun Newspaper*, 1st *April* 1834.

3. NORTH-AMERICAN REVIEWER

. . . 'After a careful survey of the whole ground, our belief is that no such persons as Professor Teufelsdröckh or Counsellor Heuschrecke ever existed; that the six paper-bags, with their China-ink inscriptions and multifarious contents, are a mere figment of the brain; that the "present Editor" is the only person who has ever written upon the Philosophy of Clothes; and that the *Sartor Resartus* is the only treatise that has yet appeared upon that subject; – in short, that the whole account of the origin of the work before us, which the supposed Editor relates with so much gravity, and of which we have given a brief abstract, is, in plain English, a *hum*.

'Without troubling our readers at any great length with our reasons for entertaining these suspicions, we may remark, that the absence of all other information on the subject, except what is contained in the work, is itself a fact of a most significant character. The whole German press, as well as the particular one where the work purports to have been printed, seems to be under the control of *Stillschweigen & Co.* – Silence and Company. If the Clothes-Philosophy and its author are making so great a sensation throughout Germany as is pretended, how happens it that the only notice we have of the fact is contained in a few numbers of a monthly Magazine published at London? How happens it that no intelligence about the matter has come out directly to this country? We pique ourselves here in New England upon knowing at least as much of what is going on in the literary way in the old Dutch Mother-Land as our brethren of the fast-anchored Isle; but thus far we have no tidings whatever of the "extensive close-printed close-meditated volume," which forms the subject of this pretended commentary. Again, we would respectfully inquire of the "present Editor" upon what part of the map of Germany we are to look for the city of *Weissnichtwo* – "Know-not-where" – at which place the work is supposed to have been printed, and the Author to have resided. It has been our fortune to visit several portions of the German territory, and to examine pretty carefully, at different times and for various purposes, maps of the whole; but we have no recollection of any such place. We suspect that the city of *Know-not-where* might be called, with at least as much propriety, *Nobody-knows-where*, and is to be found in the kingdom of *Nowhere*. Again, the village of *Entepfuhl* – "Duck-pond" – where the supposed Author of the work is said to have passed his youth, and that of *Hinterschlag*, where he had his education, are equally foreign to our geography. Duck-ponds enough there undoubtedly are in almost every village in Germany, as the traveller in that country knows too well to his cost, but any particular village denominated Duck-pond is to us altogether *terra incognita*. The names of the personages are not less singular than those of the places. Who can refrain from a smile at the yoking together of such a pair of appellatives as Diogenes Teufelsdröckh? The supposed bearer of this strange title is represented as admitting, in his pretended autobiography, that "he had searched to no purpose through all the Heralds' books in and without the German empire, and through all manner of Subscribers'-lists, Militia-rolls, and other Name-catalogues," but had nowhere been able to find "the name Teufelsdröckh, except as appended to his own person." We can readily believe this, and we doubt very much whether any Christian parent would think of condemning a son to carry through life the burden of so unpleasant a title. That of Counsellor Heuschrecke – "Grasshopper" – though not offensive, looks much more like a piece of fancy work than a "fair business transaction." The same may be said of *Blumine* – "Flower-Goddess" – the heroine of the fable; and so of the rest.

'In short, our private opinion is, as we have remarked, that the whole story of a correspondence with Germany, a university of Nobody-knows-where, a Professor of Things in General, a Counsellor Grasshopper, a Flower-Goddess Blumine, and so forth, has about as much foundation in truth as the late entertaining account of Sir John Herschel's discoveries in the moon. Fictions of this kind are, however, not uncommon, and ought not, perhaps, to be condemned with too much severity; but we are not sure that we can exercise the same indulgence in regard to the attempt, which seems to be made to mislead the public as to the substance of the work before us, and its pretended German original. Both purport, as we have seen, to be upon the subject of Clothes, or dress. *Clothes, their Origin and Influence*, is the title of the supposed German treatise of Professor Teufelsdröckh, and the rather odd name of *Sartor Resartus* – the Tailor Patched – which the present Editor has affixed to his pretended commentary, seems to look the same way. But though there is a good deal of remark throughout the work in a half-serious, half-comic style upon dress, it seems to be in reality a treatise upon the great Science of Things in General, which Teufelsdröckh is supposed to have professed at the university of Nobody-knows-where. Now, without intending to adopt a too rigid standard of morals, we own that we doubt a little the propriety of offering to the public a treatise on Things in General, under the name and in the form of an Essay on Dress. For ourselves, advanced as we unfortunately are in the journey of life, far beyond the period when dress is practically a matter of interest, we have no hesitation in saying, that the real subject of the work is to us more attractive than the ostensible one. But this is probably not the case with the mass of readers. To the younger portion of the community, which constitutes everywhere the very great majority, the subject of dress is one of intense and paramount importance. An author who treats it appeals, like the poet, to the young men and maidens – *virginibus puerisque* – and calls upon them, by all the motives which habitually operate most strongly upon their feelings, to buy his book. When, after opening their purses for this purpose, they have carried home the work in triumph, expecting to find in it some particular instruction in regard to the tying of their neckcloths, or the cut of their corsets, and meet with nothing better than a dissertation on Things in General, they will – to use the mildest term – not be in very good humour. If the last improvements in legislation, which we have made in this country, should have found their way to England, the author, we think, would stand some chance of being *Lynched*. Whether his object in this piece of *supercherie*[1] be merely pecuniary profit, or whether he takes a malicious pleasure in quizzing the Dandies, we shall not undertake to say. In the latter part of the work, he devotes a separate chapter to this class of persons, from the tenour of

1 *supercherie*: hoax

which we should be disposed to conclude, that he would consider any mode of divesting them of their property very much in the nature of a spoiling of the Egyptians.

'The only thing about the work, tending to prove that it is what it purports to be, a commentary on a real German treatise, is the style, which is a sort of Babylonish dialect, not destitute, it is true, of richness, vigour, and at times a sort of singular felicity of expression, but very strongly tinged throughout with the peculiar idiom of the German language. This quality in the style, however, may be a mere result of a great familiarity with German literature; and we cannot, therefore, look upon it as in itself decisive, still less as outweighing so much evidence of an opposite character.'
– *North-American Review, No.* 89, *October 1835.*

4. NEW-ENGLAND EDITORS

'The Editors have been induced, by the expressed desire of many persons, to collect the following sheets out of the ephemeral pamphlets[1] in which they first appeared, under the conviction that they contain in themselves the assurance of a longer date.

'The Editors have no expectation that this little Work will have sudden and general popularity. They will not undertake, as there is no need, to justify the gay costume in which the Author delights to dress his thoughts, or the German idioms with which he has sportively sprinkled his pages. It is his humour to advance the gravest speculations upon the gravest topics in a quaint and burlesque style. If his masquerade offend any of his audience, to that degree that they will not hear what he has to say, it may chance to draw others to listen to his wisdom; and what work of imagination can hope to please all? But we will venture to remark that the distaste excited by these

† *Fraser's* (London) *Magazine,* 1833–4

peculiarities in some readers is greatest at first, and is soon forgotten; and that the foreign dress and aspect of the Work are quite superficial, and cover a genuine Saxon heart. We believe, no book has been published for many years, written in a more sincere style of idiomatic English, or which discovers an equal mastery over all the riches of the language. The Author makes ample amends for the occasional eccentricity of his genius, not only by frequent bursts of pure splendour, but by the wit and sense which never fail him.

'But what will chiefly commend the Book to the discerning reader is the manifest design of the work, which is, a Criticism upon the Spirit of the Age – we had almost said, of the hour – in which we live; exhibiting in the most just and novel light the present aspects of Religion, Politics, Literature, Arts, and Social Life. Under all his gaiety the Writer has an earnest meaning, and discovers an insight into the manifold wants and tendencies of human nature, which is very rare among our popular authors. The philanthropy and the purity of moral sentiment, which inspire the work, will find their way to the heart of every lover of virtue.' – *Preface to Sartor Resartus: Boston*, 1835, 1837.

SUNT, FUERUNT VEL FUERE.[1]

London, 30th June 1838.

[1] *Sunt, Fuerunt vel Fuere*: The way they are, The way they have been

Sartor Resartus

IN THREE BOOKS

Mein Vermächtniss, wie herrlich weit und breit!
Die Zeit ist mein Vermächtniss, mein Acker ist die Zeit.
Goethe

My inheritance, how wide and fair!
Time is my estate, to Time I'm heir.

HERR DIOGENES

Book One

CHAPTER I

Preliminary

CONSIDERING our present advanced state of culture, and how the Torch of Science has now been brandished and borne about, with more or less effect, for five thousand years and upwards; how, in these times especially, not only the Torch still burns, and perhaps more fiercely than ever, but innumerable Rush-lights and Sulphur-matches, kindled thereat, are also glancing in every direction, so that not the smallest cranny or doghole in Nature or Art can remain unilluminated, – it might strike the reflective mind with some surprise that hitherto little or nothing of a fundamental character, whether in the way of Philosophy or History, has been written on the subject of Clothes.

Our Theory of Gravitation is as good as perfect: Lagrange, it is well known, has proved that the Planetary

System, on this scheme, will endure for ever; Laplace, still
more cunningly, even guesses that it could not have been
made on any other scheme. Whereby, at least, our nautical
Logbooks can be better kept; and water-transport of all
kinds has grown more commodious. Of Geology and
Geognosy we know enough: what with the labours of
our Werners and Huttons, what with the ardent genius
of their disciples, it has come about that now, to many a
Royal Society, the Creation of a World is little more
mysterious than the cooking of a Dumpling; concerning
which last, indeed, there have been minds to whom the
question, *How the apples were got in*, presented difficulties.
Why mention our disquisitions on the Social Contract, on
the Standard of Taste, on the Migrations of the Herring?
Then, have we not a Doctrine of Rent, a Theory of Value;
Philosophies of Language, of History, of Pottery, of Apparitions, of Intoxicating Liquors? Man's whole life and
environment have been laid open and elucidated; scarcely
a fragment or fibre of his Soul, Body, and Possessions, but
has been probed, dissected, distilled, desiccated, and scien-
tifically decomposed: our spiritual Faculties, of which it
appears there are not a few, have their Stewarts, Cousins,
Royer Collards: every cellular, vascular, muscular Tissue
glories in its Lawrences, Majendies, Bichâts.

How, then, comes it, may the reflective mind repeat, that
the grand Tissue of all Tissues, the only real *Tissue*, should
have been quite overlooked by Science – the vestural
Tissue, namely, of woollen or other Cloth; which Man's
Soul wears as its outmost wrappage and overall; wherein his
whole other Tissues are included and screened, his whole
Faculties work, his whole Self lives, moves, and has its
being? For if, now and then, some straggling broken-
winged thinker has cast an owl's-glance into this obscure
region, the most have soared over it altogether heedless;
regarding Clothes as a property, not an accident, as quite
natural and spontaneous, like the leaves of trees, like the

plumage of birds. In all speculations they have tacitly figured man as a *Clothed Animal*; whereas he is by nature a *Naked Animal*; and only in certain circumstances, by purpose and device, masks himself in Clothes. Shakespeare says, we are creatures that look before and after: the more surprising that we do not look round a little, and see what is passing under our very eyes.

But here, as in so many other cases, Germany, learned, indefatigable, deep-thinking Germany comes to our aid. It is, after all, a blessing that, in these revolutionary times, there should be one country where abstract Thought can still take shelter; that while the din and frenzy of Catholic Emancipations, and Rotten Boroughs, and Revolts of Paris, deafen every French and every English ear, the German can stand peaceful on his scientific watch-tower; and, to the raging, struggling multitude here and elsewhere, solemnly, from hour to hour, with preparatory blast of cowhorn, emit his *Höret ihr Herren und lasset's Euch sagen*;[1] in other words, tell the Universe, which so often forgets that fact, what o'clock it really is. Not infrequently the Germans have been blamed for an unprofitable diligence; as if they struck into devious courses, where nothing was to be had but the toil of a rough journey; as if, forsaking the gold-mines of Finance, and that political slaughter of fat oxen whereby a man himself grows fat, they were apt to run goose-hunting into regions of bilberries and crowberries, and be swallowed up at last in remote peat-bogs. Of that unwise science, which, as our Humorist expresses it,

> By geometric scale
> Doth take the size of pots of ale,

still more, of that altogether misdirected industry, which is seen vigorously enough thrashing mere straw, there can

1 *Höret ihr Herren und lasset's Euch sagen*: Listen, gentlemen, and let it be told you.

nothing defensive be said. In so far as the Germans are chargeable with such, let them take the consequence. Nevertheless be it remarked, that even a Russian Steppe has Tumuli and gold ornaments; also many a scene that looks desert and rock-bound from the distance, will unfold itself, when visited, into rare valleys. Nay, in any case, would Criticism erect not only fingerposts and turnpikes, but spiked gates and impassable barriers, for the mind of man? It is written, 'Many shall run to and fro, and knowledge shall be increased.' Surely the plain rule is, Let each considerate person have his way, and see what it will lead to. For not this man and that man, but all men make up mankind, and their united tasks the task of mankind. How often have we seen some such adventurous, and perhaps much-censured wanderer light on some outlying, neglected, yet vitally momentous province; the hidden treasures of which he first discovered, and kept proclaiming till the general eye and effort were directed thither, and the conquest was completed; – thereby, in these his seemingly so aimless rambles, planting new standards, founding new habitable colonies, in the immeasurable circumambient realm of Nothingness and Night! Wise man was he who counselled that Speculation should have free course, and look fearlessly towards all the thirty-two points of the compass, whithersoever and howsoever it listed.

Perhaps it is proof of the stinted condition in which pure Science, especially pure moral Science, languishes among us English; and how our mercantile greatness, and invaluable Constitution, impressing a political or other immediately practical tendency on all English culture and endeavour, cramps the free flight of Thought, – that this, not Philosophy of Clothes, but recognition even that we have no such Philosophy, stands here for the first time published in our language. What English intellect could have chosen such a topic, or by chance stumbled on it? But for that same unshackled, and even sequestered condition of the German Learned, which permits and induces them to fish in all manner of waters, with all manner of nets, it seems probable enough, this abstruse Inquiry might, in spite of the results it leads to, have continued dormant for indefinite periods. The Editor of these sheets, though otherwise boasting himself a man of confirmed speculative habits, and perhaps discursive enough, is free to confess, that never, till these last months, did the above very plain considerations, on our total want of a Philosophy of Clothes, occur to him; and then, by quite foreign sugges-tion. By the arrival, namely, of a new Book from Professor Teufelsdröckh of Weissnichtwo;[1] treating expressly of this subject; and in a style which, whether understood or not, could not even by the blindest be overlooked. In the present Editor's way of thought, this remarkable Treatise, with its Doctrines, whether as judicially acceded to, or judicially denied, has not remained without effect.

'*Die Kleider ihr Werden und Wirken* (Clothes, their Origin and Influence): *von Diog. Teufelsdröckh, J. U. D. etc. Stillschweigen und Co^gnie: Weissnichtwo*, 1833:[2]

'Here,' says the *Weissnichtwo'sche Anzeiger*,[3] 'comes a Volume of that extensive, close-printed, close-meditated sort, which, be it spoken with pride, is seen only in Germany, perhaps only in Weissnichtwo: issuing from the hitherto irreproachable Firm of Stillschweigen and Company, with every external furtherance, it is of such internal quality as to set Neglect at defiance.' . . . 'A work,' concludes the well nigh enthusiastic Reviewer, 'interesting alike to the antiquary, the historian, and the philosophic

---

1 *Professor Teufelsdröckh of Weissnichtwo*: Professor Devil's-excrement of Know-not-where
2 *von Diog. . . . Weissnichtwo, 1833*: by Diogenes Teufelsdröckh, Juris Utriusque Doctor, etc., Silence and Co., Know-not-where, 1833
3 *Weissnichtwo'sche Anzeiger*: Weissnichtwo Advertiser

thinker; a masterpiece of boldness, lynx-eyed acuteness, and rugged independent Germanism and Philanthropy (*derber Kerndeutschheit und Menschenliebe*); which will not, assuredly, pass current without opposition in high places; but must and will exalt the almost new name of Teufels-dröckh to the first ranks of Philosophy, in our German Temple-of-Honour.'

Mindful of old friendship, the distinguished Professor, in this the first blaze of his fame, which however does not dazzle him, sends hither a Presentation Copy of his Book; with compliments and encomiums which modesty forbids the present Editor to rehearse; yet without indicated wish or hope of any kind, except what may be implied in the concluding phrase: *Möchte es* (this remarkable Treatise) *auch im Brittischen Boden gedeihen!*[1]

---

1 *Möchte es . . . auch im Brittischen Boden gedeihen*: May it also thrive on British soil

CHAPTER 2

Editorial Difficulties

IF for a speculative man, 'whose seedfield,' in the sublime words of the Poet, 'is Time,' no conquest is important but that of new Ideas, then might the arrival of Professor Teufelsdröckh's Book be marked with chalk in the Editor's Calendar. It is indeed an 'extensive Volume,' of boundless, almost formless contents, a very Sea of Thought; neither calm nor clear, if you will; yet wherein the toughest pearl-diver may dive to his utmost depth, and return not only with sea-wreck but with true orients.

Directly on the first perusal, almost on the first deliberate inspection, it became apparent that here a quite new Branch of Philosophy, leading to as yet undescried ulterior results, was disclosed; farther, what seemed scarcely less interesting, a quite new human Individuality, an almost unexampled personal Character, that, namely, of Professor

Teufelsdröckh the Discloser. Of both which novelties, as
far as might be possible, we resolved to master the significance. But as man is emphatically a Proselytising creature, no sooner was such mastery even fairly attempted,
than the new question arose: How might this acquired good
be imparted to others, perhaps in equal need thereof; how
could the Philosophy of Clothes and the Author of such
Philosophy be brought home, in any measure, to the
business and bosoms of our own English nation? For if
new-got gold is said to burn the pockets till it be cast forth
into circulation, much more may new Truth.

Here, however, difficulties occurred. The first thought
naturally was to publish Article after Article on this remarkable volume, in such widely-circulating Critical Journals as
the Editor might stand connected with, or by money or love
procure access to. But, on the other hand, was it not clear
that such matter as must here be revealed and treated of
might endanger the circulation of any Journal extant? If,
indeed, the whole Parties of the State could have been
abolished, Whig, Tory, and Radical, embracing in discre-
pant union; and the whole Journals of the Nation could
have been jumbled into one Journal, and the Philosophy of
Clothes poured forth in incessant torrents therefrom, the
attempt had seemed possible. But, alas, what vehicle of that
sort have we, except *Fraser's Magazine?* A vehicle all
strewed (figuratively speaking) with the maddest Water-
loo-Crackers, exploding distractively and destructively,
wheresoever the mystified passenger stands or sits; nay,
in any case, understood to be, of late years, a vehicle full to
overflowing, and inexorably shut! Besides, to state the
Philosophy of Clothes without the Philosopher, the ideas
of Teufelsdröckh without something of his personality, was
it not to insure both of entire misapprehension? Now for
Biography, had it been otherwise admissible, there were no
adequate documents, no hope of obtaining such, but
rather, owing to circumstances, a special despair. Thus

did the Editor see himself, for the while, shut out from all public utterance of these extraordinary Doctrines, and constrained to revolve them, not without disquietude, in the dark depths of his own mind.

So had it lasted for some months; and now the Volume on Clothes, read and again read, was in several points becoming lucid and lucent; the personality of its Author more and more surprising, but, in spite of all that memory and conjecture could do, more and more enigmatic; whereby the old disquietude seemed fast settling into fixed discontent, – when altogether unexpectedly arrives a Letter from Herr Hofrath Heuschrecke[1], our Professor's chief friend and associate in Weissnichtwo, with whom we had not previously corresponded. The Hofrath, after much quite extraneous matter, began dilating largely on the 'agitation and attention' which the Philosophy of Clothes was exciting in its own German Republic of Letters; on the deep significance and tendency of his Friend's Volume; and then, at length, with great circumlocution, hinted at the practicability of conveying 'some knowledge of it, and of him, to England, and through England to the distant West:' a Work on Professor Teufelsdröckh 'were undoubtedly welcome to the *Family*, the *National*, or any other of those patriotic *Libraries*, at present the glory of British Literature;' might work revolutions in Thought; and so forth; – in conclusion, intimating not obscurely, that should the present Editor feel disposed to undertake a Biography of Teufelsdröckh, he, Hofrath Heuschrecke, had it in his power to furnish the requisite Documents.

As in some chemical mixture, that has stood long evaporating, but would not crystallise, instantly when the wire or other fixed substance is introduced, crystallisation commences, and rapidly proceeds till the whole is finished,

1 *Hofrath Heuschrecke*: Councillor Grasshopper

so was it with the Editor's mind and this offer of Heu-schrecke's. Form rose out of void solution and disconti-nuity; like united itself with like in definite arrangement; and soon either in actual vision and possession, or in fixed reasonable hope, the image of the whole Enterprise had shaped itself, so to speak, into a solid mass. Cautiously yet courageously, through the twopenny post, application to the famed redoubtable OLIVER YORKE was now made: an interview, interviews with that singular man have taken place; with more of assurance on our side, with less of satire (at least of open satire) on his, than we anticipated; – for the rest, with such issue as is now visible. As to those same 'patriotic *Libraries*,' the Hofrath's counsel could only be viewed with silent amazement; but with his offer of Docu-ments we joyfully and almost instantaneously closed. Thus, too, in the sure expectation of these, we already see our task begun; and this our *Sartor Resartus*, which is properly a 'Life and Opinions of Herr Teufelsdröckh,' hourly advancing.

Of our fitness for the Enterprise, to which we have such title and vocation, it were perhaps uninteresting to say more. Let the British reader study and enjoy, in simplicity of heart, what is here presented him, and with whatever metaphysical acumen, and talent for Meditation he is possessed of. Let him strive to keep a free, open sense; cleared from the mists of Prejudice, above all from the paralysis of Cant; and directed rather to the Book itself than to the Editor of the Book. Who or what such Editor may be, must remain conjectural, and even insignificant:† it is a Voice publishing tidings of the Philosophy of Clothes; undoubtedly a Spirit addressing Spirits: whoso hath ears let him hear.

On one other point the Editor thinks it needful to give

† With us even he still communicates in some sort of mask, or muffler; and, we have reason to think, under a feigned name! – O. Y.

warning: namely, that he is animated with a true though perhaps a feeble attachment to the Institutions of our Ancestors; and minded to defend these, according to ability, at all hazards; nay, it was partly with a view to such defence that he engaged in this undertaking. To stem, or if that be impossible, profitably to divert the current of Innovation, such a Volume as Teufelsdröckh's, if cunningly planted down, were no despicable pile, or floodgate, in the Logical wear.

For the rest, be it nowise apprehended that any personal connexion of ours with Teufelsdröckh, Heuschrecke, or this Philosophy of Clothes, can pervert our judgment, or sway us to extenuate or exaggerate. Powerless, we venture to promise, are those private Compliments themselves. Grateful they may well be; as generous illusions of friendship; as fair mementos of bygone unions, of those nights and suppers of the gods, when lapped in the symphonies and harmonies of Philosophic Eloquence, though with baser accompaniments, the present Editor revelled in that feast of reason, never since vouchsafed him in so full measure! But what then? *Amicus Plato, magis amica veritas;*[1] Teufelsdröckh is our friend, Truth is our divinity. In our historical and critical capacity, we hope, we are strangers to all the world; have feud or favour with no one, – save indeed the Devil, with whom as with the Prince of Lies and Darkness we do at all times wage internecine war. This assurance, at an epoch when Puffery and Quackery have reached a height unexampled in the annals of mankind, and even English Editors, like Chinese Shopkeepers, must write on their door-lintels, *No cheating here*, – we thought it good to premise.

[1] *Amicus Plato, magis amica veritas*: Plato is a friend, but truth is a greater friend

TRUTH AND THE PRINCE OF LIES

CHAPTER 3

Reminiscences

To the Author's private circle the appearance of this singular Work on Clothes must have occasioned little less surprise than it has to the rest of the world. For ourselves, at least, few things have been more unexpected. Professor Teufelsdröckh, at the period of our acquaintance with him, seemed to lead a quite still and self-contained life: a man devoted to the higher Philosophies, indeed; yet more likely, if he published at all, to publish a Refutation of Hegel and Bardili, both of whom, strangely enough, he included under a common ban; than to descend, as he has here done, into the angry noisy Forum, with an Argument that cannot but exasperate and divide. Not, that we can remember, was the Philosophy of Clothes once touched upon between us. If through the high silent, meditative Transcendentalism of our Friend we detected any practical tendency whatever, it was at most Political, and towards a certain prospective, and for the present quite speculative, Radicalism; as indeed some correspondence, on his part, with Herr Oken of Jena was now and then suspected; though his special contributions to the *Isis* could never be more than surmised at. But, at all events, nothing Moral, still less any thing Didactico-Religious, was looked for from him.

Well do we recollect the last words he spoke in our hearing; which indeed, with the Night they were uttered in, are to be forever remembered. Lifting his huge tumbler of *Gukguk*,[1] and for a moment lowering his tobacco-pipe, he stood up in full coffeehouse (it was *Zum Grünen Ganse*,[2] the largest in Weissnichtwo, where all the Virtuosity, and nearly all the Intellect, of the place assembled of an evening); and there, with low, soul-stirring tone, and the look truly of an angel, though whether of a white or of a black one might be dubious, proposed this toast: *Die Sache der Armen in Gottes und Teufels Namen* (The Cause of the Poor in Heaven's name and—'s)! One full shout, breaking the leaden silence; then a gurgle of innumerable emptying bumpers, again followed by universal cheering, returned him loud acclaim. It was the finale of the night: resuming their pipes; in the highest enthusiasm, amid volumes of tobacco-smoke; triumphant, cloudcapt without and within, the assembly broke up, each to his thoughtful pillow. *Bleibt doch ein echter Spass- und Galgen-vogel*,[3] said several; meaning thereby that, one day, he would probably be hanged for his democratic sentiments. *Wo steckt der Schalk?*[4] added they, looking round: but Teufelsdröckh had retired by private alleys, and the Compiler of these pages beheld him no more.

In such scenes has it been our lot to live with this Philosopher, such estimate to form of his purposes and powers. And yet, thou brave Teufelsdröckh, who could tell what lurked in thee? Under those thick locks of thine, so long and lank, overlapping roof-wise the gravest face we

1 *Gukguk* is unhappily only an academical – Beer
2 *Zum Grünen Ganse*: The Green Goose
3 *Bleibt doch ein echter Spass- und Galgen-vogel*: He will always be a true joker and a gallows-bird
4 *Wo steckt der Schalk?*: Where is the rascal hiding?

ever in this world saw, there dwelt a most busy brain. In thy eyes, too, deep under their shaggy brows, and looking out so still and dreamy, have we not noticed gleams of an ethereal or else a diabolic fire, and half fancied that their stillness was but the rest of infinite motion, the *sleep* of a spinning-top? Thy little figure, there as in loose, ill-brushed, threadbare habiliments, thou sattest, amid litter and lumber, whole days, to 'think and smoke tobacco,' held in it a mighty heart. The secrets of man's Life were laid open to thee; thou sawest into the mystery of the Universe, farther than another; thou hadst *in petto* thy remarkable Volume on Clothes. Nay, was there not in that clear logically-founded Transcendentalism of thine; still more, in thy meek, silent, deepseated Sansculottism,[1] combined with a true princely Courtesy of inward nature, the visible rudiments of such speculation? But great men are too often unknown, or what is worse, misknown. Already, when we dreamed not of it, the warp of thy remarkable Volume lay on the loom; and silently, mysterious shuttles were putting in the woof!

How the Hofrath Heuschrecke is to furnish biographical data, in this case, may be a curious question; the answer of which, however, is happily not our concern, but his. To us it appeared, after repeated trial, that in Weissnichtwo, from the archives or memories of the best-informed classes, no Biography of Teufelsdröckh was to be gathered; not so much as a false one. He was a Stranger there, wafted thither by what is called the course of circumstances; concerning whose parentage, birthplace, prospects or pursuits, Curiosity had indeed made inquiries, but satisfied herself with the most indistinct replies. For himself, he was a man so still and altogether unparticipating, that to question him

1 *Sansculottism*: philosophical radicalism; lit. 'without knee breeches' (trousers being a sign of social equality during the French Revolution – AG)

even afar off on such particulars was a thing of more than usual delicacy: besides, in his sly way, he had ever some quaint turn, not without its satirical edge, wherewith to divert such intrusions, and deter you from the like. Wits spoke of him secretly as if he were a kind of Melchizedek, without father or mother of any kind; sometimes, with reference to his great historic and statistic knowledge, and the vivid way he had of expressing himself like an eye-witness of distant transactions and scenes, they called him the *Ewige Jude*, Everlasting, or as we say, Wandering Jew.

To the most, indeed, he had become not so much a Man as a Thing; which Thing doubtless they were accustomed to see, and with satisfaction; but no more thought of accounting for than for the fabrication of their daily *Allgemeine Zeitung*,[1] or the domestic habits of the Sun. Both were there and welcome; the world enjoyed what good was in them, and thought no more of the matter. The man Teufelsdröckh passed and repassed, in his little circle, as one of those originals and nondescripts, more frequent in German Universities than elsewhere; of whom, though you see them alive, and feel certain enough that they must have a History, no History seems to be discoverable; or only such as men give of mountain rocks and antediluvian ruins: that they have been created by unknown agencies, are in a state of gradual decay, and for the present reflect light and resist pressure; that is, are visible and tangible objects in this phantasm world, where so much other mystery is.

It was to be remarked that though, by title and diploma, *Professor der Allerley-Wissenschaft*, or as we should say in English, 'Professor of Things in General,' he had never delivered any Course; perhaps never been incited thereto by any public furtherance or requisition. To all appearance, the enlightened Government of Weissnichtwo, in founding their New University, imagined they had done enough, if 'in times like ours,' as the half-official Program expressed it, 'when all things are, rapidly or slowly, resolving themselves into Chaos, a Professorship of this kind had been established; whereby, as occasion called, the task of bodying somewhat forth again from such Chaos might be, even slightly, facilitated.' That actual Lectures should be held,

1 *Allgemeine Zeitung*: Universal Gazette

and Public Classes for the 'Science of Things in General,' they doubtless considered premature; on which ground too they had only established the Professorship, nowise endowed it; so that Teufelsdröckh, 'recommended by the highest Names,' had been promoted thereby to a Name merely.

Great, among the more enlightened classes, was the admiration of this new Professorship: how an enlightened Government had seen into the Want of the Age (*Zeitbedürfniss*); how at length, instead of Denial and Destruction, we were to have a science of Affirmation and Re-construction; and Germany and Weissnichtwo were, where they should be, in the vanguard of the world. Considerable also was the wonder at the new Professor, dropt opportunely enough into the nascent University; so able to lecture, should occasion call; so ready to hold his peace for indefinite periods, should an enlightened Government consider that occasion did not call. But such admiration and such wonder, being followed by no act to keep them living, could last only nine days; and, long before our visit to that scene, had quite died away. The more cunning heads thought it was all an expiring clutch at popularity, on the part of a Minister, whom domestic embarrassments, court intrigues, old age, and dropsy soon afterwards finally drove from the helm.

As for Teufelsdröckh, except by his nightly appearances at the *Grünen Ganse*, Weissnichtwo saw little of him, felt little of him. Here, over his tumbler of Gukguk, he sat reading Journals; sometimes contemplatively looking into the clouds of his tobacco-pipe, without other visible employment: always, from his mild ways, an agreeable phenomenon there; more especially when he opened his lips for speech; on which occasions the whole Coffeehouse would hush itself into silence, as if sure to hear something noteworthy. Nay, perhaps to hear a whole series and river of the most memorable utterances; such as, when once thawed, he would for hours indulge in, with fit audience:

and the more memorable, as issuing from a head apparently not more interested in them, not more conscious of them, than is the sculptured stone head of some public Fountain, which through its brass mouth-tube emits water to the worthy and the unworthy; careless whether it be for cooking victuals or quenching conflagrations; indeed, maintains the same earnest assiduous look, whether any water be flowing or not.

To the Editor of these sheets, as to a young enthusiastic Englishman, however unworthy, Teufelsdröckh opened himself perhaps more than to the most. Pity only that we could not then half guess his importance, and scrutinise him with due power of vision! We enjoyed, what not three men in Weissnichtwo could boast of, a certain degree of access to the Professor's private domicile. It was the attic floor of the highest house in the Wahngasse;[1] and might truly be called the pinnacle of Weissnichtwo, for it rose sheer up above the contiguous roofs, themselves rising from elevated ground. Moreover, with its windows, it looked towards all the four *Orte*, or as the Scotch say, and we ought to say, *Airts*:[2] the Sitting-room itself commanded three; another came to view in the *Schlafgemach* (Bed-room) at the opposite end; to say nothing of the Kitchen, which offered two, as it were, *duplicates*, and showing nothing new. So that it was in fact the speculum or watch-tower of Teufelsdröckh; wherefrom, sitting at ease, he might see the whole life-circulation of that considerable City; the streets and lanes of which, with all their doing and driving (*Thun und Treiben*) were for most part visible there.

'I look down into all that wasp-nest or bee-hive,' have we heard him say, 'and witness their wax-laying and honey-making, and poison-brewing, and choking by sulphur. From the Palace esplanade, where music plays while Serene Highness is pleased to eat his victuals, down to the low

1 *Wahngasse*: Fantasy lane
2 *Orte . . . Airts*: points of the compass

lane, where in her door-sill the aged widow, knitting for a thin livelihood, sits to feel the afternoon sun, I see it all; for, except the Schlosskirche[1] weathercock, no biped stands so high. Couriers arrive bestrapped and bebooted, bearing Joy and Sorrow bagged up in pouches of leather: there, top-laden, and with four swift horses, rolls in the country Baron

1 *Schlosskirche*: Castle church

and his household; here, on timber leg, the lamed Soldier
hops painfully along, begging alms: a thousand carriages,
and wains, and cars, come tumbling in with Food, with
young Rusticity, and other Raw Produce, inanimate or
animate, and go tumbling out again with Produce manufactured. That living flood, pouring through these streets,
of all qualities and ages, knowest thou whence it is coming,
whither it is going? *Aus der Ewigkeit, zu der Ewigkeit hin*:
From Eternity, onwards to Eternity! These are Apparitions:
what else? Are they not Souls rendered visible; in Bodies,
that took shape, and will lose it; melting into air? Their solid
pavement is a Picture of the Sense; they walk on the bosom
of Nothing, blank Time is behind them and before them.
Or fanciest thou, the red and yellow Clothes-screen yonder, with spurs on its heels, and feather in its crown, is but
of To-day, without a Yesterday or a To-morrow; and had
not rather its Ancestor alive when Hengst and Horsa
overran thy Island? Friend, thou seest here a living link
in that Tissue of History, which inweaves all Being: watch
well, or it will be past thee, and seen no more.'

'*Ach, mein Lieber!*[1] said he once, at midnight, when we
had returned from the Coffeehouse in rather earnest talk, 'it
is a true sublimity to dwell here. These fringes of lamplight,
struggling up through smoke and thousandfold exhalation,
some fathoms into the ancient reign of Night, what thinks
Boötes of them, as he leads his Hunting Dogs over the
Zenith in their leash of sidereal fire? That stifled hum of
Midnight, when Traffic has lain down to rest; and the
chariot-wheels of Vanity, still rolling here and there
through distant streets, are bearing her to Halls roofed
in, and lighted to the due pitch for her; and only Vice and
Misery, to prowl or to moan like nightbirds, are abroad:
that hum, I say, like the stertorous, unquiet slumber of sick
Life, is heard in Heaven! Oh, under that hideous coverlid of

1 *Ach, mein Lieber*: Ah, my dear sir

vapours, and putrefactions, and unimaginable gases, what a
Fermenting-vat lies simmering and hid! The joyful and the
sorrowful are there; men are dying there, men are being
born; men are praying – on the other side of a brick
partition, men are cursing; and around them all is the vast,
void Night. The proud Grandee still lingers in his per-
fumed saloons, or reposes within damask curtains; Wretchedness cowers into truckle-beds, or shivers hunger-stricken
into its lair of straw: in obscure cellars, *Rouge-et-Noir*
languidly emits its voice-of-destiny to haggard hungry
Villains; while Councillors of State sit plotting, and playing
their high chess-game, whereof the pawns are Men. The
Lover whispers his mistress that the coach is ready; and she,
full of hope and fear, glides down, to fly with him over the
borders: the Thief, still more silently, sets-to his picklocks
and crowbars, or lurks in wait till the watchmen first snore
in their boxes. Gay mansions, with supper-rooms and
dancing-rooms, are full of light and music and high-
swelling hearts; but, in the Condemned Cells, the pulse
of life beats tremulous and faint, and bloodshot eyes look out
through the darkness, which is around and within, for the
light of a stern last morning. Six men are to be hanged on the
morrow: comes no hammering from the *Rabenstein?*[1] – their
gallows must even now be o' building. Upwards of five
hundred thousand two-legged animals without feathers lie
round us, in horizontal position; their heads all in night-
caps, and full of the foolishest dreams. Riot cries aloud, and
staggers and swaggers in his rank dens of shame; and the
Mother, with streaming hair, kneels over her pallid dying
infant, whose cracked lips only her tears now moisten. – All
these heaped and huddled together, with nothing but a
little carpentry and masonry between them; – crammed in,
like salted fish, in their barrel; – or weltering, shall I say, like
an Egyptian pitcher of tamed Vipers, each struggling to get

1 *Rabenstein*: raven's stone; the gallows

its *head above* the others: *such* work goes on under that smoke-counterpane! – But I, *mein Werther*,[1] sit above it all; I am alone with the Stars.'

We looked in his face to see whether, in the utterance of such extraordinary Night-thoughts, no feeling might be traced there; but with the light we had, which indeed was only a single tallow-light, and far enough from the window, nothing save that old calmness and fixedness was visible.

These were the Professor's talking seasons: most commonly he spoke in mere monosyllables, or sat altogether silent, and smoked; while the visitor had liberty either to say what he listed, receiving for answer an occasional grunt; or to look round for a space, and then take himself away. It was a strange apartment; full of books and tattered papers, and miscellaneous shreds of all conceivable substances, 'united in a common element of dust.' Books lay on tables, and below tables; here fluttered a sheet of manuscript, there a torn handkerchief, or nightcap hastily thrown aside: ink-bottles alternated with bread-crusts, coffee-pots, tobacco-boxes, Periodical Literature, and Blücher Boots. Old Lieschen (Lisekin, 'Liza), who was his bed-maker and stove-lighter, his washer and wringer, cook, errand-maid, and general lion's-provider, and for the rest a very orderly creature, had no sovereign authority in this last citadel of Teufelsdröckh; only some once in the month, she half-forcibly made her way thither, with broom and duster, and (Teufelsdröckh hastily saving his manuscripts) effected a partial clearance, a jail-delivery of such lumber as was not Literary. These were her *Erdbebungen*[2] (Earthquakes), which Teufelsdröckh dreaded worse than the pestilence; nevertheless, to such length he had been forced to comply. Glad would he have been to sit here philosophising for ever, or till the litter, by accumulation, drove him out of doors: but Lieschen was his right-arm, and spoon, and necessary

1 *mein Werther*: my good friend
2 *Erdbebungen*: lit. earth-vibrations

HERR HOFRATH HEUSCHRECKE

of life, and would not be flatly gainsayed. We can still remember the ancient woman; so silent that some thought her dumb; deaf also you would often have supposed her; for Teufelsdröckh and Teufelsdröckh only would she serve or give heed to; and with him she seemed to communicate chiefly by signs; if it were not rather by some secret divination that she guessed all his wants, and supplied them. Assiduous old dame! she scoured, and sorted, and swept, in her kitchen, with the least possible violence to the ear; yet all was tight and right there: hot and black came the coffee ever at the due moment; and the speechless Lieschen herself looked out on you, from under her clean white coif with its lappets, through her clean withered face and wrinkles, with a look of helpful intelligence, almost of benevolence.

Few strangers, as above hinted, had admittance hither: the only one we ever saw there, ourselves excepted, was the Hofrath Heuschrecke, already known, by name and expectation, to the readers of these pages. To us, at that period, Herr Heuschrecke seemed one of those purse-mouthed, crane-necked, clean-brushed, pacific individuals, perhaps sufficiently distinguished in society by this fact, that, in dry weather or in wet, 'they never appear without their umbrella.' Had we not known with what 'little wisdom' the world is governed; and how, in Germany as elsewhere, the ninety and nine Public Men can for most part be but mute train-bearers to the hundredth, perhaps but stalking-horses and willing or unwilling dupes, – it might have seemed wonderful how Herr Heuschrecke should be named a *Rath*, or Councillor, and Counsellor, even in Weissnichtwo. What counsel to any man, or to any woman, could this particular Hofrath give; in whose loose, zigzag figure; in whose thin visage, as it went jerking to and fro, in minute incessant fluctuation, – you traced rather confusion worse confounded; at most, Timidity and physical Cold? Some indeed said withal, he was 'the very Spirit

of Love embodied:' blue earnest eyes, full of sadness and
kindness; purse ever open, and so forth; the whole of which,
we shall now hope for many reasons, was not quite ground-
less. Nevertheless, friend Teufelsdröckh's outline, who
indeed handled the burin like few in these cases, was
probably the best: *Er hat Gemüth und Geist, hat wenigstens
gehabt, doch ohne Organ, ohne Schicksals-Gunst; ist gegen-
wärtig aber halb-zerrüttet, halb-erstarrt,* 'He has heart and
talent, at least has had such, yet without fit mode of
utterance, or favour of Fortune; and so is now half-cracked,
half-congealed.' – What the Hofrath shall think of this,
when he sees it, readers may wonder: we, safe in the
stronghold of Historical Fidelity, are careless.

The main point, doubtless, for us all, is his love of
Teufelsdröckh, which indeed was also by far the most
decisive feature of Heuschrecke himself. We are enabled
to assert that he hung on the Professor with the fondness of
a Boswell for his Johnson. And perhaps with the like return;
for Teufelsdröckh treated his gaunt admirer with little
outward regard, as some half-rational or altogether irrational friend, and at best loved him out of gratitude and by
habit. On the other hand, it was curious to observe with
what reverent kindness, and a sort of fatherly protection,
our Hofrath, being the elder, richer, and as he fondly
imagined far more practically influential of the two, looked
and tended on his little Sage, whom he seemed to consider
as a living oracle. Let but Teufelsdröckh open his mouth,
Heuschrecke's also unpuckered itself into a free doorway,
besides his being all eye and all ear, so that nothing might
be lost: and then, at every pause in the harangue he gurgled
out his pursy chuckle of a cough-laugh (for the machinery
of laughter took some time to get in motion, and seemed
crank and slack), or else his twanging, nasal *Bravo! Das
glaub' ich*;[1] in either case, by way of heartiest approval. In

1 *Das glaub' ich*: I believe that

short, if Teufelsdröckh was Dalai-Lama, of which except perhaps in his self-seclusion, and god-like Indifference, there was no symptom, then might Heuschrecke pass for his chief Talapoin, to whom no dough-pill he could knead and publish was other than medicinal and sacred.

In such environment, social, domestic, physical, did Teufelsdröckh, at the time of our acquaintance, and most likely does he still, live and meditate. Here, perched up in his high Wahngasse watchtower, and often, in solitude, outwatching the Bear, it was that the indomitable Inquirer fought all his battles with Dulness and Darkness; here, in all probability, that he wrote this surprising Volume on *Clothes*. Additional particulars: of his age, which was of that standing middle sort you could only guess at; of his wide surtout; the colour of his trousers, fashion of his broad-brimmed steeple-hat, and so forth, we might report, but do not. The Wisest truly is, in these times, the Greatest; so that an enlightened curiosity leaving Kings and such like to rest very much on their own basis, turns more and more to the Philosophic Class; nevertheless, what reader expects that, with all our writing and reporting, Teufelsdröckh could be brought home to him, till once the Documents arrive? His Life, Fortunes, and Bodily Presence, are as yet hidden from us, or matter only of faint conjecture. But on the other hand, does not his Soul lie enclosed in this remarkable Volume, much more truly than Pedro Garcia's did in the buried Bag of Doubloons? To the soul of Diogenes Teufelsdröckh, to his opinions namely on the 'Origin and Influence of Clothes,' we for the present gladly return.

CHAPTER 4

Characteristics

IT were a piece of vain flattery to pretend that this Work on Clothes entirely contents us; that it is not, like all works of Genius, like the very Sun, which, though the highest published Creation, or work of Genius, has nevertheless black spots and troubled nebulosities amid its effulgence, – a mixture of insight, inspiration, with dulness, double-vision, and even utter blindness.

Without committing ourselves to those enthusiastic praises and prophesyings of the *Weissnichtwo'sche Anzeiger*, we admitted that the Book had in a high degree excited us to self-activity, which is the best effect of any book; that it had even operated changes in our way of thought; nay, that it promised to prove, as it were, the opening of a new mine-shaft, wherein the whole world of Speculation might henceforth dig to unknown depths. More specially it may now be declared that Professor Teufelsdröckh's acquirements, patience of research, philosophic and even poetic vigour, are here made indisputably manifest; and unhappily no less his prolixity and tortuosity and manifold ineptitude; that, on the whole, as in opening new mine-shafts is not unreasonable, there is much rubbish in his Book, though likewise specimens of almost invaluable ore. A paramount popularity in England we cannot promise him. Apart from the choice of such a topic as Clothes, too often the manner of treating it betokens in the Author a rusticity and academic seclusion, unblamable, indeed inevitable in a German, but fatal to his success with our public.

Of good society Teufelsdröckh appears to have seen little, or has mostly forgotten what he saw. He speaks out with a strange plainness; calls many things by their mere dictionary names. To him the Upholsterer is no Pontiff, neither is any Drawing-room a Temple, were it never so begilt and overhung: 'a whole immensity of Brussels carpets, and pier-glasses, and ormolu,' as he himself expresses it, 'cannot hide from me that such Drawing-room is simply a section of Infinite Space, where so many God-created Souls do for the time meet together.' To Teufelsdröckh the highest Duchess is respectable, is venerable; but nowise for her pearl-bracelets, and Malines laces: in his eyes, the star of a Lord is little less and little more than the broad button of Birmingham spelter in a Clown's smock; 'each is an implement,' he says, 'in its kind; a tag for *hooking-together*; and, for the rest, was dug from the earth, and hammered on a stithy before smiths' fingers.' Thus does the Professor look in men's faces with a strange impartiality, a strange scientific freedom; like a man unversed in the higher circles, like a man dropped thither from the Moon. Rightly considered, it is in this peculiarity, running through his whole system of thought, that all these short-comings, over-shootings, and multiform perversities, take rise: if indeed they have not a second source, also natural enough, in his Transcendental Philosophies, and humour of looking at all Matter and Material things as Spirit; whereby truly his case were but the more hopeless, the more lamentable.

To the Thinkers of this nation, however, of which class it is firmly believed there are individuals yet extant, we can safely recommend the Work: nay, who knows but among the fashionable ranks too, if it be true, as Teufelsdröckh maintains, that 'within the most starched cravat there passes a windpipe and wesand, and under the thickliest embroidered waistcoat beats a heart,' – the force of that rapt earnestness may be felt, and here and there an arrow of the soul pierce through. In our wild Seer, shaggy, unkempt, like a Baptist living on locusts and wild honey, there is an untutored energy, a silent as it were unconscious strength, which, except in the higher walks of Literature, must be rare. Many a deep glance, and often with unspeakable precision, has he cast into mysterious Nature, and the still more mysterious Life of Man. Wonderful it is with what cutting words, now and then, he severs asunder the confusion; sheers down, were it furlongs deep, into the true centre of the matter; and there not only hits the nail on the head, but with crushing force smites it home, and buries it. – On the other hand, let us be free to admit, he is the most unequal writer breathing. Often after some such feat, he will play truant for long pages, and go dawdling and dreaming, and mumbling and maundering the merest commonplaces, as if he were asleep with eyes open, which indeed he is.

Of his boundless Learning, and how all reading and literature in most known tongues, from *Sanconiathon* to *Dr. Lingard*, from your Oriental *Shasters*, and *Talmuds*, and *Korans*, with Cassini's *Siamese Tables*, and Laplace's *Mécanique Céleste*, down to *Robinson Crusoe* and the *Belfast Town and Country Almanack*, are familiar to him, – we shall say nothing: for unexampled as it is with us, to the Germans such universality of study passes without wonder, as a thing commendable, indeed, but natural, indispensable, and there of course. A man that devotes his life to learning, shall he not be learned?

In respect of style our Author manifests the same genial capability, marred too often by the same rudeness, inequality, and apparent want of intercourse with the higher classes. Occasionally, as above hinted, we find consummate vigour, a true inspiration: his burning Thoughts step forth in fit burning Words, like so many full-formed Minervas, issuing amid flame and splendour from Jove's head; a rich, idiomatic diction, picturesque allusions, fiery poetic emphasis, or quaint tricksy turns; all the graces and terrors of a wild Imagination, wedded to the clearest Intellect, alternate in beautiful vicissitude. Were it not that sheer sleeping and soporific passages; circumlocutions, repetitions, touches even of pure doting jargon, so often intervene! On the whole, Professor Teufelsdröckh is not a cultivated writer. Of his sentences perhaps not more than nine-tenths stand straight on their legs; the remainder are in quite angular attitudes, buttressed up by props (of parentheses and dashes), and ever, with this or the other tagrag hanging from them; a few even sprawl out helplessly on all sides quite broken-backed and dismembered. Nevertheless, in almost his very worst moods, there lies in him a singular attraction. A wild tone pervades the whole utterance of the man, like its keynote and regulator; now screwing itself aloft as into the Song of Spirits, or else the shrill mockery of Fiends; now sinking in cadences, not without melodious heartiness, though sometimes abrupt enough, into the common pitch, when we hear it only as a monotonous hum; of which hum the true character is extremely difficult to fix. Up to this hour we have never fully satisfied ourselves whether it is a tone and hum of real Humour, which we reckon among the very highest qualities of genius, or some remote echo of mere Insanity and Inanity, which doubtless ranks below the very lowest.

Under a like difficulty, in spite even of our personal intercourse, do we still lie with regard to the Professor's moral feeling. Gleams of an ethereal Love burst forth from him, soft wailings of infinite Pity; he could clasp the whole Universe into his bosom, and keep it warm; it seems as if under that rude exterior there dwelt a very seraph. Then again he is so sly and still, so imperturbably saturnine; shews such indifference, malign coolness towards all that men strive after; and ever with some half-visible wrinkle of a bitter sardonic humour, if indeed it be not mere stolid callousness, – that you look on him almost with a shudder, as on some incarnate Mephistopheles, to whom this great terrestrial and celestial Round, after all, were but some huge foolish Whirligig, where kings and beggars, and angels and demons, and stars and streetsweepings, were chaotically whirled; in which only children could take interest. His look, as we mentioned, is probably the gravest ever seen: yet it is not of that cast-iron gravity frequent enough among our own Chancery suitors; but rather the gravity as of some silent, high-encircled mountain-pool, perhaps the crater of an extinct volcano; into whose black deeps you fear to gaze: those eyes, those lights that sparkle in it, may indeed be reflexes of the heavenly Stars, but perhaps also glances from the region of Nether Fire!

Certainly a most involved, self-secluded, altogether enigmatic nature, this of Teufelsdröckh! Here, however, we gladly recall to mind that once we saw him *laugh*; once only, perhaps it was the first and last time in his life; but then such a peal of laughter, enough to have awakened the Seven Sleepers! It was of Jean Paul's doing: some single billow in that vast world-Mahlstrom of Humour, with its Heaven-kissing coruscations, which is now, alas, all congealed in the frost of Death! The large-bodied Poet and the small, both large enough in soul, sat talking miscellaneously together, the present Editor being privileged to listen; and now Paul, in his serious way, was giving one of those inimitable 'Extra-harangues;' and, as it chanced, On the Proposal for a *Cast-metal King*: gradually a light kindled in our Professor's eyes and face, a beaming, mantling, loveliest light; through those murky features, a radiant ever-young Apollo looked; and he burst forth like the neighing of all Tattersall's, – tears streaming down his cheeks, pipe held aloft, foot clutched into the air, – loud, long-continuing, uncontrollable; a laugh not of the face and diaphragm only, but of the whole man from head to heel. The present Editor, who laughed indeed, yet with measure, began to fear all was not right: however, Teufelsdröckh composed himself, and sank into his old stillness; on his inscrutable countenance there was, if any thing, a slight look of shame; and Richter himself could not rouse him again. Readers who have any tincture of Psychology know how much is to be inferred from this; and that no man who has once heartily and wholly laughed can be altogether irreclaimably bad. How much lies in Laughter: the cipher-key, wherewith we decipher the whole man! Some men wear an everlasting barren simper; in the smile of others lies a cold glitter as of ice: the fewest are able to laugh, what can be called laughing, but only sniff and titter and snigger from the throat outwards; or at best, produce some whiffling husky cachinnation, as if they were laughing through wool: of none such comes good. The man who cannot laugh is not only fit for treasons, stratagems and spoils; but his whole life is already a treason and a stratagem.

Considered as an Author, Herr Teufelsdröckh has one scarcely pardonable fault, doubtless his worst: an almost total want of arrangement. In this remarkable Volume, it is true, his adherence to the mere course of Time produces, through the Narrative portions, a certain shew of outward method; but of true logical method and sequence there is too little. Apart from its multifarious sections and subdivisions, the Work naturally falls into two Parts; a Historical-Descriptive, and a Philosophical-Speculative: but falls, unhappily, by no firm line of demarcation; in that labyrinthic combination, each Part overlaps, and indents, and indeed runs quite through the other. Many sections are of a debatable rubric, or even quite nondescript and unnameable; whereby the Book not only loses in accessibility, but too often distresses us like some mad banquet, wherein all courses had been confounded, and fish and flesh, soup and solid, oyster-sauce, lettuces, Rhine-wine and French mustard, were hurled into one huge tureen or trough, and the hungry Public invited to help itself. To bring what order we can out of this Chaos shall be part of our endeavour.

CHAPTER 5

The World in Clothes

'As Montesquieu wrote a *Spirit of Laws*,' observes our Professor, 'so could I write a *Spirit of Clothes*; thus, with an *Esprit des Lois*, properly an *Esprit de Coutumes* we should have an *Esprit de Costumes*.[1] For neither in tailoring nor in legislating does man proceed by mere Accident, but the hand is ever guided on by mysterious operations of the mind. In all his Modes and habilatory endeavours an Architectural Idea will be found lurking; his Body and the Cloth are the site and materials whereon and whereby his beautified edifice, of a Person, is to be built. Whether he flow gracefully out in folded mantles, based on light sandals; tower up in high headgear, from amid peaks, spangles and bell-girdles; swell out in starched ruffs, buckram stuffings and monstrous tuberosities; or girth himself into separate sections, and front the world an Agglomeration

1 *Esprit des Lois . . . Esprit de Coutumes . . . Esprit de Costumes*: Spirit of the Laws . . . Spirit of Customs . . . Spirit of Costumes

of four limbs, – will depend on the nature of such Architectural Idea: whether Grecian, Gothic, Later-Gothic, or
altogether Modern, and Parisian or Anglo-Dandiacal.
Again, what meaning lies in Colour! From the soberest
drab to the high-flaming scarlet, spiritual idiosyncrasies
unfold themselves in choice of Colour: if the Cut betoken
Intellect and Talent, so does the Colour betoken Temper
and Heart. In all which, among nations as among individuals, there is an incessant, indubitable, though infinitely
complex working of Cause and Effect: every snip of the
Scissors has been regulated and prescribed by ever-active
Influences, which doubtless to Intelligences of a superior
order are neither invisible nor illegible.

'For such superior Intelligences a Cause-and-effect Philosophy of Clothes, as of Laws, were probably a comfortable
winter-evening entertainment: nevertheless, for inferior Intelligences, like men, such Philosophies have always seemed
to me uninstructive enough. Nay, what is your Montesquieu
himself but a clever infant spelling Letters from a hieroglyphical prophetic Book, the lexicon of which lies in Eternity,
in Heaven? – Let any Cause-and-Effect Philosopher explain,
not why I wear such and such a Garment, obey such and
such a Law; but even why *I* am *here*, to wear and obey any
thing! – Much, therefore, if not the whole, of that same
Spirit of Clothes I shall suppress, as hypothetical, ineffectual,
and even impertinent: naked Facts, and Deductions drawn
therefrom in quite another than that omniscient style, are
my humbler and proper province.'

Acting on which prudent restriction, Teufelsdröckh has
nevertheless contrived to take in a well nigh boundless
extent of field; at least, the boundaries too often lie quite
beyond our horizon. Selection being indispensable, we
shall here glance over his First Part only in the most cursory
manner. This First Part is, no doubt, distinguished by
omnivorous learning, and utmost patience and fairness:
at the same time, in its results and delineations, it is much

more likely to interest the Compilers of some *Library* of General, Entertaining, Useful, or even Useless Knowledge than the miscellaneous readers of these pages. Was it this Part of the Book which Heuschrecke had in view, when he recommended us to that joint-stock vehicle of publication, 'at present the glory of British Literature?' If so, the Library Editors are welcome to dig in it for their own behoof.

To the First Chapter, which turns on Paradise and Figleaves, and leads us into interminable disquisitions of a mythological, metaphorical, cabalistico-sartorial and quite antediluvian cast, we shall content ourselves with giving an unconcerned approval. Still less have we to do with 'Lilis, Adam's first wife, whom, according to the Talmudists, he had before Eve, and who bore him, in that wedlock, the whole progeny of aerial, aquatic, and terrestrial Devils,' – very needlessly, we think. On this portion of the Work, with its profound glances into the *Adam-Kadmon*, or Primeval Element, here strangely brought into relation with the *Nifl* and *Muspel* (Darkness and Light) of the antique North, it may be enough to say that its correctness of deduction, and depth of Talmudic and Rabbinical lore have filled perhaps not the worst Hebraist in Britain with something like astonishment.

But quitting this twilight region, Teufelsdröckh hastens from the Tower of Babel, to follow the dispersion of Mankind over the whole habitable and habilable globe. Walking by the light of Oriental, Pelasgic, Scandinavian, Egyptian, Otaheitean, Ancient and Modern researches of every conceivable kind, he strives to give us in compressed shape (as the Nürnbergers give an *Orbis Pictus*) an *Orbis Vestitus*;[1] or view of the costumes of all mankind, in all countries, in all times. It is here that to the Antiquarian, to the Historian, we can triumphantly say: Fall to! Here is

1 *Orbis Pictus*: The World in Pictures; *Orbis Vestitus*: The World in Clothes

Learning: an irregular Treasury, if you will; but inexhaustible as the Hoard of King Nibelung which twelve waggons in twelve days, at the rate of three journeys a day, could not carry off. Sheepskin cloaks and wampum belts; phylacteries, stoles, albs; chlamides, togas, Chinese silks, Afghaun shawls, trunk hose, leather breeches, Celtic philibegs (though breeches, as the name *Gallia Braccata* indicates, are the more ancient), Hussar cloaks, Vandyke tippets, ruffs, fardingales, are brought vividly before us, – even the Kilmarnock nightcap is not forgotten. For most part too we must admit that the Learning, heterogeneous as it is, and tumbled down quite pell-mell, is true concentrated and purified Learning, the drossy parts smelted out and thrown aside.

Philosophical reflections intervene, and sometimes touching pictures of human life. Of this sort the following has surprised us. The first purpose of Clothes, as our Professor imagines, was not warmth or decency, but ornament. 'Miserable indeed,' says he, 'was the condition of the Aboriginal Savage, glaring fiercely from under his fleece of hair, which with the beard reached down to his loins, and hung round him like a matted cloak; the rest of his body sheeted in its thick natural fell. He loitered in the sunny glades of the forest, living on wild fruits; or, as the ancient Caledonian, squatted himself in morasses, lurking for his bestial or human prey; without implements, without arms, save the ball of heavy Flint, to which, that his sole possession and defence might not be lost, he had attached a long cord of plaited thongs; thereby recovering as well as hurling it with deadly unerring skill. Nevertheless, the pains of Hunger and Revenge once satisfied, his next care was not Comfort but Decoration (*Putz*). Warmth he found in the toils of the chase; or amid dried leaves, in his hollow tree, in his bark shed, or natural grotto: but for Decoration he must have Clothes. Nay, among wild people, we find tattooing and painting even prior to Clothes. The first spiritual want

THE ABORIGINAL SAVAGE

of a barbarous man is Decoration; as indeed we still see among the barbarous classes in civilised countries.

'Reader, the heaven-inspired melodious Singer; loftiest Serene Highness; nay thy own amber-locked, snow-and-rose-bloom Maiden, worthy to glide sylphlike almost on air, whom thou lovest, worshippest as a divine Presence, which indeed, symbolically taken, she is, – has descended, like thyself, from that same hair-mantled, flint-hurling Aboriginal Anthropophagus! Out of the eater cometh forth meat; out of the strong cometh forth sweetness. What changes are wrought not by Time, yet in Time! For not Mankind only, but all that Mankind does or beholds, is in continual growth, re-genesis and self-perfecting vitality. Cast forth thy Act, thy Word, into the ever-living, ever-working Universe: it is a seed-grain that cannot die; unnoticed to-day (says one) it will be found flourishing as a Banyan-grove (perhaps, alas, as a Hemlock-forest!) after a thousand years.

'He who first shortened the labour of Copyists by device of *Movable Types* was disbanding hired Armies, and cash-iering most Kings and Senates, and creating a whole new Democratic world; he had invented the Art of Printing. The first ground handful of Nitre, Sulphur, and Charcoal drove Monk Schwartz's pestle through the ceiling: what will the last do? Achieve the final undisputed prostration of Force under Thought, of Animal Courage under Spiritual. A simple invention was it in the old-world Grazier, – sick of lugging his slow Ox about the country till he got it bartered for corn or oil, – to take a piece of Leather, and thereon scratch or stamp the mere Figure of an Ox (or *Pecus*); put it in his pocket, and call it *Pecunia*, Money. Yet hereby did Barter grow Sale, the Leather Money is now Golden and Paper, and all miracles have been out-miracled: for there are Rothschilds and English National Debts; and whoso has sixpence is Sovereign (to the length of sixpence) over all men; commands Cooks to feed him, Philosophers to teach him, Kings to mount guard over him, – to the length of sixpence. – Clothes too, which began in foolishest love of Ornament, what have they not become! Increased Security, and pleasurable Heat soon followed: but what of these? Shame, divine Shame (*Schaam*, Modesty), as yet a stranger to the Anthropophagous bosom, arose there mysteriously under Clothes; a mystic grove-encircled shrine for the Holy in man. Clothes gave us individuality, distinctions, social polity; Clothes have made Men of us; they are threatening to make Clothes-screens of us.

'But on the whole,' continues our eloquent Professor, 'Man is a Tool-using Animal (*Handthierendes Thier*). Weak in himself, and of small stature, he stands on a basis, at most for the flattest-soled, of some half square-foot, insecurely enough; has to straddle out his legs, lest the very wind supplant him. Feeblest of bipeds! Three quintals are a crushing load for him; the Steer of the meadow tosses him aloft, like a waste rag. Nevertheless he can use Tools, can devise Tools: with these the granite mountain melts into light dust before him; he kneads glowing iron, as if it were soft paste; seas are his smooth highway, winds and fire his unwearying steeds. Nowhere do you find him without Tools; without Tools he is nothing, with Tools he is all.'

Here may we not, for a moment, interrupt the stream of Oratory with a remark that this Definition of the Tool-using Animal, appears to us, of all that Animal-sort, considerably the precisest and best? Man is called a Laughing Animal: but do not the apes also laugh, or attempt to do it; and is the manliest man the greatest and oftenest laugher? Teufelsdröckh himself, as we said, laughed only once. Still less do we make of that other French Definition of the Cooking Animal; which, indeed, for rigorous scientific purposes, is as good as useless. Can a Tartar be said to Cook, when he only readies his steak by riding on it? Again, what Cookery does the Green-lander use, beyond stowing up his whale-blubber, as a marmot, in the like case, might do? Or how would Monsieur Ude prosper among those Orinocco Indians who, according to Humboldt, lodge in crow-nests, on the branches of trees; and, for half the year, have no victuals but pipe-clay, the whole country being under water? But on the other hand, show us the human being, of any period or climate, without his Tools: those very Caledo-nians, as we saw, had their Flint-ball, and Thong to it, such as no brute has or can have.

'Man is a Tool-using animal,' concludes Teufels-dröckh in his abrupt way; 'of which truth Clothes are but one example: and surely if we consider the interval between the first wooden Dibble fashioned by man, and those Liverpool Steam-carriages, or the British House of Commons, we shall note what progress he has made. He digs up certain black stones from the bosom of the Earth, and says to them, *Transport me, and this luggage, at the rate of five-and-thirty miles an hour*; and they do it:

he collects, apparently by lot, six hundred and fifty-eight* miscellaneous individuals, and says to them, *Make this nation toil for us, bleed for us, hunger, and sorrow, and sin for us*; and they do it.'

* The number of British Members of Parliament in 1838 – AG

CHAPTER 6

Aprons

ONE of the most unsatisfactory Sections in the whole Volume is that on *Aprons*. What though stout old Gao the Persian Blacksmith, 'whose Apron, now indeed hidden under jewels, because raised in revolt which proved successful, is still the royal standard of that country;' what though John Knox's Daughter, 'who threatened Sovereign Majesty that she would catch her Husband's head in her Apron, rather than he should lie and be a Bishop;' what though the Landgravine Elizabeth, with many other Apron worthies, – figure here? An idle wire-drawing spirit, sometimes even a tone of levity, approaching to conventional satire, is too clearly discernible. What, for example, are we to make of such sentences as the following?

'Aprons are Defences; against injury to cleanliness, to

safety, to modesty, sometimes to roguery. From the thin slip of notched silk (as it were, the Emblem and beatified Ghost of an Apron), which some highest-bred housewife, sitting at Nürnberg Workboxes and Toyboxes, has gracefully fastened on; to the thick-tanned hide, girt round him with thongs, wherein the Builder builds, and at evening sticks his trowel; or to those jingling sheet-iron Aprons, wherein your otherwise half-naked Vulcans hammer and smelt in their Smelt-furnace, – is there not range enough in the fashion and uses of this Vestment? How much has been concealed, how much has been defended in Aprons! Nay, rightly considered, what is your whole Military and Police Establishment, charged at uncalculated millions, but a huge scarlet-coloured, iron-fastened Apron, wherein Society works (uneasily enough); guarding itself from some soil and stithy-sparks, in this Devil's smithy (*Teufelsschmiede*) of a world? But of all Aprons the most puzzling to me hitherto has been the Episcopal, or Cassock. Wherein consists the usefulness of this Apron? The Overseer (*Episcopus*) of Souls, I notice, has tucked in the corner of it, as if his day's work were done: what does he shadow forth thereby?' &c. &c.

Or again, has it often been the lot of our readers to read such stuff as we shall now quote?

'I consider those printed Paper Aprons, worn by the Parisian Cooks, as a new vent, though a slight one, for Typography; therefore as an encouragement to modern Literature, and deserving of approval: nor is it without satisfaction that I hear of a celebrated London Firm having in view to introduce the same fashion, with important extensions, in England.' – We who are on the spot hear of no such thing; and indeed have reason to be thankful that hitherto there are other vents for our Literature, exuberant as it is. – Teufelsdröckh continues: 'If such supply of printed Paper should rise so far as to choke up the highways and public thoroughfares, new means must of necessity be had recourse to. In a world existing by Industry, we grudge to employ Fire as a destroying element, and not as a creating one. However, Heaven is omnipotent, and will find us an outlet. In the meanwhile, is it not beautiful to see five million quintals of Rags picked annually from the Laystall; and annually, after being macerated, hot-pressed, printed on, and sold, – returned thither; filling so many hungry mouths by the way? Thus is the Laystall, especially with its Rags or Clothes-rubbish, the grand Electric Battery, and Fountain-of-Motion, from which and to which the Social Activities (like vitreous and resinous Electricities) circulate, in larger or smaller circles, through the mighty, billowy, stormtost Chaos of Life, which they keep alive!' – Such passages fill us who love the man, and partly esteem him, with a very mixed feeling.

Farther down we meet with this: 'The Journalists are now the true Kings and Clergy: henceforth Historians, unless they are fools, must write not of Bourbon Dynasties, and Tudors and Hapsburgs; but of Stamped Broad-sheet Dynasties, and quite new successive Names, according as this or the other Able Editor, or Combination of Able Editors, gains the world's ear. Of the British Newspaper Press, perhaps the most important of all, and wonderful enough in its secret constitution and procedure, a valuable descriptive History already exists, in that language, under the title of *Satan's Invisible World Displayed**; which, however, by search in all the Weissnichtwo Libraries, I have not yet succeeded in procuring (*vermöchte nicht aufzutreiben*).'

Thus does the good Homer not only nod, but snore. Thus does Teufelsdröckh, wandering in regions where he had little business, confound the old authentic Presbyterian Witchfinder with a new, spurious, imaginary Historian of the *Brittische Journalistik*; and so stumble on perhaps the most egregious blunder in Modern Literature!

---

* *Satan's Invisible World Displayed* is actually a 16th-century history of witchcraft and witch-finding: thus Carlyle hints that British newspapers also deal in malign illusions – AG

CHAPTER 7

Miscellaneous-Historical

HAPPIER is our Professor, and more purely scientific and historic, when he reaches the Middle Ages in Europe, and down to the end of the Seventeenth Century; the true era of extravagance in Costume. It is here that the Antiquary and Student of Modes comes upon his richest harvest. Fantastic garbs, beggaring all fancy of a Teniers or a Callot, succeed each other, like monster devouring monster in a Dream. The whole too in brief authentic strokes, and touched not seldom with that breath of genius which makes even old raiment live. Indeed, so learned, precise, graphical, and every way interesting have we found these Chapters, that it may be thrown out as a pertinent question for parties concerned, Whether or not a good English Translation thereof might henceforth be profitably incorporated with

Mr. Merrick's valuable Work *On Ancient Armour*? Take, by way of example, the following sketch; as authority for which Paulinus's *Zeitkürzende Lust* (11. 678) is, with seeming confidence referred to:

'Did we behold the German fashionable dress of the Fifteenth Century, we might smile; as perhaps those bygone Germans, were they to rise again, and see our haberdashery, would cross themselves, and invoke the Virgin. But happily no bygone German, or man, rises again; thus the Present is not needlessly trammelled with the Past; and only grows out of it, like a Tree, whose roots are not intertangled with its branches, but lie peaceably under ground. Nay it is very mournful, yet not useless, to see and know, how the Greatest and Dearest, in a short while, would find his place quite filled up here, and no room for him; the very Napoleon, the very Byron, in some seven years, has become obsolete, and were now a foreigner to his Europe. Thus is the Law of Progress secured; and in Clothes, as in all other external things whatsoever, no fashion will continue.

'Of the military classes in those old times, whose buff-belts, complicated chains and gorgets, huge churn-boots, and other riding and fighting gear have been bepainted in modern Romance, till the whole has acquired somewhat of a signpost character, – I shall here say nothing: the civil and pacific classes, less touched upon, are wonderful enough for us.

'Rich men, I find, have *Teusinke*'[1] (a perhaps untranslateable article); 'also a silver girdle, whereat hang little bells; so that when a man walks it is with continual jingling. Some few, of musical turn, have a whole chime of bells (*Glockenspiel*) fastened there; which especially, in sudden whirls, and the other accidents of walking, has a grateful effect. Observe too how fond they are of peaks, and Gothic-arch

1 *Teusinke*: a bell-shaped girdle

intersections. The male world wears peaked caps, an ell-long, which hang bobbing over the side (*schief*): their shoes

are peaked in front, also to the length of an ell (and laced on the side with tags); even the wooden shoes have their ell-long noses: some also clap bells on the peak. Farther, according to my authority, the men have breeches without seat (*ohne Gesäss*): these they fasten peakwise to their shirts; and the long round doublet must overlap them.

'Rich maidens, again, flit abroad in gowns scolloped out behind and before, so that back and breast are almost bare. Wives of quality, on the other hand, have train-gowns four or five ells in length; which trains there are boys to carry. Brave cleopatras sailing in their silk-cloth Galley, with a

Cupid for steersman! Consider their welts, a handbreadth thick, which waver round them by way of hem; the long flood of silver buttons, or rather silver shells, from throat to shoe, wherewith these same welt-gowns are buttoned. The maidens have bound silver snoods about their hair, with gold spangles, and pendent flames (*Flammen*), that is, sparkling hair-drops: but of their mothers' headgear who shall speak? Neither in love of grace is comfort forgotten. In winter weather you behold the whole fair creation (that can afford it) in long mantles, with skirts wide below, and, for hem, not one but two sufficient hand-broad welts: all ending atop in a thick well-starched Ruff, some twenty inches broad: these are their Ruff-mantles (*Kragenmäntel*).

'As yet among the wo-mankind hoop-petticoats are not; but the men have doublets of fustian, under which lie multiple ruffs of cloth, pasted together with batter (*mit Teig zusammen-gekleistert*), which create protuberance enough. Thus do the two sexes vie with each other in the art of Decoration; and as usual the stronger carries it.'

Our Professor, whether he have Humour himself or not, manifests a certain feeling of the Ludicrous, a sly obser-vance of it, which, could emotion of any kind be confidently predicated of so still a man, we might call a real love. None of those bell-girdles, bushel-breeches, cornuted shoes, or other the like phenom-ena, of which the History of Dress offers so many, escape him; more espe-cially the mischances, or striking adventures, inci-

dent to the wearers of such, are noticed with due fidelity. Sir Walter Raleigh's fine mantle, which he spread in the

mud under Queen Elizabeth's feet, appears to provoke little
enthusiasm in him; he merely asks, Whether at that period
the Maiden Queen 'was red-painted on the nose, and
white-painted on the cheeks, as her tirewomen, when from
spleen and wrinkles she would no longer look in any glass,
were wont to serve her?' We can answer that Sir Walter

knew well what he was doing, and had the Maiden Queen been stuffed parchment dyed in verdigris, would have done the same.

Thus too, treating of those enormous habiliments, that were not only slashed and galooned, but artificially swollen out on the broader parts of the body, by introduction of Bran, – our Professor fails not to comment on that luckless Courtier, who having seated himself on a chair with some projecting nail on it, and therefrom rising, to pay his *devoir* on the entrance of Majesty, instantaneously emitted several pecks of dry wheatdust; and stood there diminished to a spindle, his galoons and slashes dangling sorrowful and flabby round him. Whereupon the Professor publishes this reflection:

'By what strange chances do we live in History! Erostratus by a torch; Milo by a bullock; Henry Darnley, an unfledged booby and bustard, by his limbs; most Kings and Queens by being born under such and such a bedtester; Boileau Despréaux (according to Helvetius) by the peak of a turkey; and this ill-starred individual by a rent in his breeches, – for no Memoirist of Kaiser Otto's Court omits him. Vain was the prayer of Themistocles for a talent of Forgetting: my Friends, yield cheerfully to Destiny, and read since it is written.' – Has Teufelsdröckh to be put in mind that, nearly related to the impossible talent of Forgetting, stands that talent of Silence, which even travelling Englishmen manifest?

'The simplest costume,' observes our Professor, 'which I anywhere find alluded to in History, is that used as regimental, by Bolivar's Cavalry, in the late Columbian wars. A square Blanket, twelve feet in diagonal, is provided (some were wont to cut off the corners, and make it circular): in the centre a slit is effected, eighteen inches long; through this the mother-naked Trooper introduces his head and neck; and so rides shielded from all weather, and in battle from many strokes (for he rolls it about his left arm); and not only dressed, but harnessed and draperied.'

With which picture of a State of Nature, affecting by its singularity, and Old-Roman contempt of the superfluous, we shall quit this part of our subject.

CHAPTER 8

The World out of Clothes

If in the Descriptive-Historical Portion of his Volume, Teufelsdröckh, discussing merely the *Werden* (Origin and successive Improvement) of Clothes, has astonished many a reader, much more will he in the Speculative-Philosophical Portion, which treats of their *Wirken*, or Influences. It is here that the present Editor first feels the pressure of his task; for here properly the higher and new Philosophy of Clothes commences: an untried, almost inconceivable region, or chaos; in venturing upon which, how difficult, yet how unspeakably important is it to know what course, of survey and conquest, is the true one; where the footing is firm substance and will bear us, where it is hollow, or mere cloud, and may engulf us! Teufelsdröckh undertakes no less than to expound the moral, political, even religious Influences of Clothes; he undertakes to make manifest, in its thousandfold bearings, this grand Proposition, that Man's earthly interests 'are all hooked and

buttoned together, and held up, by Clothes.' He says in so
many words, 'Society is founded upon Cloth;' and again,
'Society sails through the Infinitude on Cloth, as on a
Faust's Mantle, or rather like the Sheet of clean and
unclean beasts in the Apostle's Dream; and without such
Sheet or Mantle, would sink to endless depths, or mount to
inane limbos, and in either case be no more.'

By what chains, or indeed infinitely complected tissues,
of Meditation this grand Theorem is here unfolded, and
innumerable practical Corollaries are drawn therefrom, it
were perhaps a mad ambition to attempt exhibiting. Our
Professor's method is not, in any case, that of common
school Logic, where the truths all stand in a row, each
holding by the skirts of the other; but at best that of
practical Reason, proceeding by large Intuition over whole
systematic groups and kingdoms; whereby we might say, a
noble complexity, almost like that of Nature, reigns in his
Philosophy, or spiritual picture of Nature: a mighty maze,
yet, as faith whispers, not without a plan. Nay we com-
plained above, that a certain ignoble complexity, what we
must call mere confusion, was also discernible. Often,
too, must we exclaim: Would to Heaven those same
Biographical Documents were come! For it seems as if
the demonstration lay much in the Author's individuality;
as if it were not Argument that had taught him, but
Experience. At present it is only in local glimpses, and
by significant fragments, picked often at wide enough
intervals from the original Volume, and carefully collated,
that we can hope to impart some outline or foreshadow of
this Doctrine. Readers of any intelligence are once more
invited to favour us with their most concentrated attention: let these, after intense consideration, and not till
then, pronounce, Whether on the utmost verge of our
actual horizon there is not a looming as of Land; a
promise of new Fortunate Islands, perhaps whole undis-
covered Americas, for such as have canvass to sail thither?

– As exordium to the whole, stands here the following long citation:

'With men of a speculative turn,' writes Teufelsdröckh, 'there come seasons, meditative, sweet, yet awful hours, when in wonder and fear you ask yourself that unanswerable question: Who am *I*; the thing that can say "I" (*das Wesen das sich* ICH *nennt*)? The world, with its loud trafficking, retires into the distance; and, through the paper-hangings, and stone-walls, and thick-plied tissues of Commerce and Polity, and all the living and lifeless Integuments (of Society and a Body), wherewith your Existence sits surrounded, – the sight reaches forth into the void Deep, and you are alone with the Universe, and silently commune with it, as one mysterious Presence with another.

'Who am I; what is this ME? A Voice, a Motion, an Appearance; – some embodied, visualised Idea in the Eternal Mind? *Cogito ergo sum*. Alas, poor Cogitator, this takes us but a little way. Sure enough, I am; and lately was not: but Whence? How? Whereto? The answer lies around, written in all colours and motions, uttered in all tones of jubilee and wail, in thousand-figured, thousand-voiced, harmonious Nature: but where is the cunning eye and ear to whom that God-written Apocalypse will yield articulate meaning? We sit as in a boundless Phantasmagoria and Dream-grotto; boundless, for the faintest star, the remotest century, lies not even nearer the verge thereof: sounds and many-coloured visions flit round our sense; but Him, the Unslumbering, whose work both Dream and Dreamer are, we see not; except in rare half-waking moments, suspect not. Creation, says one, lies before us, like a glorious Rainbow; but the Sun that made it lies behind us, hidden from us. Then, in that strange Dream, how we clutch at shadows as if they were substances; and sleep deepest while fancying ourselves most awake! Which of your Philosophical Systems is other than a dream-theorem; a net quotient, confidently given out, where divisor and dividend are both unknown? What are all your national Wars, with their Moscow Retreats, and sanguinary hate-filled Revolutions, but the Somnambulism of uneasy Sleepers? This Dreaming, this Somnambulism is what we on Earth call Life; wherein the most indeed undoubtingly wander, as if they knew right hand from left; yet they only are wise who know that they know nothing.

'Pity that all Metaphysics had hitherto proved so inexpressibly unproductive! The secret of Man's Being is still like the Sphinx's secret: a riddle that he cannot rede; and for ignorance of which he suffers death, the worst death, a spiritual. What are your Axioms, and Categories, and Systems, and Aphorisms? Words, words. High Air-castles are cunningly built of Words, the Words well bedded also in good Logic-mortar; wherein, however, no Knowledge will come to lodge. *The whole is greater than the part*: how exceedingly true! *Nature abhors a vacuum*: how exceedingly false and calumnious! Again, *Nothing can act but where it is:* with all my heart; only WHERE is it? Be not the slave of Words: is not the Distant, the Dead, while I love it, and long for it, and mourn for it, Here, in the genuine sense, as truly as the floor I stand on? But that same WHERE, with its brother WHEN, are from the first the master-colours of our Dream-grotto; say rather, the Canvass (the warp and woof thereof) whereon all our Dreams and Life-visions are painted. Nevertheless, has not a deeper meditation taught certain of every climate and age, that the WHERE and WHEN, so mysteriously inseparable from all our thoughts, are but superficial terrestrial adhesions to thought; that the Seer may discern them where they mount up out of the celestial EVERY-WHERE and FOREVER: have not all nations conceived their God as Omnipresent and Eternal; as existing in a universal HERE, an everlasting Now? Think well, thou too wilt find that Space is but a mode of our human Sense, so likewise Time; there *is* no Space and no Time: WE are – we know not what; – light-sparkles floating in the æther of Deity!

'So that this so solid-seeming World, after all, were but an air-image, our ME the only reality: and Nature, with its thousandfold production and destruction, but the reflex of our own inward Force, the "phantasy of our Dream;" or what the Earth-Spirit in *Faust* names it, *the living visible Garment of God*:

In Being's floods, in Action's storm,
I walk and work, above, beneath,
Work and weave in endless motion!
Birth and Death,
An infinite ocean;
A seizing and giving
The fire of the Living:
'Tis thus at the roaring Loom of Time I ply,
And weave for God the Garment thou seest Him by.

Of twenty millions that have read and spouted this thunder-speech of the *Erdgeist*, are there yet twenty units of us that have learned the meaning thereof?'

'It was in some such mood, when wearied and foredone with these high speculations, that I first came upon the question of Clothes. Strange enough, it strikes me, is this same fact of there being Tailors and Tailored. The Horse I ride has his own whole fell: strip him of the girths and flaps and extraneous tags I have fastened round him, and the noble creature is his own sempster and weaver and spinner: nay his own bootmaker, jeweller, and man-milliner; he bounds free through the valleys, with a perennial rainproof court-suit on his body; wherein warmth and easiness of fit have reached perfection; nay, the graces also have been considered, and frills and fringes, with gay variety of colour, featly appended, and ever in the right place, are not wanting. While I – Good Heaven! – have thatched myself over with the dead fleeces of sheep, the bark of vegetables, the entrails of worms, the hides of oxen or seals, the felt of furred beasts; and walk abroad a moving Rag-screen, over-heaped with shreds and tatters raked from the Charnel-house of Nature, where they would have rotted, to rot on me more slowly! Day after day, I must thatch myself anew; day after day, this despicable thatch must lose some film of its thickness; some film of it, frayed away by tear and wear, must be brushed off into the Ashpit, into the Laystall; till by degrees the whole has been brushed thither, and I, the dust-making, patent Rag-grinder, get new material to grind down. O subter-brutish! vile! most vile! For have not I too a compact all-enclosing Skin, whiter or dingier? Am I a botched mass of tailors' and cobblers' shreds, then; or a tightly-articulated, homogeneous little Figure, automatic, nay alive?

'Strange enough how creatures of the human-kind shut their eyes to plainest facts; and, by the mere inertia of Oblivion and Stupidity, live at ease in the midst of Wonders and Terrors. But indeed man is, and was always, a block-head and dullard; much readier to feel and digest, than to think and consider. Prejudice, which he pretends to hate, is his absolute lawgiver; mere use-and-wont everywhere leads him by the nose: thus let but a Rising of the Sun, let but a Creation of the World happen *twice*, and it ceases to be marvellous, to be noteworthy, or noticeable. Perhaps not once in a lifetime does it occur to your ordinary biped, of any country or generation, be he gold-mantled Prince or russet-jerkined Peasant, that his Vestments and his Self are not one and indivisible; that *he* is naked, without vestments, till he buy or steal such, and by forethought sew and button them.

'For my own part, these considerations, of our Clothes-thatch, and how, reaching inwards even to our heart of hearts, it tailorises and demoralises us, fill me with a certain horror at myself and mankind; almost as one feels at those Dutch Cows, which, during the wet season, you see grazing deliberately with jackets and petticoats (of striped sacking), in the meadows of Gouda. Nevertheless there is something great in the moment when a man first strips himself of adventitious wrappages; and sees indeed that he is naked, and, as Swift has it, "a forked straddling animal with bandy legs;" yet also a Spirit, and unutterable Mystery of Mysteries.'

CHAPTER 9

Adamitism

LET no courteous reader take offence at the opinions broached in the conclusion of the last Chapter. The Editor himself, on first glancing over that singular passage, was inclined to exclaim: What, have we got not only a Sansculottist, but an enemy to Clothes in the abstract? A new Adamite, in this century, which flatters itself that it is the Nineteenth, and destructive both to Superstition and Enthusiasm?

Consider, thou foolish Teufelsdröckh, what benefits unspeakable all ages and sexes derive from Clothes. For example, when thou thyself, a watery, pulpy, slobbery freshman and new-comer in this Planet, sattest muling and puking in thy nurse's arms; sucking thy coral, and looking forth into the world in the blankest manner, what hadst thou been, without thy blankets, and bibs, and other

nameless hulls? A terror to thyself and mankind! Or hast
thou forgotten the day when thou first receivedst breeches,
and thy long clothes became short? The village where thou
livedst was all apprised of the fact; and neighbour after
neighbour kissed thy pudding cheek, and gave thee, as
handsel, silver or copper coins, on that the first gala-day of
thy existence. Again, wert not thou, at one period of life, a
Buck, or Blood, or Macaroni, or Incroyable, or Dandy, or
by whatever name, according to year and place, such
phenomenon is distinguished? In that one word lie included mysterious volumes. Nay, now when the reign of
folly is over, or altered, and thy clothes are not for triumph
but for defence, hast thou always worn them perforce, and
as a consequence of Man's Fall; never rejoiced in them as in
a warm moveable House, a Body round thy Body, wherein
that strange THEE of thine sat snug, defying all variations
of Climate? Girt with thick double-milled kerseys; half-
buried under shawls and broad-brims, and overalls and
mudboots, thy very fingers cased in doeskin and mittens,
thou hast bestrode that 'Horse I ride;' and, though it were
in wild winter, dashed through the world, glorying in it as if
thou wert its lord. In vain did the sleet beat round thy
temples; it lighted only on thy impenetrable, felted or
woven, case of wool. In vain did the winds howl, – forests
sounding and creaking, deep calling unto deep, – and the
storms heap themselves together into one huge Arctic
whirlpool: thou flewest through the middle thereof, striking
fire from the highway; wild music hummed in thy ears, thou
too wert as a 'sailor of the air;' the wreck of matter and the
crash of worlds was thy element and propitiously wafting
tide. Without Clothes, without bit or saddle, what hadst
thou been; what had thy fleet quadruped been? – Nature is
good, but she is not the best: here truly was the victory of
Art over Nature. A thunderbolt indeed might have pierced
thee; all short of this thou couldst defy.

Or, cries the courteous reader, has your Teufelsdröckh

forgotten what he said lately about 'Aboriginal Savages,' and their 'condition miserable indeed?' Would he have all this unsaid; and us betake ourselves again to the 'matted cloak,' and go sheeted in a 'thick natural fell?'

Nowise, courteous reader! The Professor knows full well what he is saying; and both thou and we, in our haste, do him wrong. If Clothes, in these times, 'so tailorise and demoralise us,' have they no redeeming value; can they not be altered to serve better; must they of necessity be thrown to the dogs? The truth is, Teufelsdröckh, though a Sansculottist, is no Adamite: and much perhaps as he might wish to go forth before this degenerate age 'as a Sign,' would nowise wish to do it, as those old Adamites did, in a state of Nakedness. The utility of Clothes is altogether apparent to him: nay perhaps he has an insight into their more recondite, and almost mystic qualities, what we might call the omnipotent virtue of Clothes, such as was never before vouchsafed to any man. For example:

'You see two individuals,' he writes, 'one dressed in fine Red, the other in coarse threadbare Blue: Red says to Blue, "Be hanged and anatomised;" Blue hears with a shudder, and (O wonder of wonders!) marches sorrowfully to the gallows; is there noosed up, vibrates his hour, and the surgeons dissect him, and fit his bones into a skeleton for medical purposes. How is this; or what make ye of your *Nothing can act but where it is?* Red has no physical hold of Blue, no *clutch* of him, is nowise in *contact* with him: neither are those ministering Sheriffs and Lord-Lieutenants and hangmen and Tipstaves so related to commanding Red, that he can tug them hither and thither; but each stands distinct within his own skin. Nevertheless, as it is spoken, so is it done: the articulated Word sets all hands in Action; and Rope and Improved-drop perform their work.

'Thinking reader, the reason seems to me twofold: First, that *Man is a Spirit*, and bound by invisible bonds to *All Men*; Secondly, that *he wears Clothes*, which are the visible emblems of that fact. Has not your Red, hanging individual, a horsehair wig, squirrel skins, and a plush gown; whereby all mortals know that he is a JU D G E ? – Society, which the more I think of it astonishes me the more, is founded upon Cloth.

'Often in my atrabiliar moods, when I read of pompous ceremonials, Frankfort Coronations, Royal Drawing-rooms, Levees, Couchees; and how the ushers and macers and pursuivants are all in waiting; how Duke this is presented by Archduke that, and Colonel A by General B, and innumerable Bishops, Admirals, and miscellaneous Functionaries, are advancing gallantly to the Anointed presence; and I strive, in my remote privacy, to form a clear picture of that solemnity, – on a sudden, as by some enchanter's wand, the – shall I speak it? – the Clothes fly off the whole dramatic corps; and Dukes, Grandees, Bishops, Generals, Anointed presence itself, every mother's son of them, stand straddling there, not a shirt on them; and I know not whether to laugh or weep. This physical or psychical infirmity, in which perhaps I am not singular, I have, after hesitation, thought right to publish, for the solace of those afflicted with the like.'

Would to Heaven, say we, thou hadst thought right to keep it secret! Who is there now that can read the five columns of Presentations in his Morning Newspaper without a shudder? Hypochondriac men, and all men are to a certain extent hypochondriac, should be more gently treated. With what readiness our fancy, in this shattered state of the nerves, follows out the consequences which Teufelsdröckh, with a devilish coolness, goes on to draw:

'What would Majesty do, could such an accident befall in reality; should the buttons all simultaneously start, and the solid wool evaporate, in very Deed, as here in Dream? *Ach Gott!* How each skulks into the nearest hiding-place; their high State Tragedy (*Haupt- und Staats-Action*) becomes a Pickleherring-Farce to weep at, which is the worst kind of Farce; *the tables* (according to Horace), and with them, the whole fabric of Government, Legislation, Property, Police, and Civilised Society, *are dissolved*, in wails and howls.'

Lives the man that can figure a naked Duke of Windlestraw addressing a naked House of Lords? Imagination, choked as in mephitic air, recoils on itself, and will not forward with the picture. The Woolsack, the Ministerial, the Opposition Benches – *infandum! infandum!*[1] And yet why is the thing impossible? Was not every soul, or rather every body, of these Guardians of our Liberties, naked, or nearly so, last night; 'a forked Radish with a head fantastically carved?' And why might he not, did our stern Fate so order it, walk out to St. Stephen's, as well as into bed, in that no-fashion; and there, with other similar Radishes, hold a Bed of Justice? 'Solace of those afflicted with the like!' Unhappy Teufelsdröckh, had man ever such a 'physical or psychical infirmity' before? And now how many, perhaps, may thy unparalleled confession (which we, even to the sounder British world, and goaded on by Critical and Biographical duty, grudge to re-impart) incurably infect therewith! Art thou the malignest of Sansculottists, or only the maddest?

'It will remain to be examined,' adds the inexorable Teufelsdröckh, 'in how far the SCARECROW, as a Clothed Person, is not also entitled to benefit of clergy, and English trial by jury: nay, perhaps considering his high function (for is not he too a Defender of Property, and Sovereign armed with the *terrors* of the Law?), to a certain royal Immunity and Inviolability; which, however, misers and the meaner class of persons are not always voluntarily disposed to grant him.' . . . 'O my Friends, we are (in Yorick Sterne's words) but as "turkeys driven, with a stick and red clout, to the market:" or if some drivers, as they do in Norfolk, take a dried bladder and put peas in it, the rattle thereof terrifies the boldest!'

---

1 *infandum! infandum!*: unspeakable, unspeakable

CHAPTER 10

Pure Reason

IT must now be apparent enough that our Professor, as above hinted, is a speculative Radical, and of the very darkest tinge; acknowledging, for most part, in the solemnities and paraphernalia of civilised Life, which we make so much of, nothing but so many Cloth-rags, turkey-poles, and 'Bladders with dried Peas.' To linger among such speculations, longer than mere Science requires, a discerning public can have no wish. For our purposes the simple fact that such a *Naked World* is possible, nay actually exists (under the Clothed one), will be sufficient. Much, therefore, we omit about 'Kings wrestling naked on the green with Carmen,' and the Kings being thrown: 'dissect them with scalpels,' says Teufelsdröckh; 'the same viscera, tissues, livers, lights, and other Life-tackle are there: examine their spiritual

mechanism; the same great Need, great Greed, and little
Faculty; nay ten to one but the Carman, who understands
draught-cattle, the rimming of wheels, something of the
laws of unstable and stable equilibrium, with other
branches of waggon-science, and has actually put forth
his hand and operated on Nature, is the more cunningly
gifted of the two. Whence, then, their so unspeakable
difference? From Clothes.' Much also we shall omit about
confusion of Ranks, and Joan and My Lady, and how it
would be every where 'Hail fellow well met,' and Chaos
were come again: all which to any one that has once fairly
pictured out the grand mother-idea, *Society in a state of
Nakedness*, will spontaneously suggest itself. Should some
sceptical individual still entertain doubts whether in a
World without Clothes, the smallest Politeness, Polity,
or even Police, could exist, let him turn to the original
Volume, and view there the boundless Serbonian Bogs of
Sansculottism, stretching sour and pestilential: over which
we have lightly flown; where not only whole armies but
whole nations might sink! If indeed the following argument, in its brief rivetting emphasis, be not of itself incon-
trovertible and final:

'Are we Opossums; have we natural Pouches, like the
Kangaroo? Or how, without Clothes, could we possess the
master-organ, soul's-seat, and true pineal gland of the
Body Social: I mean, a PURSE?'

Nevertheless it is impossible to hate Professor Teufelsdröckh; at worst, one knows not whether to hate or to love
him. For though in looking at the fair tapestry of human
Life, with its royal and even sacred figures, he dwells not on
the obverse alone, but here chiefly on the reverse; and
indeed turns out the rough seams, tatters, and manifold
thrums of that unsightly wrong-side, with an almost diabolic patience and indifference, which must have sunk him
in the estimation of most readers, – there is that within
which unspeakably distinguishes him from all other past

and present Sansculottists. The grand unparalleled peculiarity of Teufelsdröckh is, that with all this Descendentalism, he combines a Transcendentalism no less superlative; whereby if on the one hand he degrade man below most animals, except those jacketted Gouda Cows, he, on the other, exalts him beyond the visible Heavens, almost to an equality with the gods.

'To the eye of vulgar Logic,' says he, 'what is man? An omnivorous Biped that wears Breeches. To the eye of Pure Reason what is he? A Soul, a Spirit, and divine Apparition. Round his mysterious ME, there lies, under all those woolrags, a Garment of Flesh (or of Senses), contextured in the Loom of Heaven; whereby he is revealed to his like, and dwells with them in UNION and DIVISION; and sees and fashions for himself a universe, with azure Starry Spaces, and long Thousands of Years. Deep-hidden is he under that strange Garment; amid Sounds and Colours and Forms, as it were, swathed in, and inextricably overshrouded: yet is it sky-woven, and worthy of a God. Stands he not thereby in the centre of Immensities, in the conflux of Eternities? He feels; power has been given him to Know, to Believe; nay does not the spirit of Love, free in its celestial primeval brightness, even here, though but for moments, look through? Well said Saint Chrysostom, with his lips of gold, "the true SHEKINAH is Man:" where else is the GOD's–PRESENCE manifested not to our eyes only, but to our hearts, as in our fellow man?'

In such passages, unhappily too rare, the high Platonic Mysticism of our Author, which is perhaps the fundamental element of his nature, bursts forth, as it were, in full flood: and, through all the vapour and tarnish of what is often so perverse, so mean in his exterior and environment, we seem to look into a whole inward Sea of Light and Love; – though, alas, the grim coppery clouds soon roll together again, and hide it from view.

Such tendency to Mysticism is every where traceable in

this man; and indeed, to attentive readers, must have been long ago apparent. Nothing that he sees but has more than a common meaning, but has two meanings: thus, if in the highest Imperial Sceptre and Charlemagne-Mantle, as well as in the poorest Ox-goad and Gipsy-Blanket, he finds Prose, Decay, Contemptibility; there is in each sort Poetry also, and a reverend Worth. For Matter, were it never so despicable, is Spirit, the manifestation of Spirit: were it never so honourable, can it be more? The thing Visible, nay the thing Imagined, the thing in any way conceived as Visible, what is it but a Garment, a Clothing of the higher, celestial Invisible, 'unimaginable, formless, dark with excess of bright?' Under which point of view the following passage, so strange in purport, so strange in phrase, seems characteristic enough:

'The beginning of all Wisdom is to look fixedly on Clothes, or even with armed eyesight, till they become *transparent*. "The Philosopher," says the wisest of this age, "must station himself in the middle:" how true! The Philosopher is he to whom the Highest has descended, and the Lowest has mounted up; who is the equal and kindly brother of all.

'Shall we tremble before clothwebs and cobwebs, whether woven in Arkwright looms, or by the silent Arachnes that weave unrestingly in our Imagination? Or, on the other hand, what is there that we cannot love; since all was created by God?

'Happy he who can look through the Clothes of a Man (the woollen, and fleshly, and official Bank-paper and State-paper Clothes), into the Man himself; and discern, it may be, in this or the other Dread Potentate, a more or less incompetent Digestive-apparatus; yet also an inscrutable venerable Mystery, in the meanest Tinker that sees with eyes!'

For the rest, as is natural to a man of this kind, he deals much in the feeling of Wonder; insists on the necessity and high worth of universal Wonder, which he holds to be the only reasonable temper for the denizen of so singular a Planet as ours. 'Wonder,' says he, 'is the basis of Worship: the reign of Wonder is perennial, indestructible in Man; only at certain stages (as the present), it is, for some short season, a reign *in partibus infidelium*.'[1] That progress of Science, which is to destroy Wonder, and in its stead substitute Mensuration and Numeration, finds small favour with Teufelsdröckh, much as he otherwise venerates these two latter processes.

1 *in partibus infidelium*: in the country of the unbelievers

'Shall your Science,' exclaims he, 'proceed in the small chink-lighted, or even oil-lighted, underground workshop of Logic alone; and man's mind become an Arithmetical Mill, whereof Memory is the Hopper, and mere Tables of Sines and Tangents, Codification, and Treatises of what you call Political Economy, are the Meal? And what is that Science, which the scientific Head alone, were it screwed off, and (like the Doctor's in the Arabian Tale) set in a basin, to keep it alive, could prosecute without shadow of a heart, – but one other of the mechanical and menial handicrafts, for which the Scientific Head (having a Soul in it) is too noble an organ? I mean that Thought without Reverence is barren, perhaps poisonous; at best, dies like Cookery with the day that called it forth; does not live, like sowing, in successive tilths and wider-spreading harvests, bringing food and plenteous increase to all Time.'

In such wise does Teufelsdröckh deal hits, harder or softer, according to ability; yet ever, as we would fain persuade ourselves, with charitable intent. Above all, that class of 'Logic-choppers, and treble-pipe Scoffers, and professed Enemies to Wonder; who, in these days, so numerously patrol as night-constables about the Mechanics' Institute of Science, and cackle, like true Old-Roman geese and goslings round their Capitol, on any alarm, or on none; nay who often, as illuminated Sceptics, walk abroad into peaceable society, in full daylight, with rattle and lantern, and insist on guiding you and guarding you therewith, though the Sun is shining, and the street populous with mere justice-loving men:' that whole class is inexpressibly wearisome to him. Hear with what uncommon animation he perorates:

'The man who cannot wonder, who does not habitually wonder (and worship), were he President of innumerable Royal Societies, and carried the whole *Mécanique Céleste* and *Hegel's Philosophy*, and the epitome of all Laboratories and Observatories with their results, in his single head, – is but a Pair of Spectacles behind which there is no Eye. Let those who have Eyes look through him, then he may be useful.

'Thou wilt have no Mystery and Mysticism; wilt walk through thy world by the sunshine of what thou callest Truth, or even by the Hand-lamp of what I call Attorney Logic; and "explain" all, "account" for all, or believe nothing of it? Nay, thou wilt attempt laughter; whoso recognises the unfathomable, all-pervading domain of Mystery, which is everywhere under our feet and among our hands; to whom the Universe is an Oracle and Temple, as well as a Kitchen and Cattle-stall, – he shall be a (delirious) Mystic; to him thou, with sniffing charity, wilt protrusively proffer thy Handlamp, and shriek, as one injured, when he kicks his foot through it? – *Armer Teufel!*[1] Doth not thy Cow calve, doth not thy Bull gender? Thou thyself, wert thou not Born, wilt thou not Die? "Explain" me all this, or do one of two things: Retire into private places with thy foolish cackle; or, what were better, give it up, and weep, not that the reign of wonder is done, and God's world all disembellished and prosaic, but that thou hitherto art a Dilettante and sandblind Pedant.'

1 *Armer Teufel*: Poor devil

CHAPTER II

Prospective

THE Philosophy of Clothes is now to all readers, as we predicted it would do, unfolding itself into new boundless expansions, of a cloudcapt, almost chimerical aspect, yet not without azure loomings in the far distance, and streaks as of an Elysian brightness; the highly questionable purport and promise of which it is becoming more and more important for us to ascertain. Is that a real Elysian brightness, cries many a timid wayfarer, or the reflex of Pandemonian lava? Is it of a truth leading us into beatific Asphodel meadows, or the yellow-burning marl of a Hell-on-Earth?

Our Professor, like other Mystics, whether delirious or inspired, gives an Editor enough to do. Ever higher and dizzier are the heights he leads us to; more piercing, all-comprehending, all-confounding are his views and glances. For example, this of Nature being not an Aggregate but a Whole:

'Well sang the Hebrew Psalmist: "If I take the wings of the morning and dwell in the uttermost parts of the universe, God is there." Thou too, O cultivated reader, who too probably art no Psalmist, but a Prosaist, knowing GOD only by tradition, knowest thou any corner of the world where at least FORCE is not? The drop which thou shakest from thy wet hand, rests not where it falls, but to-morrow thou findest it swept away; already, on the wings of the Northwind, it is nearing the Tropic of Cancer. How came it to evaporate, and not lie motionless? Thinkest thou there is aught motionless; without Force, and utterly dead?

'As I rode through the Schwarzwald, I said to myself; That little fire which glows star-like across the dark-growing (*nachtende*) moor, where the sooty smith bends over his anvil, and thou hopest to replace thy lost horse-shoe, – is it a detached, separated speck, cut off from the whole universe; or indissolubly joined to the whole? Thou fool, that smithy-fire was (primarily) kindled at the Sun; is fed by air that circulates from before Noah's Deluge, from beyond the Dogstar; therein, with Iron Force, and Coal Force, and the far stronger Force of Man, are cunning affinities and battles and victories of Force brought about: it is a little ganglion, or nervous centre, in the great vital system of Immensity. Call it, if thou wilt, an unconscious Altar, kindled on the bosom of the All; whose iron sacrifice, whose iron smoke and influence reach quite through the All; whose Dingy Priest, not by word, yet by brain and sinew, preaches forth the mystery of Force; nay preaches forth (exoterically enough) one little textlet from the Gospel of Freedom, the Gospel of Man's Force, commanding, and one day to be all-commanding.

'Detached, separated! I say there is no such separation: nothing hitherto was ever stranded, cast aside; but all, were it only a withered leaf, works together with all; is borne forward on the bottomless, shoreless flood of Action, and lives through perpetual metamorphoses. The withered leaf is not dead and lost, there are Forces in it and around it, though working in inverse order; else how could it *rot?* Despise not the rag from which man makes Paper, or the litter from which the Earth makes Corn. Rightly viewed no meanest object is insignificant; all objects are as windows, through which the philosophic eye looks into Infinitude itself.'

Again, leaving that wondrous Schwarzwald Smithy-Altar, what vacant, high-sailing air-ships are these, and whither will they sail with us?

'All visible things are Emblems; what thou seest is not there on its own account; strictly taken, is not there at all: Matter exists only spiritually, and to represent some Idea, and *body* it forth. Hence Clothes, as despicable as we think them, are so unspeakably significant. Clothes, from the King's-mantle downwards, are Emblematic, not of want only, but of a manifold cunning Victory over Want. On the other hand, all Emblematic things are properly Clothes, thought-woven or hand-woven: must not the Imagination weave Garments, visible Bodies, wherein the else invisible creations and inspirations of our Reason are, like Spirits, revealed, and first become all-powerful; – the rather if, as we often see, the Hand too aid her, and (by wool Clothes or otherwise) reveal such even to the outward eye?

'Men are properly said to be clothed with Authority, clothed with Beauty, with Curses, and the like. Nay, if you consider it, what is Man himself, and his whole terrestrial Life, but an Emblem; a Clothing or visible Garment for that divine ME of his, cast hither, like a light-particle, down from Heaven? Thus is he said also to be clothed with a Body.

'Language is called the Garment of Thought: however, it should rather be, Language is the Flesh-Garment, the Body, of Thought. I said that Imagination wove this Flesh-Garment; and does she not? Metaphors are her stuff: examine Language; what, if you except some few primitive elements (of natural sound), what is it all but Metaphors, recognised as such, or no longer recognised; still fluid and florid, or now solid-grown and colourless? If those same primitive elements are the osseous fixtures in the Flesh-

Garment, Language, – then are Metaphors its muscles and
tissues and living integuments. An unmetaphorical style
you shall in vain seek for: is not your very *Attention* a
Stretching-to? The difference lies here: some styles are lean,
adust, wiry, the muscle itself seems osseous; some are even
quite pallid, hunger-bitten, and dead-looking; while others
again glow in the flush of health and vigorous self-growth,
sometimes (as in my own case) not without an apoplectic
tendency. Moreover, there are sham Metaphors, which
overhanging that same Thought's-Body (best naked),
and deceptively bedizening, or bolstering it out, may be
called its false stuffings, superfluous show-cloaks (*Putz-
Mäntel*), and tawdry woollen rags: whereof he that runs and
reads may gather whole hampers, – and burn them.'

Than which paragraph on Metaphors did the reader ever
chance to see a more surprisingly metaphorical? However,
that is not our chief grievance; the Professor continues:

'Why multiply instances? It is written the Heavens and
the Earth shall fade away like a Vesture; which indeed they
are: the Time-vesture of the Eternal. Whatsoever sensibly
exists, whatsoever represents Spirit to Spirit, is properly a
Clothing, a suit of Raiment, put on for a season, and to be
laid off. Thus in this one pregnant subject of CLOTHES,
rightly understood, is included all that men have thought,
dreamed, done, and been: the whole external Universe and
what it holds is but Clothing; and the essence of all Science
lies in the PHILOSOPHY OF CLOTHES.'

Towards these dim infinitely-expanded regions, close-
bordering on the impalpable Inane, it is not without apprehension, and perpetual difficulties, that the Editor sees
himself journeying and struggling. Till lately a cheerful
daystar of hope hung before him, in the expected Aid of
Hofrath Heuschrecke; which daystar, however, melts now,
not into the red of morning, but into a vague, gray, half-
light, uncertain whether dawn of day or dusk of utter
darkness. For the last week, these so-called Biographical

Documents are in his hand. By the kindness of a Scottish Hamburgh Merchant, whose name, known to the whole mercantile world, he must not mention; but whose honourable courtesy, now and often before spontaneously manifested to him, a mere literary stranger, he cannot soon forget, – the bulky Weissnichtwo Packet, with all its Customhouse seals, foreign hieroglyphs, and miscellaneous tokens of Travel, arrived here in perfect safety, and free of cost. The reader shall now fancy with what hot haste it was broken up, with what breathless expectation glanced over; and, alas, with what unquiet disappointment it has, since then, been often thrown down, and again taken up.

Hofrath Heuschrecke, in a too long-winded Letter, full of compliments, Weissnichtwo politics, dinners, dining repartees, and other ephemeral trivialities, proceeds to remind us of what we knew well already: that however it may be with Metaphysics, and other abstract Science originating in the Head (*Verstand*) alone, no Life-Philosophy (*Lebensphilosophie*), such as this of Clothes pretends to be, which originates equally in the Character (*Gemüth*), and equally speaks thereto, can attain its significance till the Character itself is known and seen; 'till the Author's View of the World (*Weltansicht*), and how he actively and passively came by such view, are clear: in short, till a Biography of him has been philosophico-poetically written, and philosophico-poetically read.' 'Nay,' adds he, 'were the speculative scientific Truth even known, you still, in this inquiring age, ask yourself, Whence came it, and Why, and How? and rest not, till, if no better may be, Fancy have shaped out an answer; and, either in the authentic lineaments of Fact, or the forged ones of Fiction, a complete picture and Genetical History of the Man and his spiritual Endeavour lies before you. But why,' says the Hofrath, and indeed say we, 'do I dilate on the uses of our Teufelsdröckh's Biography? The great Herr Minister von Goethe has penetratingly remarked that "Man is properly the *only* object that interests man:" thus I too have noted, that in Weissnichtwo our whole conversation is little or nothing else but Biography or Autobiography; ever humano-anecdotical (*menschlich-anekdotisch*). Biography is by nature the most universally profitable, universally pleasant of all things: especially Biography of distinguished individuals.

'By this time, *mein Verehrtester* (my Most Esteemed),' continues he, with an eloquence which, unless the words be purloined from Teufelsdröckh, or some trick of his, as we suspect, is well-nigh unaccountable, 'by this time, you are fairly plunged (*vertieft*) in that mighty forest of Clothes-Philosophy; and looking round, as all readers do, with astonishment enough. Such portions and passages as you have already mastered, and brought to paper, could not but awaken a strange curiosity touching the mind they issued from; the perhaps unparalleled psychical mechan-ism, which manufactured such matter, and emitted it to the light of day. Had Teufelsdröckh also a father and mother; did he, at one time, wear drivel-bibs, and live on spoon-meat? Did he ever, in rapture and tears, clasp a friend's bosom to his; looks he also wistfully into the long burial-aisle of the Past, where only winds, and their low harsh moan, give inarticulate answer? Has he fought duels; – good Heaven! how did he comport himself when in Love? By what singular stair-steps, in short, and subterranean passages, and sloughs of Despair, and steep Pisgah hills, has he reached this wonderful prophetic Hebron (a true Old-Clothes Jewry) where he now dwells?

'To all these natural questions the voice of public History is as yet silent. Certain only that he has been, and is, a Pilgrim, and Traveller from a far Country; more or less footsore and travel-soiled; has parted with road-companions; fallen among thieves, been poisoned by bad cookery, blistered with bugbites; nevertheless, at every stage (for they have let him pass), has had the Bill to discharge. But the whole particulars of his Route, his Weather-observations, the picturesque Sketches he took, though all regularly jotted down (in indelible sympathetic-ink by an invisible interior Penman), are these nowhere forthcoming? Perhaps quite lost: one other leaf of that mighty Volume (of human Memory) left to fly abroad, unprinted, unpublished, unbound up, as waste paper; and rot, the sport of rainy winds?

'No, *verehrtester Herr Herausgeber*,[1] in no wise! I here, by the unexampled favour you stand in with our Sage, send not a Biography only, but an Autobiography: at least the materials for such; wherefrom, if I misreckon not, your perspicacity will draw fullest insight; and so the whole Philosophy and Philosopher of Clothes stand clear to the wondering eyes of England; nay thence, through America, through Hindostan, and the antipodal New Holland, finally conquer (*einnehmen*) great part of this terrestrial Planet!'

And now let the sympathising reader judge of our feeling when, in place of this same Autobiography with 'fullest insight,' we find – Six considerable PAPER-BAGS, carefully sealed, and marked successively, in gilt China-ink, with the symbols of the Six southern Zodiacal Signs, beginning at Libra; in the inside of which sealed Bags, lie miscellaneous masses of Sheets, and oftener Shreds and Snips, written in Professor Teufelsdröckh's scarce-legible *cursiv-schrift*; and treating of all imaginable things under the Zodiac and above it, but of his own personal history only at rare intervals, and then in the most enigmatic manner!

Whole fascicles there are, wherein the Professor, or, as he here speaking in the third person calls himself, 'the Wanderer,' is not once named. Then again, amidst what seems to be a Metaphysico-theological Disquisition, 'Detached Thoughts on the Steam-engine,' or 'The continued

---

1 *verehrtester Herr Herausgeber*: most esteemed Mr. Editor

Possibility of Prophecy,' we shall meet with some quite
private, not unimportant Biographical fact. On certain
sheets stand Dreams, authentic or not, while the circum-
jacent waking Actions are omitted. Anecdotes, oftenest
without date of place or time, fly loosely on separate slips,
like Sibylline leaves. Interspersed also are long purely
Autobiographical delineations, yet without connexion,
without recognisable coherence; so unimportant, so super-
fluously minute, they almost remind us of 'P. P. Clerk of
this Parish.' Thus does famine of intelligence alternate with
waste. Selection, order appears to be unknown to the
Professor. In all Bags the same imbroglio; only perhaps
in the Bag *Capricorn*, and those near it, the confusion a little
worse confounded. Close by a rather eloquent Oration 'On
receiving the Doctor's-Hat,' lie washbills marked *bezahlt*
(settled). His Travels are indicated by the Street-
Advertisements of the various cities he has visited; of which
Street-Advertisements, in most living tongues, here is
perhaps the completest collection extant.

So that if the Clothes Volume itself was too like a Chaos,
we have now instead of the solar Luminary that should still
it, the airy Limbo which by intermixture will farther vo-
latilise and discompose it! As we shall perhaps see it our
duty ultimately to deposit these Six Paper Bags in the
British Museum, farther description, and all vituperation
of them, may be spared. Biography or Autobiography of
Teufelsdröckh there is, clearly enough, none to be gleaned
here: at most some sketchy, shadowy, fugitive likeness of
him may, by unheard-of efforts, partly of intellect partly of
imagination, on the side of Editor and of Reader, rise up
between them. Only as a gaseous-chaotic Appendix to that
aqueous-chaotic Volume can the contents of the Six Bags
hover round us, and portions thereof be incorporated with
our delineation of it.

Daily and nightly does the Editor sit (with green spectacles) deciphering these unimaginable Documents from

CHAOS

their perplexed *cursiv-schrift*; collating them with the almost equally unimaginable Volume, which stands in legible print. Over such a universal medley of high and low, of hot, cold, moist and dry, is he here struggling (by union of like with like, which is Method) to build a firm Bridge for British travellers. Never perhaps since our first Bridge-builders, Sin and Death, built that stupendous Arch from Hell-gate to the Earth, did any Pontifex, or Pontiff, undertake such a task as the present Editor. For in this Arch too, leading as we humbly presume, far otherwards than that grand primeval one, the materials are to be fished up from the weltering deep, and down from the simmering air, here one mass, there another, and cunningly cemented, while the elements boil beneath: nor is there any supernatural force to do it with; but simply the Diligence and feeble thinking Faculty of an English Editor, endeavouring to evolve printed Creation out of a German printed and written Chaos, wherein, as he shoots to and fro in it, gathering clutching, piecing the Why to the far-distant Wherefore, his whole Faculty and Self are like to be swallowed up.

Patiently, under these incessant toils and agitations, does the Editor, dismissing all anger, see his otherwise robust health declining; some fraction of his allotted natural sleep nightly leaving him, and little but an inflamed nervous-system to be looked for. What is the use of Health, or of Life, if not to do some work therewith? And what work nobler than transplanting foreign Thought into the barren domestic soil; except indeed planting Thought of your own, which the fewest are privileged to do? Wild as it looks, this Philosophy of Clothes, can we ever reach its real meaning, promises to reveal newcoming Eras, the first dim rudiments and already-budding germs of a nobler Era, in Universal History. Is not such a prize worth some striving? Forward with us, courageous reader; be it towards failure, or towards success! The latter thou sharest with us, the former also is not all our own.

Book Two

THE OLD ADAM AND EVE

Genesis

IN a psychological point of view, it is perhaps questionable whether from birth and genealogy, how closely scrutinised soever, much insight is to be gained. Nevertheless, as in every phenomenon the Beginning remains always the most notable moment; so, with regard to any great man, we rest not till, for our scientific profit or not, the whole circumstances of his first appearance in this Planet, and what manner of Public Entry he made, are with utmost completeness rendered manifest. To the Genesis of our Clothes-Philosopher, then, be this First Chapter consecrated. Unhappily, indeed, he seems to be of quite obscure extraction; uncertain, we might almost say, whether of any: so that this Genesis of his can properly be nothing but an Exodus (or transit out of Invisibility into Visibility); whereof the preliminary portion is nowhere forthcoming.

'In the village of Entepfuhl,'[1] thus writes he, in the Bag *Libra*, on various Papers, which we arrange with difficulty,

1 *Entepfuhl*: duck-pond

'dwelt Andreas Futteral and his wife; childless, in still
seclusion, and cheerful though now verging towards old
age. Andreas had been grenadier Sergeant, and even regimental Schoolmaster under Frederick the Great; but now,
quitting the halbert and ferule for the spade and pruning-
hook, cultivated a little Orchard, on the produce of which
he, Cincinnatus-like, lived not without dignity. Fruits, the
peach, the apple, the grape, with other varieties came in
their season; all which Andreas knew how to sell: on
evenings he smoked largely, or read (as be seemed a
regimental Schoolmaster), and talked to neighbours that
would listen about the Victory of Rossbach; and how Fritz
the Only (*der Einzige*) had once with his own royal lips
spoken to him, had been pleased to say, when Andreas as
camp-sentinel demanded the pass-word, *Schweig Du Hund*
(Peace, hound!) before any of his staff-adjutants could
answer. "*Das nenn' ich mir einen König*, there is what I call
a King," would Andreas exclaim: "but the smoke of
Kunersdorf was still smarting his eyes."

'Gretchen, the housewife, won like Desdemona by the
deeds rather than the looks of her now veteran Othello,
lived not in altogether military subordination; for, as Andreas said, "the womankind will not drill (*wer kann die
Weiberchen dressiren*):" nevertheless she at least loved him
both for valour and wisdom; to her a Prussian grenadier
Sergeant and Regiment's-Schoolmaster was little other
than a Cicero and Cid: what you see, yet cannot see over,
is as good as infinite. Nay, was not Andreas in very deed a
man of order, courage, downrightness (*Geradheit*); that
understood Büsching's Geography, had been in the victory
of Rossbach, and left for dead in the camisade of Hoch-
kirch? The good Gretchen, for all her fretting, watched over
him and hovered round him, as only a true housemother
can: assiduously she cooked and sewed and scoured
for him; so that not only his old regimental sword and
grenadier-cap, but the whole habitation and environment

where, on pegs of honour, they hung, looked ever trim and gay: a roomy painted Cottage, embowered in fruit-trees and forest-trees, evergreens and honeysuckles; rising many-coloured from amid shaven grass-plots, flowers struggling in through the very windows; under its long projecting eaves nothing but garden-tools in methodic piles (to screen them from rain), and seats, where, especially on summer nights, a King might have wished to sit and smoke and call it his. Such a *Bauergut* (Copyhold) had Gretchen given her veteran; whose sinewy arms, and long-disused gardening talent, had made it what you saw.

'Into this umbrageous Man's-nest, one meek yellow evening or dusk, when the Sun, hidden indeed from terrestrial Entepfuhl, did nevertheless journey visible and radiant along the celestial Balance (*Libra*), it was that a Stranger of reverend aspect entered; and, with grave salutation, stood before the two rather astonished house-mates. He was close-muffled in a wide mantle; which without farther parley unfolding, he deposited therefrom what seemed some Basket, overhung with green Persian silk; saying only: *Ihr lieben Leute, hier bringe ein unschätz-bares Verleihen; nehmt es in aller Acht, sorgfältigst benützt es: mit hohem Lohn, oder wohl mit schweren Zinsen, wird's einst zurückgefordert,* 'Good Christian people, here lies for you an invaluable Loan; take all heed thereof, in all careful-ness employ it: with high recompense, or else with heavy penalty, will it one day be required back.' Uttering which singular words, in a clear, bell-like, forever memorable tone, the Stranger gracefully withdrew; and before An-dreas or his wife gazing in expectant wonder, had time to fashion either question or answer, was clean gone. Neither out of doors could aught of him be seen or heard; he had vanished in the thickets, in the dusk; the Orchard-gate stood quietly closed: the Stranger was gone once and always. So sudden had the whole transaction been, in the autumn stillness and twilight, so gentle, noiseless, that the Futterals could have fancied it all a trick of Imagination, or some visit from an authentic Spirit. Only that the green-silk Basket, such as neither Imagination nor authentic Spirits are wont to carry, still stood visible and tangible on their little parlour-table. Towards this the astonished couple, now with lit candle, hastily turned their attention. Lifting the green veil, to see what invaluable it hid, they descried there, amid down and rich white wrappages, no Pitt Diamond or Hapsburg Regalia, but in the softest sleep, a little red-coloured Infant! Beside it, lay a roll of gold Friedrichs,[1] the exact amount of which was never publicly known; also a *Taufschein* (baptismal certificate), wherein unfortunately nothing but the Name was decipherable; other document or indication none whatever.

'To wonder and conjecture was unavailing, then and always thenceforth. Nowhere in Entepfuhl, on the morrow or next day, did tidings transpire of any such figure as the Stranger; nor could the Traveller, who had passed through the neighbouring Town in coach-and-four, be connected with this Apparition, except in the way of gratuitous surmise. Meanwhile, for Andreas and his wife, the grand practical problem was: What to do with this little sleeping red-coloured Infant? Amid amazements and curiosities, which had to die away without external satisfying, they resolved, as in such circumstances charitable prudent people needs must, on nursing it, though with spoon-meat, into whiteness, and if possible into manhood. The Heavens smiled on their endeavour: thus has that same mysterious Individual ever since had a status for himself, in this visible Universe, some modicum of victual and lodging and parade-ground; and now expanded in bulk, faculty, and knowledge of good and evil, he, as HERR DIOGENES TEUFELSDRÖCKH, professes or is ready to profess,

1 *Friedrichs*: Prussian gold coins

perhaps not altogether without effect, in the new University of Weissnichtwo, the new Science of Things in General.'

Our Philosopher declares here, as indeed we should think he well might, that these facts, first communicated, by the good Gretchen Futteral, in his twelfth year, 'produced on the boyish heart and fancy a quite indelible impression. Who this reverend Personage,' he says, 'that glided into the Orchard Cottage when the Sun was in Libra, and then, as on spirit's wings, glided out again, might be? An inexpressible desire, full of love and of sadness, has often since struggled within me to shape an answer. Ever, in my distresses and my loneliness, has Fantasy turned, full of longing (*sehnsuchts-voll*), to that unknown Father, who perhaps far from me, perhaps near, either way invisible, might have taken me to his paternal bosom, there to lie screened from many a woe. Thou beloved Father, dost thou still, shut out from me only by thin penetrable curtains of earthly Space, wend to and fro among the crowd of the living? Or art thou hidden by those far thicker curtains of the Everlasting Night, or rather of the Everlasting Day, through which my mortal eye and out-stretched arms need not strive to reach? Alas! I know not, and in vain vex myself to know. More than once, heart-deluded, have I taken for thee this and the other noble-looking Stranger; and approached him wistfully, with infinite regard: but he too must repel me, he too was not thou.

'And yet, O Man born of Woman,' cries the Auto-biographer, with one of his sudden whirls, 'wherein is my case peculiar? Hadst thou, any more than I, a Father whom thou knowest? The Andreas and Gretchen, or the Adam and Eve, who led thee into Life, and for a time suckled and pap-fed thee there, whom thou namest Father and Mother; these were, like mine, but thy nursing-father and nursing-mother: thy true Beginning and Father is in Heaven, whom with the bodily eye thou shalt never behold, but only with the spiritual.'

'The little green veil,' adds he, among much similar

moralising, and embroiled discoursing, 'I yet keep; still more inseparably the Name, Diogenes Teufelsdröckh. From the veil can nothing be inferred: a piece of now quite faded Persian silk, like thousands of others. On the Name I have many times meditated and conjectured; but neither in this lay there any clue. That it was my unknown Father's name I must hesitate to believe. To no purpose have I searched through all the Herald's Books, in and without the German Empire, and through all manner of Subscriber-Lists (*Pränumeranten*), Militia-Rolls, and other Name-catalogues; extraordinary names as we have in Germany, the name Teufelsdröckh, except as appended to my own person, nowhere occurs. Again, what may the unchristian rather than Christian "Diogenes" mean? Did that reverend Basket-bearer intend, by such designation, to shadow forth my future destiny, or his own present malign humour? Perhaps the latter, perhaps both. Thou ill-starred Parent, who like an Ostrich must leave thy ill-starred offspring to be hatched into self-support by the mere sky-influences of Chance, can thy pilgrimage have been a smooth one? Beset by Misfortune thou doubtless hast been; or indeed by the worst figure of Misfortune, by Misconduct. Often have I fancied how, in thy hard life-battle, thou wert shot at and slung at, wounded, hand-fettered, hamstrung, browbeaten and bedevilled, by the Time-Spirit (*Zeitgeist*) in thyself and others, till the good soul first given thee was seared into grim rage; and thou hadst nothing for it but to leave in me an indignant appeal to the Future, and living speaking Protest against the Devil, as that same Spirit not of the Time only, but of Time itself, is well named! Which Appeal and Protest, may I now modestly add, was not perhaps quite lost in air.

'For indeed as Walter Shandy often insisted, there is much, nay almost all, in Names. The Name is the earliest Garment you wrap round the Earth-visiting ME; to which it thenceforth cleaves, more tenaciously (for there are Names that have lasted nigh thirty centuries) than the very skin. And now from without, what mystic influences does it not send inwards, even to the centre; especially in those plastic first-times, when the whole soul is yet infantine, soft, and the invisible seed-grain will grow to be an all overshadowing tree! Names? Could I unfold the influence of Names, which are the most important of all Clothings, I were a second greater Trismegistus. Not only all common Speech, but Science, Poetry itself is no other, if thou consider it, than a right *Naming*. Adam's first task was giving names to natural Appearances: what is ours still but a combination of the same; be the Appearances exotic-vegetable, organic, mechanic, stars, or starry movements (as in Science); or (as in Poetry) passions, virtues, calamities, God-attributes, Gods? – In a very plain sense the Proverb says, *Call one a thief and he will steal*; in an almost similar sense, may we not perhaps say, *Call one Diogenes Teufelsdröckh and he will open the Philosophy of Clothes*.'

'Meanwhile the incipient Diogenes, like others, all ignorant of his Why, his How or Whereabout, was opening his eyes to the kind Light; sprawling out his ten fingers and toes; listening, tasting, feeling; in a word, by all his Five Senses, still more by his Sixth Sense of Hunger, and a whole infinitude of inward, spiritual, half awakened Senses, endeavouring daily to acquire for himself some knowledge of this strange Universe where he had arrived, be his task therein what it might. Infinite was his progress; thus in some fifteen months, he could perform the miracle of – Speech! To breed a fresh Soul, is it not like brooding a fresh (celestial) Egg; wherein as yet all is formless, powerless; yet by degrees organic elements and fibres shoot through the watery albumen; and out of vague Sensation, grows Thought, grows Fantasy and Force, and we have Philosophies, Dynasties, nay Poetries and Religions!

'Young Diogenes, or rather young Gneschen, for by such diminutive had they in their fondness named him, travelled forward to those high consummations, by quick yet easy stages. The Futterals, to avoid vain talk, and moreover keep the roll of gold Friedrichs safe, gave out that he was a grand-nephew; the orphan of some sister's daughter, suddenly deceased, in Andreas's distant Prussian birth-land; of whom, as of her indigent sorrowing widower, little enough was known at Entepfuhl. Heedless of all which, the Nurseling took to his spoon-meat, and throve. I have heard him noted as a still infant, that kept his mind much to himself; above all, that seldom or never cried. He already felt that Time was precious; that he had other work cut out for him than whimpering.'

Such, after utmost painful search and collation among these miscellaneous Paper-masses, is all the notice we can gather of Herr Teufelsdröckh's genealogy. More imperfect, more enigmatic it can seem to few readers than to us. The Professor, in whom truly we more and more discern a certain satirical turn, and deep undercurrents of roguish whim, for the present stands pledged in honour, so we will not doubt him: but seems it not conceivable that, by the 'good Gretchen Futteral,' or some other perhaps interested party, he has himself been deceived? Should these Sheets, translated or not, ever reach the Entepfuhl Circulating-Library, some cultivated native of that district might feel called to afford explanation. Nay, since Books, like invisible scouts, permeate the whole habitable globe, and Tombuctoo itself is not safe from British Literature, may not some Copy find out even the mysterious Basket-bearing Stranger, who in a state of extreme senility perhaps still exists; and gently force even him to disclose himself; to claim openly a son, in whom any father may feel pride?

CHAPTER 2

Idyllic

'HAPPY season of Childhood!' exclaims Teufelsdröckh: 'Kind Nature, that art to all a bountiful mother; that visitest the poor man's hut with auroral radiance; and for thy Nurseling hast provided a soft swathing of Love and infinite Hope, wherein he waxes and slumbers, danced-round (*umgaukelt*) by sweetest Dreams! If the paternal Cottage still shuts us in, its roof still screens us; with a Father we have as yet a prophet, priest and king, and an Obedience that makes us Free. The young spirit has awakened out of Eternity, and knows not what we mean by Time; as yet Time is no fast-hurrying stream, but a sportful sunlit ocean; years to the child are as ages: ah! the secret of Vicissitude, of that slower or quicker decay and ceaseless downrushing of the universal World-fabric, from the granite mountain to the man or day-moth, is yet unknown; and in a motionless Universe we taste, what afterwards in this quick-whirling Universe is forever denied us, the balm of Rest. Sleep on, thou fair Child, for thy long rough journey is at hand! A little while, and thou too shalt sleep no more, but thy very dreams shall be mimic battles; thou too, with old Arnauld, must say in stern patience: "Rest? Rest? Shall I not have all

Eternity to rest in?" Celestial Nepenthe! though a Pyrrhus conquer empires, and an Alexander sack the world, he finds thee not; and thou hast once fallen gently, of thy own accord, on the eyelids, on the heart of every mother's child. For as yet, sleep and waking are one: the fair Life-garden rustles infinite around, and everywhere is dewy fragrance, and the budding of Hope; which budding, if in youth, too frost-nipt, it grow to flowers, will in manhood yield no fruit, but a prickly, bitter-rinded stone-fruit, of which the fewest can find the kernel.'

In such rose-coloured light does our Professor, as Poets are wont, look back on his childhood; the historical details of which (to say nothing of much other vague oratorical matter) he accordingly dwells on, with an almost wearisome minuteness. We hear of Entepfuhl standing 'in trustful derangement' among the woody slopes; the paternal Orchard flanking it as extreme outpost from below; the little Kuhbach[1] gushing kindly by, among beech-rows, through river after river, into the Donau, into the Black Sea, into the Atmosphere and Universe; and how 'the brave old Linden, stretching like a parasol of twenty ells in radius, overtopping all other rows and clumps, towered up from the central *Agora* and *Campus Martius* of the Village, like its Sacred Tree; and how the old men sat talking under its shadow (Gneschen often greedily listening), and the wearied labourers reclined, and the unwearied children sported, and the young men and maidens often danced to flute-music. 'Glorious summer twilights,' cries Teufelsdröckh, 'when the Sun like a proud Conqueror and Imperial Task-master turned his back, with his gold-purple emblazonry, and all his fire-clad bodyguard (of Prismatic Colours); and the tired brickmakers of this clay Earth might steal a little frolic, and those few meek Stars would not tell of them!'

Then we have long details of the *Weinlesen* (Vintage), the

1 *Kuhbach*: Cow-brook

Harvest-Home, Christmas, and so forth; with a whole cycle of the Entepfuhl Children's-games, differing apparently by mere superficial shades from those of other countries. Concerning all which, we shall here, for obvious reasons, say nothing. What cares the world for our as yet miniature Philosopher's achievements under that 'brave old Linden?' Or even where is the use of such practical reflections as the following? 'In all the sports of Children, were it only in their wanton breakages and defacements, you shall discern a creative instinct (*schaffenden Trieb*): the Mankin feels that he is a born Man, that his vocation is to Work. The choicest present you can make him is a Tool; be it knife or pengun, for construction or for destruction; either way it is for Work, for Change. In gregarious sports of skill or strength, the Boy trains himself to Cooperation, for war or peace, as governor or governed: the little Maid again, provident of her domestic destiny, takes with preference to Dolls.'

Perhaps, however, we may give this anecdote, considering who it is that relates it: 'My first short-clothes were of yellow serge; or rather, I should say, my first short-cloth, for the vesture was one and indivisible, reaching from neck to ankle, a mere body with four limbs: of which fashion how little could I then divine the architectural, how much less the moral significance!'

More graceful is the following little picture: 'On fine evenings I was wont to carry forth my supper (bread-crumb boiled in milk), and eat it out of doors. On the coping of the Orchard-wall, which I could reach by climbing, or still more easily if Father Andreas would set up the pruning-ladder, my porringer was placed: there, many a sunset, have I, looking at the distant western Mountains, consumed, not without relish, my evening meal. Those hues of gold and azure, that hush of World's expectation as Day died, were still a Hebrew Speech for me; nevertheless I was looking at the fair illuminated Letters, and had an eye for their gilding.'

With 'the little one's friendship for the cattle and poultry' we shall not much intermeddle. It may be that hereby he acquired 'a certain deeper sympathy with animated Nature:' but when, we would ask, saw any man, in a collection of Biographical Documents, such a piece as this: 'Impressive enough (*bedeutungsvoll*) was it to hear, in early morning, the Swineherd's horn; and know that so many hungry, happy quadrupeds, were on all sides starting in hot haste to join him, for breakfast on the Heath. Or to see them, at eventide, all marching in again, with short squeak, almost in military order; and each, topographically correct, trotting off in succession to the right or left, through its own lane, to its own dwelling; till old Kunz, at the Village-head, now left alone, blew his last blast, and retired for the night. We are wont to love the Hog chiefly in the form of Ham: yet did not these bristly thick-skinned beings here manifest intelligence, perhaps humour of character; at any rate, a touching, trustful submissiveness to Man, – who were he but a Swineherd, in darned gabardine, and leather breeches more resembling slate or discoloured tin breeches, is still the Hierarch of this lower world?'

It is maintained, by Helvetius and his set, that an infant of genius is quite the same as any other infant, only that certain surprisingly favourable influences accompany him through life, especially through childhood, and expand him, while others lie close-folded and continue dunces. Herein, say they, consists the whole difference between an inspired Prophet and a double-barrelled Game-preserver: the inner man of the one has been fostered into generous development; that of the other, crushed down perhaps by vigour of animal digestion, and the like, has exuded and evaporated, or at best sleeps now irresuscitably stagnant at the bottom of his stomach. 'With which opinion,' cries Teufelsdröckh, 'I should as soon agree as with this other, that an acorn might, by favourable or unfavourable influences of soil and climate, be nursed into a cabbage, or the cabbage-seed into an oak.

'Nevertheless,' continues he, 'I too acknowledge the all but omnipotence of early culture and nurture: hereby we have either a doddered dwarf bush, or a high-towering, wide-shadowing tree; either a sick yellow cabbage, or an edible, luxuriant, green one. Of a truth, it is the duty of all men, especially of all philosophers, to note down with accuracy the characteristic circumstances of their Education, what furthered, what hindered, what in any way modified it: to which duty, now-a-days so pressing for many a German Autobiographer, I also zealously address myself.' – Thou rogue! Is it by short-clothes of yellow serge, and swineherd horns, that an infant of genius is educated? And yet, as usual, it ever remains doubtful whether he is laughing in his sleeve at these Autobiographical times of ours, or writing from the abundance of his own fond ineptitude. For he continues: 'If among the ever-streaming currents of Sights, Hearings, Feelings for Pain or Pleasure, whereby, as in a Magic Hall, young Gneschen went about environed, I might venture to select and specify, perhaps these following were also of the number:

'Doubtless, as childish sports call forth Intellect, Activity, so the young creature's Imagination was stirred up, and a Historical tendency given him by the narrative habits of Father Andreas; who, with his battle-reminiscences, and gray, austere, yet hearty patriarchal aspect, could not but appear another Ulysses and "Much-enduring Man." Eagerly I hung upon his tales, when listening neighbours enlivened the hearth: from these perils and these travels, wild and far almost as Hades itself, a dim world of Adventure expanded itself within me. Incredible also was the knowledge I acquired in standing by the Old Men under the Linden-tree: the whole of Immensity was yet new to me; and had not these reverend seniors, talkative enough, been employed in partial surveys thereof for nigh fourscore years? With amazement I began to discover that Entepfuhl stood in the middle of a Country, of a World; that there was such a thing as History, as Biography; to which I also, one day, by hand and tongue, might contribute.

'In a like sense worked the *Postwagen* (Stage-Coach), which, slow-rolling under its mountains of men and luggage, wended through our Village: northwards, truly, in the dead of night; yet southwards visibly at eventide. Not till my eighth year, did I reflect that this Postwagen could be other than some terrestrial Moon, rising and setting by mere Law of Nature, like the heavenly one; that it came on

made highways, from far cities towards far cities; weaving
them like a monstrous shuttle into closer and closer union.
It was then that, independently of Schiller's *Wilhelm Tell*, I
made this not quite insignificant reflection (so true also in
spiritual things): *Any road, this simple Entepfuhl road, will
lead you to the end of the World!*

'Why mention our Swallows, which, out of far Africa as I
learned, threading their way over seas and mountains,
corporate cities and belligerent nations, yearly found themselves, with the month of May, snug-lodged in our Cottage
Lobby? The hospitable Father (for cleanliness' sake) had
fixed a little bracket, plumb under their nest: there they
built, and caught flies, and twittered, and bred; and all, I
chiefly, from the heart loved them. Bright, nimble creatures, who taught *you* the mason-craft; nay, stranger still,
gave you a masonic incorporation, almost social police? For
if, by ill chance, and when time pressed, your House fell,
have I not seen five neighbourly Helpers appear next day;
and swashing to and fro, with animated, loud, long-drawn
chirpings, and activity almost super-hirundine, complete it
again before nightfall?

'But undoubtedly the grand summary of Entepfuhl
child's-culture, where as in a funnel its manifold influences
were concentrated and simultaneously poured down on us,
was the annual Cattle-fair. Here, assembling from all the
four winds, came the elements of an unspeakable hurly-
burly. Nutbrown maids and nutbrown men, all clear-
washed, loud-laughing, bedizened and be-ribanded; who
came for dancing, for treating, and if possible, for happiness. Topbooted Graziers from the North; Swiss Brokers,
Italian Drovers, also topbooted, from the South; these with
their subalterns in leather jerkins, leather skullcaps, and
long oxgoads; shouting in half-articulate speech, amid the
inarticulate barking and bellowing. Apart stood Potters
from far Saxony, with their crockery in fair rows; Nürnberg
Pedlars, in booths that to me seemed richer than Ormuz

bazaars; Showmen from the Lago Maggiore; detachments of the *Wiener Schub* (Offscourings of Vienna) vociferously superintending games of chance. Ballad-singers brayed, Auctioneers grew hoarse; cheap New Wine (*heuriger*) flowed like water, still worse confounding the confusion; and high over all, vaulted, in ground-and-lofty tumbling, a particoloured Merry Andrew, like the genius of the place and of Life itself.

'Thus encircled by the mystery of Existence; under the deep heavenly Firmament; waited on by the four golden Seasons, with their vicissitudes of contribution, for even grim Winter brought its skating-matches and shooting-matches, its snow-storms and Christmas carols, – did the Child sit and learn. These things were the Alphabet, whereby in after-time he was to syllable and partly read the grand Volume of the World: what matters it whether such Alphabet be in large gilt letters or in small ungilt ones, so you have an eye to read it? For Gneschen, eager to learn, the very act of looking thereon was a blessedness that gilded all: his existence was a bright, soft element of Joy; out of which, as in Prospero's Island, wonder after wonder bodied itself forth, to teach by charming.

'Nevertheless I were but a vain dreamer to say, that even then my felicity was perfect. I had, once for all, come down from Heaven into the Earth. Among the rainbow colours that glowed on my horizon, lay even in childhood a dark ring of Care, as yet no thicker than a thread, and often quite overshone; yet always it reappeared, nay, ever waxing broader and broader; till in after-years it almost overshadowed my whole canopy, and threatened to engulf me in final night. It was the ring of Necessity, whereby we are all begirt: happy he for whom a kind heavenly Sun brightens it into a ring of Duty, and plays round it with beautiful prismatic diffractions; yet ever, as basis and as bourne for our whole being, it is there.

'For the first few years of our terrestrial Apprenticeship, we have not much work to do; but, boarded and lodged gratis, are set down mostly to look about us over the workshop, and see others work, till we have understood the tools a little, and can handle this and that. If good Passivity alone, and not good Passivity and good Activity together, were the thing wanted, then was my early position favourable beyond the most. In all that respects openness of Sense, affectionate Temper, ingenuous Curiosity, and the fostering of these, what more could I have wished? On the other side, however, things went not so well. My Active Power (*Thatkraft*) was unfavourably hemmed in; of which misfortune how many traces yet abide with me! In an orderly house, where the litter of children's sports is hateful enough, your training is too stoical; rather to bear and forbear than to make and do. I was forbid much: wishes in any measure bold I had to renounce; every where a strait bond of Obedience inflexibly held me down. Thus already Freewill often came in painful collision with Necessity; so that my tears flowed, and at seasons the Child itself might taste that root of bitterness, wherewith the whole fruitage of our life is mingled and tempered.

'In which habituation to Obedience, truly, it was beyond measure safer to err by excess than by defect. Obedience is our universal duty and destiny; wherein whoso will not bend must break: too early and too thoroughly we cannot be trained to know that Would, in this world of ours, is as mere zero to Should, and for most part as the smallest of fractions even to Shall. Hereby was laid for me the basis of worldly Discretion, nay, of Morality itself. Let me not quarrel with my upbringing! It was rigorous, too frugal, compressively secluded, every way unscientific: yet in that very strictness and domestic solitude might there not lie the root of deeper Earnestness, of the stem from which all noble fruit must grow? Above all, how unskilful soever, it was loving, it was well-meant, honest; whereby every deficiency was helped. My kind Mother, for as such I must ever love the good Gretchen, did me one altogether invaluable service: she taught me, less indeed by word than by act and daily reverent look and habitude, her own simple version of the Christian Faith. Andreas, too, attended Church; yet more like a parade-duty, for which he in the other world expected pay with arrears, – as, I trust, he has received: but my Mother, with a true woman's heart, and fine though uncultivated sense, was in the strictest acceptation Religious. How indestructibly the Good grows, and propagates itself, even among the weedy entanglements of Evil! The highest whom I knew on Earth I here saw bowed down, with awe unspeakable, before a Higher in Heaven: such things, especially in infancy, reach inwards to the very core of your being; mysteriously does a Holy of Holies build itself into visibility in the mysterious deeps; and Reverence, the divinest in man, springs forth undying from its mean envelopment of Fear. Wouldst thou rather be a peasant's son that knew, were it never so rudely, there was a God in Heaven and in Man; or a duke's son that only knew there were two and thirty quarters on the family-coach?'

To which last question we must answer: Beware, O Teufelsdröckh, of spiritual pride!

CHAPTER 3

Pedagogy

HITHERTO we see young Gneschen, in his indivisible case of yellow serge, borne forward mostly on the arms of kind Nature alone; seated, indeed, and much to his mind, in the terrestrial workshop; but (except his soft hazel eyes, which we doubt not already gleamed with a still intelligence) called upon for little voluntary movement there. Hitherto accordingly his aspect is rather generic, that of an incipient Philosopher and Poet in the abstract: perhaps it would puzzle Herr Heuschrecke himself to say wherein the special Doctrine of Clothes is as yet foreshadowed or betokened. For with Gneschen, as with others, the Man may indeed stand pictured in the Boy (at least, all the pigments are there); yet only some half of the Man stands in the Child, or young Boy, namely his Passive endowment, not his Active. The more impatient are we to discover what figure he cuts in this latter capacity; how when, to use his own words, 'he understands the tools a little, and can handle this or that,' he will proceed to handle it.

Here, however, may be the place to state that, in much of our Philosopher's history, there is something of an almost Hindoo character: nay, perhaps in that so well-fostered and every-way excellent 'Passivity' of his, which, with no free development of the antagonist Activity, distinguished his childhood, we may detect the rudiments of much that, in afterdays, and still in these present days, astonishes the world. For the shallow-sighted, Teufelsdröckh is oftenest a man without Activity of any kind, a No-man; for the deep-sighted, again, a man with Activity almost superabundant, yet so spiritual, close-hidden, enigmatic, that no mortal can foresee its explosions, or even when it has exploded, so much as ascertain its significance. A dangerous, difficult temper for the modern European; above all, disadvantageous in the hero of a Biography! Now as heretofore it will behove the Editor of these pages, were it never so unsuccessfully, to do his endeavour.

Among the earliest tools of any complicacy which a man, especially a man of letters, gets to handle, are his Class-books. On this portion of his History, Teufelsdröckh looks down professedly as indifferent. Reading he 'cannot remember ever to have learned;' so perhaps had it by nature. He says generally: 'Of the insignificant portion of my Education, which depended on Schools, there need almost no notice be taken. I learned what others learn; and kept it stored by in a corner of my head, seeing as yet no manner of use in it. My Schoolmaster, a downbent, brokenhearted, underfoot martyr, as others of that guild are, did little for me, except discover that he could do little: he, good soul, pronounced me a genius, fit for the learned professions; and that I must be sent to the Gymnasium, and one day to

the University. Meanwhile, what printed thing soever I
could meet with I read. My very copper pocket-money I
laid out on stall-literature; which, as it accumulated, I with
my own hands sewed into volumes. By this means was the
young head furnished with a considerable miscellany of
things and shadows of things: History in authentic fragments lay mingled with Fabulous chimeras, wherein also
was reality; and the whole not as dead stuff, but as living
pabulum, tolerably nutritive for a mind as yet so peptic.'

That the Entepfuhl Schoolmaster judged well we now
know. Indeed, already in the youthful Gneschen, with all
his outward stillness, there may have been manifest an
inward vivacity that promised much; symptoms of a spirit
singularly open, thoughtful, almost poetical. Thus, to say
nothing of his Suppers on the Orchard-wall, and other
phenomena of that earlier period, have many readers of
these pages stumbled, in their twelfth year, on such
reflections as the following? 'It struck me much, as I
sat by the Kuhbach, one silent noontide, and watched
it flowing, gurgling, to think how this same streamlet had
flowed and gurgled, through all changes of weather and of
fortune, from beyond the earliest date of History. Yes,
probably on the morning when Joshua forded Jordan;
even as at the mid-day when Cæsar, doubtless with
difficulty, swam the Nile, yet kept his *Commentaries* dry,
– this little Kuhbach, assiduous as Tiber, Eurotas, or
Siloa, was murmuring on across the wilderness, as yet
unnamed, unseen: here, too, as in the Euphrates and the
Ganges, is a Vein or Veinlet of the grand World-
circulation of Waters, which, with its atmospheric
Arteries, has lasted and lasts simply with the World. Thou
fool! Nature alone is antique, and the oldest Art a mush-
room; that idle crag thou sittest on is six thousand years of
age.' In which little thought, as in a little fountain, may
there not lie the beginning of those well-nigh unutterable
meditations on the grandeur and the mystery of TIME,

and its relation to ETERNITY, which play such a part in this Philosophy of Clothes?

Over his Gymnasic and Academic years the Professor by no means lingers so lyrical and joyful as over his childhood. Green sunny tracts there are still; but intersected by bitter rivulets of tears, here and there stagnating into sour marshes of discontent. 'With my first view of the Hinter-schlag[1] Gymnasium,' writes he, 'my evil days began. Well do I still remember the red sunny Whitsuntide morning, when trotting full of hope, by the side of Father Andreas, I entered the main street of the place, and saw its steeple-clock (then striking Eight), and *Schuldthurm* (Jail), and the aproned or disaproned Burghers moving in to breakfast: a little dog, in mad terror, was rushing past; for some human imps had tied a tin kettle to its tail; thus did the agonised creature loud-jingling career through the whole length of the Borough, and become notable enough. Fit emblem of many a Conquering Hero, to whom Fate (wedding Fantasy to Sense, as it often elsewhere does) has malignantly appended a tin kettle of Ambition, to chase him on; which, the faster he runs, urges him the faster, the more loudly and more foolishly! Fit emblem also of much that awaited myself, in that mischievous Den; as in the World, whereof it was a portion and epitome!

'Alas, the kind beech-rows of Entepfuhl were hidden in the distance: I was among strangers, harshly, at best in-differently, disposed towards me; the young heart felt, for the first time, quite orphaned and alone.' His school-fellows, as is usual, persecuted him: 'They were Boys,' he says, 'mostly rude Boys, and obeyed the impulse of rude Nature, which bids the deerherd fall upon any stricken hart, the duck-flock put to death any broken-winged brother or sister, and on all hands the strong tyrannise over the weak.' He admits that though 'perhaps in an unusual degree

[1] *Hinterschlag*: Slap-behind

morally courageous,' he succeeded ill in battle, and would fain have avoided it; a result, as would appear, owing less to his small personal stature (for, in passionate seasons, he was 'incredibly nimble'), than to his 'virtuous principles:' 'if it was disgraceful to be beaten,' says he, 'it was only a shade less disgraceful to have so much as fought; thus was I drawn two ways at once, and in this important element of school history, the war-element, had little but sorrow.' On the whole, that same excellent 'Passivity,' so notable in Teufelsdröckh's childhood, is here visibly enough again getting nourishment. 'He wept often; indeed to such a degree, that he was nick-named *Der Weinende* (the Tearful), which epithet, till towards his thirteenth year, was indeed not quite unmerited. Only at rare intervals did the young soul burst forth into fire-eyed rage, and, with a Stormfulness (*Ungestüm*) under which the boldest quailed, assert that he too had Rights of Man, or at least of Mankin.' In all which, who does not discern a fine flower-tree and cinnamon-tree (of genius) nigh choked among pumpkins, reedgrass, and ignoble shrubs; and forced, if it would live, to struggle upwards only, and not outwards; into a *height* quite sickly and disproportioned to its *breadth?*

We find, moreover, that his Greek and Latin were 'mechanically' taught; Hebrew scarce even mechanically; much else which they called History, Cosmography, Philosophy, and so forth, no better than not at all. So that, except inasmuch as Nature was still busy; and he himself 'went about, as was of old his wont, among the Craftsmen's workshops, there learning many things;' and farther lighted on some small store of curious reading, in Hans Wachtel the Cooper's house, where he lodged, – his time, it would appear, was utterly wasted. Which facts the Professor has not yet learned to look upon with any contentment. Indeed, throughout the whole of this Bag *Scorpio*, where we now are, and often in the following Bag, he shews himself unusually animated on the matter of Education, and not without some touch of what we might presume to be anger.

'My Teachers,' says he, 'were hide-bound Pedants, without knowledge of man's nature or of boy's; or of aught save their lexicons and quarterly account-books. Innumerable dead Vocables (no dead Language, for they themselves knew no Language) they crammed into us, and called it fostering the growth of mind. How can an inanimate, mechanical Gerund-grinder, the like of whom will, in a subsequent century, be manufactured, at Nürnberg, out of wood and leather, foster the growth of any thing; much more of Mind, which grows, not like a vegetable (by having its roots littered with etymological compost), but like a Spirit, by mysterious contact of Spirit; Thought kindling itself at the fire of living Thought? How shall *he* give kindling, in whose own inward man there is no live coal, but all is burnt out to a dead grammatical cinder? The Hinterschlag Professors knew Syntax enough; and of the human soul thus much: that it had a faculty called Memory, and could be acted on through the muscular integument by appliance of birch rods.

'Alas, so is it every where, so will it ever be; till the Hodman is discharged, or reduced to Hod-bearing; and an Architect is hired, and on all hands fitly encouraged: till communities and individuals discover, not without surprise, that fashioning the souls of a generation by Knowledge can rank on a level with blowing their bodies to pieces by Gunpowder; that with Generals and Field-marshals for killing, there should be world-honoured Dignitaries, and were it possible, true God-ordained Priests, for teaching. But as yet, though the Soldier wears openly, and even parades, his butchering-tool, nowhere, far as I have travelled, did the Schoolmaster make show of his instructing-tool: nay, were he to walk abroad with birch girt on thigh, as if he therefrom expected honour, would not, among the idler class, a certain levity be excited?'

In the third year of this Gymnasic period, Father Andreas seems to have died: the young Scholar, otherwise so

THE SCHOOLMASTER OF THE FUTURE

maltreated, saw himself for the first time clad outwardly in sables, and inwardly in quite inexpressible melancholy. 'The dark boundless Abyss, that lies under our feet, had yawned open; the pale kingdoms of Death, with all their innumerable silent nations and generations stood before him; the inexorable word, NEVER! now first showed its meaning. My mother wept, and her sorrow got vent; but in my heart there lay a whole lake of tears, pent up in silent desolation. Nevertheless, the unworn Spirit is strong, Life is so healthful that it even finds nourishment in Death: these stern experiences, planted down by Memory in my Imagination, rose there to a whole cypress forest, sad but beautiful; waving, with not unmelodious sighs, in dark luxuriance, in the hottest sunshine, through long years of youth: – as in manhood also it does, and will do; for I have now pitched my tent under a Cypress tree; the Tomb is now my inexpugnable Fortress, ever close by the gate of which I look upon the hostile armaments, and pains and penalties, of tyrannous Life placidly enough, and listen to its loudest threatenings with a still smile. O ye loved ones, that already sleep in the noiseless Bed of Rest, whom in life I could only weep for and never help; and ye, who wide-scattered still toil lonely in the monster-bearing Desert, dyeing the flinty ground with your blood, – yet a little while, and we shall all meet THERE, and our Mother's bosom will screen us all; and Oppression's harness, and Sorrow's fire-whip, and all the Gehenna Bailiffs that patrol and inhabit ever-vexed Time, cannot thenceforth harm us any more!'

Close by which rather beautiful apostrophe, lies a la-boured Character of the deceased Andreas Futteral; of his natural ability, his deserts in life (as Prussian Sergeant); with long historical inquiries into the genealogy of the Futteral family, here traced back as far as Henry the Fowler: the whole of which we pass over, not without astonishment. It only concerns us to add that now was the time when Mother Gretchen revealed to her foster-son that he was not at all of this kindred; or indeed of any kindred, having come into historical existence in the way already known to us. 'Thus was I doubly orphaned,' says he; 'bereft not only of Possession, but even of Remembrance. Sorrow and Wonder, here suddenly united, could not but produce abundant fruit. Such a disclosure, in such a season, struck its roots through my whole nature: ever till the years of mature manhood, it mingled with my whole thoughts, was as the stem whereon all my day-dreams and night-dreams grew. A certain poetic elevation, yet also a corresponding civic depression, it naturally imparted: *I was like no other*; in which fixed-idea, leading sometimes to highest, and oftener to frightfullest results, may there not lie the first spring of Tendencies, that in my Life have become remarkable enough? As in birth, so in action, speculation, and social position, my fellows are perhaps not numerous.'

In the Bag *Sagittarius*, as we at length discover, Teufelsdröckh has become a University man; though how, when, or of what quality, will nowhere disclose itself with the smallest certainty. Few things, in the way of confusion and capricious indistinctness, can now surprise our readers; not even the total want of dates, almost without parallel in a Biographical work. So enigmatic, so chaotic we have always found, and must always look to find, these scattered Leaves. In *Sagittarius*, however, Teufelsdröckh begins to shew himself even more than usually Sibylline: fragments of all sorts; scraps of regular Memoir, College Exercises, Programs, Professional Testimoniums, Milkscores, torn Billets, sometimes to appearance of an amatory cast; all blown together as if by merest chance, henceforth bewilder the sane Historian. To combine any picture of these University, and the subsequent, years; much more, to decipher therein any illustrative primordial elements of the Clothes-Philosophy, becomes such a problem as the reader may imagine.

So much we can see; darkly, as through the foliage of some wavering thicket: a youth of no common endowment, that has passed happily through Childhood, less happily yet still vigorously through Boyhood, now at length perfect in 'dead vocables,' and set down, as he hopes, by the living Fountain, there to superadd Ideas and Capabilities. From such Fountain he draws, diligently, thirstily, yet nowise with his whole heart, for the water nowise suits his palate; discouragements, entanglements, aberrations are discoverable or supposable. Nor perhaps are even pecuniary distresses wanting; for 'the good Gretchen, who in spite of advices from not disinterested relatives has sent him hither, must after a time withdraw her willing but too feeble hand.' Nevertheless in an atmosphere of Poverty and manifold Chagrin, the Humour of that young Soul, what character is in him, first decisively reveals itself; and, like strong sunshine in weeping skies, gives out variety of colours, some of which are prismatic. Thus with the aid of Time, and of what Time brings, has the stripling Diogenes Teufelsdröckh waxed into manly stature; and into so questionable an aspect, that we ask with new eagerness How he specially came by it, and regret anew that there is no more explicit answer. Certain of the intelligible and partially significant fragments, which are few in number, shall be extracted from that Limbo of a Paperbag, and presented with the usual preparation.

As if, in the Bag *Scorpio*, Teufelsdröckh had not already expectorated his antipedagogic spleen; as if, from the name *Sagittarius*, he had thought himself called upon to shoot arrows, we here again fall in with such matter as this: 'The University where I was educated still stands vivid enough in my remembrance, and I know its name well; which name, however, I from tenderness to existing interests and persons, shall in no wise divulge. It is my painful duty to say that, out of England and Spain, ours was the worst of all hitherto discovered Universities. This is indeed a time when right Education is, as nearly as may be, impossible: however, in degrees of wrongness there is no limit; nay, I can conceive a worse system than that of the Nameless itself; as poisoned victual may be worse than absolute hunger.

'It is written, When the blind lead the blind, both shall fall into the ditch: wherefore, in such circumstances, may it not sometimes be safer, if both leader and led simply – sit still? Had you, any where in Crim Tartary, walled in a square enclosure; furnished it with a small, ill-chosen Library; and then turned loose into it eleven hundred Christian striplings, to tumble about as they listed, from three to seven years; certain persons, under the title of Professors, being stationed at the gates, to declare aloud that it was a University, and exact considerable admission-fees, – you had, not indeed in mechanical structure, yet in spirit and result, some imperfect resemblance of our High Seminary. I say, imperfect; for if our mechanical structure was quite other, so neither was our result altogether the same: unhappily, we were not in Crim Tartary, but in a corrupt European city, full of smoke and sin; moreover, in the middle of a Public, which, without far costlier apparatus, than that of the Square Enclosure, and Declaration aloud, you could not be sure of gulling.

'Gullible, however, by fit apparatus, all Publics are; and gulled, with the most surprising profit. Towards any thing like a *Statistics of Imposture*, indeed, little as yet has been done: with a strange indifference, our Economists, nigh buried under Tables for minor Branches of Industry, have altogether overlooked the grand all-overtopping Hypocrisy Branch; as if our whole arts of Puffery, of Quackery, Priestcraft, Kingcraft, and the innumerable other crafts and mysteries of that genus, had not ranked in Productive Industry at all! Can any one, for example, so much as say, What monies, in Literature and Shoeblacking, are realised by actual Instruction and actual jet Polish; what by fictitious-persuasive Proclamation of such; specifying, in distinct items, the distributions, circulations, disbursements, incomings of said monies, with the smallest approach to accuracy? But to ask, How far, in all the several infinitely complected departments of social business, in government, education, in manual, commercial, intellectual fabrication of every sort, man's Want is supplied by true Ware; how far by the mere Appearance of true Ware: – in other words, To what extent, by what methods, with what effects, in various times and countries, Deception takes the place and wages of Performance: here truly is an Inquiry big with results for the future time, but to which hitherto only the vaguest answer can be given. If for the present, in our Europe, we estimate the ratio of Ware to

Appearance of Ware so high even as at One to a Hundred
(which, considering the Wages of a Pope, Russian Auto-
crat, or English Game-Preserver, is probably not far from
the mark), – what almost prodigious saving may there not
be anticipated, as the *Statistics of Imposture* advances, and
so the manufacturing of Shams (that of Realities rising
into clearer and clearer distinction therefrom) gradually
declines, and at length becomes all but wholly unnecessary!

'This for the coming golden ages. What I had to remark,
for the present brazen one, is, that in several provinces, as
in Education, Polity, Religion, where so much is wanted
and indispensable, and so little can as yet be furnished,
probably Imposture is of sanative, anodyne nature, and
man's Gullibility not his worst blessing. Suppose your
sinews of war quite broken; I mean your military chest
insolvent, forage all but exhausted; and that the whole army
is about to mutiny, disband, and cut your and each other's
throat, – then were it not well could you, as if by miracle,
pay them in any sort of fairy-money, feed them on coagu-
lated water, or mere imagination of meat; whereby, till the
real supply came up, they might be kept together, and
quiet? Such perhaps was the aim of Nature, who does
nothing without aim, in furnishing her favourite, Man,
with this his so omni-potent or rather omnipatient Talent
of being Gulled.

'How beautifully it works, with a little mechanism; nay,
almost makes mechanism for itself! These Professors in the
Nameless lived with ease, with safety, by a mere Reputation, constructed in past times, and then too with no great
effort, by quite another class of persons. Which Reputation,
like a strong, brisk-going, undershot-wheel, sunk into the
general current, bade fair, with only a little annual repaint-
ing on their part, to hold long together, and of its own
accord, assiduously grind for them. Happy that it was so for
the Millers! They themselves needed not to work; their

attempts at working, at what they called Educating, now when I look back on it, fill me with a certain mute admiration.

'Besides all this, we boasted ourselves a Rational University; in the highest degree, hostile to Mysticism: thus was the young vacant mind furnished with much talk about Progress of the Species, Dark Ages, Prejudice, and the like; so that all were quickly enough blown out into a state of windy argumentativeness; whereby the better sort must soon end in sick, impotent Scepticism; the worser sort explode (*crepiren*) in finished Self-conceit, and to all spiritual intents become dead. – But this too is portion of mankind's lot. If our era is the Era of Unbelief, why murmur under it; is there not a better coming, nay come? As in longdrawn Systole and longdrawn Diastole, must the period of Faith alternate with the period of Denial; must the vernal growth, the summer luxuriance of all Opinions, Spiritual Representations and Creations, be followed by, and again follow, the autumnal decay, the winter dissolution. For man lives in Time, has his whole earthly being, endeavour, and destiny shaped for him by Time: only in the transitory Time-Symbol is the ever-motionless Eternity we stand on made manifest. And yet, in such winter-seasons of Denial, it is for the nobler-minded perhaps a comparative misery to have been born, and to be awake, and work; and for the duller a felicity, if like hibernating animals, safe-lodged in some Salamanca University, or Sybaris City, or other superstitious or voluptuous Castle of Indolence, they can slumber through, in stupid dreams, and only awaken when the loud-roaring hailstorms have all done their work, and to our prayers and martyrdoms the new Spring has been vouchsafed.'

That in the environment, here mysteriously enough shadowed forth, Teufelsdröckh must have felt ill at ease, cannot be doubtful. 'The hungry young,' he says, 'looked up to their spiritual Nurses; and, for food, were bidden eat

MOUNT PARNASSUS

the east wind. What vain jargon of controversial Meta-physic, Etymology, and mechanical Manipulation, falsely named Science, was current there, I indeed learned, better perhaps than the most. Among eleven hundred Christian youths, there will not be wanting some eleven eager to learn. By collision with such, a certain warmth, a certain polish was communicated; by instinct and happy accident, I took less to rioting (*renommiren*), than to thinking and reading, which latter also I was free to do. Nay from the chaos of that Library, I succeeded in fishing up more books perhaps than had been known to the very keepers thereof. The foundation of a Literary Life was hereby laid: I learned, on my own strength, to read fluently in almost all cultivated languages, on almost all subjects, and sciences; farther, as man is ever the prime object to man, already it was my favourite employment to read character in speculation, and from the Writing to construe the Writer. A certain groundplan of Human Nature and Life began to fashion itself in me; wondrous enough, now when I look back on it; for my whole Universe, physical and spiritual, was as yet a Machine! However, such a conscious, recognised groundplan, the truest I had, *was* beginning to be there, and by additional experiments, might be cor-rected and indefinitely extended.'

Thus from poverty does the strong educe nobler wealth; thus in the destitution of the wild desert, does our young Ishmael acquire for himself the highest of all possessions, that of Self-help. Nevertheless a desert this was, waste, and howling with savage monsters. Teufelsdröckh gives us long details of his 'fever-paroxysms of Doubt;' his Inquiries concerning Miracles, and the Evidences of religious Faith; and how 'in the silent night-watches, still darker in his heart than over sky and earth, he has cast himself before the All-seeing, and with audible prayers, cried vehemently for Light, for deliverance from Death and the Grave. Not till after long years, and unspeakable agonies, did the believing heart surrender; sink into spell-bound sleep, under the nightmare, Unbelief; and, in this hagridden dream, mistake God's fair living world for a pallid, vacant Hades and extinct Pandemonium. But through such Purgatory pain,' continues he, 'it is appointed us to pass: first must the dead Letter of Religion own itself dead, and drop piecemeal into dust, if the living Spirit of Religion, freed from this its charnel-house, is to arise on us, newborn of Heaven, and with new healing under its wings.'

To which Purgatory pains, seemingly severe enough, if we add a liberal measure of Earthly distresses, want of practical guidance, want of sympathy, want of money, want of hope; and all this in the fervid season of youth, so exaggerated in imagining, so boundless in desires, yet here so poor in means, – do we not see a strong incipient spirit oppressed and overloaded from without and from within; the fire of genius struggling up among fuel-wood of the greenest, and as yet with more of bitter vapour than of clear flame?

From various fragments of Letters and other documentary scraps, it is to be inferred that Teufelsdröckh, isolated, shy, retiring as he was, had not altogether escaped notice: certain established men are aware of his existence; and, if stretching out no helpful hand, have at least their eyes on him. He appears, though in dreary enough humour, to be addressing himself to the Profession of Law; – whereof, indeed, the world has since seen him a public graduate. But omitting these broken, unsatisfactory thrums of Economical relation, let us present rather the following small thread of Moral relation; and therewith, the reader for himself weaving it in at the right place, conclude our dim arras-picture of these University years.

'Here also it was that I formed acquaintance with Herr Towgood, or, as it is perhaps better written, Herr Toughgut; a young person of quality (*von Adel*), from the interior parts of England. He stood connected, by blood and hospitality, with the Counts von Zähdarm,[1] in this quarter of Germany; to which noble Family I likewise was, by his means, with all friendliness, brought near. Towgood had a fair talent, unspeakably ill-cultivated; with considerable humour of character: and, bating his total ignorance, for he knew nothing except Boxing and a little Grammar, shewed less of that aristocratic impassivity and silent fury than for most part belongs to Travellers of his nation. To him I owe my first practical knowledge of the English and their ways; perhaps also something of the partiality with which I have ever since regarded that singular people. Towgood was not without an eye, could he have come at any light. Invited doubtless by the presence of the Zähdarm Family, he had travelled hither, in the almost frantic hope of perfecting his studies; he, whose studies had been as yet those of infancy, hither to a University where so much as the notion of perfection, not to say the effort after it, no longer existed! Often we would condole over the hard destiny of the Young in this era: how, after all our toil, we were to be turned out into the world, with beards on our chins, indeed, but with few other attributes of manhood; no existing thing that we were trained to Act on, nothing that we could so much as Believe. "How has our Head on the outside a polished Hat," would Towgood exclaim, "and in the inside Vacancy, or a froth of Vocables and Attorney Logic! At a small cost men are educated to make leather into shoes; but, at a great cost, what am I educated to make? By Heaven, Brother! what I have already eaten and worn, as I came thus far, would endow a considerable Hospital of Incurables." – "Man, indeed," I would answer, "has a Digestive faculty, which must be kept working, were it even partly by stealth. But as for our Miseducation, make not bad worse; waste not the time yet ours, in trampling on thistles because they have yielded us no figs. *Frisch zu,*

1 *Zähdarm*: Tough-gut

Bruder![1] Here are Books, and we have brains to read them; here is a whole Earth and a whole Heaven and we have eyes to look on them: *Frisch zu!*'

'Often also our talk was gay; not without brilliancy, and even fire. We looked out on Life, with its strange scaffolding, where all at once harlequins dance, and men are beheaded and quartered: motley, not unterrific was the aspect; but we looked on it like brave youths. For myself, these were perhaps my most genial hours. Towards this young warmhearted, strong-headed and wrongheaded Herr Towgood, I was even near experiencing the now obsolete sentiment of Friendship. Yes, foolish Heathen that I was, I felt that, under certain conditions, I could have loved this man, and taken him to my bosom, and been his brother once and always. By degrees, however, I understood the new time, and its wants. If man's *Soul* is indeed, as in the Finnish Language, and Utilitarian Philosophy, a kind of *Stomach*, what else is the true meaning of Spiritual Union but an Eating together? Thus we, instead of Friends, are Dinner-guests; and here as elsewhere have cast away chimeras.'

So ends, abruptly as is usual, and enigmatically, this little incipient romance. What henceforth becomes of the brave Herr Towgood, or Toughgut? He has dived under, in the Autobiographical Chaos, and swims we see not where. Does any reader 'in the interior parts of England' know of such a man?

---

1 *Frisch zu, Bruder*: Get on with it, brother

CHAPTER 4

Getting under Way

'THUS nevertheless,' writes our Autobiographer, apparently as quitting College, 'was there realised Somewhat; namely, I, Diogenes Teufelsdröckh: a visible Temporary Figure (*Zeitbild*), occupying some cubic feet of Space, and containing within it Forces both physical and spiritual; hopes, passions, thoughts; the whole wondrous furniture, in more or less perfection, belonging to that mystery, a Man. Capabilities there were in me to give battle, in some small degree, against the great Empire of Darkness: Does not the very Ditcher and Delver, with his spade, extinguish many a thistle and puddle; and so leave a little Order, where he found the opposite? Nay your very Daymoth has capabilities in this kind; and ever organises something (into its own Body, if no otherwise), which was before Inorganic;

and of mute dead air makes living music, though only of the faintest, by humming.

'How much more, one whose capabilities are spiritual; who has learned or begun learning the grand thaumaturgic art of Thought! Thaumaturgic I name it; for hitherto all Miracles have been wrought thereby, and henceforth innumerable will be wrought; whereof we, even in these days, witness some. Of the Poet's and Prophet's inspired Message, and how it makes and unmakes whole worlds, I shall forbear mention: but cannot the dullest hear Steam-engines clanking around him? Has he not seen the Scottish Brassmith's IDEA (and this but a mechanical one) travelling on fire-wings round the Cape, and across two Oceans; and stronger than any other Enchanter's Familiar, on all hands unweariedly fetching and carrying: at home, not only weaving Cloth; but rapidly enough overturning the whole old system of Society; and, for Feudalism and Preservation of the Game, preparing us, by indirect but sure methods, Industrialism and the Government of the Wisest. Truly a Thinking Man is the worst enemy the Prince of Darkness can have; every time such a one announces himself, I doubt not, there runs a shudder through the Nether Empire; and new Emissaries are trained, with new tactics, to, if possible, entrap him, and hoodwink and handcuff him.

'With such high vocation had I too, as denizen of the Universe, been called. Unhappy it is, however, that though born to the amplest Sovereignty, in this way, with no less than sovereign right of Peace and War against the Time-Prince (*Zeitfürst*), or Devil, and all his Dominions, your coronation ceremony costs such trouble, your sceptre is so difficult to get at, or even to get eye on!'

By which last wiredrawn similitude, does Teufelsdröckh mean no more than that young men find obstacles in what we call 'getting under way?' 'Not what I Have,' continues he, 'but what I Do is my Kingdom. To each is given a certain inward Talent, a certain outward Environment of

Fortune; to each, by wisest combination of these two, a certain maximum of Capability. But the hardest problem were ever this first: To find by study of yourself, and of the ground you stand on, what your combined inward and outward Capability specially is. For, alas, our young soul is all budding with Capabilities, and we see not yet which is the main and true one. Always too the new man is in a new time, under new conditions; his course can be the *facsimile* of no prior one, but is by its nature original. And then how seldom will the outward Capability fit the inward: though talented wonderfully enough, we are poor, unfriended, dyspeptical, bashful; nay what is worse than all, we are foolish. Thus, in a whole imbroglio of Capabilities, we go stupidly groping about, to grope which is ours, and often clutch the wrong one: in this mad work, must several years of our small term be spent, till the purblind Youth, by practice, acquire notions of distance, and become a seeing Man. Nay, many so spend their whole term, and in ever new expectation, ever new disappointment, shift from enterprise to enterprise, and from side to side; till at length, as exasperated striplings of threescore and ten, they shift into their last enterprise, that of getting buried.

'Such, since the most of us are too ophthalmic, would be the general fate; were it not that one thing saves us: our Hunger. For on this ground, as the prompt nature of Hunger is well known, must a prompt choice be made: hence have we, with wise foresight, Indentures and Apprenticeships for our irrational young; whereby, in due season, the vague universality of a Man shall find himself ready-moulded into a specific Craftsman; and so thenceforth work, with much or with little waste of Capability, as it may be; yet not with the worst waste, that of time. Nay even in matters spiritual, since the spiritual artist too is born blind, and does not, like certain other creatures, receive sight in nine days, but far later, sometimes never, – is it not well that there should be what we call Professions, or

Bread-studies (*Brod-zwecke*), preappointed us? Here, circling like the gin-horse, for whom partial or total blindness is no evil, the Bread-artist can travel contentedly round and round, still fancying that it is forward and forward, and realise much: for himself victual; for the world an additional horse's power in the grand corn-mill or hemp-mill of Economic Society. For me too had such a leading-string been provided; only that it proved a neck-halter, and had nigh throttled me, till I broke it off. Then, in the words of Ancient Pistol, did the World generally become mine oyster, which I, by strength or cunning, was to open, as I would and could. Almost had I deceased (*fast wär ich umgekommen*), so obstinately did it continue shut.'

We see here, significantly foreshadowed, the spirit of much that was to befall our Autobiographer; the historical embodyment of which, as it painfully takes shape in his Life, lies scattered, in dim disastrous details, through this Bag *Pisces*, and those that follow. A young man of high talent, and high though still temper, like a young mettled colt, 'breaks off his neck-halter,' and bounds forth, from his peculiar manger, into the wide world; which, alas, he finds all rigorously fenced in. Richest clover-fields tempt his eye; but to him they are forbidden pasture: either pining in progressive starvation, he must stand; or, in mad exasperation, must rush to and fro, leaping against sheer stonewalls, which he cannot leap over, which only lacerate and lame him; till at last, after thousand attempts and endurances, he, as if by miracle, clears his way; not indeed into luxuriant and luxurious clover, yet into a certain bosky wilderness where existence is still possible, and Freedom though waited on by Scarcity is not without sweetness. In a word, Teufelsdröckh having thrown up his legal Profession, finds himself without landmark of outward guidance; whereby his previous want of decided Belief, or inward guidance, is frightfully aggravated. Necessity urges him on; Time will not stop, neither can he, a Son of Time; wild passions without solacement, wild faculties without employment, ever vex and agitate him. He too must enact that stern Monodrama, *No Object and no Rest*; must front its successive destinies, work through to its catastrophe, and deduce therefrom what moral he can.

Yet let us be just to him, let us admit that his 'neck-halter' sat nowise easy on him; that he was in some degree forced to break it off. If we look at the young man's civic position, in this Nameless Capital, as he emerges from its Nameless University, we can discern well that it was far from enviable. His first Law Examination he has come through triumphantly; and can even boast that the *Examen Rigorosum* need not have frightened him: but though he is hereby 'an *Auscultator* of respectability,' what avails it? There is next to no employment to be had. Neither, for a youth without connexions is the process of Expectation very hopeful in itself; nor for one of his disposition much cheered from without. 'My fellow Auscultators,' he says, 'were Auscultators: they dressed, and digested, and talked articulate words; other vitality shewed they almost none. Small speculation in those eyes, that they did glare withal! Sense neither for the high nor for the deep, nor for aught human or divine, save only for the faintest scent of coming Preferment.' In which words, indicating a total estrangement on the part of Teufelsdröckh, may there not also lurk traces of a bitterness as from wounded vanity? Doubtless these prosaic Auscultators may have sniffed at him, with his strange ways; and tried to hate, and, what was much more impossible, to despise him. Friendly communion, in any case, there could not be: already has the young Teufelsdröckh left the other young geese; and swims apart, though as yet uncertain whether he himself is cygnet or gosling.

Perhaps too what little employment he had was performed ill, at best unpleasantly. 'Great practical method and expertness' he may brag of; but is there not also great practical pride, though deep-hidden, only the deeper-seated? So shy a man can never have been popular. We figure to ourselves, how in those days he may have played strange freaks with his Independence, and so forth: do not his own words betoken as much? 'Like a very young person, I imagined it was with Work alone, and not also with Folly and Sin, in myself and others, that I had been appointed to struggle.' Be this as it may, his progress from the passive Auscultatorship, towards any active Assessorship, is evidently of the slowest. By degrees, those same established men, once partially inclined to patronise him, seem to withdraw their countenance, and give him up as 'a man of genius;' against which procedure he, in these Papers loudly protests. 'As if,' says he, 'the higher did not presuppose the lower; as if he who can fly into heaven, could not also walk post if he resolved on it! But the world is an old woman, and mistakes any gilt farthing for a gold coin; whereby being often cheated she will thenceforth trust nothing but the common copper.'

How our winged sky-messenger, unaccepted as a terrestrial runner, contrived, in the meanwhile, to keep himself from flying skyward without return, is not too clear from these Documents. Good old Gretchen seems to have vanished from the scene, perhaps from the Earth; other Horn of Plenty, or even of Parsimony, no where flows for him; so that 'the prompt nature of Hunger being well known,' we are not without our anxiety. From private Tuition, in never so many languages and sciences, the aid derivable is small; neither, to use his own words, 'does the young Adventurer hitherto suspect in himself any literary gift; but at best earns bread-and-water wages, by his wide faculty of Translation. Nevertheless,' continues he, 'that I subsisted is clear, for you find me even now alive.' Which fact, however, except upon the principle of our truehearted, kind old Proverb, that 'there is ever Life for the Living,' we must profess ourselves unable to explain.

Certain Landlords' Bills, and other economic Documents, bearing the mark of Settlement, indicate that he was not without money; but, like an independent Hearth-holder, if not House-holder, paid his way. Here also occur, among many others, two little mutilated Notes, which perhaps throw light on his condition. The first has now no date, or writer's name, but a huge Blot; and runs to this effect: 'The (*Inkblot*), tied down by previous promise, cannot, except by best wishes, forward the Herr Teufelsdröckh's views on the Assessorship in question; and sees himself under the cruel necessity of forbearing for the present, what were otherwise his duty and joy, to assist in opening the career for a man of genius, on whom far higher triumphs are yet waiting.' The other is on gilt paper; and interests us like a sort of epistolary mummy now dead, yet which once lived and beneficently worked. We give it in the original: '*Herr Teufelsdröckh wird von der Frau Gräfinn, auf Donnerstag, zum ÆSTHETISCHEN THEE, schönstens eingeladen.*'[1]

Thus, in answer to a cry for solid pudding, whereof there is the most urgent need, comes, epigrammatically enough, the invitation to a wash of quite fluid *Æsthetic Tea!* How Teufelsdröckh, now at actual handgrips with Destiny herself, may have comported himself among these Musical and Literary Dilettanti of both sexes, like a hungry lion invited to a feast of chickenweed, we can only conjecture. Perhaps in expressive silence, and abstinence: otherwise if the lion, in such case, is to feast at all, it cannot be on the chickenweed, but only on the chickens. For the rest, as this Frau Gräfinn dates from the *Zähdarm House*, she can be no other than the Countess and mistress of the same; whose intellectual tendencies, and good will to Teufelsdröckh, whether on the footing of Herr Towgood, or on his own footing, are hereby manifest. That some sort of relation, indeed, continued, for a time, to connect our Autobiographer, though

1 *Herr Teufelsdröckh . . . eingeladen*: Mr Teufelsdröckh is cordially invited by the Countess on Thursday to an aesthetic tea

perhaps feebly enough, with this noble House, we have elsewhere express evidence. Doubtless, if he expected patronage, it was in vain; enough for him if he here obtained occasional glimpses of the great world, from which we at one time fancied him to have been always excluded. 'The Zähdarms,' says he, 'lived in the soft, sumptuous garniture of Aristocracy; whereto Literature and Art, attracted and attached from without, must serve as the handsomest fringing. It was to the *Gnädigen Frau* (her Ladyship) that this latter improvement was due: assiduously she gathered, dexterously she fitted on, what fringing was to be had; lace or cobweb, as the place yielded.' Was Teufelsdröckh also a fringe, of lace or cobweb; or promising to be such? 'With His *Excellenz* (the Count),' continues he, 'I have more than once had the honour to converse; chiefly on general affairs, and the aspect of the world, which he, though now past middle life, viewed in no unfavourable light; finding indeed, except the Outrooting of Journalism (*die auszurottende Journalistik*), little to desiderate therein. On some points, as his *Excellenz* was not uncholeric, I found it more pleasant to keep silence. Besides, his occupation being that of Owning Land, there might be faculties enough, which, as superfluous for such use, were little developed in him.'

That to Teufelsdröckh the aspect of the world was nowise so faultless, and many things, besides 'the Outrooting of Journalism,' might have seemed improvements, we can readily conjecture. With nothing but a barren Auscultatorship from without, and so many mutinous thoughts and wishes from within, his position was no easy one. 'The Universe,' he says, 'was as a mighty Sphinx-riddle, which I knew so little of, yet must rede, or be devoured. In red streaks of unspeakable grandeur, yet also in the blackness of darkness, was Life, to my too-unfurnished Thought, unfolding itself. A strange contradiction lay in me; and I as yet knew not the solution of it; knew not that spiritual music can spring only from discords set in unison; that but for Evil there were no Good, as Victory is only possible by Battle.'

'I have heard affirmed (surely in jest),' observes he elsewhere, 'by not unphilanthropic persons, that it were a real increase of human happiness, could all young men from the age of nineteen be covered under barrels, or rendered otherwise invisible; and there left to follow their lawful studies and callings, till they emerged, sadder and wiser, at the age of twenty-five. With which suggestion, at least as considered in the light of a practical scheme, I need scarcely say that I nowise coincide. Nevertheless it is plausibly urged that, as young ladies (*Mädchen*) are, to mankind, precisely the most delightful in those years; so young gentlemen (*Bübchen*) do then attain their maximum of detestability. Such gawks (*Gecken*) are they, and foolish peacocks, and yet with such a vulturous hunger for self-indulgence; so obstinate, obstreperous, vainglorious; in all senses, so froward and so forward. No mortal's endeavour or attainment will in the smallest content the as yet unendeavouring, unattaining young gentleman; but he could make it all infinitely better, were it worthy of him. Life every where is the most manageable matter, simple as a question in the Rule of Three: multiply your second and third term together, divide the product by the first, and your quotient will be the answer, – which you are but an ass if you cannot come at. The booby has not yet found out, by any trial, that, do what one will, there is ever a cursed fraction, oftenest a decimal repeater, and no net integer quotient so much as to be thought of.'

In which passage, does there not lie an implied confession that Teufelsdröckh himself, besides his outward obstructions, had an inward, still greater, to contend with; namely, a certain temporary, youthful, yet still afflictive derangement of head? Alas! on the former side alone, his case was hard enough. 'It continues ever true,' says he, 'that Saturn, or Chronos, or what we call TIME, devours all his Children: only by incessant Running, by incessant Working, may you (for some threescore and ten years) escape him; and you too he devours at last. Can any Sovereign, or Holy Alliance of Sovereigns, bid Time stand still; even in thought, shake themselves free of Time? Our whole terrestrial being is based on Time, and built of Time; it is wholly a Movement, a Time-impulse; Time is the author of it, the material of it. Hence also our Whole Duty, which is to Move, to Work, – in the right direction. Are not our Bodies and our Souls in continual movement, whether we will or not; in a continual Waste, requiring a continual Repair? Utmost satisfaction of our whole outward and inward Wants were but satisfaction for a space of Time; thus whatso we have done, is done, and for us annihilated, and ever must we go and do anew. O Time-Spirit, how hast thou environed and imprisoned us, and sunk us so deep in thy troublous dim Time-Element; that, only in lucid moments, can so much as glimpses of our upper Azure Home be revealed to us! Me, however, as a Son of Time, unhappier than some others, was Time threatening to eat quite prematurely; for strive as I might, there was no good Running, so obstructed was the path, so gyved were the feet.' That is to say, we presume, speaking in the dialect of this lower world, that Teufelsdröckh's whole duty and necessity was, like other men's, 'to work, – in the right direction,' and that no work was to be had; whereby he became wretched enough. As was natural: with haggard Scarcity threatening him in the distance; and so vehement a soul languishing in restless inaction, and forced thereby, like Sir Hudibras's sword by rust,

> To eat into itself, for lack
> Of something else to hew and hack!

But on the whole, that same 'excellent Passivity,' as it has all along done, is here again vigorously flourishing; in which circumstance, may we not trace the beginnings of much that now characterises our Professor; and perhaps, in faint rudiments, the origin of the Clothes-Philosophy itself? Already the attitude he has assumed towards the World is too defensive; not, as would have been desirable, a bold attitude of attack. 'So far hitherto,' he says, 'as I had mingled with mankind, I was notable, if for any thing, for a certain stillness of manner, which, as my friends often rebukingly declared, did but ill express the keen ardour of my feelings. I, in truth, regarded men with an excess both of love and of fear. The mystery of a Person, indeed, is ever divine, to him that has a sense for the Godlike. Often, notwithstanding, was I blamed, and by half-strangers hated, for my so-called Hardness (*Härte*), my Indifferentism towards men; and the seemingly ironic tone I had adopted, as my favourite dialect in conversation. Alas, the panoply of Sarcasm was but as a buckram-case, wherein I had striven to envelope myself; that so my own poor Person might live safe there; and in all friendliness, being no longer exasperated by wounds. Sarcasm I now see to be, in general, the language of the Devil; for which reason I have, long since, as good as renounced it. But how many individuals did I, in those days, provoke into some degree of hostility thereby! An ironic man, with his sly stillness, and ambuscading ways, more especially an ironic young man, from whom it is least expected, may be viewed as a pest to society. Have we not seen persons of weight and name, coming forward, with gentlest indifference, to tread such a one out of sight, as an insignificancy and worm, start ceiling-high (*balkenhoch*), and thence fall shattered and supine, to be borne home on shutters, not without indignation, when he proved electric and a torpedo!'

Alas, how can a man with this devilishness of temper make way for himself in Life; where the first problem, as Teufelsdröckh too admits, is 'to unite yourself with some one and with somewhat (*sich anzuschliessen*)?' Division, not union, is written on most part of his procedure. Let us add too that, in no great length of time, the only important connexion he had ever succeeded in forming, his connexion

with the Zähdarm Family, seems to have been paralysed, for
all practical uses, by the death of the 'not uncholeric' old
Count. This fact stands recorded, quite incidentally, in a
certain *Discourse on Epitaphs*, huddled into the present Bag,
among so much else; of which Essay the learning and
curious penetration are more to be approved of than the
spirit. His grand principle is, that lapidary inscriptions, of
what sort soever, should be Historical rather than Lyrical.
'By request of that worthy Nobleman's survivors,' says he, 'I
undertook to compose his Epitaph; and not unmindful of
my own rules, produced the following; which, however, for
an alleged defect of Latinity, a defect never yet fully visible
to myself, still remains unengraven;' – wherein, we may
predict, there is more than the Latinity that will surprise an
English reader:

HIC JACET

PHILIPPUS ZAEHDARM, COGNOMINE MAGNUS,
ZAEHDARMI COMES,
EX IMPERII CONCILIO,
VELLERIS AUREI, PERISCELIDIS, NECNON VULTURIS NIGRI
EQUES.
QUI DUM SUB LUNA AGEBAT,

QUINQUIES MILLE PERDICES
PLUMBO CONFECIT:

VARII CIBI
CENTUMPONDIA MILLIES CENTENA MILLIA,
PER SE, PERQUE SERVOS QUADRUPEDES BIPEDESVE,
HAUD SINE TUMULTU DEVOLVENS,
IN STERCUS
PALAM CONVERTIT.

NUNC A LABORE REQUIESCENTEM
OPERA SEQUUNTUR.

SI MONUMENTUM QUÆRIS
FIMETUM ADSPICE.

PRIMUM IN ORBE DEJECIT [*sub dato*]; POSTREMUM
[*sub dato*].*

*HERE LIES

PHILIP ZAHDARM, SURNAMED THE GREAT
ZAHDARM'S COUNT,
COUNCILOR OF THE EMPIRE,
& OF THE GOLDEN FLEECE, ANKLE RING & BLACK VULTURE
A KNIGHT.
WHO DURING HIS EARTHLY LIFE

FIVE THOUSAND PARTRIDGES
SLEW WITH LEAD SHOT.

VARIOUS FOODSTUFF
TEN THOUSAND MILLION POUNDS OF IT,
THROUGH HIMSELF, HIS FOUR-FOOTED & TWO-FOOTED SERVANTS,
NOT WITHOUT UPROAR IN THE PROCESS,
INTO SHIT
HE PUBLICLY CONVERTED.

NOW HE RESTS FROM HIS LABOUR
HIS WORKS FOLLOWING HIM.
IF YOU ASK FOR HIS MONUMENT,
LOOK AT A DUNGHILL.

HIS FIRST KILL ON EARTH WAS [*date below*] HIS LAST [*date below*]

Parliamentary legislation in the 18th and early 19th centuries
enlarged the property and power of landowners, whose main
activity in rural areas was hunting, besides working as Justices
of the Peace whose main activity was condemning poachers.
Cottagers who killed rabbits or birds feeding on their kitchen
gardens could be transported to Australia for poaching, because
only their landlords had the right to kill wild creatures – AG

CHAPTER 5

Romance

'FOR long years,' writes Teufelsdröckh, 'had the poor Hebrew, in this Egypt of an Auscultatorship, painfully toiled, baking bricks without stubble, before ever the question once struck him with entire force: For what? – *Beym Himmel!* For Food and Warmth! And are Food and Warmth nowhere else, in the whole wide Universe, discoverable? – Come of it what might, I resolved to try.'

Thus then are we to see him in a new independent capacity, though perhaps far from an improved one. Teufelsdröckh is now a man without Profession. Quitting the common Fleet of herring-busses and whalers, where indeed his leeward, laggard condition was painful enough, he desperately steers off, on a course of his own, by sextant and compass of his own. Unhappy Teufelsdröckh! Though neither Fleet, nor Traffic, nor Commodores pleased thee, still was it not *a Fleet*, sailing in prescribed track, for fixed objects; above all, in combination, wherein, by mutual guidance, by all manner of loans and borrowings, each could manifoldly aid the other? How wilt thou sail in unknown seas; and for thyself find that shorter, Northwest Passage to thy fair Spice-country of a Nowhere? – A solitary rover, on such a voyage, with such nautical tactics, will meet with adventures. Nay, as we forthwith discover, a certain Calypso-Island detains him at the very outset; and as it were falsifies and oversets his whole reckoning.

'If in youth,' writes he once, 'the Universe is majestically unveiling, and everywhere Heaven revealing itself on Earth, nowhere to the Young Man does this Heaven on Earth so immediately reveal itself as in the Young Maiden. Strangely enough, in this strange life of ours, it has been so appointed. On the whole, as I have often said, a Person (*Persönlichkeit*) is ever holy to us; a certain orthodox Anthropomorphism connects my *Me* with all *Thees* in bonds of Love: but it is in this approximation of the Like and Unlike, that such heavenly attraction, as between Negative and Positive, first burns out into a flame. Is the pitifullest mortal Person, think you, indifferent to us? Is it not rather our heartfelt wish to be made one with him; to unite him to us, by gratitude, by admiration, even by fear; or failing all these, unite ourselves to him? But how much more, in this case of the Like-Unlike! Here is conceded us the higher mystic possibility of such a union, the highest in our Earth; thus, in the conducting medium of Fantasy, flames forth that *fire*-development of the universal Spiritual Electricity, which, as unfolded between man and woman, we first emphatically denominate LOVE.

'In every well-conditioned stripling, as I conjecture, there already blooms a certain prospective Paradise, cheered by some fairest Eve; nor in the stately vistas, and flowerage and foliage, of that Garden is a Tree of Knowledge, beautiful and awful in the midst thereof, wanting. Perhaps too the whole is but the lovelier if Cherubim and a flaming sword divide it from all footsteps of men; and grant him, the imaginative stripling, only the view, not the entrance. Happy season of virtuous youth, when Shame is still an impassable celestial barrier; and the sacred air-cities of Hope have not shrunk into the mean clay-hamlets of Reality; and man, by his nature, is yet infinite and free!

'As for our young Forlorn,' continues Teufelsdröckh, evidently meaning himself, 'in his secluded way of life, and with his glowing Fantasy, the more fiery that it burnt under cover, as in a reverberating furnace, his feeling towards the Queens of this Earth was, and indeed is, altogether unspeakable. A visible Divinity dwelt in them; to our young Friend all women were holy, were heavenly. As yet he but saw them flitting past, in their many-coloured angel-plumage; or hovering mute and inaccessible on the outskirts of *Æsthetic Tea*: all of air they were, all Soul and Form; so lovely, like mysterious priestesses, in whose hand was the invisible Jacob's-ladder, whereby man might mount into very Heaven. That he, our poor Friend, should ever win for himself one of these Gracefuls (*Holden*) – *Ach Gott!* how could he hope it; should he not have died under it? There was a certain delirious vertigo in the thought.

'Thus was the young man, if all sceptical of Demons and Angels, such as the vulgar had once believed in, nevertheless not unvisited by hosts of true Skyborn, who visibly and audibly hovered round him whereso he went; and they had that religious worship in his thought, though as yet it was by their mere earthly and trivial name that he named them. But now, if on a soul so circumstanced, some actual

Air-maiden, incorporated into tangibility and reality, should cast any electric glance of kind eyes, saying thereby, "Thou too mayest love and be loved;" and so kindle him, – good Heaven, what a volcanic, earthquake-bringing, all-consuming fire were probably kindled!'

Such a fire, it afterwards appears, did actually burst forth, with explosions more or less Vesuvian, in the inner man of Herr Diogenes; as indeed how could it fail? A nature, which, in his own figurative style, we might say, had now not a little carbonised tinder, of Irritability; with so much nitre of latent Passion, and sulphurous Humour enough; the whole lying in such hot neighbourhood, close by 'a reverberating furnace of Fantasy:' have we not here the components of driest Gunpowder, ready, on occasion of the smallest spark, to blaze up? Neither, in this our Life-element, are sparks anywhere wanting. Without doubt, some Angel, whereof so many hovered round, must one day, leaving 'the outskirts of *Æsthetic Tea*,' flit nigher; and, by electric Promethean glance, kindle no despicable fire-work. Happy, if it indeed proved a Firework, and flamed off rocket-wise, in successive beautiful bursts of splendour, each growing naturally from the other, through the several stages of a happy Youthful Love; till the whole were safely burnt out; and the young soul relieved, with little damage! Happy, if it did not rather prove a Conflagration and mad Explosion; painfully lacerating the heart itself; nay perhaps bursting the heart in pieces (which were Death); or at best, bursting the thin walls of your 'reverberating furnace,' so that it rage thenceforth all unchecked among the contig-uous combustibles (which were Madness): till of the so fair and manifold internal world of our Diogenes, there re-mained Nothing, or only the 'Crater of an extinct volcano!'

From multifarious Documents in this Bag *Capricornus*, and in the adjacent ones on both sides thereof, it becomes manifest that our Philosopher, as stoical and cynical as he now looks, was heartily and even franticly in Love: here therefore may our old doubts whether his heart were of stone or of flesh, give way. He loved once; not wisely but too well. And once only: for as your Congreve needs a new case or wrappage for every new rocket, so each human heart can properly exhibit but one Love, if even one; the 'First Love which is infinite' can be followed by no second like unto it. In more recent years, accordingly, the Editor of these Sheets was led to regard Teufelsdröckh as a man not only who would never wed, but who would never even flirt; whom the grand-climacteric itself, and *St. Martin's Summer* of incipient Dotage, would crown with no new myrtle garland. To the Professor, women are henceforth Pieces of Art; of Celestial Art, indeed; which celestial pieces he glories to survey in galleries, but has lost thought of purchasing.

Psychological readers are not without curiosity to see how Teufelsdröckh, in this for him unexampled predicament, demeans himself; with what specialities of successive configuration, splendour and colour, his Firework blazes off. Small, as usual, is the satisfaction that such can meet with here. From amid these confused masses of Eulogy and Elegy, with their mad Petrarchan and Werterean ware lying madly scattered among all sorts of quite extraneous matter, not so much as the fair one's name can be deciphered. For, without doubt, the title *Blumine*, whereby she is here designated, and which means simply Goddess of Flowers, must be fictitious. Was her real name Flora, then? But what was her surname, or had she none? Of what station in Life was she; of what parentage, fortune, aspect? Specially, by what Pre-established Harmony of occurrences did the Lover and the Loved meet one another in so wide a world; how did they behave in such meeting? To all which questions, not unessential in a Biographic work, mere Conjecture must for most part return answer. 'It was appointed,' says your Philosopher, 'that the high celestial orbit of Blumine should intersect the low sublunary one of our Forlorn; that he, looking in her empyrean eyes, should fancy the upper Sphere of Light was come down into this nether sphere of Shadows; and finding himself mistaken, make noise enough.'

We seem to gather that she was young, hazel-eyed, beautiful, and some one's Cousin; highborn, and of high spirit; but unhappily dependent and insolvent; living, perhaps, on the not too gracious bounty of monied relatives. But how came 'the Wanderer' into her circle? Was it by the humid vehicle of *Æsthetic Tea*, or by the arid one of mere Business? Was it on the hand of Herr Towgood; or of the Gnädige Frau, who, as an ornamental Artist, might sometimes like to promote flirtation, especially for young cynical Nondescripts? To all appearance, it was chiefly by Accident, and the grace of Nature.

'Thou fair Waldschloss,' writes our Autobiographer, 'what stranger ever saw thee, were it even an absolved Auscultator, officially bearing in his pocket the last *Relatio ex Actis*[1] he would ever write; but must have paused to wonder! Noble Mansion! There stoodest thou, in deep Mountain Amphitheatre, on umbrageous lawns, in thy serene solitude; stately, massive, all of granite; glittering in the western Sunbeams, like a palace of El Dorado, overlaid with precious metal. Beautiful rose up, in wavy curvature, the slope of thy guardian Hills: of the greenest was their sward, embossed with its dark-brown frets of crag, or spotted by some spreading solitary Tree and its shadow. To the unconscious Wayfarer thou wert also as an Ammon's Temple, in the Libyan Waste; where, for joy and woe, the tablet of his Destiny lay written. Well might he pause and gaze; in that glance of his were prophecy and nameless forebodings.'

But now let us conjecture that the so presentient Auscultator has handed in his *Relatio ex Actis*; been invited to a

[1] *Relatio ex Actis*: official reports

glass of Rhine-wine; and so, instead of returning dispirited and athirst to his dusty Town-home, is ushered into the Gardenhouse, where sit the choicest party of dames and cavaliers; if not engaged in Æsthetic Tea, yet in trustful evening conversation, and perhaps Musical Coffee, for we hear of 'harps and pure voices making the stillness live.' Scarcely, it would seem, is the Gardenhouse inferior in respectability to the noble Mansion itself. 'Embowered amid rich foliage, rose-clusters, and the hues and odours of thousand flowers, here sat that brave company; in front, from the wide-opened doors, fair outlook over blossom and bush, over grove and velvet green, stretching, undulating onwards to the remote Mountain peaks: so bright, so mild, and everywhere the melody of birds and happy creatures: it was all as if man had stolen a shelter from the Sun in the bosom-vesture of Summer herself. How came it that the Wanderer advanced thither with such forecasting heart (*ahnungsvoll*), by the side of his gay host? Did he feel that to these soft influences his hard bosom ought to be shut; that here, once more, Fate had it in view to try him; to mock him, and see whether there were Humour in him?

'Next moment he finds himself presented to the party; and specially by name to – Blumine! Peculiar among all dames and damosels, glanced Blumine, there in her modesty, like a star among earthly lights. Noblest maiden! whom he bent to, in body and in soul; yet scarcely dared look at, for the presence filled him with painful yet sweetest embarrassment.

'Blumine's was a name well known to him; far and wide, was the fair one heard of, for her gifts, her graces, her caprices: from all which vague colourings of Rumour, from the censures no less than from the praises, had our Friend painted for himself a certain imperious Queen of Hearts, and blooming, warm Earth-angel, much more enchanting than your mere white Heaven-angels of women, in whose placid veins circulates too little naphtha-fire. Herself also he had seen in public places; that light yet so stately form; those dark tresses, shading a face where smiles and sunlight played over earnest deeps: but all this he had seen only as a magic vision, for him inaccessible, almost without reality. Her sphere was too far from his; how should she ever think of him; O Heaven! How should they so much as once meet together? And now that Rose-goddess sits in the same circle with him; the light of *her* eyes has smiled on him, if he speak she will hear it! Nay, who knows, since the heavenly Sun looks into lowest valleys, but Blumine herself might have aforetime noted the so unnotable; perhaps, from his very gainsayers, as he had from hers, gathered wonder, gathered favour for him? Was the attraction, the agitation mutual, then; pole and pole trembling towards contact, when once brought into neighbourhood? Say rather, heart swelling in presence of the Queen of Hearts; like the Sea swelling when once near its Moon! With the Wanderer it was even so: as in heavenward gravitation, suddenly as at the touch of a Seraph's wand, his whole soul is roused from its deepest recesses; and all that was painful, and that was blissful there, dim images, vague feelings of a whole Past and a whole Future are heaving in unquiet eddies within him.

'Often, in far less agitating scenes, had our still Friend shrunk forcibly together; and shrouded up his tremours and flutterings, of what sort soever, in a safe cover of Silence, and perhaps of seeming Stolidity. How was it, then, that here, when trembling to the core of his heart, he did not sink into swoons, but rose into strength, into fearlessness and clearness? It was his guiding Genius (*Dä-mon*) that inspired him; he must go forth and meet his Destiny. Shew thyself now, whispered it, or be forever hid. Thus sometimes it is even when your anxiety becomes transcendental, that the soul first feels herself able to transcend it; that she rises above it, in fiery victory; and, borne on new-found wings of victory, moves so calmly, even because so rapidly, so irresistibly. Always must the Wanderer remember, with a certain satisfaction and sur-prise, how in this case he sat not silent, but struck adroitly into the stream of conversation; which thenceforth, to speak with an apparent not a real vanity, he may say that he continued to lead. Surely, in those hours, a certain inspiration was imparted him, such inspiration as is still possible in our late era. The self-secluded unfolds himself in noble thoughts, in free, glowing words; his soul is as one sea of light, the peculiar home of Truth and Intellect; wherein also Fantasy bodies forth form after form, radiant with all prismatic hues.'

It appears, in this otherwise so happy meeting, there talked one 'Philistine,' who even now, to the general weariness, was dominantly pouring forth Philistinism (*Philistriositäten*); little witting what hero was here entering to demolish him! We omit the series of Socratic, or rather Diogenic utterances, not unhappy in their way, whereby the monster, 'persuaded into silence,' seems soon after to have withdrawn for the night. 'Of which dialectic marauder,' writes our hero, 'the discomfiture was visibly felt as a benefit by most: but what were all applauses to the glad smile, threatening every moment to become a laugh, wherewith Blumine herself repaid the victor? He ventured to address her, she answered with attention: nay, what if there were a slight tremour in that silver voice; what if the red glow of evening were hiding a transient blush!

'The conversation took a higher tone, one fine thought called forth another: it was one of those rare seasons, when the soul expands with full freedom, and man feels himself brought near to man. Gaily in light, graceful abandonment, the friendly talk played round that circle: for the burden was rolled from every heart; the barriers of Ceremony, which are indeed the laws of polite living, had melted as into vapour; and the poor claims of *Me* and *Thee*, no longer parted by rigid fences, now flowed softly into one another; and Life lay all harmonious, many-tinted, like some fair royal champaign, the sovereign and owner of which were Love only. Such music springs from kind hearts, in a kind environment of place and time. And yet as the light grew more aërial on the mountain tops, and the shadows fell longer over the valley, some faint tone of sadness may have breathed through the heart; and, in whispers more or less audible, reminded every one that as this bright day was drawing towards its close, so likewise must the Day of man's Existence decline into dusk and darkness; and with all its sick toilings, and joyful and mournful noises, sink in the still Eternity.

'To our Friend the hours seemed moments; holy was he and happy: the words from those sweetest lips came over him like dew on thirsty grass; all better feelings in his soul seemed to whisper: It is good for us to be here. At parting, the Blumine's hand was in his: in the balmy twilight, with the kind stars above them, he spoke something of meeting again, which was not contradicted; he pressed gently those small soft fingers, and it seemed as if they were not hastily, not angrily withdrawn.'

Poor Teufelsdröckh! it is clear to demonstration thou art smit: the Queen of Hearts would see a 'man of genius' also sigh for her; and there, by art magic, in that preternatural hour, has she bound and spell-bound thee. 'Love is not altogether a Delirium,' says he elsewhere; 'yet has it many points in common therewith. I call it rather a discerning of the Infinite in the Finite, of the Idea made Real; which discerning again may be either true or false, either seraphic or demoniac, Inspiration or Insanity. But in the former case, too, as in common Madness, it is Fantasy that super-adds itself to Sight; on the so petty domain of the Actual, plants its Archimedes-lever, whereby to move at will the infinite Spiritual. Fantasy I might call the true Heaven-gate and Hell-gate of man: his sensuous life is but the small temporary stage (*Zeitbühne*), whereon thick-streaming in-fluences from both these far yet near regions meet visibly, and act tragedy and melodrama. Sense can support herself handsomely, in most countries, for some eighteenpence a-day; but for Fantasy planets and solar-systems will not suffice. Witness your Pyrrhus conquering the world, yet drinking no better red wine than he had before.' Alas, witness also your Diogenes, flame-clad, scaling the upper Heaven, and verging towards Insanity, for prize of a 'high-souled Brunette,' as if the Earth held but one, and not several of these!

He says that, in Town, they met again: 'day after day, like his heart's sun, the blooming Blumine shone on him. Ah! a little while ago, and he was yet all in darkness: him what Graceful (*Holde*) would ever love? Disbelieving all things, the poor youth had never learned to believe in himself. Withdrawn, in proud timidity, within his own fastnesses; solitary from men, yet baited by night-spectres enough, he saw himself, with a sad indignation, constrained to renounce the fairest hopes of existence. And now, O now! "She looks on thee," cried he: "she the fairest, noblest; do not her dark eyes tell thee, thou are not despised? The Heaven's-Messenger! All Heaven's blessings be hers!" Thus did soft melodies flow through his heart; tones of an infinite gratitude; sweetest intimations that he also was a man, that for him also unutterable joys had been provided.

'In free speech, earnest or gay, amid lambent glances, laughter, tears, and often with the inarticulate mystic speech of Music: such was the element they now lived in; in such a many-tinted, radiant Aurora, and by this fairest of Orient Lightbringers must our Friend be blandished, and the new Apocalypse of Nature unrolled to him. Fairest Blumine! And, even as a Star, all Fire and humid Softness, a very Light-ray incarnate! Was there so much as a fault, a "caprice," he could have dispensed with? Was she not to him in very deed a Morning-Star; did not her presence bring with it airs from Heaven? As from Æolean Harps in the breath of dawn, as from the Memnon's Statue struck by the rosy-finger of Aurora, unearthly music was around him, and lapped him into untried balmy Rest. Pale Doubt fled away to the distance; Life bloomed up with happiness and hope. The Past, then, was all a haggard dream; he had been in the Garden of Eden, then, and could not discern it! But lo now! the black walls of his prison melt away; the captive is alive, is free. If he loved his Disen-chantress? *Arh Gott!* His whole heart and soul and life were hers, but never had he named it Love: existence was all a Feeling, not yet shaped into a Thought.'

Nevertheless, into a Thought, nay into an Action, it must be shaped; for neither Disenchanter nor Disenchantress, mere 'Children of Time,' can abide by Feeling alone. The Professor knows not, to this day, 'how in her soft, fervid bosom, the Lovely found determination, even on hest of Necessity, to cut asunder these so blissful bonds.' He even appears surprised at the 'Duenna Cousin,' whoever she may have been, 'in whose meagre, hunger-bitten philoso-phy, the religion of young hearts was, from the first, faintly approved of.' We, even at such distance, can explain it without necromancy. Let the Philosopher answer this one question: What figure, at that period, was a Mrs. Teufels-dröckh likely to make in polished society? Could she have driven so much as a brass-bound Gig, or even a simple iron-spring one? Thou foolish 'absolved Auscultator,' be-fore whom lies no prospect of capital, will any yet known 'religion of young hearts' keep the human Kitchen warm? Pshaw! thy divine Blumine, when she 'resigned herself to wed some richer,' shews more philosophy, though but 'a woman of genius,' than thou, a pretended man.

Our readers have witnessed the origin of this Love-mania, and with what royal splendour it waxes, and rises. Let no one ask us to unfold the glories of its dominant state; much less the horrors of its almost instantaneous dissolu-tion. How from such inorganic masses, henceforth madder than ever, as lie in these Bags, can even fragments of a living delineation be organised? Besides, of what profit were it? We view, with a lively pleasure, the gay silk Montgolfier start from the ground, and shoot upwards, cleaving the liquid deeps, till it dwindle to a luminous star: but what is there to look longer on, when once, by natural elasticity, or accident of fire, it has exploded? A hapless air-navigator, plunging, amid torn parachutes, sandbags, and confused wreck, fast enough, into the jaws of the Devil! Suffice it to know that Teufelsdröckh rose into the highest regions of the Empyrean, by a natural parabolic track, and returned thence in a quick perpendicular one. For the rest, let any feeling reader who has been unhappy enough to do the like, paint it out for himself; considering only that if he, for his perhaps comparatively insignificant mistress, underwent such agonies and frenzies, what must Teufelsdröckh's have been, with a fire-heart, and for a nonpareil Blumine! We glance merely at the final scene:

'One morning, he found his Morning-star all dimmed and dusky-red; the fair creature was silent, absent, she seemed to have been weeping. Alas, no longer a Morning-star, but a troublous skyey Portent, announcing that the Doomsday had dawned! She said, in a tremulous voice, they were to meet no more.' The thunderstruck Air-sailor is not wanting to himself in this dread hour: but what avails it?

We omit the passionate expostulations, entreaties, indignations, since all was vain, and not even an explanation was conceded him; and hasten to the catastrophe. 'Farewell, then, Madam! said he, not without sternness, for his stung pride helped him. She put her hand in his, she looked in his face, tears started to her eyes: in wild audacity he clasped her to his bosom; their lips were joined, their two souls, like two dew-drops, rushed into one, – for the first time, and for the last!' Thus was Teufelsdröckh made immortal by a kiss. And then? Why, then – 'thick curtains of Night rushed over his soul, as rose the immeasurable Crash of Doom; and through the ruins as of a shivered Universe, was he falling, falling, towards the Abyss.'

CHAPTER 6

Sorrows of Teufelsdröckh

WE have long felt that, with a man like our Professor, matters must often be expected to take a course of their own; that, in so multiplex, intricate a nature, there might be channels, both for admitting and emitting, such as the Psychologist had seldom noted; in short, that on no grand occasion and convulsion, neither in the joy-storm nor in the woe-storm, could you predict his demeanour.

To our less philosophical readers, for example, it is now clear that the so passionate Teufelsdröckh, precipitated through 'a shivered Universe' in this extraordinary way, has only one of three things which he can next do: Establish himself in Bedlam; begin writing Satanic Poetry; or blow out his brains. In the progress towards any of which consummations, do not such readers anticipate extravagance enough: breast-beating, brow-beating (against walls), lion-bellowings of blasphemy and the like, stampings, smitings, breakages of furniture, if not arson itself?

Nowise so does Teufelsdröckh deport him. He quietly

lifts his *Pilgerstab* (Pilgrim-staff), 'old business being soon
wound up;' and begins a perambulation and circumambu-
lation of the terraqueous Globe! Curious it is, indeed, how
with such vivacity of conception, such intensity of feeling;
above all, with these unconscionable habits of Exaggeration
in speech, he combines that wonderful stillness of his, that
stoicism in external procedure. Thus if his sudden bereave-
ment, in this matter of the Flower-goddess, is talked of as a
real Doomsday and Dissolution of Nature, in which light
doubtless it partly appeared to himself, his own nature is
nowise dissolved thereby; but rather is compressed closer.
For once, as we might say, a Blumine by magic appliances
has unlocked that shut heart of his, and its hidden things
rush out tumultuous, boundless, like genii enfranchised
from their glass phial: but no sooner are your magic appliances withdrawn, than the strange casket of a heart springs-
to again; and perhaps there is now no key extant that will
open it; for a Teufelsdröckh, as we remarked, will not love a
second time. Singular Diogenes! No sooner has that heart-
rending occurrence fairly taken place, than he affects to
regard it as a thing natural, of which there is nothing more to
be said. 'One highest Hope, seemingly legible in the eyes of
an Angel, had recalled him as out of Death-shadows into
celestial Life: but a gleam of Tophet passed over the face of
his Angel; he was rapt away in whirlwinds, and heard the
laughter of Demons. It was a Calenture,' adds he, 'whereby
the Youth saw green Paradise-groves in the waste Ocean-
waters: a lying vision, yet not wholly a lie, for *he* saw it.' But
what things soever passed in him, when he ceased to see it;
what ragings and despairings soever Teufelsdröckh's soul
was the scene of, he has the goodness to conceal under a
quite opaque cover of Silence. We know it well; the first mad
paroxysm past, our brave Gneschen collected his dismembered philosophies, and buttoned himself together; he was
meek, silent, or spoke of the weather, and the Journals: only
by a transient knitting of those shaggy brows, by some deep

flash of those eyes, glancing one knew not whether with tear-dew or with fierce fire, – might you have guessed what a Gehenna was within; that a whole Satanic School were spouting, though inaudibly, there. To consume your own choler, as some chimneys consume their own smoke; to keep a whole Satanic School spouting, if it must spout, inaudibly, is a negative yet no slight virtue, nor one of the commonest in these times.

Nevertheless, we will not take upon us to say, that in the strange measure he fell upon, there was not a touch of latent Insanity; whereof indeed the actual condition of these Documents in *Capricornus* and *Aquarius* is no bad emblem. His so unlimited Wanderings, toilsome enough, are without assigned or perhaps assignable aim; internal Unrest seems his sole guidance; he wanders, wanders, as if that curse of the Prophet had fallen on him, and he were 'made like unto a wheel.' Doubtless, too, the chaotic nature of these Paper-bags aggravates our obscurity. Quite without note of pre-paration, for example, we come upon the following slip: 'A peculiar feeling is it that will rise in the Traveller, when turning some hill-range in his desert road, he descries lying far below, embosomed among its groves and green natural bulwarks, and all diminished to a toybox, the fair Town, where so many souls, as it were seen and yet unseen, are driving their multifarious traffic. Its white steeple is then truly a starward-pointing finger; the canopy of blue smoke seems like a sort of Life-breath: for always, of its own unity, the soul gives unity to whatso it looks on with love: thus does the little Dwellingplace of men, in itself a congeries of houses and huts, become for us an individual, almost a person. But what thousand other thoughts unite thereto, if the place has to ourselves been the arena of joyous or mournful experi-ences; if perhaps the cradle we were rocked in still stands there, if our Loving ones still dwell there, if our Buried ones there slumber!' Does Teufelsdröckh, as the wounded eagle is said to make for its own eyrie, and indeed military deserters, and all hunted outcast creatures, turn as if by instinct in the direction of their birthland, – fly first, in this extremity, towards his native Entepfuhl; but reflecting that there no help awaits him, take but one wistful look from the distance, and then wend elsewhither?

Little happier seems to be his next flight: into the wilds of Nature; as if in her mother-bosom he would seek healing. So at least we incline to interpret the following Notice, separated from the former by some considerable space, wherein, however, is nothing noteworthy:

'Mountains were not new to him; but rarely are Mountains seen in such combined majesty and grace as here. The rocks are of that sort called Primitive by the mineralogists, which always arrange themselves in masses of a rugged, gigantic character; which ruggedness, however, is here tempered by a singular airiness of form, and softness of environment: in a climate favourable to vegetation, the gray cliff, itself covered with lichens, shoots up through a garment of foliage or verdure; and white, bright cottages, tree-shaded, cluster round the everlasting granite. In fine vicissitude, Beauty alternates with Grandeur: you ride through stony hollows, along strait passes, traversed by torrents, overhung by high walls of rock; now winding amid broken shaggy chasms, and huge fragments; now suddenly emerging into some emerald valley, where the streamlet collects itself into a Lake, and man has again found a fair dwelling, and it seems as if Peace had established herself in the bosom of Strength.

'To Peace, however, in this vortex of existence, can the son of Time not pretend: still less if some Spectre haunt him from the Past; and the Future is wholly a Stygian Darkness, spectre-bearing. Reasonably might the Wanderer exclaim to himself: Are not the gates of this world's Happiness inexorably shut against thee; hast thou a hope that is not mad? Nevertheless, one may still murmur audibly, or in the original Greek if that suit better: "Whoso can look on Death will start at no shadows?"

'From such meditations is the Wanderer's attention called outwards: for now the Valley closes in abruptly, intersected by a huge mountain mass, the stony water-worn ascent of which is not to be accomplished on horse-back. Arrived aloft, he finds himself again lifted into the evening sunset light; and cannot but pause, and gaze round him, some moments there. An upland irregular expanse of wold, where valleys in complex branchings are suddenly or slowly arranging their descent towards every quarter of the sky. The mountain-ranges are beneath your feet, and folded together; only the loftier summits look down here and there as on a second plain; lakes also lie clear and earnest in their solitude. No trace of man now visible; unless indeed it were he who fashioned that little visible link of Highway, here, as would seem, scaling the inaccessible to unite Province with Province. But sunwards, lo you! how it towers sheer up, a world of Mountains, the diadem and centre of the mountain region! A hundred and a hundred savage peaks, in the last light of Day; all glowing, of gold and amethyst, like giant spirits of the wilderness; there in their silence, in their solitude, even as on the night when Noah's deluge first dried! Beautiful, nay solemn, was the sudden aspect to our Wanderer. He gazed over those stupendous masses with wonder, almost with longing de-sire; never till this hour had he known Nature, that she was One, that she was his Mother and divine. And as the ruddy glow was fading into clearness in the sky, and the Sun had now departed, a murmur of Eternity and Immensity, of Death and of Life, stole through his soul; and he felt as if Death and Life were one, as if the Earth were not dead, as if the Spirit of the Earth had its throne in that splendour, and his own spirit were therewith holding communion.

'The spell was broken by a sound of carriage-wheels. Emerging from the hidden Northward, to sink soon into the hidden Southward, came a gay barouche-and-four: it was open; servants and postilions wore wedding-favours:

that happy pair, then, had found each other, it was their marriage-evening! Few moments brought them near: *Du Himmel!*[1] It was Herr Towgood and———Blumine! With slight, unrecognising salutation they passed me; plunged down amid the neighbouring thickets, onwards, to Heaven, and to England; and I, in my friend Richter's words, *I remained alone, behind them, with the Night.*'

Were it not cruel in these circumstances, here might be the place to insert an observation, gleaned long ago from the great *Clothes-Volume*, where it stands with quite other intent: 'Some time before Small-pox was extirpated,' says the Professor, 'there came a new malady of the spiritual sort on Europe: I mean the epidemic, now endemical, of view-hunting. Poets of old date, being privileged with Senses, had also enjoyed external Nature; but chiefly as we enjoy the crystal cup which holds good or bad liquor for us; that is to say, in silence, or with slight incidental commentary: never, as I compute, till after the *Sorrows of Werter*, was there man found who would say: Come let us make a Description! Having drunk the liquor, come let us eat the glass! Of which endemic the Jenner is unhappily still to seek.' Too true!

We reckon it more important to remark that the Professor's Wanderings, so far as his stoical and cynical envelopement admits us to clear insight, here first take their permanent character, fatuous or not. That basilisk-glance of the Barouche-and-four seems to have withered up what little remnant of a purpose may have still lurked in him: Life has become wholly a dark labyrinth; wherein, through long years, our Friend, flying from spectres, must stumble about at random, and naturally with more haste than progress.

Foolish were it in us to attempt following him, even from afar, in this extraordinary world-pilgrimage of his; the simplest record of which, were clear record possible, would

1 *Du Himmel*: Good Heavens

fill volumes. Hopeless is the obscurity, unspeakable the confusion. He glides from country to country, from condition to condition; vanishing and reappearing, no man can calculate how or where. Through all quarters of the world he wanders, and apparently through all circles of society. If in any scene, perhaps difficult to fix geographically, he settles for a time, and forms connexions, be sure he will snap them abruptly asunder. Let him sink out of sight as Private Scholar (*Privatisirender*), living by the grace of God, in some European capital, you may next find him as Hadjee in the neighbourhood of Mecca. It is an inexplicable Phantasmagoria, capricious, quick-changing; as if our Traveller, instead of limbs and highways, had transported himself by some wishing-carpet, or Fortunatus' Hat. The whole too imparted emblematically, in dim multifarious tokens (as that collection of Street-Advertisements); with only some touch of direct historical notice sparingly interspersed: little light-islets in the world of haze! So that from this point, the Professor is more of an enigma than ever. In figurative language, we might say he becomes, not indeed a spirit, yet spiritualised, vaporised. Fact unparalleled in Biography! The river of his History, which we have traced from its tiniest fountains, and hoped to see flow onward, with increasing current, into the ocean, here dashes itself over that terrific Lover's Leap; and, as a mad-foaming cataract, flies wholly into tumultuous clouds of spray! Low down it indeed collects again into pools and plashes; yet only at a great distance, and with difficulty, if at all, into a general stream. To cast a glance into certain of those pools and plashes, and trace whither they run, must, for a chapter or two, form the limit of our endeavour.

For which end doubtless those direct historical Notices, where they can be met with, are the best. Nevertheless, of this sort too there occurs much, which, with our present light, it were questionable to emit. Teufelsdröckh, vibrating everywhere between the highest and the lowest levels, comes into contact with Public History itself. For example, those conversations and relations with illustrious Persons, as Sultan Mahmoud, the Emperor Napoleon, and others, are they not as yet rather of a diplomatic character, than of a biographic? The Editor, appreciating the sacredness of crowned heads, nay perhaps suspecting the possible trickeries of a Clothes-Philosopher, will eschew this province for the present: a new time may bring new insight and a different duty.

If we ask now, not indeed with what ulterior Purpose, for there was none, yet with what immediate outlooks; at all events, in what mood of mind, the Professor undertook and prosecuted this world-pilgrimage, – the answer is more distinct than favourable. 'A nameless Unrest,' says he, 'urged me forward; to which the outward motion was some momentary lying solace. Whither should I go? My Loadstars were blotted out; in that canopy of grim fire shone no star. Yet forward must I; the ground burnt under me; there was no rest for the sole of my foot. I was alone! alone! Ever too the strong inward longing shaped Fantasms for itself: towards these, one after the other, must I fruitlessly wander. A feeling I had that, for my fever-thirst, there was and must be somewhere a healing Fountain. To many fondly imagined Fountains, the Saints' Wells of these days, did I pilgrim; to great Men, to great Cities, to great Events: but found there no healing. In strange countries, as in the well-known; in savage deserts as in the press of corrupt civilisation, it was ever the same: how could your Wanderer escape from – *his own Shadow?* Nevertheless still Forward! I felt as if in great haste; to do I saw not what. From the depths of my own heart, it called to me, Forwards! The winds and the streams, and all Nature sounded to me, Forwards! *Ach Gott!* I was even, once for all, a Son of Time.'

From which is it not clear that the internal Satanic School was still active enough? He says elsewhere: 'The *Enchiridion* of Epictetus I had ever with me, often as my sole rational companion; and regret to mention that the nourishment it yielded was trifling.' Thou foolish Teufelsdröckh! How could it else? Hadst thou not Greek enough to understand thus much: *The end of Man is an Action, and not a Thought*, though it were the noblest?

'How I lived?' writes he once: 'Friend, hast thou considered the "rugged all-nourishing Earth," as Sophocles well names her; how she feeds the sparrow on the housetop, much more her darling, man? While thou stirrest and livest, thou hast a probability of victual. My breakfast of tea has been cooked by a Tartar woman, with water of the Amur, who wiped her earthen-kettle with a horse-tail. I have roasted wild eggs in the sand of Sahara; I have awakened in Paris *Estrapades* and Vienna *Malzleins*, with no prospect of breakfast beyond elemental liquid. That I had my Living to seek saved me from Dying, – by suicide. In our busy Europe, is there not an everlasting demand for Intellect, in the chemical, mechanical, political, religious, educational, commercial departments? In Pagan countries, cannot one write Fetishes? Living! Little knowest thou what alchemy is in an inventive Soul; how, as with its little finger, it can create provision enough for the body (of a Philosopher); and then, as with both hands, create quite other than provision; namely, spectres to torment itself withal.'

Poor Teufelsdröckh! Flying with Hunger always parallel to him; and a whole Infernal Chace in his rear; so that the countenance of Hunger is comparatively a friend's! Thus must he, in the temper of ancient Cain, or of the modern Wandering Jew, save only that he feels himself not guilty and but suffering the pains of guilt, – wend to and fro with aimless speed. Thus must he, over the whole surface of the Earth (by foot-prints), write his *Sorrows of Teufelsdröckh*; even as the great Goethe, in passionate words, must write his *Sorrows of Werter*, before the spirit freed herself, and he could become a Man. Vain truly is the hope of your swiftest Runner 'to escape from his own Shadow!' Nevertheless, in these sick days, when the Born of Heaven first descries himself (about the age of twenty) in a world such as ours, richer than usual in two things: in Truths grown obsolete, and Trades grown obsolete, – what can the fool think but that it is all a Den of Lies, wherein whoso will not speak Lies and act Lies, must stand Idle, and despair? Whereby it happens that, for your nobler minds, the publishing of some such Work of Art, in one or the other dialect, becomes almost a necessity. For what is it properly but an Altercation with the Devil, before you begin honestly Fighting him? Your Byron publishes his *Sorrows of Lord George*, in verse and in prose, and copiously otherwise: your Bonaparte represents his *Sorrows of Napoleon* Opera, in an all-too stupendous style; with music of cannon-vollies, and murder-shrieks of a world; his stage-lights are the fires of Conflagration; his rhyme and recitative are the tramp of embattled Hosts and the sound of falling Cities. – Happier is he who, like our Clothes-Philosopher, can write such matter, since it must be written, on the insensible Earth, with his shoe-soles only; and also survive the writing thereof!

CHAPTER 7

The Everlasting No

UNDER the strange nebulous envelopment, wherein our Professor has now shrouded himself, no doubt but his spiritual nature is nevertheless progressive, and growing: for how can the 'Son of Time,' in any case, stand still? We behold him, through those dim years, in a state of crisis, of transition: his new Pilgrimings, and general solution into aimless Discontinuity, what is all this but a mad Fermentation; wherefrom, the fiercer it is, the clearer product will one day evolve itself?

Such transitions are ever full of pain: thus the Eagle, when he moults, is sickly; and, to attain his new beak, must harshly dash off the old one upon rocks. What Stoicism soever our Wanderer, in his individual acts and motions may affect, it is clear that there is a hot fever of anarchy and misery raging within; coruscations of which flash out: as, indeed, how could there be other? Have we not seen him disappointed, bemocked of Destiny, through long years? All that the young heart might desire and pray for has been denied; nay, as in the last worst instance, offered and then snatched away. Ever an 'excellent Passivity;' but of useful, reasonable Activity, essential to the former as Food to Hunger, nothing granted: till at length, in this wild Pilgrimage, he must forcibly seize for himself an Activity, though useless, unreasonable. Alas! his cup of bitterness, which had been filling drop by drop, ever since that first 'ruddy morning' in the Hinterschlag Gymnasium, was at the very lip; and then with that poison-drop, of the Towgood-and-Blumine business, it runs over, and even hisses over in a deluge of foam.

He himself says once, with more justness than originality: 'Man is, properly speaking, based upon Hope, he has no other possession but Hope; this world of his is emphatically the Place of Hope.' What then was our Professor's possession? We see him, for the present, quite shut out from Hope; looking not into the golden orient, but vaguely all round into a dim copper firmament, pregnant with earthquake and tornado.

Alas, shut out from Hope, in a deeper sense than we yet dream of! For as he wanders wearisomely through this world, he has now lost all tidings of another and higher. Full of religion, or at least of religiosity, as our Friend has since exhibited himself, he hides not that, in those days, he was wholly irreligious: 'Doubt had darkened into Unbelief,' says he; 'shade after shade goes grimly over your soul, till you have the fixed, starless, Tartarean black.' To such readers as have reflected, what can be called reflecting, on man's life, and happily discovered, in contradiction to much Profit-and-Loss Philosophy, speculative and practical, that Soul is *not* synonymous with Stomach; who understand, therefore, in our Friend's words, 'that, for man's well-being, Faith is properly the one thing needful; how, with it, Martyrs, otherwise weak, can cheerfully endure the shame and the cross; and, without it, Wordlings puke up their sick existence, by suicide, in the midst of luxury:' to such it will be clear that, for a pure moral nature, the loss of his religious Belief was the loss of every thing. Unhappy young man! All wounds, the crush of long-continued Destitution, the stab of false Friendship, and of false Love, all wounds in thy so genial heart would have healed again, had not its life-warmth been withdrawn. Well might he exclaim, in his wild way: 'Is there no God, then; but at best an absentee God, sitting idle, ever since the first Sabbath, at

the outside of his Universe, and *see*ing it go? Has the word
Duty no meaning: is what we call Duty no divine Messenger and Guide, but a false earthly Fantasm, made up of
Desire and Fear, of emanations from the Gallows and from
Doctor Graham's Celestial-Bed? Happiness of an approv-
ing Conscience! Did not Paul of Tarsus, whom admiring
men have since named Saint, feel that *he* was "the chief of
sinners;" and Nero of Rome, jocund in spirit (*wohlgemuth*),
spend much of his time in fiddling? Foolish Word-monger,
and Motive-grinder, that in thy Logic-mill hast an earthly
mechanism for the Godlike itself, and wouldst fain grind
me out Virtue from the husks of Pleasure, – I tell thee, Nay!
To the unregenerate Prometheus Vinctus of a man, it is
even the bitterest aggravation of his wretchedness that he is
conscious of Virtue, that he feels himself the victim not of
suffering only, but of injustice. What then? Is the heroic
inspiration we name Virtue but some Passion; some bubble
of the blood, bubbling in the direction others *profit* by? I
know not: only this I know, If what thou namest Happiness
be our true aim, then are we all astray. With Stupidity and
sound Digestion man may front much. But what, in these
dull unimaginative days, are the terrors of Conscience to
the diseases of the Liver! Not on Morality, but on Cookery
let us build our stronghold: there brandishing our frying-
pan, as censer, let us offer sweet incense to the Devil, and
live at ease on the fat things which *he* has provided for his
Elect!'

Thus must the bewildered Wanderer stand, as so many
have done, shouting question after question into the Sibyl-
cave of Destiny, and receive no Answer but an Echo. It is all
a grim Desert, this once fair world of his; wherein is heard
only the howling of wild beasts, or the shrieks of despairing,
hate-filled men; and no Pillar of Cloud by day, and no Pillar
of Fire by night, any longer guides the Pilgrim. To such
length has the spirit of Inquiry carried him. 'But what boots
it (*was thut's*)?' cries he: 'it is but the common lot in this era.

Not having come to spiritual majority prior to the *Siècle de Louis Quinze*, and not being born purely a Loghead (*Dummkopf*), thou hadst no other outlook. The whole world is, like thee, sold to Unbelief: their old Temples of the Godhead, which for long have not been rainproof, crumble down; and men ask now: Where is the Godhead; our eyes never saw him!'

Pitiful enough were it, for all these wild utterances, to call our Diogenes wicked. Unprofitable Servants as we all are, perhaps at no era of his life was he more decisively the Servant of Goodness, the Servant of God, than even now when doubting God's existence. 'One circumstance I note,' says he: 'after all the nameless woe that Inquiry, which for me, what it is not always, was genuine Love of Truth, had wrought me, I nevertheless still loved Truth, and would bate no jot of my allegiance to her. "Truth!" I cried, "though the Heavens crush me for following her: no Falsehood! though a whole celestial Lubberland were the price of Apostacy." In conduct it was the same. Had a divine Messenger from the clouds, or miraculous Handwriting on the wall, convincingly proclaimed to me, *This shalt thou do*, with what passionate readiness, as I often thought, would I have done it, had it been leaping into the infernal Fire! Thus, in spite of all Motive-grinders, and Mechanical Profit-and-Loss Philosophies, with the sick ophthalmia and hallucination they had brought on, was the Infinite nature of Duty still dimly present to me: living without God in the world, of God's light I was not utterly bereft; if my as yet sealed eyes, with their unspeakable longing, could nowhere see Him, nevertheless in my heart He was present, and His Heaven-written Law still stood legible and sacred there.'

Meanwhile, under all these tribulations, and temporal and spiritual destitutions, what must the Wanderer, in his silent soul, have endured! 'The painfullest feeling,' writes he, 'is that of your own Feebleness (*Unkraft*); ever, as the

English Milton says, to be weak is the true misery. And yet of your Strength there is and can be no clear feeling, save by what you have prospered in, by what you have done. Between vague wavering Capability and fixed indubitable Performance, what a difference! A certain inarticulate Self-consciousness dwells dimly in us; which only our Works can render articulate and decisively discernible. Our Works are the mirror wherein the spirit first sees its natural lineaments. Hence, too, the folly of that impossible Precept, *Know thyself;* till it be translated into this partially possible one, *Know what thou canst work at.*

'But for me, so strangely unprosperous had I been, the net result of my Workings amounted as yet simply to – Nothing. How then could I believe in my Strength, when there was as yet no mirror to see it in? Ever did this agitating, yet as I now perceive, quite frivolous question, remain to me insoluble: Hast thou a certain Faculty, a certain Worth, such even as the most have not; or art thou the completest Dullard of these modern times? Alas! the fearful Unbelief is unbelief in yourself; and how could I believe? Had not my first, last Faith in myself, when even to me the Heavens seemed laid open, and I dared to love, been all too-cruelly belied? The speculative Mystery of Life grew ever more mysterious to me: neither in the practical Mystery had I made the slightest progress, but been everywhere buffeted, foiled, and contemptuously cast out. A feeble unit in the middle of a threatening Infinitude, I seemed to have nothing given me but eyes, whereby to discern my own wretchedness. Invisible yet impenetrable walls, as of Enchantment, divided me from all living: was there, in the wide world, any true bosom I could press trustfully to mine? O Heaven, No, there was none! I kept a lock upon my lips; why should I speak much with that shifting variety of so-called Friends, in whose withered, vain, and too-hungry souls, Friendship was but an incredible tradition? In such cases, your resource is to talk little, and that little mostly from the Newspapers. Now when I look back, it was a strange isolation I then lived in. The men and women round me, even speaking with me, were but Figures; I had, practically, forgotten that they were alive, that they were not merely automatic. In midst of their crowded streets, and assemblages, I walked solitary; and (except as it was my own heart, not another's, that I kept devouring) savage also, as the tiger in his jungle. Some comfort it would have been, could I, like a Faust, have fancied myself tempted and tormented of the Devil; for a Hell, as I imagine, without Life, though only Diabolic Life, were more frightful: but in our age of Downpulling and Disbelief, the very Devil has been pulled down, you cannot so much as believe in a Devil. To me the Universe was all void of Life, of Purpose, of Volition, even of Hostility: it was one huge, dead, immeasurable Steam-engine, rolling on, in its dead indifference, to grind me limb from limb. O the vast, gloomy, solitary Golgotha, and Mill of Death! Why was the Living banished thither companionless, conscious? Why if there is no Devil; nay, unless the Devil is your God?'

A prey incessantly to such corrosions, might not, moreover, as the worst aggravation to them, the iron constitution even of a Teufelsdröckh threaten to fail? We conjecture that he has known sickness; and, in spite of his locomotive habits, perhaps sickness of the chronic sort. Hear this, for example: 'How beautiful to die of broken-heart, on Paper! Quite another thing in Practice; every window of your Feeling, even of your Intellect, as it were, begrimed and mud-bespattered, so that no pure ray can enter; a whole Drugshop in your inwards; the foredone soul drowning slowly in quagmires of Disgust!'

Putting all which external and internal miseries together, may we not find in the following sentences, quite in our Professor's still vein, significance enough: 'From Suicide a certain after-shine (*Nachschein*) of Christianity withheld me; perhaps also a certain indolence of character; for, was not that a remedy I had at any time within reach? Often, however, was there a question present to me: Should some one now, at the turning of that corner, blow thee suddenly out of Space, into the other World, or other No-world, by pistol-shot, – how were it? On which ground, too, I have often, in sea-storms and sieged cities and other death-scenes, exhibited an imperturbability, which passed, falsely enough, for courage.'

'So had it lasted,' concludes the Wanderer, 'so had it lasted, as in bitter protracted Death-agony, through long years. The heart within me, unvisited by any heavenly dew-drop, was smouldering in sulphurous, slow-consuming fire. Almost since earliest memory I had shed no tear; or once only when I, murmuring half-audibly, recited Faust's Deathsong, that wild *Selig der den er im Siegesglanze findet* (Happy whom He finds in Battle's splendour), and thought that of this last Friend even I was not forsaken, that Destiny itself could not doom me not to die. Having no Hope, neither had I any definite Fear, were it of Man or of Devil: nay, I often felt as if it might be solacing, could the Arch-Devil himself, though in Tartarean terrors, but rise to me, that I might tell him a little of my mind. And yet, strangely enough, I lived in a continual, indefinite, pining Fear; tremulous, pusillanimous, apprehensive of I knew not what: it seemed as if all things in the Heavens above and the Earth beneath would hurt me; as if the heavens and the Earth were but boundless Jaws of a devouring Monster, wherein I, palpitating, waited to be devoured.

'Full of such humour, and perhaps the miserablest man in the whole French Capital or Suburbs, was I, one sultry Dogday, after much perambulation, toiling along the dirty little *Rue Saint Thomas de l'Enfer*, among civic rubbish enough, in a close atmosphere, and over pavements hot as Nebuchadnezzar's Furnace; whereby doubtless my spir-its were little cheered; when, all at once, there rose a

Thought in me, and I asked myself: "What *art* thou afraid of? Wherefore, like a coward, dost thou for ever pip and whimper, and go cowering and trembling? Despicable biped! what is the sum-total of the worst that lies before thee? Death? Well, Death; and say the pangs of Tophet too, and all that the Devil and Man may, will, or can do against thee! Hast thou not a heart; canst thou not suffer whatso it be; and, as a Child of Freedom, though outcast, trample Tophet itself under thy feet, while it consumes thee? Let it come, then; I will meet it and defy it!" And as I so thought, there rushed like a stream of fire over my whole soul; and I shook base Fear away from me for ever. I was strong, of unknown strength; a spirit, almost a god. Ever from that time, the temper of my misery was changed: not Fear or whining Sorrow was it, but Indignation and grim fire-eyed Defiance.

'Thus had the EVERLASTING NO (*das Ewige Nein*) pealed authoritatively through all the recesses of my Being, of my ME; and then was it that my whole ME stood up, in native God-created majesty, and with emphasis recorded its Protest. Such a Protest, the most important transaction in Life, may that same Indignation and Defiance, in a psychological point of view, be fitly called. The Everlasting No had said: "Behold, thou art fatherless, outcast, and the Universe is mine (the Devil's);" to which my whole Me now made answer: "*I* am not thine, but Free, and for ever hate thee!"

'It is from this hour that I incline to date my Spiritual New-birth, or Baphometic* Fire-baptism; perhaps I directly thereupon began to be a Man.'

---

* Enemies of the mediaeval order of Knights Templar claimed that these secretly worshipped an idol called Baphomet; using a hell-fire ceremony to undo a new member's Christian baptism – AG

CHAPTER 8

Centre of Indifference

THOUGH, after this 'Baphometic Fire-baptism' of his, our Wanderer signifies that his Unrest was but increased; as, indeed, 'Indignation and Defiance,' especially against things in general, are not the most peaceable inmates; yet can the Psychologist surmise that it was no longer a quite hopeless Unrest; that henceforth it had at least a fixed centre to revolve round. For the fire-baptised soul, long so scathed and thunder-riven, here feels its own Freedom, which feeling is its Baphometic Baptism: the citadel of its whole kingdom it has thus gained by assault, and will keep inexpugnable; outwards from which the remaining dominions, not indeed without hard battling, will doubtless by degrees be conquered and pacificated. Under another figure, we might say, if in that great moment, in the *Rue*

Saint Thomas de l'Enfer, the old inward Satanic School was not yet thrown out of doors, it received peremptory judicial notice to quit; – whereby, for the rest, its howl-chauntings, Ernulphus-cursings, and rebellious gnashings of teeth, might, in the meanwhile, become only the more tumultuous, and difficult to keep secret.

Accordingly, if we scrutinize these Pilgrimings well, there is perhaps discernible henceforth a certain incipient method in their madness. Not wholly as a Spectre does Teufelsdröckh now storm through the world; at worst as a spectre-fighting Man, nay that will one day be a Spectre-queller. If pilgriming restlessly to so many 'Saints' Wells,' and ever without quenching of his thirst, he nevertheless finds little secular wells, whereby from time to time some alleviation is ministered. In a word, he is now, if not ceasing, yet intermitting to 'eat his own heart;' and clutches round him outwardly, on the NOT-ME for wholesomer food. Does not the following glimpse exhibit him in a much more natural state?

'Towns also and Cities, especially the ancient, I failed not to look upon with interest. How beautiful to see thereby, as through a long vista, into the remote Time; to have, as it were, an actual section of almost the earliest Past brought safe into the Present, and set before your eyes! There, in that old City, was a live ember of Culinary Fire put down, say only two thousand years ago; and there, burning more or less triumphantly, with such fuel as the region yielded, it has burnt, and still burns, and thou thyself seest the very smoke thereof. Ah! and the far more mysterious live ember of Vital Fire was then also put down there; and still miraculously burns and spreads; and the smoke and ashes thereof (in these Judgment-Halls and Church-yards), and its bellows-engines (in these Churches), thou still seest; and its flame, looking out from every kind countenance, and every hateful one, still warms thee or scorches thee.

'Of Man's Activity and Attainment the chief results are aeriform, mystic, and preserved in Tradition only: such are his Forms of Government, with the Authority they rest on; his Customs, or Fashions both of Cloth-habits and of Soul-habits; much more his collective stock of Handicrafts, the whole Faculty he has required of manipulating Nature: all these things, as indispensable and priceless as they are, cannot in any way be fixed under lock and key, but must flit, spirit-like, on impalpable vehicles, from Father to Son; if you demand sight of them, they are nowhere to be met with. Visible Ploughmen and Hammermen there have been, ever from Cain and Tubalcain downwards: but where does your accumulated Agricultural, Metallurgic, and other Manufacturing SKILL lie warehoused? It trans-mits itself on the atmospheric air, on the sun's rays (by Hearing and by Vision); it is a thing aeriform, impalpable, of quite spiritual sort. In like manner, ask me not, Where are the LAWS; where is the GOVERNMENT? In vain wilt thou go to Schönbrunn, to Downing Street, to the Palais Bourbon: thou findest nothing there, but brick or stone houses, and some bundles of Papers tied with tape. Where then is that same cunningly-devised almighty GOVERN-MENT of theirs to be laid hands on? Everywhere, yet nowhere: seen only in its works, this too is a thing aeriform, invisible; or if you will, mystic and miraculous. So spiritual (*geistig*) is our whole daily Life: all that we do springs out of Mystery, Spirit, invisible Force; only like a little Cloud-image, or Armida's Palace, airbuilt, does the Actual body itself forth from the great mystic Deep.

'Visible and tangible products of the Past, again, I reckon up to the extent of three: Cities, with their Cabinets and Arsenals; then tilled Fields, to either or to both of which divisions Roads with their Bridges may belong; and thirdly—Books. In which third truly, the last-invented, lies a worth far surpassing that of the two others. Wondrous indeed is the virtue of a true Book. Not like a dead City of stones, yearly crumbling, yearly needing repair; more like a tilled Field, but then a spiritual Field: like a spiritual Tree, let me rather say, it stands from year to year, and from age to age (we have Books that already number some hundred-and-fifty human ages); and yearly comes its new produce of Leaves (Commentaries, Deductions, Philosophical, Political Systems; or were it only Sermons, Pamphlets, Journalistic Essays), every one of which is talismanic and thaumaturgic, for it can persuade men. O thou who art able to write a Book, which once in the two centuries or oftener there is a man gifted to do, envy not him whom they name City-builder, and inexpressibly pity him whom they name Conqueror or City-burner! Thou too art a Conqueror and Victor; but of the true sort, namely over the Devil: thou too hast built what will outlast all marble and metal, and be a wonder-bringing City of the Mind, a Temple and Seminary and Prophetic Mount, whereto all kindreds of the Earth will pilgrim. – Fool! why journeyest thou wearisomely, in thy antiquarian fervour, to gaze on the stone Pyramids of Geeza, or the clay ones of Sacchara? These stand there, as I can tell thee, idle and inert, looking over the Desart, foolishly enough, for the last three thousand years: but canst thou not open thy Hebrew BIBLE, then, or even Luther's Version thereof?'

No less satisfactory is his sudden appearance not in Battle, yet on some Battle-field; which, we soon gather, must be that of Wagram; so that here, for once, is a certain approximation to distinctness of date. Omitting much, let us impart what follows:

'Horrible enough! A whole Marchfeld strewed with shell-splinters, cannon-shot, ruined tumbrils, and dead men and horses; stragglers still remaining not so much as buried. And those red mould heaps: aye, there lie the Shells of Men, out of which all the Life and Virtue has been blown; and now are they swept together, and crammed down out of sight, like blown Egg-shells! – Did Nature, when she bade the Donau bring down his mould-cargos from the Carinthian and Carpathian Heights, and spread them out here into the softest, richest level, – intend thee, O March-feld, for a corn-bearing Nursery, whereon her children might be nursed; or for a Cockpit, wherein they might the more commodiously be throttled and tattered? Were thy three broad Highways, meeting here from the ends of Europe, made for Ammunition-waggons, then? Were thy Wagrams and Stillfrieds but so many ready-built Case-mates, wherein the house of Hapsburg might batter with artillery, and with artillery be battered? König Ottokar, amid yonder hillocks, dies under Rodolf's truncheon; here Kaiser Franz falls a-swoon under Napoleon's: within which five centuries, to omit the others, how has thy breast, fair Plain, been defaced and defiled! The greensward is torn up and trampled down; man's fond care of it, his fruit–trees, hedgerows, and pleasant dwellings, blown away with gun-powder; and the kind seedfield lies as a desolate, hideous Place-of-Sculls. – Nevertheless, Nature is at work; neither shall these Powder-Devilkins with their utmost devilry gainsay her: but all that gore and carnage will be shrouded in, absorbed into manure; and next year the Marchfeld will be green, nay greener. Thrifty unwearied Nature, ever out of our great waste educing some little profit of thy own, – how dost thou, from the very carcass of the Killer, bring Life for the Living!

'What, speaking in quite unofficial language, is the net purport and upshot of War? To my own knowledge, for example, there dwell and toil, in the British village of Dumdrudge, usually some five hundred souls. From these, by certain 'Natural Enemies' of the French, there are successively selected, during the French war, say thirty able-bodied men: Dumdrudge, at her own expense, has suckled and nursed them; she has, not without difficulty and sorrow, fed them up to manhood, and even trained them to crafts, so that one can weave, another build,

WAR

another hammer, and the weakest can stand under thirty stone avoirdupois. Nevertheless, amid much weeping and swearing, they are selected; all dressed in red; and shipped away, at the public charges, some two thousand miles, or say only to the south of Spain; and fed there till wanted. And now, to that same spot in the south of Spain, are thirty similar French artisans, from a French Dumdrudge, in like manner wending: till at length, after infinite effort, the two parties come into actual juxta-position; and Thirty stands fronting Thirty, each with a gun in his hand. Straightway the word "Fire!" is given; and they blow the souls out of one another; and in place of sixty brisk useful craftsmen, the world has sixty dead carcasses, which it must bury, and anew shed tears for. Had these men any quarrel? Busy as the Devil is, not the smallest! They lived far enough apart; were the entirest strangers; nay, in so wide a Universe, there was even, unconsciously, by Commerce, some mutual helpfulness between them. How then? Simpleton! Their Governors had fallen out; and, instead of shooting one another, had the cunning to make these poor blockheads shoot. – Alas so is it in Deutschland, and hitherto in all other lands; still as of old, "what devilry soever Kings do, the Greeks must pay the piper!" – In that fiction of the English Smollett, it is true, the final Cessation of War is perhaps prophetically shadowed forth; where the two Natural Enemies, in person, take each a Tobacco-pipe, filled with Brimstone; light the same, and smoke in one another's faces, till the weaker gives in: but from such predicted Peace-Era, what blood-filled trenches, and contentious centuries, may still divide us!'

Thus can the Professor, at least in lucid intervals, look away from his own sorrows, over the many-coloured world, and pertinently enough note what is passing there. We may remark, indeed, that for the matter of spiritual culture, if for nothing else, perhaps few periods of his life were richer than this. Internally, there is the most momentous instructive

Course of Practical Philosophy, with Experiments, going on; towards the right comprehension of which his Peripatetic habits, favourable to Meditation, might help him rather than hinder. Externally, again, as he wanders to and fro, there are, if for the longing heart little substance, yet for the seeing eye Sights enough: in these so boundless Travels of his, granting that the Satanic School was even partially kept down, what an incredible Knowledge of our Planet, and its Inhabitants and their Works, that is to say, of all knowable things, might not Teufelsdröckh acquire!

'I have read in most Public Libraries,' says he, 'including those of Constantinople and Samarcand: in most Colleges, except the Chinese Mandarin ones, I have studied, or seen that there was no studying. Unknown Languages have I oftenest gathered from their natural repertory, the Air, by my organ of Hearing; Statistics, Geographics, Topographics came, through the Eye, almost of their own accord. The ways of Man, how he seeks food, and warmth, and protection for himself, in most regions, are ocularly known to me. Like the great Hadrian, I meted out much of the terraqueous Globe with a pair of Compasses that belonged to myself only.

'Of great Scenes, why speak? Three summer days, I lingered reflecting, and even composing (*dichtete*), by the Pine-chasms of Vaucluse; and in that clear Lakelet moistened my bread. I have sat under the palm-trees of Tadmor; smoked a pipe among the ruins of Babylon. The great Wall of China I have seen; and can testify that it is of grey brick, coped and covered with granite, and shows only second-rate masonry. – Great Events, also, have I not witnessed? Kings sweated down (*ausgemergelt*) into Berlin-and-Milan Customhouse-officers; the World well won, and the World well lost; oftener than once a hundred thousand individuals shot (by each other) in one day. All kindreds and peoples and nations dashed together, and shifted and shovelled into heaps, that they might ferment there, and in time unite. The birth-pangs of Democracy, wherewith convulsed Europe was groaning in cries that reached Heaven, could not escape me.

'For great Men I have ever had the warmest predilection; and can perhaps boast that few such in this era have wholly escaped me. Great Men are the inspired (speaking and acting) Texts of that divine BOOK OF REVELATIONS, whereof a Chapter is completed from epoch to epoch, and by some named HISTORY; to which inspired Texts your numerous talented men, and your innumerable un-talented men, are the better or worse exegetic Commentaries, and waggon-load of too-stupid, heretical or orthodox, weekly Sermons. For my study, the inspired Texts themselves! Thus, did I not, in very early days, having disguised me as tavern-waiter, stand behind the field-chairs, under that shady Tree at Treisnitz by the Jena Highway; waiting upon the great Schiller and greater Goethe; and hearing what I have not forgotten. For————'

————But at this point the Editor recalls his principle of caution, some time ago laid down, and must suppress much. Let not the sacredness of Laurelled, still more, of Crowned Heads, be tampered with. Should we, at a future day, find circumstances altered, and the time come for Publication, then may these glimpses into the privacy of the Illustrious be conceded; which for the present were little better than treacherous, perhaps traitorous Eavesdrop-pings. Of Lord Byron, therefore, of Pope Pius, Emperor Tarakwang, and the 'White Water-roses' (Chinese Carbo-nari) with their mysteries, no notice here! Of Napoleon himself we shall only, glancing from afar, remark that Teufelsdröckh's relation to him seems to have been of very varied character. At first we find our poor Professor on the point of being shot as a spy; then taken into private con-versation, even pinched on the ear, yet presented with no money; at last indignantly dismissed, almost thrown out of doors, as an 'Ideologist.' 'He himself,' says the Professor, 'was among the completest Ideologists, at least Ideoprax-ists: in the Idea (*in der Idee*) he lived, moved, and fought. The man was a divine Missionary, though unconscious of it; and preached, through the cannon's throat, that great doctrine, *La carrière ouverte aux talens* (The Tools to him that can handle them), which is our ultimate Political Evangile, wherein alone can Liberty lie. Madly enough he preached, it is true, as Enthusiasts and first Missionaries are wont, with imperfect utterance, amid much frothy rant; yet as articulately perhaps as the case admitted. Or call him, if you will, an American Backwoods-man, who had to fell unpenetrated forests, and battle with innumerable wolves, and did not entirely forbear strong liquor, rioting, and even theft; whom, notwithstanding, the peaceful Sower will follow, and, as he cuts the boundless harvest, bless.'

More legitimate and decisively authentic is Teufels-dröckh's appearance and emergence (we know not well whence) in the solitude of the North Cape, on that June Midnight. He has a 'light-blue Spanish cloak' hanging round him, as his 'most commodious, principal, indeed sole upper-garment;' and stands there, on the World-promontory, looking over the infinite Brine, like a little blue Belfry (as we figure), now motionless indeed, yet ready, if stirred, to ring quaintest changes.

'Silence as of Death,' writes he; 'for Midnight, even in the Arctic latitudes, has its character: nothing but the granite cliffs ruddy-tinged, the peaceable gurgle of that slow-heaving Polar Ocean, over which in the utmost North the great Sun hangs low and lazy, as if he too were slumbering. Yet is his cloud-couch wrought of crimson and cloth of gold; yet does his light stream over the mirror of waters, like a tremulous fire-pillar, shooting downwards to the abyss, and hide itself under my feet. In such mo-ments, Solitude also is invaluable; for who would speak, or be looked on, when behind him lies all Europe and Africa, fast asleep, except the watchmen; and before him the silent Immensity, and Palace of the Eternal, whereof our Sun is but a porch-lamp.

'Nevertheless, in this solemn moment, comes a man, or monster, scrambling from among the rock-hollows; and, shaggy, huge as the Hyperborean Bear, hails me in Russian speech: most probably, therefore, a Russian Smuggler. With courteous brevity, I signify my indifference to contraband trade, my humane intentions, yet strong wish to be private. In vain: the monster, counting doubtless on his superior stature, and minded to make sport for himself, or perhaps profit, were it with murder, continues to advance; ever assailing me with his importunate train-oil breath; and now has advanced till we stand both on the verge of the rock, the deep Sea rippling greedily down below. What argument will avail? On the thick Hyperborean, cherubic reasoning, seraphic eloquence were lost. Prepared for such extremity, I, deftly enough, whisk aside one step; draw out, from my interior reservoirs, a sufficient Birmingham Horse-pistol, and say: "Be so obliging as retire, Friend (*Er ziehe sich zurück, Freund*), and with promptitude!" This logic even the Hyperborean understands: fast enough, with apologetic, petitionary growl, he sidles off; and, except for suicidal, as well as homicidal purposes, need not return.

'Such I hold to be the genuine use of Gunpowder: that it makes all men alike tall. Nay, if thou be cooler, cleverer than I, if thou have more *Mind*, though all but no *Body* whatever, then canst thou kill me first, and art the taller. Hereby, at least, is the Goliath powerless, and the David resistless; savage Animalism is nothing, inventive Spiritualism is all.

'With respect to Duels, indeed, I have my own ideas. Few things, in this so surprising world, strike me with more surprise. Two little visual Spectra of men, hovering with insecure enough cohesion in the midst of the UNFATHOM-ABLE, and to dissolve therein, at any rate, very soon, –

make pause at the distance of twelve paces asunder; whirl round; and, simultaneously by the cunningest mechanism, explode one another into Dissolution; and off-hand become Air, and Non-extant! Deuce on it (*verdammt*)! The little spitfires! – Nay, I think with old Hugo von Trimberg; "God must needs laugh outright, could such a thing be, to see his wondrous Mannikins here below." '

But amid these specialities, let us not forget the great generality, which is our chief quest here: How prospered the inner man of Teufelsdröckh under so much outward shifting? Does Legion still lurk in him, though repressed; or has he exorcised that Devil's Brood? We can answer that the symptoms continue promising. Experience is the grand spiritual Doctor; and with him Teufelsdröckh has now been long a patient, swallowing many a bitter bolus. Unless our poor Friend belong to the numerous class of Incurables, which seems not likely, some cure will doubtless be effected. We should rather say that Legion, or the Satanic School, was now pretty well extirpated and cast out, but next to nothing introduced in its room; whereby the heart remains, for the while, in a quiet but no comfortable state.

'At length, after so much roasting,' thus writes our Autobiographer, 'I was what you might name calcined. Pray only that it be not rather, as is the more frequent issue, reduced to a *caput-mortuum!*[1] But in any case, by mere dint of practice, I had grown familiar with many things. Wretchedness was still wretched; but I could now partly see through it, and despise it. Which highest mortal, in this inane Existence; had I not found a Shadow-hunter, or Shadow-hunted; and, when I looked through his brave garnitures, miserable enough? Thy wishes have all been sniffed aside, thought I: but what, had they even been all granted! Did not the Boy Alexander weep because he had

1 *caput-mortuum*: death's-head

not two Planets to conquer; or a whole Solar System; or after that, a whole Universe? *Ach Gott!* when I gazed into these Stars, have they not looked down on me as if with pity from their serene spaces; like Eyes glistening with heavenly tears over the little lot of man! Thousands of human generations, all as noisy as our own, have been swallowed up of Time, and there remains no wreck of them any more; and Arcturus and Orion and Sirius and the Pleiades are still shining in their courses, clear and young, as when the Shepherd first noted them in the plain of Shinar. Pshaw! what is this paltry little Dog-cage of an Earth; what art thou that sittest whining there? Thou art still Nothing, Nobody: true; but who then is Something, Somebody? For thee the Family of Man has no use; it rejects thee; thou art wholly as a dissevered limb: so be it; perhaps it is better so!'

Too heavy-laden Teufelsdröckh! Yet surely his bands are loosening; one day he will hurl the burden far from him, and bound forth free, and with a second youth.

'This,' says our Professor, 'was the CENTRE OF INDIF- FERENCE I had now reached; through which whoso travels from the Negative Pole to the Positive must necessarily pass.'

CHAPTER 9

The Everlasting Yea

'TEMPTATIONS in the Wilderness!' exclaims Teufelsdröckh: 'Have we not all to be tried with such? Not so easily
can the old Adam, lodged in us by birth, be dispossessed.
Our Life is compassed round with Necessity; yet is the
meaning of Life itself no other than Freedom, than Voluntary Force: thus have we a warfare; in the beginning, especially, a hard-fought Battle. For the God-given mandate,
Work thou in Welldoing, lies mysteriously written, in Promethean, Prophetic Characters, in our hearts; and leaves us
no rest, night or day, till it be deciphered and obeyed; till it
burn forth, in our conduct, a visible, acted Gospel of Freedom. And as the clay-given mandate, *Eat thou and be filled*, at
the same time, persuasively proclaims itself through every
nerve, – must there not be a confusion, a contest, before the
better Influence can become the upper?

'To me nothing seems more natural than that the Son of
Man, when such God-given mandate first prophetically stirs
within him, and the Clay must now be vanquished or van-
quish, – should be carried of the spirit into grim Solitudes,
and there fronting the Tempter do grimmest battle with him;
defiantly setting him at nought, till he yield and fly. Name it as
we choose; with or without visible Devil, whether in the
natural Desart of rocks and sands, or in the populous, moral
Desart of selfishness and baseness, – to such Temptation are
we all called. Unhappy if we are not! Unhappy if we are but
Half-men, in whom that divine handwriting has never blazed
forth, all-subduing, in true sun-splendour; but quivers du-
biously amid meaner lights; or smoulders, in dull pain, in
darkness, under earthly vapours! – Our Wilderness is the
wide World in an Atheistic Century; our Forty Days are long
years of suffering and fasting: nevertheless, to these also
comes an end. Yes, to me also was given, if not Victory,
yet the consciousness of Battle, and the resolve to persevere
therein while life or faculty is left. To me also, entangled in the
enchanted forests, demon-peopled, doleful of sight and of
sound, it was given, after weariest wanderings, to work out
my way into the higher sunlit slopes – of that Mountain which
has no summit, or whose summit is in Heaven only!'

He says elsewhere, under a less ambitious figure; as
figures are, once for all, natural to him: 'Has not thy Life
been that of most sufficient men (*tüchtigen Männer*) thou
hast known in this generation? An outflush of foolish young
Enthusiasm, like the first fallow-crop, wherein are as many
weeds as valuable herbs: this all parched away, under the
Droughts of practical and spiritual Unbelief; as Disappointment, in thought and act, often-repeated gave rise
to Doubt, and Doubt gradually settled into Denial! If I have
had a second-crop, and now see the perennial greensward,
and sit under umbrageous cedars, which defy all Drought
(and Doubt): herein too, be the Heavens praised I am not
without examples, and even exemplars.'

So that for Teufelsdröckh also there has been a 'glorious revolution:' these mad shadow-hunting and shadow-hunted Pilgrimings of his, were but some purifying 'Temptation in the Wilderness,' before his apostolic work (such as it was) could begin; which Temptation is now happily over, and the Devil once more worsted! Was 'that high moment in the *Rue de l'Enfer*,' then, properly the turning point of the battle; when the Fiend said, *Worship me or be torn in shreds*, and was answered valiantly with an *Apage Satanas?*[1] – Singular Teufelsdröckh, would thou hadst told thy singular story in plain words! But it is fruitless to look there, in those Paper-bags, for such. Nothing but innuendoes, figurative crotchets: a typical Shadow, fitfully wavering, prophetico-satiric; no clear logical Picture. 'How paint to the sensual eye,' asks he once, 'what passes in the Holy-of-Holies of Man's Soul; in what words, known to these profane times, speak even afar off of the Unspeakable?' We ask in turn: Why perplex these times, profane as they are, with needless obscurity, by omission and by commission? Not mystical only is our Professor, but whimsical; and involves himself, now more than ever, in eye-bewildering *chiaroscuro*. Successive glimpses, here faithfully imparted, our more gifted readers must endeavour to combine for their own behoof.

He says: 'The hot Harmattan-wind had raged itself out; its howl went silent within me; and the long-deafened soul could now hear. I paused in my wild wanderings; and sat me down to wait, and consider; for it was as if the hour of change drew nigh. I seemed to surrender, to renounce utterly, and say: Fly, then, false shadows of Hope; I will chase you no more, I will believe you no more. And ye too, haggard spectres of Fear, I care not for you; ye too are all shadows and a lie. Let me rest here; for I am way-weary and life-weary; I will rest here, were it but to die: to die or to live is alike to me; alike insignificant.' – And again: 'Here, then,

1 *Apage Satanas*: Get thee hence, Satan

as I lay in that CENTRE OF INDIFFERENCE; cast, doubtless, by benignant upper Influence, into a healing sleep, the
heavy dreams rolled gradually away, and I awoke to a new
Heaven and a new Earth. The first preliminary moral Act,
Annihilation of Self (*Selbst-tödtung*), had been happily
accomplished; and my mind's eyes were now unsealed,
and its hands ungyved.'

Might we not also conjecture that the following passage
refers to his Locality, during this same 'healing sleep;' that
his Pilgrim-staff lies cast aside here, on 'the high table-land;'
and indeed that the repose is already taking wholesome
effect on him? Were it not that the tone, in some parts, has
more of riancy, even of levity, than we could have expected.
However, in Teufelsdröckh, there is always the strangest
Dualism: light dancing, with guitar-music, will be going on
in the forecourt, while by fits from within comes the faint
whimpering of woe and wail. We transcribe the piece entire:

'Beautiful it was to sit there, as in my skyey Tent, musing
and meditating; on the high table-land, in front of the
Mountains; over me, as roof, the azure Dome; and around
me, for walls, four azure flowing curtains, – namely, of the
Four azure Winds, on whose bottom-fringes also I have
seen gilding. And then to fancy the fair Castles that stood
sheltered in these Mountain hollows; with their green
flower-lawns, and white dames and damosels, lovely enough: or better still, the straw-roofed Cottages, wherein
stood many a Mother baking bread, with her children
round her: – all hidden and protectingly folded up in the
valley-folds; yet there and alive, as sure as if I beheld them.
Or to see, as well as fancy, the nine Towns and Villages,
that lay round my mountain-seat, which, in still weather,
were wont to speak to me (by their steeple-bells) with metal
tongue; and, in almost all weather, proclaimed their vitality
by repeated Smoke-clouds; whereon, as on a culinary
horologe, I might read the hour of the day. For it was
the smoke of cookery, as kind housewives, at morning,

midday, eventide, were boiling their husbands' kettles; and
ever a blue pillar rose up into the air, successively or
simultaneously, from each of the nine, saying, as plainly
as smoke could say: Such and such a meal is getting ready
here. Not uninteresting! For you have the whole Borough,
with all its love-makings and scandal-mongeries, conten-
tions and contentments, as in miniature, and could cover it
all with your hat. – If, in my wide Wayfarings, I had learned
to look into the business of the World in its details, here
perhaps was the place for combining it into general propositions, and deducing inferences therefrom.

'Often also could I see the black Tempest marching in
anger through the Distance: round some Schreckhorn, as yet
grim-blue, would the eddying vapour gather, and there
tumultuously eddy, and flow down like a mad witch's hair;
till, after a space, it vanished, and, in the clear sunbeam, your
Schreckhorn stood smiling grim-white, for the vapour had
held snow. How thou fermentest and elaboratest, in thy great
fermenting-vat and laboratory of an Atmosphere, of a
World, O Nature! – Or what is Nature? Ha! why do I not
name thee GOD? Art thou not the "Living Garment of
God?" O Heavens, is it, in very deed, HE, then, that ever
speaks through thee; that lives and loves in thee, that lives and
loves in me?

'Foreshadows, call them rather fore-splendours, of that
Truth, and Beginning of Truths, fell mysteriously over my
soul. Sweeter than Dayspring to the Shipwrecked in Nova
Zembla; ah! like the mother's voice to her little child that
strays bewildered, weeping, in unknown tumults; like soft
streamings of celestial music to my too exasperated heart,
came that Evangile. The Universe is not dead and demo-
niacal, a charnel-house with spectres; but god-like, and my
Father's!

'With other eyes too could I now look upon my fellow
man; with an infinite Love, an infinite Pity. Poor, wandering, wayward man! Art thou not tried, and beaten with

stripes, even as I am? Ever, whether thou bear the Royal
mantle or the Beggar's gabardine, art thou not so weary, so
heavy-laden; and thy Bed of Rest is but a Grave. O my
Brother, my Brother! why cannot I shelter thee in my
bosom, and wipe away all tears from thy eyes. – Truly,
the din of many-voiced Life, which, in this solitude, with
the mind's organ, I could hear, was no longer a maddening
discord, but a melting one: like inarticulate cries, and
sobbings of a dumb creature, which in the ear of Heaven
are prayers. The poor Earth, with her poor joys, was now
my needy Mother, not my cruel Stepdame; Man, with his
so mad Wants and so mean Endeavours, had become the
dearer to me; and even for his sufferings and his sins, I now
first named him Brother. Thus was I standing in the porch
of that "*Sanctuary of Sorrow*;" by strange, steep ways, had I
too been guided thither; and ere long its sacred gates would
open, and the "*Divine Depth of Sorrow*" lie disclosed to me.'

The Professor says, he here first got eye on the Knot that
had been strangling him, and straightway could unfasten it,
and was free. 'A vain interminable controversy,' writes he,
'touching what is at present called Origin of Evil, or some
such thing, arises in every soul, since the beginning of the
world; and in every soul, that would pass from idle Suffering into actual Endeavouring, must first be put an end to.
The most, in our time, have to go content with a simple,
incomplete enough Suppression of this controversy; to a
few some Solution of it is indispensable. In every new era,
too, such Solution comes out in different terms; and ever
the Solution of the last era has become obsolete, and is
found unserviceable. For it is man's nature to change his
Dialect from century to century; he cannot help it though
he would. The authentic *Church-Catechism* of our present
century has not yet fallen into my hands: meanwhile, for my
own private behoof, I attempt to elucidate the matter so.
Man's Unhappiness, as I construe, comes of his Greatness;
it is because there is an Infinite in him, which with all his

cunning he cannot quite bury under the Finite. Will the whole Finance Ministers and Upholsterers and Confectioners of modern Europe undertake, in joint-stock company, to make one Shoeblack HAPPY? They cannot accomplish it, above an hour or two; for the Shoeblack also has a Soul quite other than his Stomach; and would require, if you consider it, for his permanent satisfaction and saturation, simply this allotment, no more, and no less: *God's infinite Universe altogether to himself*, therein to enjoy infinitely, and fill every wish as fast as it rose. Oceans of Hochheimer, a Throat like that Ophiuchus! Speak not of them; to the infinite Shoeblack they are as nothing. No sooner is your ocean filled, than he grumbles that it might have been of better vintage. Try him with half of a Universe, of an Omnipotence, he sets to quarrelling with the proprietor of the other half, and declares himself the most maltreated of men. – Always there is a black spot in our sunshine: it is even, as I said, the *Shadow of Ourselves*.

'But the whim we have of Happiness is somewhat thus. By certain valuations, and averages, of our own striking, we come upon some sort of average terrestrial lot; this we fancy belongs to us by nature, and of indefeasible right. It is simple payment of our wages, of our deserts; requires neither thanks nor complaint: only such *overplus* as there may be do we account Happiness; any *deficit* again is Misery. Now consider that we have the valuation of our own deserts ourselves, and what a fund of Self-conceit there is in each of us, – do you wonder that the balance should so often dip the wrong way, and many a Blockhead cry: See there, what a payment; was ever worthy gentleman so used! – I tell thee, Blockhead, it all comes of thy Vanity; of what thou *fanciest* those same deserts of thine to be. Fancy that thou deservest to be hanged (as is most likely), thou wilt feel it happiness to be only shot: fancy that thou deservest to be hanged in a hairhalter, it will be a luxury to die in hemp.

'So true is it, what I then said, that *the Fraction of Life can be increased in value not so much by increasing your Numerator, as by lessening your Denominator.* Nay, unless my Algebra deceive me, *Unity* itself divided by *Zero* will give *Infinity*. Make thy claim of wages a zero, then; thou hast the world under thy feet. Well did the Wisest of our time write: "It is only with Renunciation (*Entsagen*) that Life, properly speaking, can be said to begin."

'I asked myself: What is this that, ever since earliest years, thou hast been fretting and fuming, and lamenting and self-tormenting, on account of? Say it in a word: is it not because thou art not HAPPY? Because the THOU (sweet gentleman) is not sufficiently honoured, nourished, soft-bedded, and lovingly cared for? Foolish soul! What Act of Legislature was there that *thou* shouldst be Happy? A little while ago thou hadst no right to *be* at all. What if thou wert born and predestined not to be Happy, but to be Unhappy! Art thou nothing other than a Vulture, then, that fliest through the Universe seeking after somewhat to *eat*; and shrieking dolefully because carrion enough is not given thee? Close thy *Byron*; open thy *Goethe*.'

'*Es leuchtet mir ein*, I see a glimpse of it!' cries he elsewhere: 'there is in man a HIGHER than Love of Happiness: he can do without Happiness, and instead thereof find Blessedness! Was it not to preach forth this same HIGHER that sages and martyrs, the Poet and the Priest, in all times, have spoken and suffered; bearing testimony, through life and through death, of the Godlike that is in Man, and how in the Godlike only has he Strength and Freedom? Which God-inspired Doctrine art thou too honoured to be taught; O Heavens! and broken with manifold merciful Afflictions, even till thou become contrite, and learn it! O thank thy Destiny for these; thankfully bear what yet remain: thou hadst need of them; the Self in thee needed to be annihilated. By benignant fever-paroxysms is Life rooting out the deep-seated chronic Disease, and triumphs over Death. On the roaring billows of Time, thou art not engulphed, but borne aloft into the azure of Eternity. Love not Pleasure; love God. This is the EVERLASTING YEA, wherein all contradiction is solved; wherein whoso walks and works, it is well with him.'

And again: 'Small is it that thou canst trample the Earth with its injuries under thy feet, as old Greek Zeno trained thee: thou canst love the Earth while it injures thee, and even because it injures thee; for this a Greater than Zeno was needed, and he too was sent. Knowest thou that "*Worship of Sorrow*?" The Temple thereof, opened some eighteen centuries ago, now lies in ruins, overgrown with jungle, the habitation of doleful creatures: nevertheless, venture forward; in a low crypt, arched out of falling fragments, thou findest the Altar still there, and its sacred Lamp perennially burning.'

Without pretending to comment on which strange utterances, the Editor will only remark that there lies beside them, much of a still more questionable character; unsuited to the general apprehension; nay wherein he himself does not see his way. Nebulous disquisitions on Religion, yet not without bursts of splendour; on the 'perennial continuance of Inspiration;' on Prophecy; that there are 'true Priests, as well as Baal-Priests, in our own day:' with more of the like sort. We select some fractions, by way of finish to this farrago.

'Cease, my much-respected Herr von Voltaire,' thus apostrophises the Professor: 'shut thy sweet voice; for the task appointed thee seems finished. Sufficiently hast thou demonstrated this proposition, considerable or otherwise: That the Mythus of the Christian Religion looks not in the eighteenth century as it did in the eighth. Alas, were thy six-and-thirty quartos, and the six-and-thirty thousand other quartos and folios, and flying sheets or reams, printed before and since on the same subject, all needed to convince us of so little! But what next? Wilt thou help us to embody the divine Spirit of that Religion in a new Mythus, in a new vehicle and vesture, that our Souls, otherwise too

like perishing, may live? What! thou hast no faculty in that
kind? Only a torch for burning, no hammer for building?
Take our thanks, then, and ——— thyself away.

'Meanwhile what are antiquated Mythuses to me? Or is
the God present, felt in my own Heart a thing which Herr
von Voltaire will dispute out of me; or dispute into me? To
the "*Worship of Sorrow*" ascribe what origin and genesis
thou pleasest, *has* not that Worship originated, and been
generated; is it not *here?* Feel it in thy heart, and then say
whether it is of God! This is Belief; all else is Opinion, – for
which latter whoso will let him worry and be worried.'

'Neither,' observes he elsewhere, 'shall ye tear out one
another's eyes, struggling over "Plenary Inspiration," and
such like: try rather to get a little even Partial Inspiration,
each of you for himself. One BIBLE I know, of whose
Plenary Inspiration doubt is not so much as possible; nay
with my own eyes I saw the God's-Hand writing it: thereof
all other Bibles are but Leaves, – say, in Picture-Writing to
assist the weaker faculty.'

Or to give the wearied reader relief, and bring it to an
end, let him take the following perhaps more intelligible
passage:

'To me, in this our Life,' says the Professor, 'which is an
internecine warfare with the Time-spirit, other warfare
seems questionable. Hast thou in any way a Contention with
thy brother, I advise thee, think well what the meaning thereof
is. If thou gauge it to the bottom, it is simply this: "Fellow, see!
thou art taking more than thy share of Happiness in the world,
something from *my* share: which, by the Heavens, thou shalt
not; nay I will fight thee rather." – Alas! and the whole lot to be
divided is such a beggarly matter, truly a "feast of shells," for
the substance has been spilled out: not enough to quench one
Appetite; and the collective human species clutching at
them! – Can we not, in all such cases, rather say: "Take it,
thou too-ravenous individual; take that pitiful additional
fraction of a share, which I reckoned mine, but which thou

so wantest; take it with a blessing: would to Heaven I had enough for thee!'' – If Fichte's *Wissenschaftslehre*[1] be ''to a certain extent, Applied Christianity,'' surely to a still greater extent, so is this. We have here not a Whole Duty of Man, yet a Half Duty, namely the Passive half: could we but do it, as we can demonstrate it!

'But indeed Conviction, were it never so excellent, is worthless till it convert itself into Conduct. Nay properly Conviction is not possible till then; inasmuch as all Speculation is by nature endless, formless, a vortex amid vortices: only, by a felt indubitable certainty of Experience, does it find any centre to revolve round, and so fashion itself into a system. Most true is it, as a wise man teaches us, that ''Doubt of any sort cannot be removed except by Action.'' On which ground too let him who gropes painfully in darkness or uncertain light, and prays vehemently that the dawn may ripen into day, lay this other precept well to heart, which to me was of invaluable service: ''*Do the Duty which lies nearest thee*,'' which thou knowest to be a Duty! Thy second Duty will already have become clearer.

'May we not say, however, that the hour of Spiritual Enfranchisement is even this: When your Ideal World, wherein the whole man has been dimly struggling and inexpressibly languishing to work, becomes revealed, and thrown open; and you discover, with amazement enough, like the Lothario in *Wilhelm Meister*, that your ''America is here or nowhere?'' The Situation that has not its Duty, its Ideal, was never yet occupied by man. Yes here, in this poor, miserable, hampered, despicable Actual, wherein thou even now standest, here or nowhere is thy Ideal: work it out therefrom; and working, believe, live, be free. Fool! The Ideal is in thyself, the Impediment too is in thyself: thy Condition is but the stuff thou art to shape that same Ideal out of: what matters whether such stuff be of this sort or of

1 *Wissenschaftslehre*: The Theory of Knowledge

that, so the Form thou give it be heroic, be poetic? O thou that pinest in the imprisonment of the Actual, and criest bitterly to the gods for a kingdom wherein to rule and create, know this of a truth: the thing thou seekest is already with thee, "here or nowhere," couldst thou only see!

'But it is with man's Soul as it was with Nature: the beginning of Creation is – Light. Till the eye have vision, the whole members are in bonds. Divine moment, when over the tempest-tost Soul, as once over the wild-weltering Chaos, it is spoken: Let there be Light! Ever to the greatest that has felt such moment, is it not miraculous and God-announcing; even, as under simpler figures, to the simplest and least? The mad primeval Discord is hushed; the rudely-jumbled conflicting elements bind themselves into separate Firmaments: deep silent rock-foundations are built beneath; and the skyey vault with its everlasting Luminaries above: instead of a dark wasteful Chaos, we have a blooming, fertile, Heaven-encompassed World.

'I too could now say to myself: Be no longer a Chaos, but a World, or even Worldkin. Produce! Produce! Were it but the pitifullest infinitesimal fraction of a Product, produce it in God's name! 'Tis the utmost thou hast in thee; out with it then. Up, up! Whatsoever thy hand findeth to do, do it with thy whole might. Work while it is called To-day, for the Night cometh wherein no man can work.'

CHAPTER 10

Pause

THUS have we, as closely and perhaps satisfactorily as, in such circumstances, might be, followed Teufelsdröckh through the various successive states and stages of Growth, Entanglement, Unbelief, and almost Reprobation, into a certain clearer state of what he himself seems to consider as Conversion. 'Blame not the word,' says he; 'rejoice rather that such a word, signifying such a thing, has come to light in our Modern Era, though hidden from the wisest Ancients. The Old World knew nothing of Conversion: instead of an *Ecce Homo*, they had only some *Choice of Hercules*. It was a new-attained progress in the Moral Development of man: hereby has the Highest come home to the bosoms of the most Limited; what to Plato was but a hallucination, and to Socrates a chimera, is now clear and certain to your Zinzendorfs, your Wesleys, and the poorest of their Pietists and Methodists.'

It is here then that the spiritual majority of Teufelsdröckh commences: we are henceforth to see him 'Work in Well-doing,' with the spirit and clear aims of a Man. He has discovered that the Ideal Workshop he so panted for, is even this same Actual ill-furnished Workshop he has so long been stumbling in. He can say to himself: 'Tools? Thou hast no Tools? Why, there is not a Man, or a Thing, now alive but has tools. The basest of created animalcules, the Spider itself, has a spinning-jenny, and warping-mill, and power-loom, within its head; the stupidest of Oysters has a Papin's-Digester, with stone-and-lime house to hold it in: every being that can live can do something; this let him *do*. – Tools? Hast thou not a Brain, furnished, furnishable with some glimmerings of Light; and three fingers to hold a Pen withal? Never since Aaron's Rod went out of practice, or even before it, was there such a wonder-working Tool: greater than all recorded miracles have been performed by Pens. For strangely in this so solid-seeming World, which nevertheless is in continual restless flux, it is appointed that *Sound*, to appearance the most fleeting, should be the most continuing of all things. The WORD is well said to be omnipotent in this world; man, thereby divine, can create as by a *Fiat*. Awake, arise! Speak forth what is in thee; what God has given thee, what the Devil shall not take away. Higher task than that of Priesthood was allotted to no man: wert thou but the meanest in that sacred Hierarchy, is it not honour enough therein to spend and be spent?

'By this Art, which whoso will may sacrilegiously degrade into a handicraft,' adds Teufelsdröckh, 'have I thenceforth abidden. Writings of mine, not indeed known as mine (for what am *I*?), have fallen, perhaps not altogether void, into the mighty seedfield of Opinion; fruits of my unseen sowing gratifyingly meet me here and there. I thank the Heavens that I have now found my Calling; wherein, with or without perceptible result, I am minded diligently to persevere.

'Nay how knowest thou,' cries he, 'but this and the other pregnant Device, now grown to be a world-renowned far-working Institution; like a grain of right mustard-seed once cast into the right soil, and now stretching out strong boughs to the four winds, for the birds of the air to lodge in, – may have been properly my doing? Some one's doing it without doubt was; from some Idea in some single Head it did first of all take beginning: why not from some Idea in mine?' Does Teufelsdröckh here glance at that 'SOCIETY FOR THE CONSERVATION OF PROPERTY (*Eigenthums-conservirende Gesellschaft*),' of which so many ambiguous notices glide spectre-like through these inexpressible Paperbags? 'An Institution,' hints he, 'not unsuitable to the wants of the time; as indeed such sudden extension proves: for already can the Society number, among its office-bearers or corresponding members, the highest Names, if not the highest Persons, in Germany, England, France; and contributions, both of money and of meditation, pour in from all quarters; to, if possible, enlist the remaining Integrity of the world, and, defensively and with fore-thought, marshal it round this Palladium.' Does Teufels-dröckh mean, then, to give himself out as the originator of that so notable *Eigenthums-conservirende* ('Owndom-conserving') *Gesellschaft*; and, if so, what, in the Devil's name, is it? He again hints: 'At a time when the divine Commandment, *Thou shalt not steal*, wherein truly, if well understood, is comprised the whole Hebrew Decalogue, with Solon's and Lycurgus's Constitutions, Justinian's Pandects, the Code Napoléon, and all Codes, Catechisms, Divinities, Moralities whatsoever, that man has hitherto devised (and enforced with Altar-fire and Gallows-ropes) for his social guidance: at a time, I say, when this divine Commandment has all but faded away from the general remembrance; and, with little disguise, a new opposite Commandment, *Thou shalt steal*, is every where promul-gated – it perhaps behoved, in this universal dotage and deliration, the sound portion of mankind to bestir them-selves and rally. When the widest and wildest violations of that divine right of Property, the only divine right now extant or conceivable, are sanctioned and recommended by a vicious Press, and the world has lived to hear it asserted that *we have no Property in our very Bodies, but only an accidental Possession, and Liferent,* what is the issue to be looked for? Hangmen and Catchpoles may, by their noose-gins and baited fall-traps, keep down the smaller sort of vermin: but what, except perhaps some such Universal Association, can protect us against whole meat-devouring and man-devouring hosts of Boa Constrictors? If, therefore, the more sequestered Thinker have wondered, in his privacy, from what hand that perhaps not ill-written *Program* in the Public Journals, with its high *Prize-Questions* and so liberal *Prizes,* could have proceeded, – let him now cease such wonder; and, with undivided faculty, betake himself to the *Concurrenz* (Competition).'

We ask: Has this same 'perhaps not ill-written *Program,*' or any other authentic Transaction of that Property-conserving Society, fallen under the eye of the British Reader, in any Journal, foreign or domestic? If so, what are those *Prize-Questions*; what are the terms of Competition, and when, and where? No printed Newspaper leaf, no farther light of any sort, to be met with in these Paperbags! Or is the whole business one other of those whimsicalities, and perverse inexplicabilities, whereby Herr Teufels-dröckh, meaning much or nothing, is pleased so often to play fast and loose with us?

Here, indeed, at length, must the Editor give utterance to a painful suspicion which, through late Chapters, has begun to haunt him; paralysing any little enthusiasm, that might still have rendered his thorny Biographical task a labour of love. It is a suspicion grounded perhaps on trifles, yet confirmed almost into certainty by the more and more discernible humouristico-satirical tendency of Teufels-dröckh, in whom underground humours, and intricate sardonic rogueries, wheel within wheel, defy all reckoning: a suspicion, in one word, that these Autobiographical

Documents are partly a Mystification! What if many a so-called Fact were little better than a Fiction; if here we had no direct Camera-obscura Picture of the Professor's History; but only some more or less fantastic Adumbration, symbolically, perhaps significantly enough, shadowing forth the same! Our theory begins to be that, in receiving as literally authentic what was but hieroglyphically so, Hofrath Heuschrecke, whom in that case we scruple not to name Hofrath Nose-of-Wax, was made a fool of, and set adrift to make fools of others. Could it be expected, indeed, that a man so known for impenetrable reticence as Teufelsdröckh, would all at once frankly unlock his private citadel to an English Editor and a German Hofrath; and not rather deceptively *in*lock both Editor and Hofrath, in the labyrinthic tortuosities and covered ways of said citadel (having enticed them thither), to see, in his half-devilish way, how the fools would look?

Of one fool, however, the Herr Professor will perhaps find himself short. On a small slip, formerly thrown aside as blank, the ink being all but invisible, we lately notice, and with effort decipher, the following: 'What are your historical Facts; still more your biographical? Wilt thou know a Man, above all, a Mankind, by stringing together beadrolls of what thou namest Facts? The Man is the spirit he worked in; not what he did, but what he became. Facts are engraved Hierograms, for which the fewest have the key. And then how your Blockhead (*Dummkopf*) studies not their Meaning; but simply whether they are well or ill cut, what he calls Moral or Immoral! Still worse is it with your Bungler (*Pfuscher*): such I have seen reading some Rousseau, with pretences of interpretation; and mistaking the ill-cut Serpent-of-Eternity for a common poisonous Reptile.' Was the Professor apprehensive lest an Editor, selected as the present boasts himself, might mistake the Teufelsdröckh Serpent-of-Eternity in like manner? For which reason it was to be altered, not without underhand satire, into a plainer

Symbol? Or is this merely one of his half-sophisms, half-truisms, which if he can but set on the back of a Figure, he cares not whither it gallop? We say not with certainty; and indeed, so strange is the Professor, can never say. If our Suspicion be wholly unfounded, let his own questionable ways, not our necessary circumspectness, bear the blame.

But be this as it will, the somewhat exasperated and indeed exhausted Editor determines here to shut these Paper-bags, for the present. Let it suffice that we know of Teufelsdröckh, so far, if 'not what he did, yet what he became:' the rather, as his character has now taken its ultimate bent, and no new revolution, of importance, is to be looked for. The imprisoned Chrysalis is now a winged Psyche; and such, wheresoever be its flight, it will continue. To trace by what complex gyrations (flights or involuntary waftings) through the mere external Life-element, Teufels-dröckh reaches his University Professorship, and the Psyche clothes herself in civic Titles, without altering her now fixed nature, – would be comparatively an unproductive task; were we even unsuspicious of its being, for us at least, a false and impossible one. His outward Biography, there-fore, which, at the Blumine Lover's-Leap, we saw churned utterly into spray-vapour, may hover in that condition, for aught that concerns us here. Enough that by survey of certain 'pools and plashes,' we have ascertained its general direction: do we not already know that, by one way and other, it *has* long since rained down again into a stream; and even now, at Weissnichtwo, flows deep and still, fraught with the *Philosophy of Clothes*, and visible to whoso will cast eye thereon? Over much invaluable matter that lies scattered, like jewels among quarry-rubbish, in those Paper-catacombs, we may have occasion to glance back, and somewhat will demand insertion at the right place: meanwhile be our toilsome diggings therein suspended.

If now, before reopening the great *Clothes-Volume*, we ask what our degree of progress, during these Ten Chapters, has been, towards right understanding of the *Clothes-Philosophy*, let not our discouragement become total. To speak in that old figure of the Hell-gate Bridge over Chaos, a few flying pontoons have perhaps been added, though as yet they drift straggling on the Flood; how far they will reach, when once the chains are straightened and fastened, can, at present, only be matter of conjecture.

So much we already calculate. Through many a little loophole, we have had glimpses into the internal world of Teufelsdröckh: his strange mystic, almost magic Diagram of the Universe, and how it was gradually drawn, is not henceforth altogether dark to us. Those mysterious ideas on TIME, which merit consideration, and are not wholly unintelligible with such, may by and by prove significant. Still more may his somewhat peculiar view of Nature; the decisive Oneness he ascribes to Nature. How all Nature and Life are but one *Garment*, a 'Living Garment,' woven and ever a-weaving in the 'Loom of Time:' is not here, indeed, the outline of a whole *Clothes-Philosophy*; at least the arena it is to work in? Remark too that the Character of the man, nowise without meaning in such a matter, becomes less enigmatic: amid so much tumultuous obscurity, almost like diluted madness, do not a certain indomitable Defiance and yet a boundless Reverence seem to loom forth, as the two mountain summits, on whose rock-strata all the rest were based and built?

Nay farther, may we not say that Teufelsdröckh's Biography, allowing it even, as suspected, only a hieroglyphical truth, exhibits a man, as it were pre-appointed for Clothes-Philosophy? To look through the Shows of things into Things themselves he is led and compelled. The 'Passivity' given him by birth is fostered by all turns of his fortune. Everywhere cast out, like oil out of water, from mingling in any Employment, in any public Communion, he has no portion but Solitude, and a life of Meditation. The whole energy of his existence is directed, through long years, on one task: that of enduring pain, if he cannot cure it. Thus everywhere do the Shows of things oppress him, withstand him, threaten him with fearfullest destruction: only by victoriously penetrating into Things themselves can he find peace and a stronghold. But is not this same looking through the Shows or Vestures into the Things even the first preliminary to a *Philosophy of Clothes*? Do we not, in all this, discern some beckonings towards the true higher purport of such a Philosophy; and what shape it must assume with such a man, in such an era?

Perhaps in entering on Book Third, the courteous Reader is not utterly without guess whither he is bound: nor, let us hope, for all the fantastic Dream-Grottoes through which, as is our lot with Teufelsdröckh, he must wander, will there be wanting between whiles some twinkling of a steady Polar Star.

Book Three

ADAM AND EVE

CHAPTER I

Incident in Modern History

As a wonder-loving and wonder-seeking man, Teufelsdröckh, from an early part of this Clothes-Volume, has more and more exhibited himself. Striking it was, amid all his perverse cloudiness, with what force of vision and of heart he pierced into the mystery of the World; recognising in the highest sensible phenomena, so far as Sense went, only fresh or faded Raiment; yet ever, under this, a celestial Essence thereby rendered visible: and while, on the one hand, he trod the old rags of Matter, with their tinsels, into the mire, he on the other every where exalted Spirit above all earthly principalities and powers, and worshipped it, though under the meanest shapes, with a true Platonic Mysticism. What the man ultimately purposed by this casting his Greek-fire into the general Wardrobe of the

Universe; what such more or less complete rending and burning of Garments throughout the whole compass of Civilised Life and Speculation, should lead to; the rather as he was no Adamite, in any sense, and could not, like Rousseau, recommend either bodily or intellectual Nudity, and a return to the savage state: all this our readers are now bent to discover; this is, in fact, properly the gist and purport of Professor Teufelsdröckh's Philosophy of Clothes.

Be it remembered, however, that such purport is here not so much evolved as detected to lie ready for evolving. We are to guide our British Friends into the new Gold-country, and shew them the mines; nowise to dig out and exhaust its wealth, which indeed remains for all time inexhaustible. Once there, let each dig for his own behoof, and enrich himself.

Neither, in so capricious inexpressible a Work as this of the Professor's, can our course now more than formerly be straightforward, step by step, but at best leap by leap. Significant Indications stand out here and there; which for the critical eye, that looks both widely and narrowly, shape themselves into some ground-scheme of a Whole: to select these with judgement, so that a leap from one to the other be possible, and (in our old figure) by chaining them together, a passable Bridge be effected: this as heretofore continues our only method. Among such light-spots, the following, floating in much wild matter about *Perfectibility*, has seemed worth clutching at:

'Perhaps the most remarkable incident in Modern History,' says Teufelsdröckh, 'is not the Diet of Worms, still less the Battle of Austerlitz, Waterloo, Peterloo, or any other Battle; but an incident passed carelessly over by most Historians, and treated with some degree of ridicule by others; namely, George Fox's making to himself a Suit of Leather. This man, the first of the Quakers, and by trade a Shoemaker, was one of those, to whom, under ruder or purer form, the Divine Idea of the Universe is pleased to manifest itself; and, across all the hulls of Ignorance and earthly Degradation, shine through, in unspeakable Awfulness, unspeakable Beauty, on their souls: who therefore are rightly accounted Prophets, God-possessed; or even Gods, as in some periods it has chanced. Sitting in his stall; working on tanned hides, amid pincers, paste-horns, rosin, swine-bristles, and a nameless flood of rubbish, this youth had nevertheless a Living Spirit belonging to him; also an antique Inspired Volume, through which, as through a window, it could look upwards, and discern its celestial Home. The task of a daily pair of shoes, coupled even with some prospect of victuals, and an honourable Mastership in Cordwainery, and perhaps the post of Thirdborough in his Hundred, as the crown of long faithful sewing, – was nowise satisfaction enough to such a mind: but ever amid the boring and hammering, came tones from that far country, came Splendours and Terrors; for this poor Cordwainer, as we said, was a Man; and the Temple of Immensity, wherein as Man he had been sent to minister, was full of holy mystery to him.

'The Clergy of the neighbourhood, the ordained Watchers and Interpreters of that same holy mystery, listened with unaffected tedium to his consultations, and advised him, as the solution of such doubts, to "drink beer, and dance with the girls." Blind leaders of the blind! For what end were their tithes levied and eaten; for what were their shovel-hats scooped out, and their surplices and cassock-aprons girt on; and such a church-repairing, and chaffering, and organing, and other racketting, held over that spot of God's Earth, – if Man were but a Patent Digester, and the Belly with its adjuncts the grand Reality? Fox turned from them, with tears and a sacred scorn, back to his Leather-parings and his Bible. Mountains of encumbrance, higher than Ætna, had been heaped over that Spirit: but it was a Spirit, and would not lie buried there. Through long days and nights of silent agony, it struggled and wrestled, with a man's force, to be free: how its prison-mountains heaved and swayed tumultuously, as the giant spirit shook them to this hand and that, and emerged into the light of Heaven! That Leicester shoe-shop, had men known it, was a holier place than any Vatican or Loretto-shrine. – "So bandaged, and hampered, and hemmed in," groaned he, "with thousand requisitions, obligations, straps, tatters, and tagrags, I can neither see nor move: not my own am I, but the World's; and Time flies fast, and Heaven is high, and Hell is deep: Man! bethink thee, if thou hast power of Thought! Why not; what binds me here? Want! Want! – Ha, of what? Will all the shoe-wages under the Moon ferry me across into that far Land of Light? Only Meditation can, and devout Prayer to God. I will to the woods: the hollow of a tree will lodge me, wild berries feed me; and for Clothes, cannot I stitch myself one perennial Suit of Leather!"

'Historical Oil-painting,' continues Teufelsdröckh, 'is one of the Arts I never practised; therefore shall I not decide whether this subject were easy of execution on the canvass. Yet often has it seemed to me as if such first outflashing of man's Freewill, to lighten, more and more into Day, the Chaotic Night that threatened to engulph him in its hindrances and its horrors, were properly the only grandeur there is in history. Let some living Angelo or Rosa, with seeing eye and understanding heart, picture George Fox on that morning, when he spreads out his cutting-board for the last time, and cuts cowhides by unwonted patterns, and stitches them together into one continuous all-including Case, the farewell service of his awl! Stitch away, thou noble Fox: every prick of that little instrument is pricking into the heart of Slavery, and World-worship, and the Mammon-god. Thy elbows jerk, as in strong swimmer-strokes, and every stroke is bearing thee across the Prison-ditch, within which Vanity holds her Workhouse and Rag-fair, into lands of true Liberty; were the work done, there is in broad Europe one Free Man, and thou art he!

'Thus from the lowest depth there is a path to the loftiest height: and for the Poor also a Gospel has been published. Surely, if, as D'Alembert asserts, my illustrious namesake, Diogenes, was the greatest man of Antiquity, only that he wanted Decency, then by stronger reason is George Fox the greatest of the Moderns; and greater than Diogenes himself: for he too stands on the adamantine basis of his Manhood, casting aside all props and shoars; yet not, in half-savage Pride, undervaluing the Earth; valuing it rather, as a place to yield him warmth and food, he looks Heaven-ward from his Earth, and dwells in an element of Mercy and Worship, with a still Strength, such as the Cynic's Tub did nowise witness. Great, truly, was that Tub; a temple from which man's dignity and divinity was scornfully preached abroad: but greater is the Leather Hull, for the same sermon was preached there, and not in Scorn but in Love.'

George Fox's 'perennial suit,' with all that it held, has been worn quite into ashes for nigh two centuries; why, in a discussion on the *Perfectibility of Society*, reproduce it now? Not out of blind sectarian partisanship: Teufelsdröckh himself is no Quaker; with all his pacific tendencies, did we not see him, in that scene at the North Cape, with the Archangel Smuggler, exhibit fire-arms?

For us, aware of his deep Sansculottism, there is more meant in this passage than meets the ear. At the same time, who can avoid smiling at the earnestness and Bœotian simplicity (if indeed there be not an underhand satire in it), with which that 'Incident' is here brought forward; and, in the Professor's ambiguous way, as clearly perhaps as he durst in Weissnichtwo, recommended to imitation! Does Teufelsdröckh anticipate that, in this age of refinement, any considerable class of the community, by way of testifying against the 'Mammon-god,' and escaping from what he calls 'Vanity's Workhouse and Ragfair,' where doubtless some of them are toiled and whipped and hoodwinked sufficiently, – will sheathe themselves in close-fitting cases of Leather? The idea is ridiculous in the extreme. Will Majesty lay aside its robes of state, and Beauty its frills, and train-gowns, for a second-skin of tanned hide? By which change Huddersfield and Manchester, and Coventry and Paisley, and the Fancy-Bazaar were reduced to hungry solitudes; and only Day and Martin could profit. For neither would Teufelsdröckh's mad daydream, here as we presume covertly intended, of levelling Society (*levelling* it indeed with a vengeance, into one huge drowned marsh!), and so attaining the political effects of Nudity without its frigorific or other consequences, – be thereby realized. Would not the rich man purchase a waterproof suit of Russia Leather; and the highborn Belle step forth in red or azure morocco, lined with shamoy: the black cowhide being left to the Drudges and Gibeonites of the world; and so all the old Distinctions re-established?

Or has the Professor his own deeper intention; and laughs in his sleeve at our strictures and glosses, which indeed are but a part thereof?

Church Clothes

NOT less questionable is his Chapter on *Church Clothes*, which has the farther distinction of being the shortest in the Volume. We here translate it entire:

'By Church Clothes, it need not be premised, that I mean infinitely more than Cassocks and Surplices; and do not at all mean the mere haberdasher Sunday Clothes that men go to Church in. Far from it! Church Clothes are, in our vocabulary, the Forms, the *Vestures*, under which men have at various periods embodied and represented for themselves the Religious Principle; that is to say, invested the Divine Idea of the World with a sensible and practically active Body, so that it might dwell among them as a living and life-giving WORD.

'These are unspeakably the most important of all the vestures and garnitures of Human Existence. They are first spun and woven, I may say, by that wonder of wonders, SOCIETY; for it is still only when "two or three are gathered together" that Religion, spiritually existent, and indeed indestructible however latent, in each, first outwardly manifests itself (as with "cloven tongues of fire"), and seeks to be embodied in a visible Communion and Church Militant. Mystical, more than magical, is that Communing of Soul with Soul, both looking heavenward: here properly Soul first speaks with Soul; for only in looking heavenward, take it in what sense you may, not in looking earthward, does what we can call Union, mutual Love, Society, begin to be possible. How true is that of Novalis: "It is certain, my Belief gains quite *infinitely* the moment I can convince another mind thereof!" Gaze thou in the face of thy Brother, in those eyes where plays the lambent fire of Kindness, or in those where rages the lurid conflagration of Anger; feel how thy own so quiet Soul is straightway involuntarily kindled with the like, and ye blaze and re-verberate on each other, till it is all one limitless confluent flame (of embracing Love, or of deadly-grappling Hate); and then say what miraculous virtue goes out of man into man. But if so, through all the thick-plied hulls of our Earthly Life; how much more when it is of the Divine Life we speak, and inmost ME is, as it were, brought into contact with inmost ME!

'Thus was it that I said, the Church Clothes are first spun and woven by Society; outward Religion originates by Society, Society becomes possible by Religion. Nay, per-haps every conceivable Society, past and present, may well be figured as properly and wholly a Church, in one or other of these three predicaments: an audibly preaching and prophesying Church, which is the best; second, a Church that struggles to preach and prophesy, but cannot as yet, till its Pentecost come; and third and worst, a Church gone dumb with old age, or which only mumbles delirium prior to dissolution. Whoso fancies that by Church is here meant Chapterhouses and Cathedrals, or by preaching and prophesying, mere speech and chaunting, let him,' says the oracular Professor, 'read on light of heart (*getrosten Muthes*).

'But with regard to your Church proper, and the Church Clothes specially recognised as Church Clothes, I remark, fearlessly enough, that without such Vestures and sacred Tissues Society has not existed, and will not exist. For if Government is, so to speak, the outward SKIN of the Body Politic, holding the whole together and protecting it; and all your Craft-Guilds, and Associations for Industry, of hand or of head, are the Fleshly Clothes, the muscular and osseous Tissues (lying *under* such SKIN), whereby Society stands and works; – then is Religion the inmost Pericardial and Nervous Tissue, which ministers Life and warm Circulation to the whole. Without which Pericardial Tissue the Bones and Muscles (of Industry) were inert, or animated only by a Galvanic vitality; the SKIN would become a shrivelled pelt, or fast-rotting raw-hide; and Society itself a dead carcass, – deserving to be buried. Men were no longer Social, but Gregarious; which latter state also could not continue, but must gradually issue in universal selfish discord, hatred, savage isolation, and dispersion; – whereby, as we might continue to say, the very dust and dead body of Society would have evaporated and become abolished. Such, and so all-important, all-sustaining, are the Church Clothes, to civilised or even to rational man.

'Meanwhile, in our era of the World, those same Church Clothes have gone sorrowfully out at elbows: nay, far worse, many of them have become mere hollow Shapes, or Masks, under which no living Figure or Spirit any longer dwells; but only spiders and unclean beetles, in horrid accumulation, drive their trade; and the Mask still glares on you with its glass-eyes, in ghastly affectation of Life, – some generation and half after Religion has quite withdrawn from it, and in unnoticed nooks is weaving for herself new Vestures, wherewith to reappear, and bless us, or our sons or grandsons. As a Priest, or Interpreter of the Holy, is the noblest and highest of all men, so is a Shampriest (*Scheinpriester*) the falsest and basest: neither is it doubtful that his Canonicals, were they Popes' Tiaras, will one day be torn from him, to make bandages for the wounds of mankind; or even to burn into tinder, for general scientific or culinary purposes.

'All which, as out of place here, falls to be handled in my Second Volume, *On the Palingenesia, or Newbirth of Society*; which volume, as treating practically of the Wear, Destruction, and Re-texture of Spiritual Tissues, or Garments, forms, properly speaking, the Transcendental or ultimate Portion of this my Work *on Clothes*, and is already in a state of forwardness.'

And herewith, no farther exposition, note, or commentary being added, does Teufelsdröckh, and must his Editor now, terminate the Singular Chapter on Church Clothes!

Symbols

PROBABLY it will elucidate the drift of these foregoing obscure utterances, if we here insert somewhat of our Professor's speculations on *Symbols*. To state his whole doctrine, indeed, were beyond our compass: nowhere is he more mysterious, impalpable, than in this of 'Fantasy being the organ of the Godlike;' and how 'Man thereby, though based, to all seeming, on the small Visible, does nevertheless extend down into the infinite deeps of the Invisible, of which Invisible, indeed, his Life is properly the bodying forth.' Let us, omitting these high transcendental aspects of the matter, study to glean (whether from the Paperbags or the Printed Volume) what little seems logical and practical, and cunningly arrange it into such degree of coherence as it will assume. By way of proem, take the following not injudicious remarks:

'The benignant efficacies of Concealment,' cries our Professor, 'who shall speak or sing? SILENCE and SECRECY! Altars might still be raised to them (were this an altar-building time) for universal worship. Silence is the element in which great things fashion themselves together; that at length they may emerge, full-formed and majestic, into the daylight of Life, which they are thenceforth to rule. Not William the Silent only, but all the considerable men I have known, and the most undiplomatic and unstrategic of these, forbore to babble of what they were creating and projecting. Nay, in thy own mean perplexities, do thou thyself but *hold thy tongue for one day*: on the morrow, how much clearer are thy purposes, and duties; what wreck and rubbish have those mute workmen within thee swept away, when intrusive noises were shut out! Speech is too often not, as the Frenchman defined it, the art of concealing Thought; but of quite stifling and suspending Thought, so that there is none to conceal. Speech too is great, but not the greatest. As the Swiss Inscription says: *Sprechen ist silbern, Schweigen ist golden* (Speech is silvern, Silence is golden); or as I might rather express it: Speech is of Time, Silence is of Eternity.

'Bees will not work except in darkness; Thought will not work except in Silence: neither will Virtue work except in Secrecy. Let not thy right hand know what thy left hand doeth! Neither shalt thou prate even to thy own heart of "those secrets known to all." Is not Shame the soil of all Virtue, of all good manners, and good morals? Like other plants, Virtue will not grow unless its root be hidden, buried from the eye of the sun. Let the Sun shine on it, nay, do but look at it privily thyself, the root withers, and no flower will glad thee. O my Friends, when we view the fair clustering flowers that overwreathe, for example, the Marriage-bower, and encircle man's life with the fragrance and hues of Heaven, what hand will not smite the foul plunderer that grubs them up by the roots, and, with grinning, grunting satisfaction, shews us the dung they flourish in! Men speak much of the Printing Press with its Newspapers: *du Himmel!* what are these to Clothes and the Tailor's Goose?

'Of kin to the so incalculable influences of Concealment,

and connected with still greater things, is the wondrous agency of *Symbols*. In a Symbol there is concealment and yet revelation: here, therefore, by Silence and by Speech acting together, comes a doubled significance. And if both the Speech be itself high, and the Silence fit and noble, how expressive will their union be! Thus in many a painted Device, or simple Seal-emblem, the commonest Truth stands out to us proclaimed with quite new emphasis.

'For it is here that Fantasy with her mystic wonderland plays into the small prose domain of Sense, and becomes incorporated therewith. In the Symbol proper, what we can call a Symbol, there is ever, more or less distinctly and directly, some embodyment and revelation of the Infinite; the Infinite is made to blend itself with the Finite, to stand visible, and as it were attainable, there. By Symbols, accordingly, is man guided and commanded, made happy, made wretched. He every where finds himself encompassed with Symbols, recognised as such or not recognised: the Universe is but one vast Symbol of God; nay, if thou wilt have it, what is man himself but a Symbol of God, is not all that he does symbolical; a revelation to Sense of the mystic god-given Force that is in him; a "Gospel of Freedom," which he, the "Messias of Nature," preaches, as he can, by act and word? Not a Hut he builds but is the visible embodyment of a Thought; but bears visible record of invisible things; but is, in the transcendental sense, symbolical as well as real.'

'Man,' says the Professor elsewhere, in quite antipodal contrast with these high-soaring delineations, which we have here cut short on the verge of the inane, 'man is by birth somewhat of an owl. Perhaps too of all the owleries that ever possessed him, the most owlish, if we consider it, is that of your actually existing Motive-Millwrights. Fantastic tricks enough has man played in his time; has fancied himself to be most things, down even to an animated heap of Glass: but to fancy himself a dead Iron-Balance for weighing Pains and Pleasures on, was reserved for this

his latter era. There stands he, his Universe one huge
Manger, filled with hay and thistles to be weighed against
each other; and looks long-eared enough. Alas, poor devil!
spectres are appointed to haunt him: one age, he is
hagridden, bewitched; the next, priestridden, befooled;
in all ages, bedevilled. And now the Genius of Mechanism
smothers him worse than any Nightmare did; till the Soul is
nigh choked out of him, and only a kind of Digestive,
Mechanic life remains. In Earth and in Heaven he can see
nothing but Mechanism; has fear for nothing else, hope in
nothing else: the world would indeed grind him to pieces;
but cannot he fathom the Doctrine of Motives, and cunningly compute them to grind the other way?

'Were he not, as has been said, purblinded by enchantment, you had but to bid him open his eyes and look. In
which country, in which time, was it hitherto that man's
history, or the history of any man, went on by calculated or

calculable "Motives?" What make ye of your Christianities, and Chivalries, and Reformations, and Marseillese Hymns, and Reigns of Terror? Nay, has not perhaps the Motive-grinder himself been *in Love*? Did he never stand so much as a contested Election? Leave him to Time, and the medicating virtue of Nature.'

'Yes, Friends,' elsewhere observes the Professor, 'not our Logical, Mensurative faculty, but our Imaginative one is King over us; I might say, Priest and Prophet to lead us heavenward; or Magician and Wizard to lead us hellward. Nay, even for the basest Sensualist, what is Sense but the implement of Fantasy; the vessel it drinks out of? Ever in the dullest existence, there is a sheen either of Inspiration or of Madness (thou partly hast it in thy choice, which of the two) that gleams in from the circumambient Eternity, and colours with its own hues our little islet of Time. The Understanding is indeed thy window, too clear thou canst not make it; but Fantasy is thy eye, with its colour-giving retina, healthy or diseased. Have not I myself known five hundred living soldiers sabred into crows' meat, for a piece of glazed cotton, which they called their Flag; which, had you sold it at any market-cross, would not have brought above three groschen? Did not the whole Hungarian Nation rise, like some tumultuous moon-stirred Atlantic, when Kaiser Joseph pocketed their Iron Crown; an implement, as was sagaciously observed, in size and commercial value, little differing from a horse-shoe? It is in and through *Symbols* that man, consciously or unconsciously, lives, works, and has his being: those ages, moreover, are accounted the noblest which can the best recognise symbolical worth, and prize it the highest. For is not a Symbol ever, to him who has eyes for it, some dimmer or clearer revelation of the Godlike?

'Of Symbols, however, I remark farther, that they have both an extrinsic and intrinsic value; oftenest the former only. What, for instance, was in that clouted Shoe which

the Peasants bore aloft with them as ensign in their
Bauernkrieg (Peasants' War)? Or in the Wallet-and-staff
round which the Netherland *Gueux*, glorying in that nick-
name of Beggars, heroically rallied and prevailed, though
against King Philip himself? Intrinsic significance these had
none: only extrinsic; as the accidental Standards of multi-
tudes more or less sacredly uniting together; in which
union itself, as above noted, there is ever something mystical and borrowing of the Godlike. Under a like category
too, stand, or stood, the stupidest heraldic coats-of-arms;
military Banners every where; and generally all national or
other sectarian Costumes and Customs: they have no
intrinsic, necessary divineness, or even worth; but have
acquired an extrinsic one. Nevertheless through all these
there glimmers something of a Divine Idea; as through
military Banners themselves, the Divine Idea of Duty, of
heroic Daring; in some instances of Freedom, of Right.
Nay, the highest ensign that men ever met and embraced
under, the Cross itself, had no meaning save an accidental
extrinsic one.

'Another matter it is, however, when your Symbol has
intrinsic meaning, and is of itself *fit* that men should unite
round it. Let but the Godlike manifest itself to Sense; let
but Eternity look, more or less visibly, through the Time-
Figure (*Zeitbild*)! Then is it fit that men unite there; and
worship together before such Symbol; and so from day to
day, and from age to age, superadd to it new divineness.

'Of this latter sort are all true Works of Art: in them (if
thou know a Work of Art from a Daub of Artifice) wilt thou
discern Eternity looking through Time; the Godlike rendered visible. Here too may an extrinsic value gradually
superadd itself: thus certain *Iliads*, and the like, have, in
three thousand years, attained quite new significance. But
nobler than all in this kind are the Lives of heroic, god-
inspired Men; for what other Work of Art is so divine? In
Death too, in the Death of the Just, as the last perfection of

a Work of Art, may we not discern symbolic meaning? In that divinely transfigured Sleep, as of Victory, resting over the beloved face which now knows thee no more, read (if thou canst for tears) the confluence of Time with Eternity, and some gleam of the latter peering through.

'Highest of all Symbols are those wherein the Artist or Poet has risen into Prophet, and all men can recognise a present God, and worship the same: I mean religious Symbols. Various enough have been such religious Symbols, what we call *Religions*; as men stood in this stage of culture or the other, and could worse or better body forth the Godlike: some Symbols with a transient intrinsic worth; many with only an extrinsic. If thou ask to what height man has carried it in this matter, look on our divinest Symbol: on Jesus of Nazareth, and his Life, and his Biography, and what followed therefrom. Higher has the human Thought not yet reached: this is Christianity and Christendom; a Symbol of quite perennial, infinite character; whose significance will ever demand to be anew inquired into, and anew made manifest.

'But, on the whole, as Time adds much to the sacredness of Symbols, so likewise in his progress he at length defaces, or even desecrates them; and Symbols, like all terrestrial Garments, wax old. Homer's Epos has not ceased to be true; yet it is no longer *our* Epos, but shines in the distance, if clearer and clearer, yet also smaller and smaller, like a receding Star. It needs a scientific telescope, it needs to be reinterpreted and artificially brought near us, before we can so much as know that it *was* a Sun. So likewise a day comes when the Runic Thor, with his Eddas, must withdraw into dimness; and many an African Mumbo-Jumbo, and Indian Wau-Wau be utterly abolished. For all things, even Celestial Luminaries, much more atmospheric meteors, have their rise, their culmination, their decline.

'Small is this which thou tellest me that the Royal Sceptre is but a piece of gilt wood; that the Pyx has become a most foolish box, and truly, as Ancient Pistol thought, "of little price." A right Conjuror might I name thee, couldst thou conjure back into these wooden tools the divine virtue they once held.

'Of this thing however be certain: wouldst thou plant for Eternity, then plant into the deep infinite faculties of man, his Fantasy and Heart; wouldst thou plant for Year and Day, then plant into his shallow superficial faculties, his Self-love and Arithmetical Understanding, what will grow there. A Hierarch, therefore, and Pontiff of the World will we call him, the Poet and inspired Maker; who, Prometheus-like, can shape new Symbols, and bring new Fire from Heaven to fix it there. Such too will not always be wanting; neither perhaps now are. Meanwhile, as the average of matters goes, we account him Legislator and wise who can so much as tell when a Symbol has grown old, and gently remove it.

'When, as the last English† Coronation was preparing,' concludes this wonderful Professor, 'I read in their Newspapers that the "Champion of England," he who must offer battle to the Universe for his new King, had brought it so far that he could now "mount his horse with little assistance," I said to myself: Here also have we a Symbol well nigh superannuated. Alas, move whithersoever you may, are not the tatters and rags of superannuated worn-out Symbols (in this Ragfair of a World) dropping off every where, to hoodwink, to halter, to tether you; nay, if you shake them not aside, threatening to accumulate, and perhaps produce suffocation!'

† *Now* last but one – ED.

CHAPTER 4

Helotage

AT this point we determine on adverting shortly, or rather reverting, to a certain Tract of Hofrath Heuschrecke's, entitled *Institute for the Repression of Population;* which lies, dishonourably enough (with torn leaves, and a perceptible smell of aloetic drugs), stuffed into the Bag *Pisces*. Not indeed for sake of the Tract itself, which we admire little; but of the marginal Notes, evidently in Teufelsdröckh's hand, which rather copiously fringe it. A few of these may be in their right place here.

Into the Hofrath's *Institute*, with its extraordinary schemes, and machinery of Corresponding Boards and the like, we shall not so much as glance. Enough for us to understand that Heuschrecke is a disciple of Malthus; and so zealous for the doctrine, that his zeal almost literally eats him up. A deadly fear of Population possesses the Hofrath; something like a fixed-idea; undoubtedly akin to the more diluted forms of Madness. Nowhere, in that quarter of his intellectual world, is there light; nothing but a grim shadow of Hunger; open mouths opening wider

and wider; a world to terminate by the frightfullest consummation: by its too dense inhabitants, famished into
delirium, universally eating one another. To make air for
himself in which strangulation, choking enough to a ben-
evolent heart, the Hofrath founds, or proposes to found,
this *Institute* of his, as the best he can do. It is only with our
Professor's comments thereon that we concern ourselves.

First, then, remark that Teufelsdröckh, as a speculative
Radical, has his own notions about human dignity; that the
Zähdarm palaces and courtesies have not made him forgetful
of the Futteral cottages. On the blank cover of Heuschrecke's
Tract, we find the following, indistinctly engrossed:

'Two men I honour, and no third. First, the toilworn
Craftsman that with earth-made Implement laboriously
conquers the Earth, and makes her man's. Venerable to
me is the hard Hand; crooked, coarse; wherein notwithstanding lies a cunning virtue, indefeasibly royal, as of the
Sceptre of this Planet. Venerable too is the rugged face, all
weather-tanned, besoiled, with its rude intelligence; for it is
the face of a Man living manlike. Oh, but the more venerable
for thy rudeness, and even because we must pity as well as
love thee! Hardly-entreated Brother! For us was thy back so
bent, for us were thy straight limbs and fingers so deformed:
thou wert our Conscript, on whom the lot fell, and fighting
our battles wert so marred. For in thee too lay a god-created
Form, but it was not to be unfolded; encrusted must it stand
with the thick adhesions and defacements of Labour; and thy
body like thy soul was not to know freedom. Yet toil on, toil
on: *thou* art in thy duty, be out of it who may; thou toilest for
the altogether indispensable, for daily bread.

'A second man I honour, and still more highly: Him who
is seen toiling for the spiritually indispensable; not daily
bread, but the Bread of Life. Is not he too in his duty;
endeavouring towards inward Harmony; revealing this, by
act or by word, through all his outward endeavours, be they
high or low? Highest of all, when his outward and his

inward endeavour are one: when we can name him Artist; not earthly Craftsman only, but inspired Thinker, that with heaven-made Implement conquers Heaven for us! If the poor and humble toil that we have Food, must not the high and glorious toil for him in return that he have Light and Guidance; Freedom, Immortality? – These two, in all their degrees, I honour: all else is chaff and dust, which let the wind blow whither it listeth.

'Unspeakably touching is it, however, when I find both dignities united; and he that must toil outwardly for the lowest of man's wants, is also toiling inwardly for the highest. Sublimer in this world know I nothing than a Peasant Saint, could such now any where be met with. Such a one will take thee back to Nazareth itself; thou wilt see the splendour of Heaven spring forth from the humblest depths of Earth, like a light shining in great darkness.'

And again: 'It is not because of his toils that I lament for the poor: we must all toil, or steal (howsoever we name our stealing) which is worse; no faithful workman finds his task a pastime. The poor is hungry and athirst, but for him also there is food and drink: he is heavy-laden and weary; but for him also the Heavens send Sleep, and of the deepest; in his smoky cribs, a clear dewy heaven of Rest envelopes him, and fitful glitterings of cloud-skirted Dreams. But what I do mourn over is that the lamp of his soul should go out; that no ray of heavenly, or even of earthly knowledge, should visit him; but, only in the haggard darkness, like two spectres, Fear and Indignation. Alas, while the Body stands so broad and brawny, must the Soul lie blinded, dwarfed, stupified, almost annihilated! Alas, was this too a Breath of God: bestowed in Heaven, but on Earth never to be unfolded! – That there should one Man die ignorant who had capacity for Knowledge, this I call a tragedy, were it to happen more than twenty times in the minute, as by some computations it does. The miserable fraction of Science which united mankind, in a wide Universe of Nescience, has acquired, why is not this, with all diligence, imparted to all?'

Quite in an opposite strain is the following: 'The old Spartans had a wiser method; and went out and hunted down their Helots, and speared and spitted them, when they grew too numerous. With our improved fashions of hunting, Herr Hofrath, now after the invention of fire-arms, and standing armies, how much easier were such a hunt! Perhaps in the most thickly-peopled country, some three days annually might suffice to shoot all the able-bodied Paupers that had accumulated within the year. Let

Governments think of this. The expense were trifling: nay, the very carcasses would pay it. Have them salted and barrelled; could not you victual therewith, if not Army and Navy, yet richly such infirm Paupers, in workhouses and elsewhere, as enlightened Charity, dreading no evil of them, might see good to keep alive?'

'And yet,' writes he farther on, 'there must be something wrong. A full-formed Horse will, in any market, bring from twenty to as high as two hundred Friedrichs d'or: such is his worth to the world. A full-formed Man is not only worth nothing to the world, but the world could afford him a round sum would he simply engage to go and hang himself. Nevertheless, which of the two was the more cunningly-devised article, even as an Engine? Good Heavens! A white European Man, standing on his two Legs, with his two five-fingered Hands at his shackle-bones, and miraculous Head on his shoulders, is worth, I should say, from fifty to a hundred Horses!'

'True, thou Gold-Hofrath!' cries the Professor else-where: 'Too crowded indeed. Meanwhile, what portion of this inconsiderable terraqueous Globe have ye actually tilled and delved, till it will grow no more? How thick stands your Population in the Pampas and Savannas of America; round ancient Carthage, and in the interior of Africa; on both slopes of the Altaic chain, in the central Platform of Asia; in Spain, Greece, Turkey, Crim Tartary, the Curragh of Kildare? One man, in one year, as I have understood it, if you lend him Earth, will feed himself and nine others. Alas, where now are the Hengsts and Alarics of our still glowing, still expanding Europe; who, when their home is grown too narrow, will enlist and, like Fire-pillars, guide onwards those superfluous masses of indomitable living Valour; equipped, not now with the battle-axe and war-chariot, but with the steam-engine and ploughshare? Where are they? – Preserving their Game!'

CHAPTER 5

The Phœnix

PUTTING which four singular Chapters together, and alongside of them numerous hints, and even direct utterances, scattered over these Writings of his, we come upon the startling yet not quite unlooked-for conclusion, that Teufelsdröckh is one of those who consider Society, properly so called, to be as good as extinct; and that only the Gregarious feelings, and old inherited habitudes, at this juncture, hold us from Dispersion, and universal national, civil, domestic and personal war! He says expressly: 'For the last three centuries, above all, for the last three quarters of a century, that same Pericardial Nervous Tissue (as we named it) of Religion, where lies the Life-essence of Society, has been smote at and perforated, needfully and needlessly; till now it is quite rent into shreds; and Society, long pining, diabetic, consumptive, can be regarded as defunct; for those spasmodic, galvanic sprawlings are not life, neither indeed will they endure, galvanise as you may, beyond two days.'

'Call ye that a Society,' cries he again, 'where there is no longer any Social Idea extant; not so much as the Idea of a common Home, but only of a common, over-crowded Lodging-house? Where each, isolated, regardless of his neighbour, turned against his neighbour, clutches what he can get, and cries "Mine!" and calls it Peace, because, in the cut-purse and cut-throat Scramble, no steel knives, but only a far cunninger sort, can be employed? Where Friendship, Communion, has become an incredible tradition; and your holiest Sacramental Supper is a smoking Tavern Dinner, with Cook for Evangelist? Where your Priest has no tongue but for plate-licking: and your high Guides and Governors cannot guide; but on all hands hear it passionately proclaimed: *Laissez faire*; Leave us alone of your guidance, such light is darker than darkness; eat your wages, and sleep!

'Thus, too,' continues he, 'must an observant eye discern everywhere that saddest spectacle: The Poor perishing, like neglected, foundered Draught-Cattle, of Hunger and Overwork; the Rich, still more wretchedly, of Idleness, Satiety, and Overgrowth. The Highest in rank, at length, without honour from the Lowest; scarcely, with a little mouth-honour, as from tavern-waiters who expect to put it in the bill. Once sacred Symbols fluttering as empty Pageants, whereof men grudge even the expense; a World becoming dismantled: in one word, the CHURCH fallen speechless, from obesity and apoplexy; the STATE shrunken into a Police-Office, straitened to get its pay!'

We might ask, are there many 'observant eyes,' belonging to Practical men, in England or elsewhere, which have descried these phenomena; or is it only from the mystic elevation of a German *Wahngasse* that such wonders are visible? Teufelsdröckh contends that the aspect of a 'deceased or expiring Society' fronts us everywhere, so that whoso runs may read. 'What, for example,' says he, 'is the universally-arrogated Virtue, almost the sole remaining Catholic Virtue, of these days? For some half century, it has been the thing you name "Independence." Suspicion of "Servility," of reverence for Superiors, the very dogleech is anxious to disavow. Fools! Were your Superiors worthy to govern, and you worthy to obey, reverence for them were even your only possible freedom. Independence, in all kinds, is rebellion; if unjust rebellion, why parade it, and every where prescribe it?'

But what then? Are we returning, as Rousseau prayed, to the state of Nature? 'The Soul Politic having departed,' says Teufelsdröckh, 'what can follow but that the Body Politic be decently interred, to avoid putrescence? Liberals, Economists, Utilitarians enough I see marching with its bier, and chaunting loud pæans, towards the funeral-pile, where, amid wailings from some, and saturnalian revelries from the most, the venerable Corpse is to be burnt. Or, in plain words, that these men, Liberals, Utilitarians, or whatsoever they are called, will ultimately carry their point, and dissever and destroy most existing Institutions of Society, seems a thing which has some time ago ceased to be doubtful.

'Do we not see a little subdivision of the grand Utilitarian Armament come to light even in insulated England? A living nucleus, that will attract and grow, does at length appear there also; and under curious phasis; properly as the inconsiderable fag-end, and so far in rear of the others as to fancy itself the van. Our European Mechanisers are a Sect of boundless diffusion, activity, and co-operative spirit: has not Utilitarianism flourished in high places of Thought, here among ourselves, and in every European country, at some time or other, within the last fifty years? If now in all countries, except perhaps England, it has ceased to flour-

ish, or indeed to exist, among Thinkers, and sunk to
Journalists and the popular mass, – who sees not that, as
hereby it no longer preaches, so the reason is, it now needs
no Preaching, but is in full universal Action, the doctrine
every where known and enthusiastically laid to heart? The
fit pabulum, in these times, for a certain rugged workshop-
intellect and heart, nowise without their corresponding
workshop-strength and ferocity, it requires but to be stated
in such scenes to make proselytes enough. – Admirably
calculated for destroying, only not for rebuilding! It spreads
like a sort of Dog-madness; till the whole World-kennel will
be rabid: then woe to the Huntsmen, with or without their
whips! They should have given the quadrupeds water,'
adds he, 'the water, namely, of Knowledge and of Life,
while it was yet time.'

Thus, if Professor Teufelsdröckh can be relied on, we are
at this hour in a most critical condition; beleaguered by that
boundless 'Armament of Mechanisers' and Unbelievers,
threatening to strip us bare! 'The World,' says he, 'as it
needs must, is under a process of devastation and waste,
which, whether by silent assiduous corrosion, or open
quicker combustion, as the case chances, will effectually
enough annihilate the past Forms of Society; replace them
with what it may. For the present, it is contemplated that
when man's whole Spiritual Interests are once *divested*,
these innumerable stript-off Garments shall mostly be
burnt; but the sounder Rags among them be quilted
together into one huge Irish watch-coat for the defence
of the Body only!' – This, we think, is but Job's news to the
humane reader.

'Nevertheless,' cries Teufelsdröckh, 'who can hinder it;
who is there that can clutch into the wheel-spokes of
Destiny, and say to the Spirit of the Time: Turn back, I
command thee? – Wiser were it that we yielded to the
Inevitable and Inexorable, and accounted even this the
best.'

Nay, might not an attentive Editor, drawing his own inferences from what stands written, conjecture that Teufelsdröckh individually had yielded to this same 'Inevitable and Inexorable' heartily enough; and now sat waiting the issue, with his natural diabolico-angelical Indifference, if not even Placidity? Did we not hear him complain that the World was a 'huge Ragfair,' and the 'rags and tatters of old Symbols' were raining down every where, like to drift him in, and suffocate him? What with those 'unhunted Helots' of his; and the uneven *sic-vos-non-vobis*[1] pressure, and hard crashing collision he is pleased to discern in existing things; what with the so hateful 'empty Masks,' full of beetles and spiders, yet glaring out on him, from their glass-eyes, 'with a ghastly affectation of life,' – we feel entitled to conclude him even willing that much should be thrown to the Devil, so it were but done gently! Safe himself in that 'Pinnacle of Weissnichtwo,' he would consent, with a tragic solemnity, that the monster UTILITARIA, held back, indeed, and moderated by nose-rings, halters, foot-shackles, and every conceivable modification of rope, should go forth to do her work; – to tread down old ruinous Palaces and Temples, with her broad hoof, till the whole were trodden down, that new and better might be built! Remarkable in this point of view are the following sentences.

'Society,' says he, 'is not dead: that Carcass, which you call dead Society, is but her mortal coil which she has shuffled off, to assume a nobler; she herself, through perpetual metamorphoses, in fairer and fairer development, has to live till Time also merge in Eternity. Wheresoever two or three Living Men are gathered together, there is Society; or there it will be, with its cunning mechanisms and stupendous structures, overspreading this little Globe, and reaching upwards to Heaven and downwards to Gehenna: for always, under one or the other figure, has it two authentic Revelations, of a God and of a Devil; the Pulpit, namely, and the Gallows.'

Indeed, we already heard him speak of 'Religion, in unnoticed nooks, weaving for herself new Vestures;' – Teufelsdröckh himself being one of the loom-treaddles? Elsewhere he quotes without censure that strange aphorism

1 *sic-vos-non-vobis*: thus you labour not for yourselves

of Saint-Simon's, concerning which and whom so much were to be said: *L'age d'or qu'une aveugle tradition a placé jusqu'ici dans le passé est devant nous;* The golden age which a blind tradition has hitherto placed in the Past is Before us. – But listen again:

'When the Phœnix is fanning her funeral pyre, will there not be sparks flying? Alas, some millions of men, and among them such as a Napoleon, have already been licked into that high-eddying Flame, and like moths, consumed there. Still also have we to fear that incautious beards will get singed.

'For the rest, in what year of grace such Phœnix-cremation will be completed, you need not ask. The law of Perseverance is among the deepest in man: by nature he hates change; seldom will he quit his old house till it has actually fallen about his ears. Thus have I seen Solemnities linger as Ceremonies, sacred Symbols as idle Pageants, to the extent of three hundred years and more after all life and sacredness had evaporated out of them. And then, finally, what time the Phœnix Death-Birth itself will require depends on unseen contingencies. – Meanwhile, would Destiny offer Mankind that after, say two centuries of convulsion and conflagration, more or less vivid, the fire-creation should be accomplished, and we find ourselves again in a Living Society, and no longer fighting but working, – were it not perhaps prudent in Mankind to strike the bargain?'

Thus is Teufelsdröckh content that old sick Society should be deliberately burnt (alas! with quite other fuel than spicewood); in the faith that she is a Phœnix; and that a new heavenborn young one will rise out of her ashes! We ourselves, restricted to the duty of Indicator, shall forbear commentary. Meanwhile, will not the judicious reader shake his head, and reproachfully, yet more in sorrow than in anger, say or think: From a *Doctor Utriusque Juris*, titular Professor in a University, and man to whom hitherto, for his services, Society, bad as she is, has given not only food and raiment (of a kind), but books, tobacco and gukguk, we expected more gratitude to his benefactress; and less of a blind Trust in the future, which resembles that rather of a philosophical Fatalist and Enthusiast, than of a solid house-holder paying scot and lot in a Christian country.

CHAPTER 6

Old Clothes

As mentioned above, Teufelsdröckh, though a Sansculottist, is in practice probably the politest man extant: his whole heart and life are penetrated and informed with the spirit of Politeness; a noble natural Courtesy shines through him, beautifying his vagaries; like sun-light, making a rosy-fingered, rainbow-dyed Aurora out of mere aqueous clouds; nay, brightening London smoke itself into gold vapour, as from the crucible of an alchemist. Hear in what earnest though fantastic wise he expresses himself on this head:

'Shall Courtesy be done only to the rich, and only by the rich? In Good-breeding, which differs, if at all, from High-breeding, only as it gracefully remembers the rights of others, rather than gracefully insists on its own rights, I discern no special connexion with wealth or birth: but rather that it lies in human nature itself, and is due from all men towards all men. Of a truth, were your Schoolmaster at his post, and worth any thing when there, this, with so much else, would be reformed. Nay, each man were then also his neighbour's schoolmaster; till at length a rude-visaged, unmannered Peasant, could no more be met with than a Peasant unacquainted with botanical Physiology, or who felt not that the clod he broke was created in Heaven.

'For whether thou bear a sceptre or a sledge-hammer, art thou not ALIVE; is not this thy brother ALIVE? "There is but one Temple in the world," says Novalis, "and that Temple is the Body of Man. Nothing is holier than this high Form. Bending before men is a reverence done to this Revelation in the Flesh. We touch Heaven, when we lay our hands on a human Body."

'On which ground, I would fain carry it farther than most do; and whereas the English Johnson only bowed to every Clergyman, or man with a shovel-hat, I would bow to every Man with any sort of hat, or with no hat whatever. Is he not a Temple, then; the visible Manifestation and Impersonation of the Divinity? And yet, alas, such indiscriminate bowing serves not. For there is a Devil dwells in man, as well as a Divinity; and too often the bow is but pocketed by the *former*. It would go to the pocket of Vanity (which is your clearest phasis of the Devil, in these times); therefore must we withhold it.

'The gladder am I, on the other hand, to do reverence to those Shells and outer Husks of the Body, wherein no devilish passion any longer lodges, but only the pure emblem and effigies of Man: I mean, to Empty, or even to Cast Clothes. Nay, is it not to Clothes that most men do reverence; to the fine frogged broad-cloth, nowise to the "straddling animal with bandy legs" which it holds, and makes a Dignitary of? Who ever saw any Lord my-lorded in tattered blanket, fastened with wooden skewer? Nevertheless, I say, there is in such worship a shade of hypocrisy, a

practical deception: for how often does the Body appropriate what was meant for the Cloth only! Whoso would
avoid Falsehood, which is the essence of all Sin, will
perhaps see good to take a different course. That reverence
which cannot act without obstruction and perversion when
the Clothes are full, may have free course when they are
empty. Even as, for Hindoo Worshippers, the Pagoda is not
less sacred than the God; so do I too worship the hollow
cloth Garment with equal fervour, as when it contained the
Man: nay, with more, for I now fear no deception, of myself
or of others.

'Did not King *Toomtabard*, or, in other words, John
Balliol, reign long over Scotland; the man John Balliol
being quite gone, and only the "Toom Tabard" (Empty
Gown) remaining? What still dignity dwells in a suit of Cast
Clothes! How meekly it bears its honours! No haughty

looks, no scornful gesture; silent and serene, it fronts the world; neither demanding worship, nor afraid to miss it. The Hat still carries the physiognomy of its Head: but the vanity and the stupidity, and goose-speech which was the sign of these two, are gone. The Coat-arm is stretched out, but not to strike; the Breeches, in modest simplicity, depend at ease, and now at last have a graceful flow; the Waistcoat hides no evil passion, no riotous desire; hunger or thirst now dwells not in it. Thus all is purged from the grossness of Sense, from the carking Cares and foul Vices of the World; and rides there, on its Clothes-horse; as, on a Pegasus, might some skyey Messenger, or purified Apparition, visiting our low Earth.

'Often, while I sojourned in that monstrous Tuberosity of Civilised Life, the Capital of England; and meditated, and questioned Destiny, under that ink-sea of vapour, black, thick, and multifarious as Spartan broth; and was one lone Soul amid those grinding millions; – often have I turned into their Old-Clothes Market to worship. With awe-struck heart I walk through that Monmouth Street, with its empty Suits, as through a Sanhedrim of stainless Ghosts. Silent are they, but expressive in their silence: the past witnesses and instruments of Woe and Joy, of Passions, Virtues, Crimes, and all the fathomless tumult of Good and Evil in "the Prison called Life." Friends! trust not the heart of that man for whom Old Clothes are not venerable. Watch too, with reverence, that bearded Jewish Highpriest, who with hoarse voice, like some Angel of Doom, summons them from the four winds! On his head, like the Pope, he has three Hats, – a real triple tiara; on either hand, are the similitude of Wings, whereon the summoned Garments come to alight; and ever, as he slowly cleaves the air, sounds forth his deep fateful note, as if through a trumpet he were proclaiming: "Ghosts of Life, come to Judgment!" Reck not, ye fluttering Ghosts: he will purify you in his Purgatory, with fire and with water; and, one day, new-created ye shall reappear. Oh! let him in whom the flame of Devotion is ready to go out, who has never worshipped, and knows not what to worship, pace and repace, with austerest thought, the pavement of Monmouth Street, and say whether his heart and his eyes still continue dry. If Field Lane, with its long fluttering rows of yellow handkerchiefs, be a Dionysius' Ear, where, in stifled jarring hubbub, we hear the Indictment which Poverty and Vice bring against lazy Wealth, that it has left them there cast out and trodden under foot of Want, Darkness, and the Devil, – then is Monmouth Street a Mirza's Hill, where, in motley vision, the whole Pageant of Existence passes awfully before us; with its wail and jubilee, mad loves and mad hatreds, church-bells and gallows-ropes, farce-tragedy, beast-godhood, – the Bedlam of Creation!' To most men, as it does to ourselves, all this will seem over-charged. We too have walked through Monmouth Street; but with little feeling of 'Devotion:' probably in part because the contemplative process is so fatally broken in upon by the brood of money-changers, who nestle in that Church, and importune the worshipper with merely secular proposals. Whereas Teufelsdröckh might be in that happy middle-state, which leaves to the Clothes-broker no hope either of sale or of purchase, and so be allowed to linger there without molestation. – Something we would have given to see the little philosophical Figure, with its steeple-hat and loose-flowing skirts, and eyes in a fine frenzy, 'pacing and repacing in austerest thought' that foolish Street; which to him was a true Delphic avenue, and supernatural Whispering-gallery, where the 'Ghosts of Life' rounded strange secrets in his ear. O thou philosophic Teufelsdröckh, that listenest while others only gabble, and with thy quick tympanum hearest the grass grow!

At the same time, is it not strange that, in Paperbag Documents, destined for an English Work, there exists nothing like an authentic diary of this his sojourn in London; and of his Meditations among the Clothes-shops only the obscurest emblematic shadows? Neither, in conversation (for, indeed, he was not a man to pester you with his Travels), have we heard him more than allude to the subject.

For the rest, however, it cannot be uninteresting that we here find how early the significance of Clothes had dawned on the now so distinguished Clothes-Professor. Might we but fancy it to have been even in Monmouth Street, at the bottom of our own English 'ink-sea,' that this remarkable Volume first took being, and shot forth its salient point in his soul, – as in Chaos did the Egg of Eros, one day to be hatched into a Universe!

CHAPTER 7

Organic Filaments

FOR us, who happen to live while the World-Phœnix is
burning herself, and burning so slowly that, as Teufelsdröckh
calculates, it were a handsome bargain would she engage to
have done 'within two centuries,' there seems to lie but an
ashy prospect. Not altogether so, however, does the Professor figure it. 'In the living subject,' says he, 'change is wont to
be gradual: thus, while the serpent sheds its old skin, the new
is already formed beneath. Little knowest thou of the burning
of a World-Phœnix, who fanciest that she must first burn out,
and lie as a dead cinereous heap; and therefrom the young
one start up by miracle, and fly heavenward. Far otherwise! In
that Firewhirlwind, Creation and Destruction proceed together; ever as the ashes of the Old are blown about, do
organic filaments of the New mysteriously spin themselves;
and amid the rushing and the waving of the Whirlwind-
Element, come tones of a melodious Deathsong, which end

not but in tones of a more melodious Birthsong. Nay, look into the Fire-whirlwind with thy own eyes, and thou wilt see.' Let us actually look, then: to poor individuals, who cannot expect to live two centuries, those same organic filaments, mysteriously spinning themselves, will be the best part of the spectacle. First, therefore, this of Mankind in general:

'In vain thou deniest it,' says the Professor; 'thou *art* my Brother. Thy very Hatred, thy very Envy, those foolish Lies thou tellest of me in thy splenetic humour: what is all this but an inverted Sympathy? Were I a Steam-engine, wouldst thou take the trouble to tell Lies of me? Not thou! I should grind all unheeded, whether badly or well.

'Wondrous truly are the bonds that unite us one and all; whether by the soft binding of Love, or the iron chaining of Necessity, as we like to choose it. More than once, have I said to myself, of some perhaps whimsically strutting Figure, such as provokes whimsical thoughts: "Wert thou, my little Brotherkin, suddenly covered up with even the largest imaginable Glass-bell, – what a thing it were, not for thyself only, but for the world! Post Letters, more or fewer, from all the four winds, impinge against thy Glass walls, but must drop unread: neither from within comes there question or response into any Postbag; thy Thoughts fall into no friendly ear or heart, thy Manufacture into no purchasing hand; thou art no longer a circulating venous-arterial Heart, that, taking and giving, circulatest through all Space and all Time: there has a Hole fallen out in the immeasurable, universal World-tissue, which must be darned up again!"

'Such venous-arterial circulation, of Letters, verbal Messages, paper and other Packages, going out from him and coming in, are a blood-circulation, visible to the eye: but the finer nervous circulation, by which all things, the minutest that he does, minutely influence all men, and the very look of his face blesses or curses whomso it lights on, and so generates ever new blessing or new cursing: all this you cannot see, but only imagine. I say, there is not a red Indian, hunting by Lake Winnipic, can quarrel with his squaw, but the whole world must smart for it: will not the price of beaver rise? It is a mathematical fact that the casting of this pebble from my hand alters the centre of gravity of the Universe.

'If now an existing generation of men stand so woven

together, not less indissolubly does generation with generation. Hast thou ever meditated on that word, Tradition: how we inherit not Life only, but all the garniture and form of Life; and work, and speak, and even think and feel, as our Fathers, and primeval grandfathers, from the beginning, have given it us? – Who printed thee, for example, this unpretending Volume on the Philosophy of Clothes? Not the Herren Stillschweigen and Company: but Cadmus of Thebes, Faust of Mentz, and innumerable others whom thou knowest not. Had there been no Mæsogothic Ulfila, there had been no English Shakespeare, or a different one. Simpleton! It was Tubalcain that made thy very Tailor's needle, and sewed that court suit of thine.

'Yes, truly, if Nature is one, and a living indivisible whole, much more is Mankind, the Image that reflects and creates Nature, without which Nature were not. As palpable life-streams in that wondrous Individual, Mankind, among so many life-streams that are not palpable, flow on those main-currents of what we call Opinion; as preserved in Institutions, Polities, Churches, above all in Books. Beautiful it is to understand and know that a Thought did never yet die; that as thou, the originator thereof, has gathered it and created it from the whole Past, so thou wilt transmit it to the whole Future. It is thus that the heroic Heart, the seeing Eye of the first times, still feels and sees in us of the latest; that the Wise Man stands ever encompassed, and spiritually embraced, by a cloud of witnesses and brothers; and there is a living, literal *Communion of Saints*, wide as the World itself, and as the History of the World.

'Noteworthy also, and serviceable for the progress of this same Individual, wilt thou find his subdivision into Generations. Generations are as the Days of toilsome Mankind; Death and Birth are the vesper and the matin bells, that summon Mankind to sleep, and to rise refreshed for new advancement. What the Father has made the Son can make and enjoy; but has also work of his own appointed him. Thus all things wax, and roll onwards; Arts, Establishments, Opinions, nothing is completed, but ever completing. Newton has learned to see what Kepler saw; but there is also a fresh heaven-derived force in Newton; he must mount to still higher points of vision. So too the Hebrew Lawgiver is, in due time, followed by an Apostle of the Gentiles. In the business of Destruction, as this also is from time to time a necessary work, thou findest a like sequence and perseverance: for Luther it was as yet hot enough to stand by that burning of the Pope's Bull; Voltaire could not warm himself at the glimmering ashes, but required quite other fuel. Thus likewise, I note, the English Whig has, in the second generation, become an English Radical; who, in the third again, it is to be hoped, will become an English Rebuilder. Find Mankind where thou wilt, thou findest it in living movement, in progress faster or slower: the Phœnix soars aloft, hovers with outstretched wings, filling Earth with her music; or, as now, she sinks, and with spheral swan-song immolates herself in flame, that she may soar the higher and sing the clearer.'

Let the friends of social order, in such a disastrous period, lay this to heart, and derive from it any little comfort they can. We subjoin another passage, concerning Titles:

'Remark, not without surprise,' says Teufelsdröckh, 'how all high Titles of Honour come hitherto from Fighting. Your *Herzog* (Duke, *Dux*) is Leader of Armies; your Earl (*Jarl*) is Strong Man; your Marshall cavalry Horseshoer. A Millennium, or reign of Peace and Wisdom, having from of old been prophesied, and becoming now daily more and more indubitable, may it not be apprehended that such Fighting-titles will cease to be palatable, and new and higher need to be devised?

'The only Title wherein I, with confidence, trace eternity, is that of King. *König* (King), anciently *Könning*, means Ken-ning (Cunning), or which is the same thing,

Can-ning. Ever must the Sovereign of Mankind be fitly
entitled King.'

'Well, also,' says he elsewhere, 'was it written by Theo-
logians: a King rules by divine right. He carries in him an
authority from God, or man will never give it him. Can I
choose my own King? I can choose my own King Popinjay,
and play what farce or tragedy I may with him: but he who
is to be my Ruler, whose will is to be higher than my will,
was chosen for me in Heaven. Neither except in such
Obedience to the Heaven-chosen is Freedom so much
as conceivable.'

The Editor will here admit that, among all the wondrous
provinces of Teufelsdröckh's spiritual world, there is none
he walks in with such astonishment, hesitation, and even
pain, as in the Political. How, with our English love of
Ministry and Opposition, and that generous conflict of
Parties, mind warming itself against mind in their mutual
wrestle for the Public Good, by which wrestle, indeed, is
our invaluable Constitution kept warm and alive; how shall
we domesticate ourselves in this spectral Necropolis, or
rather City both of the Dead and of the Unborn, where the
Present seems little other than an inconsiderable Film
dividing the Past and the Future? In those dim longdrawn
expanses, all is so immeasurable; much so disastrous,
ghastly; your very radiances, and straggling light-beams,
have a supernatural character. And then with such an
Indifference, such a prophetic peacefulness (accounting
the inevitably-coming as already here, to him all one
whether it be distant by centuries or only by days), does
he sit; – and live, you would say, rather in any other age
than in his own! It is our painful duty to announce, or
repeat, that, looking into this man, we discern a deep,
silent, slow-burning, inextinguishable Radicalism, such as
fills us with shuddering admiration.

Thus, for example, he appears to make little even of the

Elective Franchise; at least so we interpret the following: 'Satisfy yourselves,' he says, 'by universal, indubitable experiment, even as ye are now doing or will do, whether FREEDOM heavenborn and leading heavenward, and so vitally essential for us all, cannot peradventure be mechanically hatched and brought to light in that same Ballot-Box of yours; or at worst, in some other discoverable or devisable Box, Edifice, or Steam-mechanism. It were a mighty convenience; and beyond all feats of manufacture witnessed hitherto.' Is Teufelsdröckh acquainted with the British Constitution, even slightly? – He says, under another figure: 'But after all, were the problem, as indeed it now everywhere is, To rebuild your old House from the top downwards (since you must live in it the while), what better, what other, than the Representative Machine will serve your turn? Meanwhile, however, mock me not with the name of Free, "when you have but knit up my chains into ornamental festoons." ' – Or what will any member of the Peace Society make of such an assertion as this: 'The lower people everywhere desire War. Not so unwisely; there is then a demand for lower people – to be shot!'

Gladly, therefore, do we emerge from those soul-confusing labyrinths of speculative Radicalism, into somewhat clearer regions. Here, looking round, as was our hest, for 'organic filaments,' we ask, may not this, touching 'Hero-worship,' be of the number? It seems of a cheerful character; yet so quaint, so mystical, one knows not what, or how little, may lie under it. Our readers shall look with their own eyes:

'True is it that, in these days, man can do almost all things, only not obey. True likewise that whoso cannot obey cannot be free, still less bear rule; he that is the inferior of nothing, can be the superior of nothing, the equal of nothing. Nevertheless, believe not that man has lost his faculty of Reverence; that if it slumber in him, it has gone dead. Painful for man is that same rebellious Independence, when it has become inevitable; only in loving companionship with his fellows does he feel safe; only in reverently bowing down before the Higher does he feel himself exalted.

'Or what if the character of our so troublous Era lay even in this: that man had for ever cast away Fear, which is the lower; but not yet risen into perennial Reverence, which is the higher and highest?

'Meanwhile, observe with joy, so cunningly has Nature ordered it, that whatsoever man ought to obey he cannot but obey. Before no faintest revelation of the Godlike did he ever stand irreverent; least of all, when the Godlike shewed itself revealed in his fellow-man. Thus is there a true religious Loyalty for ever rooted in his heart; nay, in all ages, even in ours, it manifests itself as a more or less orthodox *Hero-worship*. In which fact, that Hero-worship exists, has existed, and will for ever exist, universally among Mankind, mayst thou discern the corner-stone of living rock, whereon all Polities for the remotest time may stand secure.'

Do our readers discern any such corner-stone, or even so much as what Teufelsdröckh is looking at? He exclaims: 'Or hast thou forgotten Paris and Voltaire? How the aged, withered man, though but a Sceptic, Mocker, and millinery Court-poet, yet because even he seemed the Wisest, Best, could drag mankind at his chariot-wheels, so that princes coveted a smile from him, and the loveliest of France would have laid their hair beneath his feet! All Paris was one vast Temple of Hero-Worship; though their Divinity, more-over, was of feature too apish.

'But if such things,' continues he, 'were done in the dry tree, what will be done in the green? If, in the most parched season of man's History, in the most parched spot of Europe, when Parisian life was at best but a scientific *Hortus Siccus*, bedizened with some Italian Gumflowers, such virtue could come out of it: what is it to be looked for when Life again waves leafy and bloomy, and your Hero-Divinity shall have nothing apelike, but be wholly human? Know that there is in man a quite indestructible Reverence for whatsoever holds of Heaven, or even plausibly counterfeits such holding. Shew the dullest clodpole, shew the haughtiest featherhead, that a soul Higher than himself is actually here; were his knees stiffened into brass, he must down and worship.'

Organic filaments, of a more authentic sort, mysteriously spinning themselves, some will perhaps discover in the following passage:

'There is no Church, sayest thou? The voice of Prophecy has gone dumb? This is even what I dispute: but, in any case, hast thou not still Preaching enough? A Preaching Friar settles himself in every village; and builds a pulpit, which he calls Newspaper. Therefrom he preaches what most momentous doctrine is in him, for man's salvation; and dost not thou listen, and believe? Look well, thou seest every where a new Clergy of the Mendicant Orders, some bare-footed, some almost bare-backed, fashion itself into shape, and teach and preach, zealously enough, for copper alms and the love of God. These break in pieces the ancient idols; and, though themselves too often reprobate, as idol-breakers are wont to be, mark out the sites of new Churches, where the true God-ordained, that are to follow, may find audience, and minister. Said I not, Before the old skin was shed, the new had formed itself beneath it?'

Perhaps, also, in the following; wherewith we now hasten to knit up this ravelled sleeve:

'But there is no Religion?' reiterates the Professor. 'Fool! I tell thee, there is. Hast thou well considered all that lies in this immeasurable froth-ocean we name LITERATURE? Fragments of a genuine Church-*Homiletic* lie scattered there, which Time will assort: nay, fractions even of a *Liturgy* could I point out. And knowest thou no Prophet, even in the vesture, environment, and dialect of this age? None to whom the Godlike had revealed itself, through all meanest and highest forms of the Common; and by him been again prophetically revealed: in whose inspired melody, even in these rag-gathering and rag-burning days, Man's Life again begins, were it but afar off, to be divine? Knowest thou none such? I know him, and name him – Goethe.

'But thou as yet standest in no Temple; joinest in no Psalm-worship; feelest well that, where there is no ministering Priest, the people perish? Be of comfort! Thou art not alone, if thou have Faith. Spake we not of a Communion of Saints, unseen, yet not unreal, accompanying and brother-like embracing thee, so thou be worthy? Their heroic Sufferings rise up melodiously together to Heaven, out of all lands, and out of all times, as a sacred *Miserere*; their heroic Actions also, as a boundless, everlasting Psalm of Triumph. Neither say that thou hast now no Symbol of the Godlike. Is not God's Universe a Symbol of the Godlike; is not Immensity a Temple; is not Man's History, and Men's History, a perpetual Evangile? Listen, and for organ-music thou wilt ever, as of old, hear the Morning Stars sing together.'

CHAPTER 8

Natural Supernaturalism

IT is in his stupendous Section, headed *Natural Supernaturalism*, that the Professor first becomes a Seer; and, after long effort, such as we have witnessed, finally subdues under his feet this refractory Clothes-Philosophy, and takes victorious possession thereof. Phantasms enough he has had to struggle with; 'Cloth-webs and Cob-webs,' of Imperial Mantles, Superannuated Symbols, and what not: yet still did he courageously pierce through. Nay, worst of all, two quite mysterious, world-embracing Phantasms, TIME and SPACE, have ever hovered round him, perplexing and bewildering: but with these also he now resolutely grapples, these also he victoriously rends asunder. In a word, he has looked fixedly on Existence, till one after the other, its earthly hulls and garnitures, have all melted away;

and now to his rapt vision the interior, celestial Holy of Holies, lies disclosed.

Here therefore properly it is that the Philosophy of Clothes attains to Transcendentalism; this last leap, can we but clear it, takes us safe into the promised land, where *Palingenesia*, in all senses, may be considered as beginning. 'Courage, then!' may our Diogenes exclaim, with better right than Diogenes the First once did. This stupendous Section we, after long, painful meditation, have found not to be unintelligible; but on the contrary to grow clear, nay radiant, and all-illuminating. Let the reader, turning on it what utmost force of speculative intellect is in him, do his part; as we, by judicious selection and adjustment, shall study to do ours:

'Deep has been, and is, the significance of Miracles,' thus quietly begins the Professor; 'far deeper perhaps than we imagine. Meanwhile, the question of questions were: What specially is a Miracle? To that Dutch King of Siam, an icicle had been a miracle; whoso had carried with him an airpump, and phial of vitriolic ether, might have worked a miracle. To my Horse again, who unhappily is still more unscientific, do not I work a miracle, and magical *'open sesame!'* every time I please to pay twopence, and open for him an impassable *Schlagbaum*, or shut Turnpike?

' "But is not a real Miracle simply a violation of the Laws of Nature?" ask several. Whom I answer by this new question: What are the Laws of Nature? To me perhaps the rising of one from the dead were no violation of these Laws, but a confirmation; were some far deeper Law, now first penetrated into, and by Spiritual Force, even as the rest have all been, brought to bear on us with its Material Force.

'Here too may some inquire, not without astonishment: On what ground shall one, that can make Iron swim, come and declare that therefore he can teach Religion? To us, truly, of the Nineteenth Century, such declaration were inept enough; which nevertheless to our fathers, of the First Century, was full of meaning.

' "But is it not the deepest Law of Nature that she be constant?" cries an illuminated class: "Is not the Machine of the Universe fixed to move by unalterable rules?" Probable enough, good friends: nay, I too must believe that the God, whom ancient, inspired men assert to be "without variableness or shadow of turning," does indeed never change; that Nature, that the Universe, which no one whom it so pleases can be prevented from calling a Machine, does move by the most unalterable rules. And now of you too I make the old inquiry: What those same unalterable rules, forming the complete Statute-Book of Nature, may possibly be?

'They stand written in our Works of Science, say you; in the accumulated records of man's Experience? – Was man with his Experience present at the Creation, then, to see how it all went on? Have any deepest scientific individuals yet dived down to the foundations of the Universe, and gauged every thing there? Did the Maker take them into His counsel; that they read His ground-plan of the incomprehensible All; and can say, This stands marked therein, and no more than this? Alas, not in anywise! These scientific individuals have been nowhere but where we also are; have seen some handbreadths deeper than we see into the Deep that is infinite, without bottom as without shore.

'Laplace's Book on the Stars, wherein he exhibits that certain Planets, with their Satellites, gyrate round our worthy Sun, at a rate and in a course, which, by greatest good fortune, he and the like of him have succeeded in detecting, – is to me as precious as to another. But is this what thou namest "Mechanism of the Heavens," and "System of the World;" this, wherein Sirius and the Pleiades, and all Herschel's Fifteen thousand Suns per minute, being left out, some paltry handful of Moons, and inert Balls, had been – looked at, nicknamed, and marked in the Zodiacal Waybill; so that we can now prate of their Whereabout; their How, their Why, their What, being hid from us as in the signless Inane?

'System of Nature! To the wisest man, wide as is his vision, Nature remains of quite *infinite* depth, of quite infinite expansion; and all Experience thereof limits itself to some few computed centuries, and measured square-miles. The course of Nature's phases, on this our little fraction of a Planet, is partially known to us; but who knows what deeper courses these depend on; what infinitely larger Cycle (of causes) our little Epicycle revolves on? To the Minnow every cranny and pebble, and quality and accident, of its little native Creek may have become familiar: but does the Minnow understand the Ocean Tides and periodic Currents, the Trade-winds, and Monsoons, and Moon's Eclipses; by all which the condition of its little Creek is regulated, and may, from time to time (*un*miraculously enough), be quite overset and reversed? Such a minnow is man; his Creek this Planet Earth; his Ocean the immeasurable All; his Monsoons and periodic Currents the mysterious Course of Providence through Æons of Æons.

'We speak of the Volume of Nature: and truly a Volume it is, – whose Author and Writer is God. To read it! Dost thou, does man, so much as well know the Alphabet thereof? With its Words, Sentences, and grand descriptive Pages, poetical and philosophical, spread out through Solar Systems, and Thousands of Years, we shall not try thee. It is a Volume written in celestial hieroglyphs, in the true Sacred-writing; of which even Prophets are happy that they can read here a line and there a line. As for your Institutes, and Academies of Science, they strive bravely; and, from amid the thick-crowded, inextricably intertwisted hieroglyphic writing, pick out, by dextrous combination, some Letters in the vulgar Character, and therefrom put together this and the other economic Recipe, of high avail in Practice. That Nature is more than some boundless Volume of such Recipes, or huge, well-nigh inexhaustible

Domestic-Cookery Book, of which the whole secret will, in this wise, one day, evolve itself, the fewest dream.

'Custom,' continues the Professor, 'doth make dotards of us all. Consider well, thou wilt find that Custom is the greatest of Weavers; and weaves air-raiment for all the Spirits of the Universe; whereby indeed these dwell with us visibly, as ministering servants, in our houses and work-shops; but their spiritual nature becomes, to the most, for ever hidden. Philosophy complains that Custom has hood-winked us, from the first; that we do every thing by Custom, even Believe by it; that our very Axioms, let us boast of Free-thinking as we may, are oftenest simply such Beliefs as we have never heard questioned. Nay, what is Philosophy throughout but a continual battle against Cus-tom; an ever-renewed effort to *transcend* the sphere of blind Custom, and so become Transcendental?

'Innumerable are the illusions and legerdemain tricks of Custom: but of all these perhaps the cleverest is her knack of persuading us that the Miraculous, by simple repetition, ceases to be Miraculous. True, it is by this means we live; for man must work as well as wonder: and herein is Custom so far a kind nurse, guiding him to his true benefit. But she is a fond foolish nurse, or rather we are false foolish nurselings, when, in our resting and reflecting hours, we prolong the same deception. Am I to view the Stupendous with stupid indifference, because I have seen it twice, or two hundred, or two million times? There is no reason in Nature or in Art why I should: unless, indeed, I am a mere Work-Machine, for whom the divine gift of Thought were no other than the terrestrial gift of Steam is to the Steam-engine; a power whereby Cotton might be spun, and money and money's worth realised.

'Notable enough too, here as elsewhere, wilt thou find the potency of Names; which indeed are but one kind of such Custom-woven, wonder-hiding garments. Witchcraft,

and all manner of Spectre-work, and Demonology, we have
now named Madness, and Diseases of the Nerves. Seldom
reflecting that still the new question comes upon us: What
is Madness, what are Nerves? Ever, as before, does Madness remain a mysterious-terrific, altogether *infernal* boiling
up of the Nether Chaotic Deep, through this fair-painted
Vision of Creation, which swims thereon, which we name
the Real. Was Luther's Picture of the Devil less a Reality,
whether it were formed within the bodily eye, or without it?
In every the wisest Soul, lies a whole world of internal
Madness, an authentic Demon-Empire; out of which,
indeed, his world of Wisdom has been creatively built
together, and now rests there, as on its dark foundations
does a habitable flowery Earth-rind.

'But deepest of all illusory Appearances, for hiding Wonder, as for many other ends, are your two grand fundamental world-enveloping Appearances, SPACE and TIME.
These, as spun and woven for us from before Birth itself, to
clothe our celestial ME for dwelling here, and yet to blind
it, – lie all-embracing, as the universal canvass, or warp and
woof, whereby all minor Illusions, in this Phantasm Existence, weave and paint themselves. In vain, while here on
Earth, shall you endeavour to strip them off; you can, at
best, but rend them asunder for moments, and look
through.

'Fortunatus had a wishing Hat, which when he put it on,
and wished himself Anywhere, behold he was There. By
this means had Fortunatus triumphed over Space, he had
annihilated Space; for him there was no Where, but all was
Here. Were a Hatter to establish himself, in the Wahngasse
of Weissnichtwo, and make felts of this sort for all mankind, what a world we should have of it! Still stranger,
should, on the opposite side of the street, another Hatter
establish himself; and, as his fellow-craftsman made Space-
annihilating Hats, make Time-annihilating! Of both would

I purchase, were it with my last groschen; but chiefly of this latter. To clap on your felt, and, simply by wishing that you were Any*where*, straightway to be *There!* Next to clap on your other felt, and, simply by wishing that you were Any*when*, straightway to be *Then!* This were indeed the grander: shooting at will from the Fire-Creation of the World to its Fire-Consummation; here historically present in the First Century, conversing face to face with Paul and Seneca; there prophetically in the Thirty-first, conversing also face to face with other Pauls and Senecas, who as yet stand hidden in the depth of that late Time!

'Or thinkest thou, it were impossible, unimaginable? Is the Past annihilated, then, or only past; is the Future non-extant, or only future? Those mystic faculties of thine, Memory and Hope, already answer: already through those mystic avenues, thou the Earth-blinded summonest both Past and Future, and communest with them, though as yet darkly, and with mute beckonings. The curtains of Yesterday drop down, the curtains of To-morrow roll up; but Yesterday and To-morrow both *are*. Pierce through the Time-Element, glance into the Eternal. Believe what thou findest written in the sanctuaries of Man's Soul, even as all Thinkers, in all ages, have devoutly read it there: that Time and Space are not God, but creations of God; that with God as it is a universal HERE, so is it an Everlasting NOW.

'And seest thou therein any glimpse of IMMORTALITY? – O heaven! Is the white Tomb of our Loved One, who died from our arms, and must be left behind us there, which rises in the distance, like a pale, mournfully receding Milestone, to tell how many toilsome uncheered miles we have journeyed on alone, – but a pale spectral Illusion! Is the lost Friend still mysteriously Here, even as we are Here mysteriously, with God! – Know of a truth that only the Time-shadows have perished, or are perishable; that the real Being of whatever was, and whatever is, and whatever will be, *is* even now and for ever. This, should it unhappily seem new, thou mayst ponder, at thy leisure; for the next twenty years, or the next twenty centuries; believe it thou must; understand it thou canst not.

'That the Thought-forms, Space and Time, wherein, once for all, we are sent into this Earth to live, should condition and determine our whole Practical reasonings, conceptions, and imagings (not imaginings), – seems altogether fit, just, and unavoidable. But that they should, farthermore, usurp such sway over pure spiritual Meditation, and blind us to the wonder every where lying close on us, seems nowise so. Admit Space and Time to their due rank as Forms of Thought; nay, even, if thou wilt, to their quite undue rank of Realities: and consider, then, with thyself how their thin disguises hide from us the brightest God-effulgences! Thus, were it not miraculous, could I stretch forth my hand, and clutch the Sun? Yet thou seest me daily stretch forth my hand, and therewith clutch many a thing, and swing it hither and thither. Art thou a grown Baby, then, to fancy that the Miracle lies in miles of distance, or in pounds avoirdupois of weight; and not to see that the true inexplicable God-revealing Miracle lies in this, that I can stretch forth my hand at all; that I have free Force to clutch aught therewith? Innumerable other of this sort are the deceptions, and wonder-hiding stupefactions, which Space practises on us.

'Still worse is it with regard to Time. Your grand anti-magician, and universal wonder-hider, is this same lying Time. Had we but the Time-annihilating Hat, to put on for once only, we should see ourselves in a World of Miracles, wherein all fabled or authentic Thaumaturgy, and feats of Magic, were outdone. But unhappily we have not such a Hat; and man, poor fool that he is, can seldom and scantily help himself without one.

'Were it not wonderful, for instance, had Orpheus built the walls of Thebes by the mere sound of his Lyre? Yet tell me, who built these walls of Weissnichtwo; summoning out all the sandstone rocks, to dance along from the *Steinbruch*[1] (now a huge Troglodyte Chasm, with frightful green-mantled pools); and shape themselves into Doric and Ionic pillars, squared ashlar houses, and noble streets? Was it not the still higher Orpheus, or Orpheuses, who, in past centuries, by the divine Music of Wisdom, succeeded in civilising Man? Our highest Orpheus walked in Judea, eighteen hundred years ago: his sphere-melody, flowing in wild native tones, took captive the ravished souls of men; and, being of a truth sphere-melody, still flows and sounds, though now with thousandfold Accompaniments, and rich symphonies, through all our hearts; and modulates, and divinely leads them. Is that a wonder, which happens in two hours; and does it cease to be wonderful if happening in two million? Not only was Thebes built by the Music of an Orpheus; but without the music of some inspired Orpheus was no city ever built, no work that man glories in ever done.

'Sweep away the Illusion of Time: glance, if thou have eyes, from the near moving-cause to its far distant Mover: The stroke that came transmitted through a whole galaxy of elastic balls, was it less a stroke than if the last ball only had been struck, and sent flying? Oh, could I (with the Time-annihilating Hat) transport thee direct from the Beginnings to the Endings, how were thy eyesight unsealed, and thy heart set flaming in the Light-sea of celestial wonder! Then sawest thou that this fair Universe, were it in the meanest province thereof, is in very deed the star-domed City of God; that through every star, through every grass-blade, and most through every Living Soul, the glory of a present God still beams. But Nature, which is the Time-vesture of God, and reveals Him to the wise, hides Him from the foolish.

[1] *Steinbruch*: quarry

'Again, could any thing be more miraculous than an actual authentic Ghost? The English Johnson longed, all his life, to see one; but could not, though he went to Cock Lane, and thence to the church-vaults, and tapped on coffins. Foolish Doctor! Did he never, with the mind's eye as well as with the body's, look round him into that full tide of human Life he so loved; did he never so much as look into Himself? The good Doctor was a Ghost, as actual and authentic as heart could wish; well nigh a million of Ghosts were travelling the streets by his side. Once more I say, sweep away the illusion of Time; compress the three-score years into three minutes: what else was he, what else are we? Are we not Spirits, shaped into a body, into an Appearance; and that fade away again into air, and Invisibility? This is no metaphor, it is a simple scientific *fact*: we start out of Nothingness, take figure, and are Apparitions; round us, as round the veriest spectre, is Eternity; and to Eternity minutes are as years and æons. Come there not tones of Love and Faith, as from celestial harp-strings, like the Song of beatified Souls? And again, do we not squeak and gibber (in our discordant, screech-owlish debatings and recriminatings); and glide bodeful, and feeble, and fearful; or uproar (*poltern*), and revel in our mad Dance of the Dead, – till the scent of the morning-air summons us to our still Home; and dreamy Night becomes awake and Day? Where now is Alexander of Macedon: does the steel Host, that yelled in fierce battle-shouts at Issus and Arbela, remain behind him; or have they all vanished utterly, even as perturbed Goblins must? Napoleon too, and his Moscow Retreats and Austerlitz Campaigns! Was it all other than the veriest Spectre-Hunt; which has now, with its howling tumult that made Night hideous, flitted away? – Ghosts! There are nigh a thousand million walking the earth openly at noontide; some half-hundred have vanished from it, some half-hundred have arisen in it, ere thy watch ticks once.

'O Heaven, it is mysterious, it is awful to consider that we not only carry each a future Ghost within him; but are, in very deed, Ghosts! These Limbs, whence had we them; this stormy Force; this life-blood with its burning Passion? They are dust and shadow; a Shadow-system gathered round our ME; wherein, through some moments or years, the Divine Essence is to be revealed in the Flesh. That warrior on his strong war-horse, fire flashes through his eyes; Force dwells in his arm and heart: but warrior and war-horse are a vision; a revealed Force, nothing more. Stately they tread the Earth, as if it were a firm substance: fool! the Earth is but a film; it cracks in twain, and warrior and war-horse sink beyond plummet's sounding. Plummet's? Fantasy herself will not follow them. A little while ago they were not; a little while and they are not, their very ashes are not.

'So has it been from the beginning, so will it be to the end. Generation after generation takes to itself the Form of a Body; and forth-issuing from Cimmerian Night, on Heaven's mission, APPEARS. What Force and Fire is in each he expends: one grinding in the mill of Industry; one hunter-like climbing the giddy Alpine heights of Science; one madly dashed in pieces on the rocks of Strife, in war with his fellow: – and then the Heaven-sent is recalled; his earthly Vesture falls away, and soon even to Sense becomes a vanished Shadow. Thus, like some wild-flaming, wild-thundering train of Heaven's Artillery, does this mysterious MANKIND thunder and flame, in long-drawn, quick-succeeding grandeur, through the unknown Deep. Thus, like a God-created, fire-breathing Spirit-host, we emerge from the Inane; haste stormfully across the astonished Earth; then plunge again into the Inane. Earth's mountains are levelled, and her seas filled up, in our passage: can the Earth, which is but dead and a vision, resist Spirits which have reality and are alive? On the hardest adamant some foot-print of us is stamped in; the last Rear of the host will read traces of the earliest Van. But whence? – O Heaven, whither? Sense knows not; Faith knows not; only that it is through Mystery to Mystery, from God and to God.

> 'We *are such stuff*
> As Dreams are made of, and our little Life
> Is rounded with a sleep!'

CHAPTER 9

Circumspective

HERE then arises the so momentous question: Have many British Readers actually arrived with us at the new promised country; is the Philosophy of Clothes now at last opening around them? Long and adventurous has the journey been: from those outmost vulgar, palpable Woollen-Hulls of Man; through his wondrous Flesh-Garments, and his wondrous Social Garnitures; inwards to the Garments of his very Soul's Soul, to Time and Space themselves! And now does the spiritual, eternal Essence of Man, and of Mankind, bared of such wrappages, begin in any measure to reveal itself? Can many readers discern, as through a glass darkly, in huge wavering outlines, some primeval rudiments of Man's Being, what is changeable divided from what is unchangeable? Does that Earth-Spirit's speech in *Faust*:

'Tis thus at the roaring Loom of Time I ply,
And weave for God the Garment thou see'st Him by;

or that other thousand-times-repeated speech of the Magician, Shakespeare:

And like the baseless fabric of this vision,
The cloudcapt Towers, the gorgeous Palaces,
The solemn Temples, the great Globe itself,
And all which it inherit, shall dissolve;
And like this unsubstantial pageant faded,
Leave not a wrack behind;

begin to have some meaning for us? In a word, do we at
length stand safe in the far region of Poetic Creation and
Palingenesia, where that Phœnix Death-Birth of Human
Society, and of all Human things, appears possible, is seen
to be inevitable?

Along this most insufficient, unheard-of Bridge, which
the Editor, by Heaven's blessing, has now seen himself
enabled to conclude, if not complete, it cannot be his sober
calculation, but only his fond hope, that many have
travelled without accident. No firm arch, overspanning
the Impassable with paved highway, could the Editor
construct; only, as was said, some zigzag series of rafts
floating tumultuously thereon. Alas, and the leaps from raft
to raft were too often of a breakneck character; the darkness, the nature of the element, all was against us!

Nevertheless, may not here and there one of a thousand,
provided with a discursiveness of intellect rare in our day,
have cleared the passage, in spite of all? Happy few, little
band of Friends, be welcome, be of courage! By degrees,
the eye grows accustomed to its new Whereabout; the hand
can stretch itself forth to work there: it is in this grand and
indeed highest work of Palingenesia that ye shall labour,
each according to ability. New labourers will arrive; new

THE REAL AND ITS IDEAL

Bridges will be built: nay, may not our own poor rope-and-raft Bridge, in your passings and repassings, be mended in many a point, till it grow quite firm, passable even for the halt?

Meanwhile, of the innumerable multitude that started with us, joyous and full of hope, where now is the innumerable remainder, whom we see no longer by our side? The most have recoiled, and stand gazing afar off, in unsympathetic astonishment, at our career: not a few, pressing forward with more courage, have missed footing, or leaped short; and now swim weltering in the Chaos-flood, some towards this shore, some towards that. To these also a helping hand should be held out; at least some word of encouragement be said.

Or, to speak without metaphor, with which mode of utterance Teufelsdröckh unhappily has somewhat infected us, – can it be hidden from the Editor that many a British Reader sits reading quite bewildered in head, and afflicted rather than instructed by the present Work? Yes, long ago has many a British Reader been, as now, demanding with something like a snarl: Whereto does all this lead; or what use is in it?

In the way of replenishing thy purse, or otherwise aiding thy digestive faculty, O British reader, it leads to nothing, and there is no use in it; but rather the reverse, for it costs thee somewhat. Nevertheless, if through this unpromising Horn-gate, Teufelsdröckh, and we by means of him, have led thee into the true Land of Dreams; and through the Clothes-Screen, as through a magical *Pierre-Pertuis*, thou lookest, even for moments, into the region of the Wonderful, and seest and feelest that thy daily life is girt with Wonder, and based on Wonder, and thy very blankets and breeches are Miracles, – then art thou profited beyond money's worth, and hast a thankfulness towards our Professor; nay, perhaps in many a literary Tea-circle, wilt open thy kind lips, and audibly express that same.

Nay, farther art not thou too perhaps by this time made aware that all Symbols are properly Clothes; that all Forms whereby Spirit manifests itself to Sense, whether outwardly or in the imagination, are Clothes; and thus not only the parchment Magna Charta, which a Tailor was nigh cutting into measures but the Pomp and Authority of Law, the sacredness of Majesty, and all inferior Worships (Worthships) are properly a Vesture and Raiment; and the Thirtynine Articles themselves are articles of wearing apparel (for the Religious Idea)? In which case, must it not also be admitted that this Science of Clothes is a high one, and may with infinitely deeper study on thy part yield richer fruit: that it takes scientific rank beside Codification, and Political Economy, and the Theory of the British Constitution; nay, rather, from its prophetic height looks down on all these, as on so many weaving-shops and spinning-mills, where the Vestures which *it* has to fashion, and consecrate, and distribute, are, too often by haggard hungry operatives who see no farther than their nose, mechanically woven and spun?

But omitting all this, much more all that concerns Natural Supernaturalism, and indeed whatever has reference to the Ulterior or Transcendental Portion of the Science, or bears never so remotely on that promised Volume of the *Palingenesie der menschlichen Gesellschaft* (Newbirth of Society), – we humbly suggest that no province of Clothes-Philosophy, even the lowest, is without its direct value, but that innumerable inferences of a practical nature may be drawn therefrom. To say nothing of those pregnant considerations, ethical, political, symbolical, which crowd on the Clothes-Philosopher from the very threshold of his Science: nothing even of those 'architectural ideas' which, as we have seen, lurk at the bottom of all Modes, and will one day, better unfolding themselves, lead to important revolutions, – let us glance, for a moment, and with the faintest light of Clothes-Philosophy, on

what may be called the Habilatory Class of our fellow-men.
Here too overlooking, whereso much were to be looked on,
the million spinners, weavers, fullers, dyers, washers, and
wringers, that puddle and muddle in their dark recesses, to
make us Clothes, and die that we may live, – let us but turn
the reader's attention upon two small divisions of mankind,
who, like moths, may be regarded as Cloth-animals, creatures that live, move, and have their being in Cloth: we
mean, Dandies and Tailors.

In regard to both which small divisions it may be asserted
without scruple that the public feeling, unenlightened by
Philosophy, is at fault; and even that the dictates of humanity are violated. As will perhaps abundantly appear to
readers of the two following Chapters.

CHAPTER 10

The Dandiacal Body

FIRST, touching Dandies, let us consider, with some scientific strictness, what a Dandy specially is. A Dandy is a Clothes-wearing Man, a Man whose trade, office, and existence consists in the wearing of Clothes. Every faculty of his soul, spirit, purse, and person is heroically consecrated to this one object, the wearing of Clothes wisely and well: so that as others dress to live, he lives to dress. The all-importance of Clothes, which a German Professor, of unequalled learning and acumen, writes his enormous Volume to demonstrate, has sprung up in the intellect of the Dandy, without effort, like an instinct of genius: he is inspired with Cloth, a Poet of Cloth. What Teufelsdröckh would call a 'Divine Idea of Cloth' is born with him; and this, like other such Ideas, will express itself outwardly, or wring his heart asunder with unutterable throes.

But, like a generous, creative enthusiast, he fearlessly makes his Idea an Action; shows himself, in peculiar guise, to mankind; walks forth, a witness and living Martyr to the eternal Worth of Clothes. We called him a Poet: is not his body the (stuffed) parchment-skin whereon he writes, with cunning Huddersfield dyes, a Sonnet to his mistress' eyebrow? Say, rather, an Epos, and *Clotha Virumque cano*,[1] to the whole world, in Macaronic verses, which he that runs may read. Nay, if you grant, what seems to be admissible, that the Dandy has a Thinking-principle in him, and some notions of Time and Space, is there not in this Life-devotedness to Cloth, in this so willing sacrifice of the Immortal to the Perishable, something (though in reverse order) of that blending and identification of Eternity with Time, which, as we have seen, constitutes the Prophetic character?

And now, for all this perennial Martyrdom, and Poesy, and even Prophecy, what is it that the Dandy asks in return? Solely, we may say, that you would recognise his existence; would admit him to be a living object; or even failing this, a visual object, or thing that will reflect rays of light. Your silver or your gold (beyond what the niggardly Law has already secured him) he solicits not; simply the glance of your eyes. Understand his mystic significance, or altogether miss and misinterpret it; do but look at him, and he is contented. May we not well cry shame on an ungrateful world, that refuses even this poor boon; that will waste its optic faculty on dried Crocodiles, and Siamese Twins; and over the domestic wonderful wonder of wonders, a live Dandy, glance with hasty indifference, and a scarcely concealed contempt! Him no Zoologist classes among the Mammalia, no Anatomist dissects with care: when did we see any injected Preparation of the Dandy, in our

1 *Clotha Virumque cano*: I sing of clothes and the man/Clothes and the man I sing

Museums; any specimen of him preserved in spirits? Lord Herringbone may dress himself in a snuff-brown suit, with snuff-brown shirt and shoes: it skills not; the undiscerning public, occupied with grosser wants, passes by regardless on the other side.

The age of Curiosity, like that of Chivalry, is indeed, properly speaking, gone. Yet perhaps only gone to sleep: for here arises the Clothes-Philosophy to resuscitate, strangely enough, both the one and the other! Should sound views of this Science come to prevail, the essential nature of the British Dandy, and the mystic significance that lies in him, cannot always remain hidden under laughable and lamentable hallucination. The following long Extract from Professor Teufelsdröckh may set the matter, if not in its true light, yet in the way towards such. It is to be regretted however that, here as so often elsewhere, the Professor's keen philosophic perspicacity is somewhat marred by a certain mixture of almost owlish purblindness, or else of some perverse, ineffectual, ironic tendency, our readers shall judge which:

'In these distracted times,' writes he, 'when the Religious Principle, driven out of most Churches, either lies unseen in the hearts of good men, looking and longing and silently working there towards some new Revelation; or else wanders homeless over the world, like a disembodied soul seeking its terrestrial organisation, – into how many strange shapes, of Superstition and Fanaticism, does it not tentatively and errantly cast itself! The higher Enthusiasm of man's nature is for the while without Exponent; yet must it continue indestructible, unweariedly active, and work blindly in the great chaotic deep: thus Sect after Sect, and Church after Church, bodies itself forth, and melts again into new metamorphosis.

'Chiefly is this observable in England, which, as the wealthiest and worst-instructed of European nations, offers precisely the elements (of Heat, namely, and of Darkness), in which such moon-calves and monstrosities are best generated. Among the newer Sects of that country, one of the most notable, and closely connected with our present subject, is that of the *Dandies*; concerning which, what little information I have been able to procure may fitly stand here.

'It is true, certain of the English Journalists, men generally without sense for the Religious Principle, or judgment for its manifestations, speak, in their brief enigmatic notices, as if this were perhaps rather a Secular Sect, and not a Religious one: nevertheless, to the psychologic eye its devotional and even sacrificial character plainly enough reveals itself. Whether it belongs to the class of Fetish-worships, or of Hero-worships or Polytheisms, or to what other class, may in the present state of our intelligence remain undecided (*schweben*). A certain touch of Manicheism, not indeed in the Gnostic shape, is discernible enough: also (for human Error walks in a cycle, and reappears at intervals) a not inconsiderable resemblance to that Superstition of the Athos Monks, who by fasting from all nourishment, and looking intensely for a length of time into their own navels, came to discern therein the true Apocalypse of Nature, and Heaven Unveiled. To my own surmise, it appears as if this Dandiacal Sect were but a new modification, adapted to the new time, of that primeval Superstition, *Self-Worship*; which Zerdusht, Quangfoutchee, Mohamed, and others, strove rather to subordinate and restrain than to eradicate; and which only in the purer forms of Religion has been altogether rejected. Wherefore, if any one chooses to name it revived Ahrimanism, or a new figure of Demon-Worship, I have, so far as is yet visible, no objection.

'For the rest, these people, animated with the zeal of a new Sect, display courage and perseverance, and what force there is in man's nature though never so enslaved. They affect great purity and separatism; distinguish themselves by a particular costume (whereof some notices were given in the earlier part of this Volume); likewise, so far as possible, by a particular speech (apparently some broken *Lingua-franca*, or English-French); and, on the whole, strive to maintain a true Nazarene deportment, and keep themselves unspotted from the world.

'They have their Temples, whereof the chief, as the Jewish Temple did, stands in their metropolis; and is named *Almack's*, a word of uncertain etymology. They worship principally by night; and have their Highpriests and Highpriestesses, who, however, do not continue for life. The rites, by some supposed to be of the Menadic sort, or perhaps with an Eleusinian or Cabiric character, are held strictly secret. Nor are Sacred Books wanting to the Sect; these they call *Fashionable Novels*: however, the Canon is not completed, and some are canonical and others not.

'Of such Sacred Books·I, not without expense, procured myself some samples; and in hope of true insight, and with the zeal which beseems an Inquirer into Clothes, set to interpret and study them. But wholly to no purpose: that tough faculty of reading, for which the world will not refuse me credit, was here for the first time foiled and set at nought. In vain that I summoned my whole energies (*mich weidlich anstrengte*), and did my very utmost: at the end of some short space, I was uniformly seized with not so much what I can call a drumming in my ears, as a kind of infinite, unsufferable Jew's-harping and scrannel-piping there; to which the frightfullest species of Magnetic Sleep soon supervened. And if I strove to shake this away, and absolutely would not yield, came a hitherto unfelt sensation, as of *Delirium Tremens*, and a melting into total deliquium: – till at last, by order of the Doctor, dreading ruin to my whole intellectual and bodily faculties, and a general breaking-up of the constitution, I reluctantly but determinedly forbore, Was there some miracle at work here; like those Fireballs, and supernal and infernal prodigies, that, in the case of the Jewish Mysteries, have also more than once scared back the Alien? Be this as it may, such failure on my part, after best efforts, must excuse the imperfection of this sketch; altogether incomplete, yet the completest I could give of a Sect too singular to be omitted.

'Loving my own life and senses as I do, no power shall induce me, as a private individual, to open another *Fashionable Novel*. But luckily, in this dilemma, comes a hand from the clouds; whereby if not victory, deliverance is held out to me. Round one of those Book-packages, which the *Stillschweigen'sche Buchhandlung*[1] is in the habit of importing from England, come, as is usual, various waste printed-sheets (*Maculatur-Blätter*), by way of interior wrappage: into these the Clothes-Philosopher, with a certain

---

1 *Stillschweigen'sche Buchhandlung*: Silence Bookshop

Mohamedan reverence even for waste paper, where curious knowledge will sometimes hover, disdains not to cast his eye. Readers may judge of his astonishment when on such a defaced stray sheet, probably the outcast fraction of some English Periodical, such as they name *Magazine*, appears something like a Dissertation on this very subject of *Fashionable Novels!* It sets out, indeed, chiefly from the Secular point of view; directing itself, not without asperity, against some to me unknown individual, named *Pelham*, who seems to be a mystagogue, and leading Teacher and Preacher of the Sect; so that, what indeed otherwise was not to be expected in such a fugitive fragmentary sheet, the true secret, the Religious physiognomy and physiology of the Dandiacal Body, is nowise laid fully open there. Nevertheless, scattered lights do from time to time sparkle out, whereby I have endeavoured to profit. Nay, in one passage selected from the Prophecies, or Mythic Theogonies, or whatever they are (for the style seems very mixed), of this Mystagogue, I find what appears to be a Confession of Faith, or Whole Duty of Man, according to the tenets of that Sect. Which Confession, or Whole Duty, therefore, as proceeding from a source so authentic, I shall here arrange under Seven distinct Articles, and in very abridged shape, lay before the German world; therewith taking leave of this matter. Observe, also, that to avoid possibility of error, I, as far as may be, quote literally from the Original:

ARTICLES OF FAITH

1. Coats should have nothing of the triangle about them; at the same time, wrinkles behind should be carefully avoided.
2. The collar is a very important point: it should be low behind, and slightly rolled.

3. No licence of fashion can allow a man of delicate taste to adopt the posterial luxuriance of a Hottentot.
4. There is safety in a swallow-tail.
5. The good sense of a gentleman is nowhere more finely developed than in his rings.
6. It is permitted to mankind, under certain restrictions, to wear white waistcoats.
7. The trowsers must be exceedingly tight across the hips.

All which Propositions, I, for the present, content myself with modestly but peremptorily and irrevocably denying.

'In strange contrast with this Dandiacal Body stands another British Sect, originally, as I understand, of Ireland, where its chief seat still is; but known also in the main Island, and indeed every where rapidly spreading. As this Sect has hitherto emitted no Canonical Books, it remains to me in the same state of obscurity as the Dandiacal, which has published Books that the unassisted human faculties are inadequate to read. The members appear to be designated by a considerable diversity of names, according to their various places of establishment: in England they are generally called the *Drudge* Sect; also, unphilosophically enough, the *White-Negroes*; and, chiefly in scorn by those of other communions, the *Ragged-Beggar* Sect. In Scotland, again, I find them entitled *Hallanshakers*,[1] or the *Stook-of-Duds* Sect; any individual communicant is named *Stook-of-Duds* (that is, Shock of Rags), in allusion, doubtless, to their professional Costume. While in Ireland, which, as mentioned, is their grand parent hive, they go by a perplexing multiplicity of designations, such as *Bogtrotters, Redshanks, Ribbonmen, Cottiers, Peep-of-day Boys, Babes of the Wood,*

1 *Hallanshakers*: beggars

Rockites, Poor-Slaves; which last, however, seems to be the primary and generic name; whereto, probably enough, the others are only subsidiary species, or slight varieties; or, at most, propagated offsets from the parent stem, whose minute subdivisions, and shades of difference, it were here loss of time to dwell on. Enough for us to understand, what seems indubitable, that the original Sect is that of the *Poor-Slaves*; whose doctrines, practices, and fundamental characteristics, pervade and animate the whole Body, howsoever denominated or outwardly diversified.

'The precise speculative tenets of this Brotherhood: how the Universe, and Man, and Man's Life, picture themselves to the mind of an Irish Poor-Slave; with what feelings and opinions he looks forward on the Future, round on the Present, back on the Past, it were extremely difficult to specify. Something Monastic there appears to be in their

Constitution: we find them bound by the two Monastic Vows, of Poverty and Obedience; which Vows, especially the former, it is said, they observe with great strictness; nay, as I have understood it, they are pledged, and be it by any solemn Nazarene ordination or not, irrevocably enough consecrated thereto, even *before* birth. That the third Monastic Vow, of Chastity, is rigidly enforced among them, I find no ground to conjecture.

'Furthermore, they appear to imitate the Dandiacal Sect in their grand principle of wearing a peculiar Costume. Of which Irish Poor-Slave Costume no description will indeed be found in the present Volume; for this reason, that by the imperfect organ of Language it seemed indescribable. Their raiment consists of innumerable skirts, lappets, and irregular wings, of all cloths and of all colours; through the labyrinthic intricacies of which their bodies are introduced by some unknown process. It is fastened together by a multiplex combination of buttons, thrums, and skewers; to which frequently is added a girdle of leather, of hempen or even of straw rope, round the loins. To straw rope, indeed, they seem partial, and often wear it by way of sandals. In head-dress they affect a certain freedom: hats with partial brim, without crown, or with only a loose, hinged, or valved crown; in the former case, they sometimes invert the hat, and wear it brim uppermost, like a University-cap, with what view is unknown.

'The name, Poor-Slaves, seems to indicate a Slavonic, Polish, or Russian origin; not so, however, the interior essence and spirit of their Superstition, which rather displays a Teutonic or Druidical character. One might fancy them worshippers of Hertha, or the Earth: for they dig and affectionately work continually in her bosom; or else, shut up in private Oratories, meditate and manipulate the substances derived from her; seldom looking up towards the Heavenly Luminaries, and then with comparative indifference. Like the Druids, on the other hand, they live in dark dwellings; often even breaking their glass-windows, where they find such, and stuffing them up with pieces of raiment, or other opaque substances, till the fit obscurity is restored. Again, like all followers of Nature-Worship, they are liable to outbreakings of an enthusiasm rising to ferocity; and burn men, if not in wicker idols, yet in sod cottages.

'In respect of diet, they have also their observances. All Poor-Slaves are Rhizophagous (or Root-eaters); a few are Ichthyophagous, and use Salted Herrings: other animal food they abstain from; except indeed, with perhaps some strange inverted fragment of a Brahminical feeling, such animals as die a natural death. Their universal sustenance is the root named Potato, cooked by fire alone; and generally without condiment or relish of any kind, save an unknown condiment named *Point*, into the meaning of which I have vainly inquired; the victual *Potatoes-and-Point* not appearing, at least not with specific accuracy of description, in any European Cookery-Book whatever. For drink they use, with an almost epigrammatic counterpoise of taste, Milk, which is the mildest of liquors, and *Potheen*, which is the fiercest. This latter I have tasted, as well as the English *Blue-Ruin*, and the Scotch *Whisky*, analogous fluids used by the Sect in those countries: it evidently contains some form of alcohol, in the highest state of concentration, though disguised with acrid oils; and is, on the whole, the most pungent substance known to me – indeed, a perfect liquid fire. In all their Religious Solemnities, Potheen is said to be an indispensable requisite, and largely consumed.

'An Irish Traveller, of perhaps common veracity, who presents himself under the to me unmeaning title of *The late John Bernard*, offers the following sketch of a domestic establishment, the inmates whereof, though such is not stated expressly, appear to have been of that Faith. Thereby shall my German readers now behold an Irish Poor-Slave, as it were with their own eyes; and even see him at meat. Moreover, in the so precious waste-paper sheet, above

mentioned, I have found some corresponding picture of a
Dandiacal Household, painted by that same Dandiacal
Mystagogue, or Theogonist: this also, by way of counter-
part and contrast, the world shall look into.

'First, therefore, of the Poor-Slave, who appears likewise
to have been a species of Innkeeper. I quote from the
original: "*The furniture of this Caravansera consisted of a
large iron Pot, two oaken Tables, two Benches, two Chairs, and
a Potheen Noggin. There was a Loft above (attainable by a
ladder), upon which the inmates slept; and the space below was
divided by a hurdle into two Apartments: the one for their cow
and pig, the other for themselves and guests. On entering the
house we discovered the family, eleven in number, at dinner: the
father sitting at the top, the mother at bottom, the children on
each side of a large oaken Board which was scooped out in the
middle, like a Trough, to receive the contents of their Pot of
Potatoes. Little holes were cut at equal distances to contain Salt;
and a bowl of Milk stood on the table: all the luxuries of meat
and beer, bread, knives, and dishes were dispensed with.*" The
Poor-Slave himself our Traveller found, as he says, broad-
backed, black-browed, of great personal strength, and
mouth from ear to ear. His Wife was a sun-browned but
well-featured woman; and his young ones, bare and chub-
by, had the appetite of ravens. Of their Philosophical, or
Religious tenets or observances, no notice or hint.

'But now, secondly, of the Dandiacal Household; in
which, truly, that often-mentioned Mystagogue and inspired Penman himself has his abode: "*A Dressing-room
splendidly furnished: violet-coloured curtains, chairs and otto-
mans of the same hue. Two full-length Mirrors are placed, one
on each side of a table, which supports the luxuries of the Toilet.
Several Bottles of Perfumes, arranged in a peculiar fashion,
stand upon a smaller table of mother-of-pearl: opposite to these
are placed the appurtenances of Lavation richly wrought in
frosted silver. A Wardrobe of Buhl is on the left; the doors of
which being partly open discover a profusion of Clothes; Shoes of*

a singularly small size monopolise the lower shelves. Fronting the
wardrobe a door ajar gives some slight glimpse of a Bathroom.
Folding-doors in the background. – Enter the Author (our
Theogonist in person), *obsequiously preceded by a French*
Valet, in white silk Jacket and cambric Apron."

'Such are the two Sects which, at this moment, divide the
more unsettled portion of the British People; and agitate
that ever-vexed country. To the eye of the political Seer,
their mutual relation, pregnant with the elements of discord and hostility, is far from consoling. These two principles of Dandiacal Self-worship or Demon-worship, and
Poor-Slavish or Drudgical Earth-worship, or whatever that
same Drudgism may be, do as yet indeed manifest themselves under distant and nowise considerable shapes:
nevertheless, in their roots and subterranean ramifications,
they extend through the entire structure of Society, and
work unweariedly in the secret depths of English national
Existence; striving to separate and isolate it into two contra-
dictory, uncommunicating masses.

'In numbers, and even individual strength, the Poor-
Slaves or Drudges, it would seem, are hourly increasing.
The Dandiacal, again, is by nature no proselytising Sect;
but it boasts of great hereditary resources, and is strong by
union: whereas the Drudges, split into parties, have as yet
no rallying-point; or at best, only co-operate by means of
partial secret affiliations. If, indeed, there were to arise a
Communion of Drudges, as there is already a Communion of
Saints, what strangest effects would follow therefrom!
Dandyism as yet affects to look down on Drudgism: but
perhaps the hour of trial, when it will be practically seen
which ought to look down, and which up, is not so distant.

'To me it seems probable that the two Sects will one day
part England between them; each recruiting itself from the
intermediate ranks, till there be none left to enlist on either
side. Those Dandiacal Manicheans, with the host of Dan-

dyising Christians, will form one body: the Drudges, gathering round them whosoever is Drudgical, be he Christian or Infidel pagan; sweeping up likewise all manner of Utilitarians, Radicals, refractory Potwalloppers, and so forth, into their general mass, will form another. I could liken Dandyism and Drudgism to two bottomless boiling Whirlpools that had broken out on opposite quarters of the firm land: as yet they appear only disquieted, foolishly bubbling wells, which man's art might cover in; yet mark them, their diameter is daily widening; they are hollow Cones that boil up from the infinite Deep, over which your firm land is but a thin crust or rind! Thus daily is the intermediate land crumbling in, daily the empire of the two Buchan-Bullers extending; till now there is but a footplank, a mere film of Land between them; this too is washed away; and then – we have the true Hell of Waters, and Noah's Deluge is outdeluged!

'Or better, I might call them two boundless, and indeed unexampled Electric Machines (turned by the "Machinery of Society"), with batteries of opposite quality; Drudgism the Negative, Dandyism the Positive: one attracts hourly towards it and appropriates all the Positive Electricity of the nation (namely, the Money thereof); the other is equally busy with the Negative (that is to say the Hunger), which is equally potent. Hitherto you see only partial transient sparkles and sputters: but wait a little, till the entire nation is in an electric state; till your whole vital Electricity, no longer healthfully Neutral, is cut into two isolated portions of Positive and Negative (of Money and of Hunger); and stands there bottled up in two World-Batteries! The stirring of a child's finger brings the two together; and then – What then? The Earth is but shivered into impalpable smoke by that Doom's-thunder-peal; the Sun misses one of his Planets in Space, and henceforth there are no eclipses of the Moon. – Or better still, I might liken'—

Oh! enough, enough of likenings and similitudes; in

excess of which, truly, it is hard to say whether Teufels-dröckh or ourselves sin the more.

We have often blamed him for a habit of wire-drawing and over-refining; from of old we have been familiar with his tendency to Mysticism and Religiosity, whereby in every thing he was still scenting out Religion: but never perhaps did these amaurosis suffusions so cloud and distort his otherwise most piercing vision, as in this of the *Dan-diacal Body!* Or was there something of intended satire; is the Professor and Seer not quite the blinkard he affects to be? Of an ordinary mortal we should have decisively answered in the affirmative; but with a Teufelsdröckh there ever hovers some shade of doubt. In the meanwhile, if satire were actually intended, the case is little better. There are not wanting men who will answer: Does your Professor take us for simpletons? His irony has overshot itself; we see through it, and perhaps through him.

CHAPTER II

Tailors

THUS, however, has our first Practical Inference from the Clothes-Philosophy, that which respects Dandies, been sufficiently drawn; and we come now to the second, concerning Tailors. On this latter our opinion happily quite coincides with that of Teufelsdröckh himself, as expressed in the concluding page of his Volume; to whom therefore we willingly give place. Let him speak his own last words, in his own way:

'Upwards of a century,' says he, 'must elapse, and still the bleeding fight of Freedom be fought, whoso is noblest perishing in the van, and thrones be hurled on altars like Pelion on Ossa and the Moloch of Iniquity have his victims,

and the Michael of Justice his Martyrs, before Tailors can
be admitted to their true prerogatives of manhood, and this
last wound of suffering Humanity be closed.

'If aught in the history of the world's blindness could
surprise us, here might we indeed pause and wonder. An idea
has gone abroad, and fixed itself down into a wide-spreading
rooted Error, that Tailors are a distinct species in Physiology,
not Men, but fractional Parts of a Man. Call any one a
Schneider (Cutter, Tailor), is it not, in our dislocated, hood-
winked, and indeed delirious condition of Society, equiva-
lent to defying his perpetual fellest enmity? The epithet
Schneidermässig (Tailorlike) betokens an otherwise unap-
proachable degree of pusillanimity: we introduce a
Tailor's-Melancholy, more opprobrious than any Leprosy,
into our Books of Medicine; and fable I know not what of his
generating it by living on Cabbage. Why should I speak of
Hans Sachs (himself a Shoemaker, or kind of Leather-
Tailor), with his *Schneider mit dem Panier*? Why of Shakespeare, in his *Taming of the Shrew*, and elsewhere? Does it not
stand on record that the English Queen Elizabeth, receiving
a deputation of Eighteen Tailors, addressed them with a:
Good morning, gentlemen both! Did not the same virago
boast that she had a Cavalry Regiment, whereof neither
horse nor man could be injured: her Regiment, namely,
of Tailors on Mares? Thus everywhere is the falsehood
taken for granted, and acted on as an indisputable fact.

'Nevertheless, need I put the question to any Physiolo-
gist, Whether it is disputable or not? Seems it not at least
presumable, that, under his Clothes, the Tailor has bones,
and viscera, and other muscles than the sartorius? Which
function of manhood is the Tailor not conjectured to
perform? Can he not arrest for Debt? Is he not in most
countries a tax-paying animal?

'To no reader of this Volume can it be doubtful which
conviction is mine. Nay, if the fruit of these long vigils, and
almost preternatural Inquiries is not to perish utterly, the

world will have approximated towards a higher Truth; and
the doctrine, which Swift, with the keen forecast of genius,
dimly anticipated, will stand revealed in clear light: that the
Tailor is not only a Man, but something of a Creator or
Divinity. Of Franklin it was said, that 'he snatched the
Thunder from Heaven and the Sceptre from Kings:' but
which is greater, I would ask, he that lends, or he that
snatches? For, looking away from individual cases, and
how a Man is by the Tailor new-created into a Nobleman,
and clothed not only with Wool but with Dignity and a Mystic
Dominion, – is not the fair fabric of Society itself, with all its
royal mantles and pontifical stoles, whereby, from nakedness
and dismemberment, we are organised into Polities, into
Nations, and a whole co-operating Mankind, the creation, as
has here been often irrefragably evinced, of the Tailor alone? –
What too are all poets, and moral Teachers, but a species of
Metaphorical Tailors? Touching which high Guild the greatest living Guild-Brother has triumphantly asked us: "Nay, if
thou wilt have it, who but the Poet first made Gods for men;
brought them down to us; and raised us up to them?"

'And this is he, whom sitting downcast, on the hard basis
of his Shop-board, the world treats with contumely, as the
ninth part of a man! Look up, thou much injured one, look
up with the kindling eye of hope, and prophetic bodings of
a noble better time. Too long hast thou sat there, on
crossed legs, wearing thy ancle-joints to horn; like some
sacred Anchorite, or Catholic Fakir, doing penance, drawing down Heaven's richest blessings, for a world that
scoffed at thee. Be of hope! Already streaks of blue peer
through our clouds; the thick gloom of Ignorance is rolling
asunder, and it will be Day. Mankind will repay with
interest their long-accumulated debt: the Anchorite that
was scoffed at will be worshipped; the Fraction will become
not an Integer only, but a Square and Cube. With astonishment the world will recognise that the Tailor is its
Hierophant, and Hierarch, or even its God.

'As I stood in the Mosque of St. Sophia, and looked upon these Four-and-Twenty Tailors, sewing and embroidering that rich Cloth, which the Sultan sends yearly for the Caaba of Mecca, I thought within myself: How many other Un-holies has your covering Art made holy, besides this Arabian Whinstone!

'Still more touching was it when, turning the corner of a lane, in the Scottish Town of Edinburgh, I came upon a Signpost, whereon stood written that such and such a one was "Breeches-Maker to his Majesty;" and stood painted the Effigies of a Pair of Leather Breeches, and between the knees these memorable words, SIC ITUR AD ASTRA.[1] Was not this the martyr prison-speech of a Tailor sighing indeed in bonds, yet sighing towards deliverance; and propheti-

1 *Sic itur ad astra*: This is the way to the stars

cally appealing to a better day? A day of justice, when the worth of Breeches would be revealed to man, and the Scissors become for ever venerable.

'Neither, perhaps, may I now say, has his appeal been altogether in vain. It was in this high moment, when the soul, rent, as it were, and shed asunder, is open to inspiring influence, that I first conceived this Work on Clothes; the greatest I can ever hope to do; which has already, after long retardations, occupied, and will yet occupy, so large a section of my Life; and of which the Primary and simpler Portion may here find its conclusion.'

CHAPTER 12

Farewell

So have we endeavoured, from the enormous, amorphous Plumpudding, more like a Scottish Haggis, which Herr Teufelsdröckh had kneaded for his fellow mortals, to pick out the choicest Plums, and present them separately on a cover of our own. A laborious, perhaps a thankless enterprise; in which, however, something of hope has occasionally cheered us, and of which we can now wash our hands not altogether without satisfaction. If hereby, though in barbaric wise, some morsel of spiritual nourishment have been added to the scanty ration of our beloved British world, what nobler recompense could the Editor desire? If it prove otherwise, why should he murmur? Was not this a Task which Destiny, in any case, had appointed him; which being now done with, he sees his general Day's-work so much the lighter, so much the shorter?

Of Professor Teufelsdröckh it seems impossible to take leave without a mingled feeling of astonishment, gratitude and disapproval. Who will not regret that talents, which might have profited in the higher walks of Philosophy, or in Art itself, have been so much devoted to a rummaging among lumber-rooms; nay, too often to a scraping in kennels, where lost rings and diamond-necklaces are nowise the sole conquests? Regret is unavoidable; yet Censure were loss of time. To cure him of his mad humours British Criticism would essay in vain: enough for her if she can, by vigilance, prevent the spreading of such among ourselves. What a result, should this piebald, entangled, hyper-metaphorical style of writing, not to say of thinking, become general among our Literary men! As it might so easily do. Thus has not the Editor himself, working over Teufelsdröckh's German, lost much of his own English purity? Even as the smaller whirlpool is sucked into the larger, and made to whirl along with it, so must the lesser mind, in this instance, become portion of the greater, and, like it, see all things figuratively: which habit time, and assiduous effort, will be needed to eradicate.

Nevertheless, wayward as our Professor shows himself, is there any reader that can part with him in declared enmity? Let us confess, there is that in the wild, much-suffering, much-inflicting man, which almost attaches us. His attitude, we will hope and believe, is that of a man who had said to Cant, Begone; and to Dilettantism, Here thou canst not be; and to Truth, Be thou in place of all to me: a man who had manfully defied the 'Time-Prince,' or Devil, to his face; nay, perhaps, Hannibal-like, was mysteriously consecrated from birth to that warfare, and now stood minded to wage the same, by all weapons, in all places, at all times.

In such a cause, any soldier, were he but a Polack Scytheman, shall be welcome.

Still the question returns on us: How could a man occasionally of keen insight, not without keen sense of propriety, who had real Thoughts to communicate, resolve to emit them in a shape bordering so closely on the absurd? Which question he were wiser than the present Editor who should satisfactorily answer. Our conjecture has sometimes been that perhaps Necessity as well as Choice was concerned in it. Seems it not conceivable that, in a Life like our Professor's, where so much bountifully given by Nature had in Practice failed and misgone, Literature also would never rightly prosper: that striving with his characteristic vehemence to paint this and the other Picture, and ever without success, he at last desperately dashes his brush, full of all colours, against the canvass, to try whether it will paint Foam? With all his stillness, there were perhaps in Teufelsdröckh desperation enough for this.

A second conjecture we hazard with even less warranty. It is that Teufelsdröckh is not without some touch of the universal feeling, a wish to proselytise. How often already have we paused, uncertain whether the basis of this so enigmatic nature were really Stoicism and Despair, or Love and Hope only seared into the figure of these! Remarkable, moreover, is this saying of his: 'How were Friendship possible? In mutual devotedness to the Good and True: otherwise impossible; except as Armed Neutrality, or hollow Commercial League. A man, be the Heavens ever praised, is sufficient for himself; yet were ten men, united in Love, capable of being and of doing what ten thousand singly would fail in. Infinite is the help man can yield to man.' And now in conjunction therewith consider this other: 'It is the Night of the World, and still long till it be Day: we wander amid the glimmer of smoking ruins, and the Sun and the Stars of Heaven are as blotted out for a season; and two immeasurable Fantoms, HYPOCRISY and

ATHEISM, with the Gowle,[1] SENSUALITY, stalk abroad over the Earth, and call it theirs: well at case are the Sleepers for whom Existence is a shallow Dream.'

But what of the awestruck Wakeful who find it a Reality? Should not these unite; since even an authentic Spectre is not visible to Two? – In which case were this enormous Clothes-Volume properly an enormous Pitchpan, which our Teufelsdröckh in his lone watchtower had kindled, that it might flame far and wide through the Night, and many a disconsolately wandering spirit be guided thither to a Brother's bosom! – We say as before, with all his malign Indifference, who knows what mad Hopes this man may harbour?

Meanwhile there is one fact to be stated here, which harmonises ill with such conjecture; and, indeed, were Teufelsdröckh made like other men, might as good as altogether subvert it. Namely, that while the Beaconfire blazed its brightest, the Watchman had quitted it; that no pilgrim could now ask him: Watchman, what of the Night? Professor Teufelsdröckh, be it known, is no longer visibly present at Weissnichtwo, but again to all appearance lost in Space! Some time ago the Hofrath Heuschrecke was pleased to favour us with another copious Epistle; wherein much is said about the 'Population-Institute;' much repeated in praise of the Paperbag Documents, the hieroglyphic nature of which our Hofrath still seems not to have surmised; and, lastly, the strangest occurrence communicated, to us for the first time, in the following paragraph:

'*Ew. Wohlgeboren*[2] will have seen, from the public Prints, with what affectionate and hitherto fruitless solicitude Weissnichtwo regards the disappearance of her Sage. Might but the united voice of Germany prevail on him

1 *Gowle*: ghoul
2 *Ew. Wohlgeboren*: Your Honour

to return; nay, could we but so much as elucidate for ourselves by what mystery he went away! But, alas, old Lieschen experiences or affects the profoundest deafness, the profoundest ignorance: in the Wahngasse all lies swept, silent, sealed up; the Privy Council itself can hitherto elicit no answer.

'It had been remarked that while the agitating news of those Parisian Three Days flew from mouth to mouth, and dinned every ear in Weissnichtwo, Herr Teufelsdröckh was not known, at the *Ganse* or elsewhere, to have spoken, for a whole week, any syllable except once these three: *Es geht an* (It is beginning). Shortly after, as *Ew. Wohlgeboren* knows, was the public tranquillity here, as in Berlin, threatened by a Sedition of the Tailors. Nor did there want Evil-wishers, or perhaps mere desperate Alarmists, who asserted that the closing Chapter of the Clothes-Volume was to blame. In this appalling crisis, the serenity of our Philosopher was indescribable: nay, perhaps, through one humble individual, something thereof might pass into the *Rath* (Council) itself, and so contribute to the country's deliverance. The Tailors are now entirely pacificated. – To neither of these two incidents can I attribute our loss: yet still comes there the shadow of a suspicion out of Paris and its Politics. For example, when the *Saint-Simonian Society* transmitted its Propositions hither, and the whole *Ganse* was one vast cackle of laughter, lamentation, and astonishment, our Sage sat mute; and at the end of the third evening, said merely: "Here also are men who have discovered, not without amazement, that Man is still Man; of which high, long-forgotten Truth you already see them make a false application." Since then, as has been ascertained by examination of the Post Director, there passed at least one Letter with its Answer between the Messieurs Bazard-Enfantin and our Professor himself; of what tenor can now only be conjectured. On the fifth night following, he was seen for the last time!

'Has this invaluable man, so obnoxious to most of the hostile Sects that convulse our Era, been spirited away by certain of their emissaries: or did he go forth voluntarily to their head-quarters to confer with them, and confront them? Reason we have, at least of a negative sort, to believe the Lost still living: our widowed heart also whispers that ere long he will himself give a sign. Otherwise, indeed, must his archives, one day, be opened by Authority; where much, perhaps the *Palingenesie* itself, is thought to be reposited.'

Thus far the Hofrath; who vanishes, as is his wont, too like an Ignis Fatuus, leaving the dark still darker. – So that Teufelsdröckh's public History were not done, then, or reduced to an even, unromantic tenor; nay, perhaps, the better part thereof were only beginning? We stand in a region of conjectures, where substance has melted into shadow, and one cannot be distinguished from the other. May Time, which solves or suppresses all problems, throw glad light on this also. Our own private conjecture, now amounting almost to certainty, is that, safe-moored in some stillest obscurity, not to lie always still, Teufelsdröckh is actually in London!

Here, however, can the present Editor, with an ambrosial joy as of over-weariness falling into sleep, lay down his pen. Well does he know, if human testimony be worth aught, that to innumerable British readers likewise, it is a satisfying consummation; that innumerable British readers consider him, during these current months, but as an uneasy interruption to their ways of thought and digestion, not without a certain irritancy and even spoken invective. For which, as for other mercies, ought he not to thank the Upper Powers? To one and all of you, O irritated readers, he, with outstretched arms and open heart, will wave a kind farewell. Thou too, miraculous Entity, that namest thyself YORKE and OLIVER, and with thy vivacities and genialities, with thy all-too Irish mirth and madness, and odour of palled punch, makest such strange work, farewell; long as thou canst, fare-*well!* Have we not, in the course of eternity, travelled some months of our Life-journey in partial sight of one another; have we not lived together, though in a state of quarrel!

Index

Invisible bonds binding all men together, 70.
Irish poor-slave, 287–90.

Jesus Christ our divinest symbol, 229.
Jewish old clothes dealer, 247.
Johnson, Dr., 245, 270.
Journalism, out-rooting of, 138.
Journalists, true kings and clergy, 53.

Kings, divine right of, 256.
Kuhbach, early reflections on, 114.

Labour, sacredness of, 232.
Land-owning as an occupation, 138.
Language, dead vocables, 117; flesh-garment of thought, 83.
Laughter, significance of, 38.
Lieschen, 23.
Life, a dream, 63–4; finds nourishment in death, 119–20; how to increase the value of, 197–8; life-battle with folly and sin, 99, 136. 138–9; most important transaction in, 177; mystery of, 138–9; nature and life a garment, 209; nothingness of, 190; pictures of human, 23, 161, 180, 194; time-spirit, life-battle with, 99, 200.
Light, beginning of creation, 202.
Literature, 259.
Logic, underground

workshops of, 78.
Logic-choppers, 78–80.
Logic-mortar and air-castles, 64.
Louis XV, ungodly age of, 173.
Love, how possible in its highest form, 220, 301; not altogether a delirium, 154; what we emphatically name, 145.
Ludicrous, the, a sense of, 57.

Madness, 266.
Magna Charta, 277.
Malthus, Heuschrecke a disciple of, 231.
Man, activity and attainment of, 180; blockhead and dullard, 66; by nature a naked animal, 7; description of by Swift, 67; divine emblem, 83, 223, 225, 245, 271; evolution in, 46; Godlike in, 198; great men too often unknown, 19; half duty of, 201; infinite in, 197; inspired text of Revelation, 186; lives of God-inspired men true works of art, 228; observations on young men, 139; religious loyalty ever rooted in his heart, 258; secret of his being, 64; spirit and a mystery, 67, 70, 75, 76, 271–2, 273; sufferings of, 196; tailorised and demoralised by clothes, 66; thinking man the worst enemy of the Prince of Darkness, 132; tool-using animal, 47–9; true